I0553254

IN THE PRESENCE OF HER ENEMIES

By Sherri Stewart

Published by Winged Publications

ISBN:978-1-968792-31-2

Chapter One

"The quality of mercy is not strain'd. It droppeth as the gentle rain from heaven upon the place beneath."

~ William Shakespeare, *Merchant of Venice*

After her last song, Tamar grinned at the young audience who sat cross-legged on the gymnasium floor of the Mennonite orphanage. "What an attentive group you are. Thank you." The children, many younger than her six-year-old twins, gave her enthusiastic applause. She had simply sung familiar children's songs, but the orphans facing her appeared appreciative of the smallest gestures. They had even sung with her, which buoyed her precarious self-confidence.

Their response brought a guilty twinge to her heart. They had no mother or father waiting for them after school, and yet they giggled with as much gusto as her own children. She should volunteer here more often, but singing soprano lead at Haarlem's opera and giving Zari and Peri, and her husband, Daniel, her full attention consumed every waking hour. And the drop in attendance hadn't been good at the opera over the last few months was all her fault.

She'd heard the producers' murmurings—if Margot van Ormer Sneider had been singing the lead, every seat would be full. So, Tamar had agreed to do public performances on her days off when the twins were in school. She agreed to use that time to drum up business for the opera and thus curry the favor of those holding the drawstrings of public funds.

Sister Adela joined her and thanked the students for their good behavior, evoking more applause. "All right, now it's time to return to your classes, then you'll be released—"

"Mama," a child's voice rang out.

Sister Adela gasped then covered her mouth. "I cannot believe it."

Again, the voice rose above the noise in the room, "Mama!"

How sad to call out for one's mother at a place like this. Tamar located the source of the voice. A small, spindly blond boy sat in the front row, his bent legs resembling a safety pin. Something about him was familiar. Was he from her synagogue? No, she knew all the kids in their shul. Since so few parents had returned from the camps after the war, most synagogues' numbers were small, and hers was even smaller since they worshipped a risen Messiah.

"What's that little boy's name?" she asked Sister Adela.

"Karl. That's the first time he's spoken since he arrived a year ago. Give me a minute. I have to help these children go back to class." Three nuns helped Sister Adela corral the children into wiggly lines forming at the gymnasium door.

Karl didn't move. Tamar's heart fluttered. Could it be? She hurried over and knelt in front of him. It *was* him, but how could this be? "Karl, do you remember me?"

He peered at her through puffy red eyes. Blue veins showed under the surface of his white skin. Frightfully thin, he sported a bruise on his cheek, and other bruises mottled his legs. What had happened in the two years since she'd last seen him?

When she swept him into her arms, he collapsed against her. "Oh, sweet boy, what happened to you? Where did you get those bruises?"

Sister Adela returned and knelt beside her. "He seems taken with you, Madame."

Tamar softly rubbed his back, his face cradled close to her neck. "I used to babysit for him years ago. He wasn't even three at the time. How did he get these bruises?"

"It's the older boys. They treat him awful even though he keeps to himself. Like I said, Karl never talks, but those eyes—they tell a story, don't they?"

Tamar noted his rheumy eyes, caked lashes, and pasty skin. Her heart bled for him.

"A ward of the state, that one. It's a shame. He won't eat, won't join any activities. Most of the kids are polite and leave him be, but a few pick on the small ones."

"That's terrible." Tamar kissed his forehead, his cheek. "What about his parents? Are they—" She couldn't verbalize his mother's name. It still stung. Margot hadn't been kind to Tamar, treating her with disdain during the war because she was a Jew, and then later as the help when she'd babysat for Karl.

Sister Adela smoothed thin strands of white-blond hair from his brow. "His mum and papa are in prison. Stolen art, I think. That's why he's here. He's got no family to speak of."

"I heard about it." She'd witnessed the houseful of stolen art when she babysat. "Didn't the papers say there were relatives in Rotterdam?"

A wistful sigh escaped the sister. "Apparently, it didn't work out. Karl's with us until the parents get out of prison. Think the director said one to two more years." She leaned close and whispered, "If he lasts that long."

Karl had snuggled his head into the space between Tamar's neck and shoulder, and he sucked his thumb, as he had so many afternoons in the past when she'd carried him up to his crib.

Sister Adela pushed to her feet. "He's what I call a failure-to-thrive child, but he surely has taken to you. Too bad you can't take him—" She covered her mouth. "I'm sorry, ma'am. Sometimes my mouth speaks of its own accord."

"When are visiting days?" Surely, she couldn't leave him, knowing how the other children treated him.

"Weekends." When Sister Adela tried to take him, he tightened his hands behind Tamar's neck, and howled.

Sister Adela's hands fidgeted. "Such a sad state of affairs. This one needs more help than we can give him."

A battle arose in Tamar's mind. This wasn't her problem. Hadn't Margot brought enough trouble into her life?

A quieter voice answered the charge. *None of Margot's doings are Karl's fault. God brings problems into your life so you can take care of them.*

She shifted him to Sister Adela's arms. "I'll be back, Karl. I promise." His longing gaze almost made her knees weak. How could she abandon him? God was presenting her with a need to meet, but shouldn't she discuss it with Daniel first? She couldn't just bring Karl home. How would the twins react? Peri and Zari had always gotten along with him, but that had only been for a few afternoons a week.

After Tamar left the orphanage to meet the children after school, second thoughts turned her steps back to the orphanage office. The sooner she rectified the situation with Karl, the sooner her conscience would stop clamoring.

No one sat at the reception desk, so she knocked on the director's door.

A tall woman with black hair pulled back into a sensible bun answered. "Yes?"

Tamar glanced up into severe eyes, then looked away, momentarily at a loss for words. "Mrs. Van Pelt? My name is Tamar Feldman…I was—"

"Ah, the opera singer. How did it go? Sorry I couldn't be there, but I had important things to attend to. Come in." The woman's stiff expression suggested that Tamar had no prayer of persuading her to reveal information about Karl. Nonetheless, she entered an office as stark as Mrs. Van Pelt who pointed to the single chair in front of her desk.

Perhaps Tamar did have a prayer. She sent a quick plea to heaven for guidance. She'd never been good with words. Melodies, yes, but not words. The woman's eyes narrowed, waiting for a response. "Yes, ma'am. It went well. The children seemed to enjoy singing the old classics. Music is…good for the soul."

Mrs. Van Pelt frowned and then peered at a file in her hand. "Well, thank you for volunteering. I'm sure you have better things to do with your time."

"Actually, I enjoyed singing for these kids. They seem to be hungry for music, and—"

The director's frown deepened. "Are you suggesting our kids look needy? That they're not well-cared for? We are *not* negligent, Mrs. Feldman. We follow the codes set forth by the government of the province of Holland."

Tamar leaned forward. "No, ma'am. I would never…That's not what I meant to say. The children look healthy and happy; that is, all but one, and that's why I'm here. I was wondering about little Karl. You see, I used to babysit for him when he was two. When his mother went for her voice lessons—" Now she was babbling. "He seems lost and scared to me. So…I was wondering if I could take him to my house for an extended visit. My kids and he got along…swimmingly."

The woman planted clenched fists on the desk. "I know of this boy. He obviously misses his parents. That is the usual pattern for kids in orphanages. They come out of it with time."

"Hasn't it been a year?"

"What are you insinuating? That we've been derelict in our duties? Why, I'll have you know we are the highest rated orphanage in the province." Her chin lifted.

Tamar breathed slowly to calm her racing heartbeat. "I have no doubt that's true, but I wonder if perhaps Karl would do better in a smaller family setting, like my family. He always got along with my twins, and he may even thrive—"

"So, by extended you mean to keep him until his parents have completed their sentences? Surely you know they won't be released for another year or so. Out of the question. Highly irregular." She stood and headed to the door.

Tamar shifted in the hard chair. "The attendant said he hasn't spoken until he saw me, and it's been a year—" She hoped she hadn't just put Sister Adela's job at risk.

"Children are often upset when they arrive. Many have lost their parents, so it's understandable, but Karl has both of them. They are just…indisposed at the present. Now if you'll excuse me, I have business to attend to." She jerked the door open.

Tamar stood, but remained near the desk. "What if I kept him until he's…better—gained some weight? He could share a room with my son. Karl loved going to the park with us and reading stories and—"She hadn't even talked to Daniel. Again, her impulsiveness reigned over her wisdom. Maybe that's where Peri inherited his outbursts.

"Again, his parents are alive. It's highly unlikely the government would permit such a thing." She opened the door wider.

Tamar went through it, stopping to look back once she was in the hall. The door had almost closed behind her, leaving only a crack open.

"Could you talk to his parents for me? A single call. Tell them Tamar Feldman would like to take him home with her for however long is needed. If they knew he had bruises—"

Only one of the director's eyes appeared at the narrow crack. "That child's always falling. He probably ran into a wall." She stared at Tamar for an uncomfortable moment. "Very well. I suppose a call wouldn't hurt. Now I have a meeting to attend. Leave your phone number with the secretary, but don't get your hopes up. The paperwork can be prohibitive." The door clicked shut.

"Cart before the horse" came to Tamar's mind once she left the orphanage. Her brother Seth had used that American adage in his letter from New York. Tamar should have been better prepared before she presented such a hard petition. She should have discussed Karl with Daniel first. He usually applied the brakes to her ideas, and his advice was prudent, not that she didn't balk sometimes.

She should have conferred with her Tante Neelie, who was a font of godly wisdom. Despite being more than twenty years older than Tamar, Neelie was always up for an adventure.

The deed was done. She'd tell Daniel when he came home from the hospital and call her aunt after the kids were in bed.

Chapter Two

"Teach me to feel another's woe, to hide the fault I see, that mercy I to others show, that mercy show to me."

~ Alexander Pope

A breeze tugged at Tamar's hat. She clamped it down. The bells of Saint Bavo's Cathedral tolled. Oh, no. The children. She was late. Again. The twins would have been waiting for ten minutes, and she still had a fifteen-minute walk to reach the school. That gave Peri twenty-five minutes to muddy his school uniform and shoes, despite Zari's warnings. At six-years-old, Zari could be trusted to behave, although she liked to voice her opinion. Tamar pictured her—tiny hands planted on hips at her brother Peri's antics.

Tamar scurried across St. Bavo's Square, side-stepping a bicycle that whizzed past. She sent up a quick call to God. Another time she needed God to fix her mistake.

Fortunately, the canal bridge was crossable. Three blocks later she reached the playground adjacent to the primary school. Zari sat alone on the bench dusting off her rucksack. Where was Peri?

Zari's tears hastened Tamar's steps. "What's wrong? Where's your brother?" She sat beside her daughter and brushed strands of hair from her face. "It's okay, Zari. Tell me what's wrong."

"Peri was by the swings—" she hiccupped. "watching the bigger boys. I started reading my library book, and when I looked up, they were all gone—even Peri." She rubbed her fists over her eyes.

"How long ago was that, honey?"

She lifted her shoulders, her lower lip protruding. "I went to tell the teacher, but the door was locked, and no one came when I knocked." Her voice rose with each word. "You told me to stay here to wait for you, so I didn't know what to do. Where were you?"

Her little rule follower. Tamar pulled her into a hug and patted her back, squelching the fears that tingled down her own spine. "You did the right thing. Your brother probably followed the other boys when they left. Let's go look for clues." If she'd been here earlier, Peri would be safe, and Zari wouldn't be so upset. Another example of Tamar shirking her duties.

They headed behind the school to the park. "I was at the orphanage longer than I expected. I'll tell you all about it later, but first let's find your brother. You know how impetuous he is."

"Im…pet…u…ous," Zari sounded out the word. "What does that mean?"

"It means acting without thinking."

"You mean like when Peri whirls around so fast he knocks over a lamp?"

"Yes, like that—impetuous."

Zari repeated the word. "I'm going to memorize—hey, look."

Straight in front of them, a shiny red bundle leaned against a linden tree. Tamar said, "It looks like your brother's rucksack."

Zari ran ahead, bent down, and looked up at Tamar. "Peri was here for sure. Wonder why he left it under the tree?"

Tamar lifted the sack and put on her most confident expression for Zari. "At least, we're going in the right direction." *Please, Lord, keep him in the palm of Your hand.*

They reached a clearing with a few picnic tables, a slide, and swings. Several boys played marbles in the dirt, and a woman on a bench faced the river while reading a book.

"Peri," Tamar called, hoping one of the boys was her son, but no blond curls bobbed in recognition. "Are those the boys who were with your brother?"

Zari shook her head. "They're too young."

Tamar slowly turned, surveying the whole clearing. Pulling Zari along, she hurried to the woman who sat a few meters from the river. Peri knew better than to get close to the water, but he was her impulsive one. Tamar quieted her fearful thoughts before interrupting the woman. "Pardon me, ma'am. Have you seen a small boy—six-years-old with blond hair? He may have been with some older boys."

The woman removed her glasses and looked up, shielding her eyes with her hand. "I heard some snickers, but I paid them no attention. I'll keep a lookout. It's hard, isn't it? They can be so—"

"Impetuous," Zari said, eliciting an understanding chuckle from the woman.

"Over here." A muffled voice came from behind them.

"Mama, it sounds like Peri."

"Yes, I heard him."

"Eema!" The faint voice called again.

"Peri? Where are you?" They hurried to the center of the clearing.

"I'm right here. Look up."

Tamar gazed through the branches of a large linden tree. Peri sat on a wobbly branch that bobbed under his weight. "How did you get up there? Come down this instant." The branch teetered. "Careful."

"I can't. Some boys from school were too 'fraid to climb up, but I showed them."

"Where are they now?" She swiped away a twig that landed on her cheek.

"They said they had to go." For all his bravado, his lower lip quivered.

Tamar looked for something to stand on, but the picnic table and two benches were bolted to the ground. "Can you back up?"

"I tried, but my pants got caught."

Forsaking modesty she hoisted herself up to a low limb, then tried to shimmy up like a monkey, but her legs chafed against the bark. Reaching up she grabbed the limb above and pulled herself to a standing position.

Crack! The limb broke and she plummeted down. She braced for impact, with her eyes squeezed shut and her teeth clenched. Strong arms grabbed her from behind, but the force of her fall tumbled them both to the ground.

"Oof," A male voice uttered close to her ear.

Once Tamar caught her breath, she rolled to the side, pushed herself upright, and spun around. A middle-aged man with a salt and pepper beard struggled to stand. His dark eyes probed hers. He retrieved his hat and glasses and quickly put them on.

She offered her hand. "Thank you, sir, for saving me from broken bones."

He took off his glasses to examine a shattered lens. "That is fine, Madame. I am glad I could help."

Her daughter stood behind her and clung to her leg. "Did you hurt yourself, Eema?"

"Nothing a warm bath won't cure." She hugged Zari's shoulder and turned her to face the gentleman. "May I ask another favor, sir?" She pointed at the tree behind her. "My son is stuck up on a limb. Would you be so kind as to help me bring him down?"

"Of course, Madame. Perhaps I can talk him down. Those branches are not so sturdy for a person my age." He moved under the tree and peered up into the shadows.

Tamar detected a whiff of cigarette smoke as he passed her. She couldn't place his accent, but it wasn't Dutch. Maybe Swedish or Bavarian. "His name is Peri."

He glanced at her and repeated the name under his breath. A tiny smile curved one side of his mouth when he stood directly below her son. "Good afternoon, Peri. I am Mr. Vogt. Would you like to come down?"

Peri whimpered in response.

"All right, when I count to three, you scoot back. One…two…three."

Peri complied, the branch bobbing with each movement. When Peri's back bumped against the trunk, Mr. Vogt said, "Reach up to grip the trunk and lift one leg over the limb." That done, a smiling Peri shimmied down.

Mr. Vogt caught Peri midair when he jumped from the lowest limb. His legs were scratched and bleeding, his pants were torn, and his face was dusty and red from exertion, but he would live to climb another tree.

Tamar approached them and extended her hand. "Thank you, Mr. Vogt, for your help."

He shook hands with her, then straightened his hat. "It was my pleasure, Mrs. Feldman."

She picked off twigs that were stuck on Peri's sweater. "What do you say to Mr. Vogt?"

Peri kicked at a stone. "Thank you for teaching me how to get down." He still hadn't looked up.

Later she and Daniel would talk with him, but she felt she had to say something in the moment. "Peri, his glasses are shattered, and we both took a tumble. All because you climbed up in that tree. Do you see how your actions caused danger to you, me, and Mr. Vogt?"

He didn't meet her eyes. "Guess so, but the boys dared me, so I couldn't say no."

Mr. Vogt took off his homburg and brushed at the crown and brim. "Sometimes, the bravest answer is no." He donned his hat. "Good day, Madame, children."

The gods must be smiling down on him. Correction—there were no gods, Erich chided himself. Hadn't Marx said religion was the opiate of the masses? No, what had smiled down on him was opportunity and his own effort. He breathed in the memory of her perfume—Tamar's exquisite scent when she fell against him. Fortune had allowed him to come upon her as she tried to shimmy up the tree of all things, and he'd been there to rescue her.

The years hadn't diminished her beauty. He remembered when he first heard her awe-inspiring voice—the voice of an angel. Only days later he viewed the sight of her beautiful face—like the face of an angel. Her image, which had remained in his dreams and waking hours ever since, had changed his life forever. He couldn't get enough of her.

His obsession to have her had spurred him to remain in the Netherlands after the war. He could have returned to Ilse and his son, Dieter, who would be nineteen now, but the thought of returning to Germany left him cold. Once he'd feasted on the finest food, it was hard to return to sandwiches. Why didn't Tamar understand that they were made for each other?

His love for her had made him careless, and he'd made mistakes. She should have understood that the art he'd stolen was to provide the means to build a future with her. The fire in the warehouse wouldn't have happened if he hadn't been distracted with thoughts about her, so in a way the calamity was her fault. He bore the pain of the burns as a small sacrifice, since it had led to him finding her, then following her to Paris. Once again, he'd become careless in his quest to rescue her from her husband. She hadn't understood.

This time he'd be more careful. In the past, he'd watched her from his seat in the opera every time she performed. Her matured voice delighted him, and her ingenuousness gave her a youthful appeal. Every thought of her filled him with desire.

The plastic surgeon had done a remarkable job of repairing the scars on his face. His glasses added a few more years. Even now, his hand shook from the skin grafts, and the twitch dragged his lip down when he was tired or anxious. Those adjustments helped disguise him.

He knew where she worked, and he knew where she lived—in that house on the canal where he'd first seen her. He'd used the vantage point of the attic to observe her all those years ago. He'd discovered she was Jewish from a picture he found of her standing by her father and brother, who wore *yarmulkes*.

Now, fortune had smiled upon him again, and they had made contact. He'd felt the stirring within him when she'd fallen against him, but she seemed unaware of his identity confirming that he had a good disguise. No one heeded a Mr. Vogt with a graying beard and thick glasses. People looked past an older man with a cane.

It didn't matter. Erich Bergman aka Mr. Vogt had made his first connection with her. What Tamar Visser Feldman didn't know was underneath this heavy coat was the virile man who owned her. Hadn't he paid the ultimate price?

Peri seemed to be free of damage from his time in the tree. He galloped ahead, almost colliding with a woman on a bicycle.

"Peri, watch where you're going. Stop on the red line." Tamar might as well have warned the wind not to blow. When he paused and peered back, his sweet smile melted her heart.

Zari swung her arm vigorously reminding Tamar they were holding hands. "Thanks for your help, Zari."

"God helped Peri, Eema. Maybe he sent an angel to stick Peri's pants on the branch so he wouldn't fall out of the tree."

Tamar spewed a laugh, but seeing Zari's solemn expression, she muffled the sound. "You might be right. That branch was bobbing up and down. He looked like a cowboy in one of those American western movies."

Zari's contemplative face resembled Daniel's. "Maybe God sent Mr. Vogt to help us get him down. Do you think Mr. Vogt is an angel?"

They'd reached Peri, who shifted from foot to foot on the red line. Bicycles whizzed past in both directions, faster than automobiles.

"Good job, Peri. You stayed on the curb."

He peered up at her with impish eyes. "Can we get an ice cream?"

Her first reaction was to say yes. Peri couldn't help his impulsiveness, and after all, she had been late, but Tamar had to send the right message. He had to learn not to yield to the suggestions of older boys. "Not this time. You left the schoolyard without permission and worried both of us."

"Yeah, and God had to send Mr. Vogt as an angel, Peri." Her daughter's hands were posted on her hips, not unlike her mother.

"He didn't help me that much," murmured Peri, taking Tamar's other hand to cross St. Bavo's Square to their house on the canal. "I could have climbed down by myself."

"No, you couldn't. The man told you how to do it," Zari said. "He was an angel. How else would he know Eema's name?"

"What?" Tamar stopped in her tracks. "What are you talking about?"

"He called you Mrs. Feldman, but you didn't tell him your name."

Chapter Three

"Who will not mercy unto others show, How can he mercy ever hope to have?"

~ Edmund Spenser

Silence reigned over the rest of their walk home. Even Peri's voice was muted in Tamar's mind, while she rehashed her conversation with Mr. Vogt. Had she introduced herself when he did? That was common practice, but her concern over Peri made it hard to remember. Although Zari was astute for six, she could be mistaken.

They reached the door to their house before Tamar was aware of it. The twins rushed up the stairs to the kitchen. "Can we have a snack before supper?" Peri called.

Supper—she hadn't even thought about what she'd prepare. Why couldn't she be more like her mother who'd always have dinner on the table even after a workday in the jewelry store? Thoughts of Peri in the tree, the man who'd helped him down, and the little blond boy at the orphanage had blocked every other thought. "How about toast?" Without waiting for an answer, she went to the cupboard to find chocolate sprinkles to spread over buttered toast.

Minutes later, while the twins snacked at the table, making dark mustaches on their faces, Tamar perused the food in the refrigerator. Leftover peas, a piece of sausage, and a few carrots would make a tasty soup. Daniel liked sausage soup with crusty bread.

When their snacks were finished, leaving the table a battlefield of crumbs, Tamar had the twins wash up before going to the parlor to practice their instruments—Zari's violin, Peri's piano. "Stop," she called before they reached the top of the stairs. "Play each of your songs three times perfectly. If you make a mistake, start over. Understood?"

"Yes, Eema," they replied in unison—always competing to be first in any goal.

Tamar listened for the strident sound of Zari tuning her violin. She was certainly following in the steps of Tante Neelie, who'd played violin in Haarlem's Opera for those few years when Tamar sang in the chorus. But that was before the war.

Neelie was the closest relationship to an aunt Tamar had ever had. Neelie had opened her home to hide Tamar and Daniel after her parents were taken to the camps. She remained her tante after her parents were gone and her brother Seth had moved to New York.

Tamar dumped the soup ingredients into a large pot and set the table for four, putting a basket of Saturday market's bread in the center. She added cinnamon to the steeping pot of tea and covered it with a towel. Tamar had so much to tell Daniel, but he was always exhausted after a day at the hospital. So many of the medical staff hadn't returned from the camps, which meant he had to fill many roles even though six years had passed since the war ended. She prayed he'd be open to offering Karl a place of peace in their house.

On cue, the door opened below, and Daniel's footsteps sounded on the steps. She could always tell by his pace if he'd had a hard day or not. Today he lumbered up to the kitchen.

When their eyes met, he smiled. The lines on his face shouldn't mark a man in his early thirties. She rushed to him, threw her arms around his tall shoulders, and nestled her head against his chest.

"I missed you," she whispered. He kissed the top of her head, then blew at a strand of her hair she'd forgotten to comb in her rush to fix dinner. She pulled away and studied his bearded face and sparkling, intelligent brown eyes that missed little. How she loved the man. From the first time she'd seen him in her dressing room at the opera, he'd been the one. Although the war and the camps had changed him, deep down she knew that a fearless Resistance fighter remained in him. He'd been her champion, her hero, and the love of her life ever since.

He kissed her temple and sniffed the air. "Is that cinnamon? You didn't. Did you make spice cookies?"

She slapped his chest. "No, silly. If you put out your shingle for your medical practice downstairs, I'll make you more cookies than you can possibly eat. You'll be drowning in cookies."

He offered an exaggerated sigh. "Mixed metaphor, my lovely, but the image of you holding a spatula is a powerful incentive. One of these days. How was yours?"

She ushered him to a chair at the table, dropped onto his lap, and loosened his tie. "I sang at the orphanage, and the kids sang right along with me, but I have so much more to tell you."

Footsteps clamored down the stairs. "Abba, you're home." The twins tripped over each other to reach him.

Tamar jumped off his lap as they took her place. She stirred the bubbling soup, then retrieved the milk from the icebox to fill the twins' glasses. She'd wait until they were in bed to tell Daniel about Karl. He'd probably balk first, but he hadn't seen the scrawny little boy with bruises.

She poured tea in two cups and sat across from him. "Children, climb off your papa and sit down for supper." After Daniel prayed a blessing, Tamar ladled soup into their bowls and passed the bread.

"Smells good," said Peri, "but the soup looks likes green mud."

"That's *snert*, Peri." Zari took a spoonful. "It doesn't taste like mud; it tastes like sausage."

"What a funny name for soup. Snert," he said, "I sound like a donkey." After he shoved a spoonful into his mouth, green residue framed his lips.

"Guess what, Papa? Peri got stuck up in a tree today."

"Oh?" Daniel looked up from buttering his bread. "What were you doing in a tree?"

A proud grin spread across Peri's face, obviously expecting his father to praise his bravado. "After school some of the older boys dared me to climb it. They didn't think I could do it, but I showed them."

"'Cept you couldn't get down." Zari stuffed a piece of bread in her mouth.

Daniel's eyes whipped to Tamar. Here it was. "I was late reaching the school after singing at the orphanage, but that's a discussion for later. When I arrived, Peri was missing." She told Daniel about tracking him down at the park. "The other boys were nowhere to be found. Peri's pants had gotten caught on a branch. A man helped me talk him down."

"Yeah, and Eema fell and knocked him over." Peri shoved a spoonful of soup into his mouth.

Daniel's eyebrows furrowed. "Why didn't you wait for Eema? You know the rules. Sometimes your mother and I will be late. It was wrong for you to leave the school with those boys. Do you understand?"

Peri's eyes studied his bowl. "Sorry, Papa. I won't do it again."

Daniel reached over and covered Peri's hand. "You worried your mother and your sister. They deserve an apology, son."

"Sorry," he croaked. "I already said sorry to Eema and Mr. Vogt, but he was no angel like Zari said."

Zari pushed her bowl away. "Then how did Mr. Vogt know Eema's name? She didn't tell him."

"What's this?" Daniel sat back.

"The man called Eema Mrs. Feldman," Zari said.

Tamar stood, removed the dishes, and carried them to the sink. She'd rather have this conversation without little ears in the room. "Children, why don't you go to your room and play with the pick-up sticks Uncle Seth and Aunt Hadassah sent you from the States."

"Excuse me, Abba," Zari dutifully said, then Peri echoed his sister's words. Their chairs scraped against the floor.

Tamar grabbed the teapot and placed it on a tray along with two cups and a plate of stroopwafels. Daniel had supported her delay in picking up the children, but there'd be questions to come. She returned to the table and sat, ready for the grilling. To busy her hands, she poured more tea and faced him.

"So, you had quite the afternoon." He stirred sugar into his cup.

She leaned forward on folded arms. "I have a lot to tell you. The twins were right. I was late to pick them up, and Peri had vanished by the time I reached the school. Zari was in tears." Tamar shook her head. "I feel like such a bad mother." Her breath whooshed out in a tremulous sigh. "Peri could've broken a bone. I tried to climb up to get him. Guess I'm not as agile as I used to be. Then this man came along and helped him down."

He sipped his tea. "Seems weird that he'd know your name."

She lifted a shoulder. "Maybe he attended the opera. Who knows? There was something familiar about him, but with all that was happening, I didn't think about it." She met Daniel's eyes. "I'll try not to be late again."

He leaned over and kissed her forehead. "I know you, Tamar. You're a wonderful mother. Things happen."

"Thank you." She squeezed his hand. Maybe he wouldn't think so after she told him the rest. "You remember little Karl, Margot and Klaus Sneider's boy?"

"Of course I remember him. He stayed with us that weekend his parents went to Amsterdam to attend a concert. He followed Peri around like a puppy." He frowned. "Did something happen to him?"

"He was at the orphanage. That's why I was late. He had a huge bruise on his face and others on his legs. Sister Adela said he's been in the orphanage for a year and hasn't spoken a single word…until today. Apparently, he remembered me babysitting him. He called me 'mama.'"

"What was he doing in the orphanage? I know his parents are in prison, but wasn't he going to live with relatives?"

She shrugged. "It didn't work out. He's so scrawny and pale now. The sister says he doesn't eat. She called his condition a 'failure to thrive,' but when I held him, he seemed to settle." She held Daniel's gaze. "I couldn't leave him like that. Apparently, the older kids pick on him. Maybe that's how he got the bruise on his cheek—"

"So, you want to bring him here?"

She nodded. "I talked to the director about bringing him home. He'd fare better here with the twins than in that awful place."

"What did the director say? He's not ours, and we don't have the best relationship with his parents."

"True, but it's not Karl's fault. He'll die there, Daniel. Margot wasn't the best parent, but I feel sure she wouldn't want him to suffer. He's a little lost boy." Her eyes glistened. "You should have seen him."

He rubbed a gentle finger under her eye. "Now, now. That heart of yours. What did the director say?"

"Mrs. Van Pelt isn't exactly a warm person. She became defensive when I mentioned the bruise—"

"That's understandable. As the head of the orphanage, the last thing she'd want was bad publicity."

"You're right. She said it was highly unlikely the government would allow us to adopt him when the parents are—"

His eyes widened and tea sloshed when he slapped his hands on the table. "Adopt? Tamar, Karl has two parents. Even though they're in prison for stealing art, they'll be out in a year or two. What were you thinking?"

Her head bobbed at a fast speed. "I never said adopt with her. It just popped out now."

Daniel covered her hand. "I'm sure there's no harm done. What else did she say?"

"When I said Karl would thrive much better in a home setting with children he knew, she agreed to contact Margot, but she also said not to get my hopes up." She peered up at Daniel. "I'm sorry I didn't wait until I checked with you, but the situation seemed so dire, and I know you. I've seen how you care for the burn victims at the hospital."

He stood and pulled her into a hug. "That's what I love about you. If it was up to you, we'd have a houseful of orphans, but in this situation, I have to agree. Just don't get your hopes up. Neither Margot nor Klaus would wish us any good will after we turned Erich Bergman, their partner in crime in to the police."

"Isn't this a God moment—the kind you and Neelie always talk about? Who would have thought I'd see Karl Sneider while singing in an orphanage? Did God put me there so I could rescue him? We might be the only adults besides his parents who would take care of him."

"At least this time you weren't breaking the law by sneaking into somebody else's house."

Tamar slapped at his chest. "That was *my* old house, silly—*my* childhood home." Her brow furrowed. "The very place where I took care of Karl. Isn't that ironic? Maybe God orchestrated my assignment to sing at the orphanage for Karl's sake. Maybe I shouldn't wait for the director to contact me. She probably won't call Margot anyway. What do you think, Daniel? Should I go to the prison and meet directly with Margot?"

He widened his eyes in mock horror and covered his heart.

"What do you mean by that gesture? I'm sure Margot would want to know if her son wasn't faring well. Even if we don't have the best relationship, she's still a mother."

He looked at the ceiling. "So many reasons come to mind I don't even know where to start. C'mon, let's go sit in the parlor." He took her hand, led her up the stairs, and pointed at Neelie's old gold and yellow brocade settee, then sat with her, their knees touching.

She felt like a child before a lecture. Whatever Daniel was going to say, she wasn't going to like it. She blurted out, "Why are you so—" His evident pain stopped her.

"I admire your zeal, Tamar, I really do. Seems I lost mine after the war. I know we were going to tell the world about what happened behind the barbed wire. You always said people would believe us because we'd been in the camps. But then life happened—the twins, my work at the hospital, and sadly for you, my inability to handle what we'd endured. I'm sorry."

She leaned against his shoulder, ready for the imminent 'but.'

"But that zeal of yours might put you in danger."

"Like when I broke into my old house and found it being used as a warehouse for stolen art?"

"Exactly." He hugged her shoulder. "And now you want to go to Margot's prison and convince her to let you take care of her child? This is the same woman who, on the arm of a Nazi, called us 'vermin.'"

She sat forward. "What am I supposed to do? It's no accident he was in the front row. If he hadn't said, 'Mama.' I wouldn't have noticed him. That's God's doing."

Daniel faced her and tipped up her chin. "If it's God's doing, we need to ask Him to show us what we should do. I'd much rather trust what I read in the Bible than random circumstances."

She considered his expression, "random circumstances," disappointed that the words minimized what she saw as an awesome chain of events. What he said was true, even if it hurt. "We could ask God for a confirmation—a double witness, so to speak. Just so we know we're not making a mistake."

"What do you mean by 'double witness'?"

"Each morning after I read a few paragraphs from the Bible, I write down whatever seems the most significant. I'm reading II Timothy. What about you?"

"The prophet Nahum. It's a hard book to understand." He yawned on cue.

"Good."

"Good?"

"Yes, if something strikes you as important for us while you're reading, it could be from the Holy Spirit. Write it down. Let's see what happens."

The next morning, after she left the twins at school, she stopped at the bakery across from her former home. Memories assailed her about the time she entered her house all those years ago, her shoes crunching over the broken glass of her parents' ransacked jewelry store. She'd called out for them, tears streaming from her eyes, but she knew that the Nazis had forced them away. Now her old house appeared devoid of life. A for sale sign hung in the window.

The Betzes who had owned the bakery where she stood had suffered the same fate as her parents—they were all gone. While Tamar waited for the new owner to finish with the customer in front of her she thought about the past. How she had loved waking to the scrumptious smell of freshly baked bread that wafted into her bedroom window.

Apparently, the baker and customer knew each other because they continued chatting. When Tamar glanced at her previous home, she admitted to herself that the place looked like it was dying of old age. It needed paint and new awnings. Her brother, Seth, who owned the house, would have gladly let her and Daniel live there, but there were too many bad memories attached to every room. The Nazi officer, Erich Bergman, had hidden in the attic, and Margot and Klaus had squatted there, using it as a temporary place to hide art stolen from Jews during the war.

Finally, the woman behind the display case took Tamar's order and filled a sack with cookies, a pastry, and a loaf of bread. Someday she'd learn how to bake bread and cookies, but not this week, or … this year. She hurried home to see if God had a message for her about visiting Margot. Nothing had popped out from the verses she'd read the three days before.

Once home, she fixed herself a cup of tea from the pot she'd made at breakfast. Although it was tepid, it would do. She opened her Bible to II Timothy, Paul's last letter to Timothy from prison in Rome, and trailed her finger down to verse 15. Rabbi Eshman had told the congregation Paul never left that prison alive where he wrote those words; Nero had him beheaded.

"*This you know, that all those in Asia have turned away from me, among whom are Phygellus and Hermogenes. The Lord grant mercy to the household of Onesiphorus, for he often refreshed me, and was not ashamed of my chain.*"

Chain? Was this reference to Paul's imprisonment what she'd been anticipating? Was God directing her to visit Margot? Tamar doubted modern-day prisoners in the Netherlands were in chains like those in ancient Rome. "*But when he arrived in Rome, he sought me out very zealously and found me.*" That seemed to align with what Tamar wanted to do—seek out Margot and find her. She read on. "*The Lord grant to him that he may find mercy from the Lord in that Day—and you know very well how many ways he ministered to me at Ephesus.*" These words seemed like clear marching orders; that is, if Daniel received a confirming message.

Chapter Four

"Once a man has truly experienced the mercy of God in his life, he will henceforth aspire only to serve."

~ Dietrich Bonhoeffer

The smell of antiseptic assailed Daniel's nose when he entered the burn department of St. Elizabeth Gasthuis—along with the faint odor of illness that no amount of cleanser could hide. After four years, he'd never become used to it.

Sister Griet's dimpled smile greeted him at the nurses' desk. "Good morning, Doctor."

"Good morning, Sister. How's Luuk doing this morning? Is he driving Sister Anna crazy?"

Sister Griet chuckled and handed him a short stack of files. "Ever since you took the bandages off the boy's hands after the most recent graft, he can't sit still. He runs up and down the hall, singing at the top of his lungs."

"Sounds like my son, Peri. A few days ago, he got stuck up in a tree. I keep learning that a healthy boy can be a lot of work." He sighed. "I'm going to miss Luuk. He's been part of this department for the last few years, but it's time to discharge him."

A cloud covered the nurse's eyes. "He doesn't have a home.

The one person left of his family—his maternal grandmother—lives in a *hofje*. You know children can't live in retirement centers. At the beginning she visited once in a while, but she hasn't been here in years. As you know, his family died in the fire. What's to become of our boy?"

"There's the Mennonite orphanage here in Haarlem, but are you sure there aren't any other relatives? Aunts, uncles?"

She shook her head. "I've checked his file, and there's only his grandmother."

"I'll ask Luuk when I do my rounds. Also, we could check with the grandmother. She'd know if there were out-of-town relatives who would be willing to provide him with a home to keep him out of an orphanage."

"I'll call her today."

Daniel headed to the patients' rooms to do rounds. Burn patients stayed so long they were more like residents. Healing required time and a sterile environment for the many grafts on their legs and arms. Working with burn patients hadn't been his dream career, but the war had changed all that. Someday, he'd realize his dream of opening his own practice on the first level of their home.

Little Luuk's blond curls bounced when he zoomed a toy truck over a closed book on his lap. He peered up, and a smile spread across his pale cheeks. "Hi, Doctor. Did you bring me a cookie?"

"Sorry. I forgot." He fished in his pockets then raised empty hands. "Next time." He approached the side of the bed. "What are you reading, or is that book just a street for your truck?"

"It's a girl's book, but Sister Griet said I had to read it for school." His eyebrows furrowed as he read the title. "*Wilde…Wietzke by Heleen.* Will you read it to me?"

Daniel ruffled his hair. Since it was a slow morning, he had time to spare. While they were together he'd ask Luuk about his family. "How about we read a few pages together, then tomorrow I'll bring you one of Peri's books about trucks." When Luuk nodded, he gestured for him to move over and joined him on the bed. "You read a page, then I'll read a page." He opened the book.

At first Luuk stumbled over the words, but soon he became immersed in the story. When his finger reached the last word, Daniel applauded. "Well done, Luuk. You're ready for chapter books. Peri's books will be too easy for you."

"No," he moaned. "I want to read about trucks."

Daniel patted his shoulder. The child was so small for a boy of ten. "You're ready to get out of here, aren't you?"

He nodded, his eyes trailing to the window. "But—"

"I know." Daniel hugged him. "Do you have any cousins?"

He lifted a shoulder, his smile vanishing. "I don't remember."

Six years had passed since the war ended. Luuk was probably three when the Nazis moved into Haarlem and took him and his parents. Who knew what he'd been through? His grandmother did, but if there were cousins or aunts and uncles somewhere, Luuk would fare better with them than in the orphanage. Still, Daniel didn't want to get Luuk's hopes up.

He stood, fluffed the pillow, and checked his hand, still scarred from the fire that had brought him to the Gasthuis years before. Daniel pulled a thick children's pencil from his pocket and a piece of paper. "Can you write your name for me?"

"Sure." He gingerly took the pencil and hummed while he scrawled his name in big letters. Good. The hand was still stiff, but the last graft had improved his mobility. He gave him a pair of children's scissors and asked him to cut a circle out of the paper.

The boy's smile radiated as he handed Daniel a discernible oval shape.

"Good job, Luuk." His upcoming departure saddened Daniel. He understood how Tamar felt about little Karl. Both Luuk and Karl deserved better than an orphanage. The older children would pick on Luuk because of the scars on his arms and hands just like they'd bullied Karl.

After he finished his rounds, Daniel pulled out his pocket Bible and read a few verses while he ate lunch in the cafeteria. Nahum spoke of judgment on the nation of Assyria for what they had done to Israel. God's gracious hand was on Israel—always had been, but He also disciplined His people. Daniel closed his eyes and prayed for God's direction. It would be easy to fall away from God as so many of the Jews had done after returning from the camps.

When he opened his eyes, he turned to the book of Matthew, written by one of Jesus's disciples. Verse 36 seemed to pop out from the verses around it: 'I was naked and you clothed Me; I was sick and you visited Me; I was in prison and you came to Me.' Was this verse confirmation that Tamar should visit Margot in prison?

He'd only encountered Margot a few times, and neither meeting had been positive. Tamar had told him about Margot's temper tantrums at the opera during rehearsals. One of those outbursts had resulted in Tamar taking Margot's place as Violetta the night he'd seen Tamar for the first time. Months later Margot was on the arm of a Nazi officer when she called him and Tamar vermin upon noticing the yellow stars on their sleeves. Even years after the war, when she and her husband, Klaus, had settled in Tamar's childhood home and hired Tamar to babysit Karl, Margot's disdain was still evident in the curl of her lip. Her arrest for housing stolen art and her subsequent prison stay most likely hadn't softened that sneer.

Nevertheless, he'd promised Tamar he'd seek God's counsel in the Word, and the message was clear. They'd also promised not to lie to each other, so he'd have to share that compelling verse. Tamar's big heart was taking her into dangerous waters once again. He'd experienced enough turbulence during the war for a lifetime, but Tamar hadn't lost her zeal for justice. Was she ready to face her enemy at the prison? He wouldn't send her there alone. Take the next step sounded in his mind. That's all he could do.

Two grafting surgeries and a debriding made the afternoon fly by. For once, the sun still shone high in the sky when Daniel left St. Elizabeth Gasthuis for home. After a few blocks in that direction, he pivoted and headed in another. He relinquished the attraction of an afternoon nap to follow up on the information he needed. With Tamar rehearsing at the opera and the twins in school, he had an hour to check out Haarlem's Mennonite orphanage for Luuk.

Daniel stepped up his pace and formulated a plan. If Tamar was right, the orphanage was no place for a child with a noticeable handicap. Like little Nazis, bullies homed in on kids like Luuk and Karl. Was he responsible as a doctor to come to the defense of children without parents?

Four blocks later, he turned onto Kleine Street, and then stared up at the imposing brownstone building that dominated the block. He headed toward the youthful voices that came from the fenced area beside the building. What was it like to grow up in an orphanage and share a room with dozens of boys?

The playground resembled many in Haarlem but lacked swings and other equipment. Two matronly women in long brown dresses with white aprons chatted at the single bench. Scarves covered their heads. The children, six to twelve, wore uniforms of the same dull brown. A circle of girls threw a beanbag back and forth while they recited a poem. The older boys played tag.

Most of them seemed normal. One tall boy zigzagging to evade another, plowed into a tiny blond boy by a bicycle rack, and knocked him on his back. Without a pause or apology, the tall boy kept running. The little boy sat up, started rocking, and sucked his thumb. Although Daniel couldn't discern his face, he had to be Karl. Was he injured?

Daniel found the gate and opened it. He wanted to go to Karl, but adherence to protocol won out, and he headed to the women to check in first.

They stopped chatting and faced him. One stood and nodded. "May we be of service?"

"Yes, I am Doctor Feldman from Elizabeth Gasthuis." He felt in his pocket for his business card, then took out a pen and wrote his contact information. "One of my patients will be released soon, and he has no family, so he'll need to be placed in an orphanage. Luuk's a wonderful ten-year-old boy who's been recovering from devastating burns to his legs, arms, and hands. He has some disfigurement, so I want to make sure this is the right place for him. I'd appreciate any information about how well a boy with disabilities would fare here."

The standing woman clasped her hands. "I'm Sister Adela, and I am so sorry to hear about your patient's suffering. What happened to his parents?"

Daniel glanced over at Karl, who still rocked silently. He needed to move the conversation along so he could tend to him. "They died in an apartment fire after they'd returned from the camps. Luuk's been in our burn unit for almost three years. He's come a long way, but I'm concerned about his future. We need to release him, but he's so vulnerable." Daniel motioned toward Karl. "See that one?"

When the two Mennonite sisters turned, the second one stood. "Oh, no," they said in unison. "What happened this time?"

This time? "One of the bigger boys knocked him over while racing away from another. He didn't stop or even look back. Do I have your permission to check on him?"

They looked at each other for a long moment. "Of course,

Doctor," Sister Adela said. He strode toward the boy, the two sisters on his heels.

"What's his name?"

"Karl."

A closer look confirmed Tamar's worries. Daniel had only seen the thin, pale boy who rocked in a frenzy twice in the past when Tamar had babysat him. The first time Karl had come for the weekend when his parents were out of town. He was two years younger than the twins, but they played well together.

The second time Daniel had entered Tamar's former house to examine Margot Sneider's irritated throat. Karl had clung to his mother's side, begging her to pick him up. Did Karl have that new illness called infantile autism that he'd read about in last year's medical journal? The author noted that many of these children fixated on a toy or an object for long periods of time, and were resistant to change. The author also hypothesized that one of the causes of the disorder was 'refrigerator mothers'—mothers who were cold and detached. Margot definitely fit that description.

With the sisters hovering so close, he couldn't mention his wife's name, so he leaned forward and touched the boy's head. "Karl, I'm Doctor Feldman. I saw that boy knock you down. It was an accident, but he should have been more careful. Can you tell me where it hurts?"

Karl looked up with rheumy eyes. His lower lip quivered, and he held up his arms to Daniel, who glanced behind him for the sisters' approval. The boy couldn't weigh more than twenty-five pounds. He carried him to the bench and sat with him.

He examined his skull for any swelling or tissue damage. When he touched a knot on the boy's left temple, Karl winced. Daniel checked his arms and torso for signs of contusions, alert to Karl's reactions. He ran his hands over his spindly, bruised legs. Daniel peered up at the sisters. "He has a bump on his head near his left temple. You'll need to ice it. Other than that, he doesn't seem to have any serious injuries, but I don't like these bruises on his cheek and legs. He's been picked on by the other kids, hasn't he?"

The taller woman sent the shorter one a warning glance, but rubbed her hands together. "We can't be watching him all the time, and the older boys find those moments when he's unattended."

He patted Karl's shoulder then stood. "Karl might not be so

lucky next time. It's too bad he doesn't have a relative who can take him."

The taller sister sent another warning look to her associate and was ignored again. "Karl's parents are alive, but they're incarcerated."

"Sister Adela, that's enough!" The tall nun gripped her arm and pulled her away.

"Wait." Daniel took a step forward. "What prison are they in?"

Sister Adela glanced back. "I'm not sure if both parents are in the same one, but word has it that Karl's mother is in Zwolle." The taller one propelled Adela away.

Zwolle—the prison that housed mentally insane inmates. Why was Margot there? She was angry and single-minded in her pursuit of reigniting her singing career, but insane? What had happened to her to be put in that prison?

Daniel checked his watch. The twins would be waiting for Tamar to meet them after school. Was there time to join them? Four blocks and a trek across the canal wouldn't even take ten minutes. He'd have liked to meet with the director, but that would have to wait for another day. He hurried out of the playground.

Zari was sitting on the curb abutting the school playground reading a book, and Peri was standing nearby tossing a ball up and down. Tamar hadn't arrived. He hastened toward Peri, who noticed him and dropped the ball.

"Papa." He ran to him. "Where's Eema? What are you doing here?"

Daniel swept him up and nuzzled his cheek. "I finished work and decided to meet you and your sister here. As soon as your mother arrives, perhaps we can stop for an ice cream cone."

"Yay," Peri shouted. Zari ran up and clung to her father's leg. "Ice cream."

Daniel stroked Zari's braids. "Your mother will be here any minute. How was your day?"

She beamed up at him, her freckles popping out like they did every spring. "We learned about fractions today. The teacher gave us each a cookie, and she told us to break it into four pieces. There were crumbs everywhere, but we got to eat them. It's kind of hard to understand that one thing can have four one-fourths." Her nose scrunched up. "Peri broke his cookie into six parts and told the class he had more than they did."

He chuckled. "That sounds like our Peri. Ah, here comes your mother."

Tamar's smile brightened her beautiful face. "What a treat to see you here." She slipped an arm around Daniel's waist. "To what do we owe this surprise?"

He picked up Zari and beckoned Peri to join them. The boy skipped over. "Hi, Eema. Papa's taking us for ice cream."

"That's where we're headed. I finished early, so I decided to check out the orphanage since little Luuk might end up there if we don't find a relative. After a quick conversation with two of the attendants, I saw Karl—" He shook his head slowly.

"Karl from the house?" Peri said.

Tamar wrapped an arm around his shoulder. "Yes, that Karl. When I sang for the children, he was in the first row. He remembered me." She peered up at Daniel. "What happened?" Tamar took his hand, and they strolled away from the school's playground.

"One of the boys ran into him and knocked him over. The older boy didn't even stop. You were right about Karl. That's no place for him or any child with a disability."

Zari wriggled to get down, her little eyebrows set in a frown. "Is Karl hurt? Where are his mama and papa? Can he come and stay with us?" Ah, that daughter of his saw and heard too much. He'd have to be more careful with his words in the future. Daniel cut a sideways glance at Tamar. She caught his eye and lifted a shoulder.

Peri, who'd skipped ahead now spun around, came back, and took Tamar's hand. "I'd like to have another boy to play with. Can he come and stay with us?"

Easy questions with difficult solutions. How much should they tell two six-year-olds? "His parents are…away for a while and can't take care of him, so that's why Karl's staying at the orphanage until they come back."

The frown deepened on his daughter's face. "So, it's kind of like when Eema babysat for Karl that time when he stayed at our house."

Tamar answered the question to Daniel's relief. "Yes, except he's been there for more than a weekend."

"So, invite him to come stay for the weekend." Zari peered up at Daniel when they stopped at a corner to wait for the bicycles to clear the road.

"It's not that easy. We'd have to ask his parents for permission, and that means we'd have to find them."

Across the street, the mauve and white striped awning welcomed them into Garonne Ice Cream shop. While the twins ran to view the colorful display of choices, Daniel took the opportunity to tell Tamar what he'd discovered. "You were right about Karl. He shouldn't be there; nor should Luuk. I didn't have time to speak with the director, but I did find out from Sister Adela that Margot is in Zwolle prison. Have you heard of the place?"

She nodded. "It's a bad one, isn't it? For the worst of the worst?"

"It's for the criminally insane. Sister Adela didn't know where Klaus Sneider was incarcerated."

She frowned. "Why would Margot be considered insane? She's many things—single-minded, disdainful, overly ambitious, but insane? No. In her own way, she loves Karl and her husband. Will the facility allow us to visit her?"

"I've been thinking about that. Maybe the prison officials will let me meet with Margot as her physician."

"Alone? Without me?"

Daniel shrugged. "She may not agree to meet with either of us since we had a part in her arrest." He pulled her close. "I don't want you to get your hopes up."

Peri's happy squeals caught their attention. He jumped up and down holding a licorice mustache over his lips. "Look at me. I look like Papa."

Zari rushed over to Daniel and grabbed his hand. "Papa, make him stop. The lady behind the counter gave him a mean look. We won't get ice cream if she makes us leave."

They hurried to the counter. "Enough, Peri," Daniel said. Tamar took the mustache away from him and dangled the licorice. "Now we'll have to buy this one. It's all wet."

He erupted in chuckles and modeled the remnants of a black mustache over his lip. Daniel said, "There's no doubt he's the culpable one." Daniel grabbed another one and led Peri to the counter. "Tell the lady you're sorry for taking the mustache."

Peri had the good sense to look contrite. He was used to apologizing, but his words didn't go too deep. "I'm sorry for making noise and jumping around."

"And?" The woman restrained her amusement and maintained a grim expression. "You shouldn't eat things you haven't paid for."

"Sorry." He shuffled from foot to foot. "But I didn't eat it; I just wore it."

Tamar mouthed an apology to her. "Now, Peri, what flavor of ice cream do you want?"

"Licorice. Then I can make a beard so I look like Papa." Great. Peri's clothes would be covered by the time they reached home. She turned to Zari. "What kind of ice cream do you want?"

"Strawberry. Can I have a mustache too?"

Daniel held up the two candies. "As you wish, but you'll both need to take a bath when you get home." After he paid for their purchases, they headed out. The twins skipped ahead, laughing as they pressed the licorice above their lips.

"Never a dull moment with those two." Tamar linked arms with Daniel. "It's so nice to walk home with you. I wish we could do it more often."

"Someday. We'll close the office on the first floor of our house, then my pretty secretary will join me for a picnic by the river."

"Pretty secretary? Is there something you want to tell me?"

He gave her a sideways hug. "She's beautiful. Not only is she the best mother in the world, but she also makes delicious chocolate chip cookies—using the recipe her sister-in-law sent from America. I can almost smell them right now." He sniffed, then shuddered. "No, that's the smell of the river."

She playfully slapped at his arm. "She'll make cookies when she's good and ready."

"I can wait. In the meantime, I'll savor them in my mind." He winked at her. "Before we reach the house, we need a plan about visiting Margot. I'll call the prison to get the visitor requirements. Since we'll have to transfer trains in Amsterdam, we'll pick a day Neelie doesn't work at the rehabilitation center. Maybe she'll agree to watch the twins. It's been a while since they've spent time with her."

"Excellent idea. Neelie might have some ideas on approaching Margot. She's so good with people—so wise." Tamar's voice grew wistful. "How I wish she could go in my place. Margot will never want to see me, even if the prison authorities grant me visitation rights."

He patted her hand. "Same for me. She still just sees us as despicable Jews." They turned onto the Barteljorisstraat, their street that ran along the canal. "Did Neelie know Margot?"

Tamar called for the children to stop at the corner then looked up at Daniel. "Of course, Neelie played violin at the opera. In fact, once Margot demanded the producers fire her because Neelie brought one of the children she babysat to rehearsal. The child's crying interrupted Margot's singing. Hopefully, the war and the recent years have dampened Margot's memory."

Chapter Five

"It is an attribute to God Himself; and earthly power doth then show likest God's when mercy seasons justice."

~ William Shakespeare

Neelie winced as she dabbed the gash on her cheek. *Thank you, Lord, that Hendrika's knife fell short of my eye.* How had she found a knife? They kept the utensil drawer locked, but one of the aides must have gotten careless. Neelie assumed the fault, because she'd suggested giving the residents tasks to do. A busy mind kept them from dwelling so much on what they'd lost.

She hurried to the bathroom for makeup to cover the spot—not that she ever wore any, but with the twins coming, she didn't want to scare them with a Frankenstein scar. Neelie looked forward to spending time with Tamar and her family. Since Neelie's son, Jan, had relocated to Paris, she'd put her efforts into the rehabilitation center. The outreach needed all her focus since the decrease in funding meant expanding the center from serving Jewish victims to becoming a halfway house for inmates. The influx of prisoners and patients with mental issues brought a whole new set of problems.

No, she refused to let their issues ruin her day off. Neelie hurried into the kitchen, grabbed some oven mitts, and removed the *boterkoeken* from the oven. She savored the scents of cinnamon and brown sugar. The potato and leek soup she'd made the night before would make the perfect lunch for the twins and their parents before they left for Zwolle.

Zwolle. The center had received a few inmates from there, even though it was hours from Amsterdam. Unlike the defeated Jews who'd returned from the camps, the inmates she'd taken in were angry. They picked fights with the quieter residents for the best seats at the tables and treated the staff with disdain. Their eyes were always on the doors and windows, looking for a way to escape.

Why did she keep thinking about the rehab center? Stop. Today she'd enjoy her adopted grandchildren, who grew taller with each visit. Zari had a quick mind and Peri had a quick body. Peri would have the apartment in shambles in minutes. She hurried to the living room to move breakable objects to higher shelves.

The doorbell rang multiple times. Peri. Of course. She smoothed white hairs away from her face and straightened her apron. With a breath of resolve, she headed to the door, her hip protesting again. At only fifty-one, she was showing her age.

A dozen rings sounded before she opened the door and bent to hug each child.

"Oma," they exclaimed before dashing past her into the house. "Mmm, it smells yummy," Zari's voice trailed behind her.

Neelie straightened to smile back at Daniel and his beautiful, blond Tamar. "Two of my favorite people. It does my heart good to see you." She embraced them. "Now don't you two run away as fast as your children ran inside."

"Tante, I've missed you so much. You don't come to Haarlem anymore, and it's only twenty minutes by train." Tamar kissed both of her cheeks.

Neelie kissed her back and framed Tamar's face with her hands. "Daniel, can you believe this one? What kind of adventure are you planning this time, Tamar?"

He chuckled. "I still have mixed feelings about our last one to Paris. It was wonderful that you were able to reconnect with your father, but…" He kissed the top of Neelie's head. "I'd better go check on the twins before they ransack your place. You two enjoy a moment of quiet before the storm." He sidestepped them and headed into the living room.

Tamar rested an arm over her tante's shoulder. "Daniel's still troubled at how easily I was kidnapped at that park in Paris. He'd rather forget it happened than talk it over. That's just his way."

"At least Bergman's dead. If ever a death was good, that Nazi's was." Neelie pretended to spit over her other shoulder. "So, what have you planned for today? You sounded cryptic on the phone."

Tamar dropped her arm. "Do you remember Margot Van Ormer?"

"How could I not? The way she treated us during *La Traviata* rehearsals? Her temper tantrums. I heard she was in prison for hiding stolen art, including the portrait my father painted of me."

"She hid the art while she and her husband squatted in *my* old house. Apparently, Klaus bought it for mere guilders in some back-alley market."

Neelie huffed. "That woman is always trouble. She needs to be in prison. Why are we talking about her?"

"It's her son, Karl. I babysat for him for a few months while she took singing lessons. She wanted to restore her voice to reclaim the head soprano role at the Haarlem Opera. You never met Karl. He was a sweet but sickly little boy. He really took to my twins, especially Peri. When I sang at the Mennonite orphanage in Haarlem the other day, he was sitting in the front row."

Neelie grabbed her arm. "Does that mean Margot and her husband are dead?"

"She's still in prison in Zwolle which is where we're headed. Back to Karl. Apparently, he hasn't spoken since he's been at the orphanage, but when he saw me, I must have jarred a memory. He said, 'Mama.' Oh, Tante, he was so thin, so pale, and covered with bruises. One of the sisters at the orphanage said the bigger kids bully him."

Neelie's hand went to her chest. "That's so sad. I've had many requests to take children from the orphanage in Amsterdam, but we're not equipped to care for little ones in the rehabilitation center. I wish we could." She'd often thought that they'd be easier to handle than the adults from the prisons, but said nothing. "So let me guess. You stormed the orphanage office, didn't you?"

Tamar rolled her eyes. "You know me. I couldn't leave Karl there. When I asked the director if I could bring him home with me temporarily, she became very defensive. Said I was accusing her of negligence. I just wanted to get him to a safe place since Sister Adela said he had something called, 'failure to thrive.'"

Neelie linked arms with her. "Having managed the center for more than five years, I understand her response. We have to answer to the government for funding, and when people are discontent, it hurts us. I doubt she could release him to your care even for a short period of time."

They headed down the short hall to join the rest of the family. Tamar sighed. "I understand that Mrs. Van Pelt assumed I wanted to keep him. She said that would be impossible since his parents were still alive and would be released in a year or two. She said she'd contact Margot, but I doubt she will."

"She wouldn't want to stir up trouble—look at that." Neelie pointed at the twins and their father. They sat on the floor in the corner a mere meter from the new television. "I bought the television for the noise. It becomes quiet in this old place at night." She pointed to the kitchen. "Why don't you give the soup a stir while I set the table."

A few minutes later, Tamar joined Neelie in the dining room. "I can't keep my eyes off the screen. The kids are spellbound by that cartoon. Even Daniel's chuckling. Maybe we should buy one."

"You'd never get them away from it, and television sets are expensive. I bought that one second-hand. It's a Telefunken from Germany—cathode-ray, whatever that means. Still cost me near 900 guilders. Can you believe that? Almost as much as a car or a house."

Once Neelie carried the tureen of soup to the table and placed a basket of fresh bread next to it, she took Tamar's hand so they could talk in private. They went to the small parlor to the left of the front door. Neelie removed books, her raincoat, and an umbrella from the settee for them to sit. "So, you and Daniel are going to visit Margot at Zwolle?"

Tamar nodded. "He visited the orphanage to assess it for one of his patients, a young burn patient at the hospital. While he was there, he saw a boy knock Karl over. It was an accident, but the older boy didn't even apologize. Daniel examined Karl and was disturbed at what he saw. That's why we're going. We hope we can convince Margot to let us take care of Karl until she's released."

Neelie patted her hand. "Zwolle is very restrictive with visitors, but Daniel might get in as a medical doctor who treated her before.

She had a sore throat, am I right?"

"Years ago. Daniel did a house call on his lunch break. Margot had asked Daniel not to tell anyone. She didn't want her husband to find out she was having throat problems because Klaus would put a stop to her singing lessons. You know how hard she tried to reestablish her career at the opera."

"So, there's no record of the house call."

Tamar nodded. "Even if he did, she'd probably refuse to meet with him after what we did—"

"Exposing her and her husband's stolen art collection." Neelie blew out a breath and squeezed Tamar's hand. "You two have God on your side. He can open doors mere humans can't, so I say give it a good try. You'll be taking the next step God's put in front of you. Karl needs your help. If Margot has any maternal instincts at all, she'll realize you're providing her son a mitzpah."

"Ah, a watchtower in Hebrew. Yes, a place of peace for him to thrive. Since she can't be there to take care of her son, we'll provide that place until she can do so herself."

Chapter Six

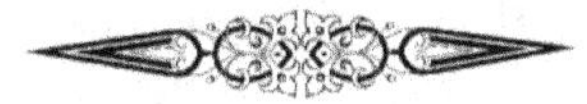

"For children are innocent and love justice,
while most of us are wicked and naturally prefer mercy."

~ G.K. Chesterton

During the train trip to Zwolle, both Tamar and Daniel were lost in their own thoughts. The journey seemed like a waste of time and money. Although Margot would never agree to meet with her, Daniel had a better chance of securing a visit. After all, he'd provided her with a prescription to heal her throat pain. Tamar was a different matter. Margot probably knew that Tamar was the lead soprano at Haarlem's opera, Margot's role until the Nazis closed down the place. Another loss Margot blamed on the Jews.

Then she had an idea. "Daniel."

"What is it, darling?" He looked up from his newspaper, his left eyebrow rising like a flag. "I'm not going to like it, am I?"

She rested her hand on his knee. "What if I offered to sing for the patients? Chances are, the inmates don't have the opportunity to attend many performances. What do you think?"

He didn't answer right away. "Hmm. Your idea has merit, but how could the prison organize an impromptu performance? We only have today."

She gave him a sly smile, then pointed to her large bag. "I packed some pajamas and toiletries just in case. We could spend the night in Zwolle. If the warden agrees, he'd have until tomorrow to organize a place for me to sing. Margot would be sure to show up. We could call Neelie and ask her to watch the children until tomorrow night."

"You're a genius." He wrapped his arm around her shoulder. "I bet they don't receive many offers for opera performances. It might just work."

Two hours later, Daniel gripped her hand while they stood in front of the warden's desk. The lines on the man's forehead indicated an unfavorable response, but Daniel intended to do his best to convince him.

The warden peered at them over glasses sitting halfway down his sharp nose. Then he stood and proffered a hand. "I'm Dr. Frank, the warden." He pointed at a tall pile of folders. "I don't have much time. How may I help you?"

A direct, honest approach was best. Daniel summoned a breath. "I'm Doctor Daniel Feldman, and this is my wife, Tamar. We come from Haarlem. I'll be quick. You have an inmate here also from Haarlem—Margot Sneider. I treated her shortly before her arrest. My wife was her understudy at the Haarlem Opera before the war, and after it ended, Tamar babysat for her son, Karl, who is now in an orphanage. Mrs. Sneider may be unaware how much her son is suffering there. He hasn't spoken a word in a year, and he's covered with bruises. We'd like her permission to bring him into our home until she is released. Otherwise, he may not make it—"

Dr. Frank frowned. "Her son's wellbeing isn't our concern, Doctor. We're here to make sure she finishes her prison time without outside interference. This information might aggravate her progress and make things worse. I'm sure the orphanage's staff is able to handle the boy's issues—"

Tamar interrupted, leaning her open hands on his desk. "I'd like to sing for your…residents, sir. Tomorrow, if that's possible. Music can be great therapy—calming them, reminding them of better times." When he didn't respond, she continued. "All I'd need is a piano, an accompanist, and a place where the residents can gather. When I performed at Karl's orphanage, the crowd sang with me and seemed to enjoy themselves. That day Karl spoke for the first time in a year."

The warden's eyebrows narrowed into a V. "We don't get many offers for performances here." He stood and paced behind his desk. "However, we can't predict inmates' reactions. Your singing might result in more harm than good." He placed his palms on the desk. "I can't take that chance. I'm sorry, but—"

Daniel said a quick prayer for a miracle, if that were possible at this late stage. "Excuse me, Warden, but I've seen audiences respond to Tamar's singing. Patients from my hospital's burn wing joined in—even some who hadn't responded to anything in years. Her voice has calmed refugees. Even drunk Nazis joined her in song. If she can handle the enemy, she can handle your patients."

Dr. Frank scrutinized him for a long moment.

Had he said too much? Was he a Nazi sympathizer? He cut a glance at Tamar. Her head was lowered. He'd said too much.

Finally, the warden spoke. "I have to say, Doctor Feldman, I'm suitably impressed. You might not believe this, but I care deeply about our inmates. I refer to them as 'guests.' It's important that they become responsible citizens again when they leave this place. Having said that, many of them are filled with anger and bitterness, which erupts at the most inopportune times. That's why we try to create a calm atmosphere—to reduce agitation."

A well-crafted no. Daniel patted Tamar's hand, stood, and led her to the door. "We've taken enough of your time."

He chuckled. "You give up too quickly, Doctor. I believe a concert by your wife is just what our guests need, and so yes, Mrs. Feldman, we would be honored to have you sing for us tomorrow—say, at eleven. Then we can release them to lunch."

Her eyes darted from Daniel to Dr. Frank. "Thank you, sir. I'll do my best not to agitate them. Would you be able to provide me with an accompanist, a lectern, and a piano? I'll provide the sheet music. As long as the room isn't too big, I won't need a microphone."

He circled his desk to join them at the door. "That can all be arranged. When you arrive tomorrow, see my secretary, and she'll get you set up." He held out his hand, and Tamar shook it. Then he shook Daniel's. "I haven't forgotten your request to meet with Mrs. Sneider. If all goes well with the concert I'll arrange a meeting for the two of you." He opened the door. "Good day."

Daniel thanked him. What had just happened? Outside the building, he finally spoke. "Can you believe it, Tamar?"

Her eyes were saucers. "I was sure he was going to kick us out. I'm a bit scared. It feels almost like when I had to sing for the Nazis during the war."

He linked her arm in his. "It seems God answered my prayer. It wasn't much of one, more like a simple 'help,' but He doesn't need length or eloquence."

"Now we need to pray that I don't get heckled tomorrow or cause a riot." She peered up at him. "You really are a salesman. I'd forgotten about singing at the Nazi bar and at the concentration camp, but I remember that same feeling of fear—panic even." She squeezed his hand. "Thank you for your kind words. I just hope I can live up to them."

Before they registered at an inn close to the prison, they called Neelie to update her.

"Of course, I'll watch the twins. I'm surprised you got anywhere with the warden. They're hard nuts to crack."

Tamar heaved a sigh. "What if they heckle me, or worse—"

"You'll be fine, Tamar. Remember you sang for drunken Nazis not once but twice—"

"That's right, but neither Daniel nor I knew what was coming, and both times I was forced to do it. I just blurted out that I'd sing tomorrow." She shook her head. "This mouth of mine."

Daniel finished her sentence. "—is beautiful. You'll sing for the prisoners, and I'll meet with Margot. We'd appreciate your prayers, Neelie. Tomorrow will be full of challenges."

The rest of the evening, they walked hand in hand down cobblestone streets off the center square that housed the town's cathedral. They climbed the gothic Sassenport gatehouse, then took pictures of each other with the new Kodak camera Tamar had given him for Christmas. They strolled along the river past lovely old houses, then bought a wooden car for Peri and a doll for Zari. Daniel wondered why they didn't do this more often. Because he let work at the hospital drain him of all his energy. By the time he returned home each evening, he was ready for a quick supper and bed.

Daniel cast a sideways glance at his beautiful wife. Tamar didn't deserve such negligence, but she never complained. He'd become a caricature of the father and husband he had vowed never to become. No more. He swept Tamar into his arms and twirled her around.

She gasped. "What are you doing?" She slapped at his chest. "Put me down."

"If you insist." He set her back down, then held her, ignoring the people who passed them on the sidewalk. "Mmm. You smell so good. I love you, Tamar Feldman. More than you'll ever know."

She grinned. "And I love you, but what brought this on?"

He stepped off the sidewalk and kept her close when a bicyclist zoomed past. "It just occurred to me that it's been a very long time since we've had a date. In fact, I can count on one hand the number of real dates we've had since we met."

Tamar's eyes sparkled. "Don't forget all those dates we had on Sunday afternoons at the labor camp. Remember meeting at our tree by the barbed wire with whatever remnants of lunch we could hide in our pockets? I lived for Sundays." She rubbed her hand against his cheek.

"So, now that we're no longer prisoners, why haven't we continued those dates? It's my fault, darling. I've let my work take my best energies instead of you and the children." He took her hand. "From now on, I'll make things right." He drew her to him and kissed her soft lips. A groan escaped. How long had it been since he'd done more than just give her a cursory peck? He opened his eyes to see tears turning her blue eyes a shade of aqua. "Tears?"

She held his waist, tucking her head under his chin. "I don't know why I'm crying. Guess I'm just happy to be with you here. Happy that you haven't fallen out of love with me. Because I couldn't stand it if that happened."

"That will never ever happen," Daniel stroked her wet cheek with his knuckle. "How about eating supper here?" He pointed to a hexagonal, glassed-in restaurant.

"Oh, Daniel. It's probably way too expensive."

He took her hand. "C'mon. We can splurge once in a while."

A waiter took them to a small table that looked out on a brook, pulled out a chair for Tamar, and handed them menus. "Welcome to

Agnieteberg. You two look like newlyweds. Are you on your honeymoon?" He filled their water glasses.

They looked at each other and laughed. "We're married with six-year-old twins." Daniel winked at Tamar, still rubbing her thumb between his fingers.

"Well, you could have fooled me. I recommend the four-course dinner for two. You'll start with an appetizer, then a bowl of our soup and a small salad. The main course is our rib roast, which is so tender you won't need a knife. Our dessert will be a surprise."

Tamar looked at Daniel with expectant eyes, and he nodded. "That sounds wonderful."

After the waiter left, she looked around the room. "Wouldn't this be the perfect place for a wedding? Ours was so…rushed, and I hardly understood the justice of the peace because my English wasn't very good."

"We didn't have a lot of choices while we were on the run, hiding out in London after we escaped from the camp." He studied her. "Tell me, would you rather have a simple wedding and a wonderful marriage or a huge bash of a wedding and not much of a marriage?"

"I don't even have to think about my answer. If I had to do it all over, I'd do it just the way we did—lining up behind servicemen and their brides-to-be."

"Me too," he said, "me too." Just then the waiter brought the first course, which he called an *amuse bouche*. Daniel waited for her to translate.

"Something fun for the mouth?"

The waiter kept bringing dishes for them to try. With the paucity of food after the war, he and Tamar always ate well but simply—soups, stews, a roast that would last a week. With twins, they didn't eat in restaurants very often.

They shared a dessert—a crème brûlée surrounded by raspberries. Tamar sipped tea while he chose coffee. They both patted their stomachs at the same time, which made them laugh. The years had made them as intuitive as their twins were. This dinner, this date, was long overdue.

"Are you ready for the walk back to the hotel?"

Her smile disappeared. "While we walk, we should discuss our plan for tomorrow."

He squeezed her hand. "Don't worry. You're a great singer. That's all you have to think about." When the waiter brought the bill, Daniel suppressed his shock at an amount almost as much as a week's pay. Feeling unsophisticated, he took bills from his wallet, counted them into the hand of the waiter, and thanked him. Some things were worth a week's pay.

They ambled back to the inn in silence. The wind had picked up, and the dark streets seemed foreboding. "Whoa," he said when Tamar sped up to the point that he held her back. "Are you nervous about tomorrow?"

She nodded. "What songs should I sing? What if they don't have an accompanist or a microphone? How many people will be watching? How am I going to get any sleep tonight?"

He clasped her shoulders. "So many questions. Let's tackle the first one. You usually do four or five songs, right?"

"Yes, but the songs I sang at the orphanage wouldn't work here."

He chuckled. "The national anthem is always a big hit."

She cut him a sideways grin. "Do you think imprisoned inmates would support a patriotic song? What was I thinking when I suggested this?"

He pulled her close to avoid a passing bicyclist. "It's all about timing."

"What do you mean?"

"If you can win them over with your first two songs, you could finish with a resounding rendition of *Het Wilhelmus*."

"Hmm. You may have a point. How about "Again" by Doris Day? It's a nightclub kind of song—not that I'd know anything about that."

"Ah, that's where you go when I fall asleep."

"Funny guy." Tamar hit his arm. "Maybe a song from the opera?"

"Good question." Would a room full of inmates appreciate a soprano's song? "You won't have an orchestra to back you up."

"To make me sound good, you mean."

"How about something upbeat, like a song from Gilbert and Sullivan? You played Mabel in the *Pirates of the Penzance* last season. People fell out of their seats laughing."

"Not at me. The guys got all the laughs." She glanced at him. "I could sing 'I Am the Very Model of a Modern Major General.' What do you think? They wouldn't get bored."

Daniel stopped. "Try it."

"Right now? Out here in the street?"

He lifted his shoulders. "They'll never see us again."

"Okay?" She started slowly, then picked up speed as the words came back to her. When they reached the corner of the square, diners at tables outside the restaurant rose to their feet, applauding and yelling, "Brava!"

Tamar stopped, her eyes lit up by their response. She laughed, curtsied, and waved. "I think I have my answer."

He held her hand the two blocks back to their hotel. "How about '*Merck toch hoe sterck*'? It's patriotic. Most people will be able to sing along."

"A song about revolution? It may start a revolt at the prison?"

"You're probably right. How about something spiritual? A calm song after the major-general song."

"I could sing a song from shul. Hey, look." She steered him to a toy store window display. "We should come here tomorrow before we catch the train to Amsterdam. Peri would love that xylophone, and there's one of those new View Masters from America. Zari would love that."

"We already bought them gifts. You're feeling guilty about leaving the kids, aren't you?"

She sighed wistfully. "I miss them. Maybe we can bring them back here when we don't have to go to prison."

Chapter Seven

"You cannot do kindness too soon, for you never know how soon it will be too late."

~ Ralph Waldo Emerson

Tamar stood behind a scarred lectern, gripping its sides. Half-opened windows reduced the breeze into the warm room where the inmates ate their meals. She swiped the back of her hand across her moist forehead.

The guards at the rear nodded at each other and opened the doors. Two lines of men filed in from the left door then rushed to the tables closest to the windows. Smaller inmates moved aside to let the more boisterous ones precede them.

Women in dark blue shifts filed in through the doors on the right and headed toward the two tables near the windows on the right. No one paid her any attention. Like the men, dozens of loud-voiced women pushed past the others and took the best seats. Strength and size dominated pecking order.

Gray uniformed attendants hovered at the periphery of the room while five guards stood in the large space between the men and the women. Tamar sensed the guards and attendants' disapproval of this impromptu performance. Had she been naïve to think she could win this crowd over through music? Her throat was dry. She should have asked for a glass of water.

A few inmates glanced her way with curious eyes, then turned to converse with the people across from them. Others rolled their eyes, as if her presence was an inconvenience. Their loud collective noise would have overwhelmed even a microphone-amplified song.

The pianist slid onto the bench, and warmed up the out-of-tune piano. Tamar hurried over with her sheet music to introduce herself. They conferred for a few minutes, and the woman didn't seem to have a problem with her choices.

Tamar returned to the podium, then searched for Daniel's face, hoping she could draw strength from seeing him. His slight nod came with a weak smile.

How could she get the inmates' attention? She recalled when she'd been duped into singing at an Amsterdam restaurant that had been turned into a Nazi hangout during the Occupation. Their beers had fueled their participation in singing with her, but there were no steins here.

A portly man in an ill-fitting suit joined her at the podium. She stepped back to let him speak. The microphone screeched its disapproval when he tapped on it and said, 'Test, test."

"Ladies and Gentlemen, we are pleased to present—" The paper he removed from his pocket crinkled loudly before he put on his glasses to read it. "Mrs. Feldman from Haarlem. She's here to sing for you, so behave…or else." He beckoned to her and knocked into the microphone, which squawked again. He shook his head and left.

She swallowed the huge lump in her throat. "Good morning…Guests. My name is Tamar, and I hope you like music—"

"Sing it, sweetheart," came from the crowd, followed by a ripple of guffaws.

"Yeah, but hurry. You're taking part of our lunchtime," another voice called.

With a short plea to heaven, she nodded at the accompanist. "I'll start with a song that you might have heard by the American singer, Doris Day."

A few men whistled, which prompted laughter. She closed her eyes, tried to feel the music, and sang "Again." At first she sounded soft and wispy, but a few words in, she found her spot by pretending to be in a nightclub with a full orchestra and patrons swirling cocktails. Her voice started to subdue the crowd which contributed hoots and whistles. One down, three to go.

When they settled down, Tamar took a deep breath and plunged into the Gilbert and Sullivan song gushing out the lyrics. She only stumbled over a few words. When she finished, she bent over to catch her breath.

From the side of the room, Daniel gave her a thumbs-up and a big grin. The crowd rose and roared their approval. She'd won them over. Relief filled her when a few yelled, "Encore." She chuckled and waved a dismissive hand. Her lungs couldn't handle singing that again.

She gestured for the pianist to start a song from shul. The risk was the pervasive intolerance of Jews, but the tune offered a reprieve from the previous fast and wordy "Major General" song. They quieted under the sound of the minor-keyed hymn. She'd made it to the third stanza when a soprano singing in the back stopped her.

The familiar voice sounded strong without a microphone. Violetta's song from *La Traviata.* Margot's voice. She sang the aria she'd sung so often before the war, as had Tamar, her understudy, during rehearsal and that one night when Margot had flounced out in a temper tantrum.

The accompanist stopped and searched for the source of the singing. Heads whipped toward the right side of the room where Margot stood.

She glided toward Tamar, singing the aria that had made her famous. Her eyes focused above Tamar's head, as if she were in a daze. If not for her familiar voice, Tamar wouldn't have recognized the thin, pallid woman. Gone was the heavily made up face. Gone were the fancy clothes and hats. Gone was the bravado, the disdain for the rest of the world. What remained was a voice, stronger and more vivid than two years earlier.

The room had quieted as if the crowd was holding its breath to see what would happen next. Guards moved toward her, but Margot waved them away without looking at them. They backed down.

Tamar swallowed and stared at Margot. This felt like a showdown—the sheriff and bandit in the middle of the dusty road. She could fight or join her. Tamar began softly singing simple harmony, letting the diva be the diva, amazed that her voice didn't break or croak because she so badly needed a drink of water.

For whatever reason, the guards kept their distance, as mesmerized by Margot's Violetta as the crowd. Tamar moved to the side so Margot could share the podium, but Margot stopped when she reached the front, whirling gracefully around in the way only a head soprano could. She held the room in her hand.

The song ended and everyone bolted to their feet, clapping, and demanding more. Tamar had seen that same ebullient smile on Margot's face after other encores. Even now, she offered a sweeping curtsey to the crowd, while they shouted "More, more, more!"

How could she follow that? Even the planned Nederlands' anthem would be a letdown after that performance. When the man in the suit tapped his watch with a frown, the decision was made.

"Ladies and Gentlemen, we—Margot and I—thank you for letting us sing for you today. You have been a wonderful audience." She motioned the pianist to her feet and thanked her. Then Tamar faced Margot. "Thank you, Margot, for your wonderful rendition of Violetta's song from *La Traviata*." Tamar swept her hand toward the soprano, who bowed with an elegance that belied her dark blue uniform.

The administrator approached, took the microphone, tapped for attention, and gave orders for the lunch staff to bring in the food. Riotous noise took over from the inmates who lined up against the wall with their food trays. Margot headed to the end of the line.

Was this a chance for Tamar to talk to her? What was the protocol? Could she approach an inmate? She'd only have this one chance.

Tamar strode to women's line. Margot took last place, her head down. Why did no one congratulate her?

A female guard stepped in front of Tamar. "Where are you going?"

"I…I just wanted to thank Margot for her song, and—"

"You have to talk to the director and get your name on the list. We have rules here." The woman nodded at the entrance.

Tamar headed toward the door. This *was* a prison, but the restrictions on contact still saddened her. They'd come all this way to tell Margot about Karl. Where was Daniel? Maybe they'd herded him to the exit as well.

With another glance back at Margot who had moved forward in the line to get her meal, Tamar passed through the waiting room full of people. A long line formed in front of the reception window. Daniel, in the far corner, thumbed through a newspaper. She hurried to him, resisting the desire to hug him. "Daniel?"

The minute he saw her, he tossed the paper onto a scarred table and took her in his arms. Uninvited tears brimmed in her eyes. "I'm sorry. It's just this has been…hard. What was I thinking to sing in front of a room of prisoners?"

He smoothed her hair as he always did to their children when they were upset or disappointed. "There, there." He tipped her face up, then brushed the tears from her cheek. "You did a brave thing today." He kissed her forehead.

"Thanks," she peered up through glistening eyes at this man she loved. Her rock. "Guess we should get going so we can catch the train."

"Not so fast." He grinned. "I scored an appointment at 1:30 with Margot when the inmates are back in their rooms."

Her mouth sagged open. "She agreed to see you?"

"I don't know why. Prisoners don't tend to get many visitors." He took her hand and found them seats. "I tried to convince the warden to let both of us meet with her, but he said only I could go because I'd been her doctor. Sorry. I'll need you to pray like crazy. She scares me."

At two o'clock, a guard called Daniel's name and ushered him down a long corridor to a large room in industrial whites and grays. A dozen long tables sat in different quadrants. The fans barely moved the stale air which smelled of disinfectant and sweat. Inmates sat across from their guests. Unsmiling guards stood at the end of each section.

A guard pointed him to a seat a few meters from a woman in a veiled black hat who dabbed at her eyes. She sat opposite a thin gray-haired man smoking a cigarette.

Margot took her seat with her arms tight against her chest. The nearby guard pointed at his watch. "Ten minutes."

Not much time to win her trust.

"Thank you for meeting with me. Your song today was beautiful. You held the audience in your hand." He smiled to soften her icy demeanor.

She leaned back and draped an arm over the chair's back. "You and your wife were the last people I expected to see today."

Daniel nodded, leaning forward. "We came just to speak with you."

She maintained a stoic face. "Then get to the point. I'm sure this isn't a friendly visit, especially after what you did."

The rancor he'd expected surfaced. "The people of Haarlem miss your singing. Tamar works at the opera part-time, but they're having a hard time filling the seats."

Faint triumph brightened Margot's eyes. She smirked. "So, why are you really here?"

He sent a prayer heavenward. "A few days ago, Tamar sang at the Mennonite orphanage, and Karl was in the first row. He's not doing well at all. I saw him the next day. He hasn't spoken a word in the last year, and he's not eating. As his mother, you should know."

Nostrils flaring, she sat back. "I don't believe you. Mrs. Van Pelt would have told me. Anyway, Karl's always been on the small side."

He reached for her hand, but she crossed her arms again. The guard pounded the table once to warn him back. "His face and his legs are bruised. I saw a boy knock him over on the playground." He lifted his palm. "Let me finish. We—Tamar and I—would like your permission to take care of Karl in our home until you're released. Our twins got along well with him when Tamar took care of him, and—"

She hissed. "You are the last people I'd trust to watch him after what you did. We didn't steal art; we simply kept it for a friend. Klaus and I were victims while the real art thief is…dead." She pushed away from the table.

"Wait. Think of Karl. We'll keep him safe, and he'll have friends. By the time you see him again, he'll be a healthy, happy boy. You know Tamar took good care of him. Let us do this for you. Think of it as penance—isn't that the word?"

"Penance, indeed. Penance couldn't pay for what you did to me," she spit out, then stared knives at Daniel. "Tell you what. I'll call Mrs. Van Pelt and see what the truth is. If her story matches yours, I'll be in touch."

He slumped. *What did I expect? Thank you for seeing me*? "I doubt she'll be forthcoming about his condition. Remember that I'm a medical doctor. I've seen Karl. The truth is he's not thriving there. He's in danger."

She sneered at him, then nodded to the guard, and left without another word.

Tamar was watching two children play jacks on the waiting-room floor when he returned. A nearby woman's head bobbed. Probably their mother. Tamar brightened when she saw him and rose to greet him. "How did it go?"

"I'm not sure." He clasped her hand. "Let's go outside. You're probably bored from sitting here."

"No, the children entertained me. We should buy the twins some jacks."

"Good idea. Why don't we stop at that toy store after we pick up our overnight bag from the hotel." He checked his watch. "We'll have time before the three o'clock train." When they were a fair distance from the prison entrance, he gave her a short version of his meeting with Margot.

She listened, eyes fastened on the sidewalk.

"What do you think?"

She peered up at him. "I'm not sure, but I'm glad the guard stopped me before I reached Margot. She'd have rejected anything I said. You handled her better than I would have."

They retrieved the overnight bag from the hotel check-in desk and went to the toy store. Tamar searched for jacks, but found a half dozen other toys she thought they'd like. After pointing to his watch more than once, Daniel grabbed jacks and a bag of marbles. "Just in case Peri doesn't catch on to jacks."

They reached the train station with ten minutes to spare and found two seats together on board. Daniel hugged their bag between his knees. "We're lucky to get seats. Clearly, more people travel to Amsterdam than from it."

Tamar rested her head against the window. "I can't wait to see the twins. Except for our trip to Paris, this was our only trip away from them."

"I hope they weren't too hard on Neelie."

"She's pretty spry for a middle-aged woman." Tamar leaned forward, elbows on her knees. "You haven't told me what you think about our day at the prison."

"I'm still thinking things through. You were a big hit with the inmates. I kept my eye on them. They resisted at first, but your Gilbert and Sullivan got them going. You made wise choices."

"I was praying like crazy. At first I was more nervous than usual. You know, children are much easier than hostile adults. It helped knowing you were there. When Margot started singing that song from *La Traviata*, I didn't know if I should sing louder or stop."

Daniel covered her hand with his. "Letting her take the lead was perfect. The warden told me she was sent to Zwolle from a woman's prison in Amsterdam because she'd become aggressive with the other inmates. Since she's been in Zwolle, she's become withdrawn and often refuses to eat. Dr. Frank was amazed that your singing drew her out. That's why he allowed me to meet with her."

"Still, she didn't believe you."

He lifted a shoulder. "Margot said she'd call the director, but we know how that will turn out."

"We've done what we can. You've told Margot about Karl. What happens now is out of our hands."

"Let's remember that the outcome is in God's hands. Let's see what He does."

Chapter Eight

"Revenge is a dish that tastes best when served cold."

~ Proverb

Margot picked at her supper, moving it around her plate with her spoon. From where Ilse Bergman sat, she hadn't seen the trollop take one bite. The women around her chattered and cackled, but the former soprano's eyes focused solely on her plate, her straggly hair providing a shield from the women around her.

Stripped of their furs and finery, divas like Margo became shadows, like most German wives of the Third Reich. Some, like Ilse, used their anger to fuel their patience—and bided their time. Ilse's anger had provided five years of fuel. Still waters.

Erich hadn't shown his face in six years, but he'd called a few times during the war, demanding that she send him his precious violin and let him speak to their son, Dieter. At first, he'd said it was just a matter of time before he'd return from the occupation in Haarlem. He'd complained about being stationed in the small town of Haarlem instead of Amsterdam. When he did call, he urged Dieter to keep practicing his violin.

In a few of his calls, Erich mentioned a soprano named Margot Sneider—stage name, Margot van Ormer, a Dutch singer. Ilse had heard the sneer in his voice. According to Erich, the soprano could be bought for a price for intel on the Jews.

Ilse knew the change in his voice when he spoke of the other soprano meant he was smitten. Music always captured his affection. Months turned into years, and the trail died, as did her hope for reconciliation with her husband. Erich always underestimated her because of her small stature and practicality, but he didn't know how deep still waters went.

Someone jarred Margot's arm, and she lashed out with a slap. Good. There was still latent ire in that woman. Ilse would ignite that anger when the time came.

The fortuitous day had shown the face of her husband's infidelity. If Erich was dead, it was Tamar Feldman's fault, a Jew of all things. One thing Ilse knew—Erich Bergman was too smart to die at anyone's hands. Her husband always said he was the master of his own fate. He'd probably escaped to South America or to a tropical island where he was sitting on an island drinking martinis. Margot would know. As long as Ilse was alive, she'd find him and make Erich and those two tramps pay for what they'd done to her and her son.

"Finish up your meals and line up. Time to go back to your rooms," a guard yelled.

An inmate pushed a wheeled tub of water behind Ilse's table for inmates to discard their plates, cups, and utensils. The soggy stew did little to whet her appetite, so she'd taken only a bite a two. She longed for a solid piece of meat—sauerbraten or a juicy German sausage. The bland Dutch food made her yearn for the honeyed sweetness of strudel and the acidic taste of sauerkraut. If she got a chance to work in the kitchen, Ilse would suggest easy changes to heighten the boring gruel, but she was stuck mopping the halls. At least it gave her access to the other female inmates, and she didn't plan on sticking around much longer.

She stood and glanced in Margot's direction. The women around her were already lining up at the door. Margot still sat, toying with her spoon, a shadow of the diva who had screamed when they took a razor to her hair. She even lunged for the guard's eyes when they clipped off her fingernails. Now Margot was a shell, a wraith of the fighter she had been in the beginning. Her spunk faded, leaving her a bag of shuffling bones—until she sang. Then a metamorphosis had taken place. Music brought Margot back to life.

Time to start her plan. She followed the women from her table to the door but lingered at the edge of Margot's table a few meters away from her. "Time to leave, Diva."

The soprano's head bobbed up, her eyes widening that she was alone at the table.

"Here, hand me your tray. I'll dump it for you." Ilse scurried forward and held out her hand.

Margot gave her the tray. "Thank you." She stood, smoothed her prison tunic, and pushed in her chair.

"I enjoyed your song today. Opera—imagine that in a place like this. You have a beautiful voice. You must be a professional singer, am I right?"

"I was. Margot van Ormer was my stage name. Perhaps, you have heard of me. I was the principal soprano at Haarlem's Opera for many years, but the war changed everything." She stared out the window for a few moments, then shook her head and offered a weak smile. "Guess we should line up."

Ilse dumped Margot's plate in the receptacle then hurried to catch up to Margot at the end of the line. "Yes, I've heard of you. Your posters were everywhere, even in my country." The last part wasn't true, but Erich had said in one of the last phone calls that the small town of Haarlem displayed posters of the diva everywhere. "You certainly outsang that other woman. What was her name?" Flattery always worked. She'd piqued the diva's interest.

Margot lifted her diva shoulder. "Just my understudy for *La Traviata.* Hardly worth mentioning." She kicked at a cup that had missed the trashcan. "What's your name? I hear a German accent. What's a German doing in Zwolle prison in the Netherlands?"

"Ilse." How much to tell her? Enough to gain her trust. "I used a fake passport to enter the Netherlands from Germany—"

Margot cast her a sideways glance as they leaned against the wall, waiting for the line to move. "So, I assume your husband was with the—"

"You assume right. I made it to Amsterdam without incident, but I became aware that I was being followed, so I ducked into an alley and shot the guy in the arm. They arrested me, so here I sit."

"Why not at a regular prison? Why in an asylum like this?"

Because I'd recognized you at the prison in Amsterdam and knew you were a link to Erich. But that piece of information was for another day. "Let's just say I didn't play according to the rules." Ilse shrugged. "I like it better here. When I arrived, I got in a fight with a guard, so they sent me to the crisis center for a week, but the staff treated me like a human. How about you?"

Margot studied her and frowned. "I don't remember seeing you at the other place, but I wasn't in the best frame of mind. They said I threw a fit. I said we had a difference of opinion. They sent me here." She blew out a breath. "Can't believe how my life has changed. I went from signing autographs one day to getting fingerprinted the next."

The line moved forward. "How long are you in for?" Ilse asked.

"Another year, but I hope I'll get out in a few months for good behavior. How about you?"

"My case is on appeal, so either very soon or ten more years."

Margot uttered a sigh. "After singing today, I couldn't believe how strong my voice was without warmup or practice. I can't wait to return to the stage. My fans want me back. That woman who performed—Tamar Feldman—can't bring in the crowds like I did. I need to get back to where I belong."

Ilse inwardly smiled. She'd made contact with her mark, and the diva was talking. Today wasn't the time to tell her about Erich. Today was the time to gain Margot's trust and find out what mattered to her. "Your family probably misses you." The grapevine in Amsterdam's prison had already informed her Margot von Ormer had a husband, and the two of them were convicted of art theft, but she'd let Margot tell her that.

"They do miss me—" Her voice trailed off, and her sparkle faded.

"I miss my husband…and my son as well. Do you have any children?"

"A four-year-old boy." Her lower lip quivered. "Karl."

The line moved forward as jail cells clinked open ahead. Margot entered a cell about six before Ilse's. The diva had glanced over her shoulder and offered a wave. It wouldn't be hard to drop a note if needed when Ilse walked past to the lunchroom. She'd make sure to connect with Margot van Ormer during recreation. A saying she'd heard in an American western came to mind. Slow and easy won the race.

Chapter Nine

"When malice has reason on its side, it looks forth bravely, and displays that reason in all its luster. When austerity and self-denial have not realized true happiness, and the soul returns to the dictates of nature, the reaction is fearfully extravagant."

~ Blaise Pascal

La Bohème was not Erich's favorite opera; in fact, it was a sacrilege. He longed for the sonorous sounds of a Mozart, a Wagner, even a Strauss, but the politics of war had made the German operas *verboten* in this country of fools. Nonetheless, he'd endured *La Bohème* at least a dozen times. He'd even awakened himself humming it after the fourteenth performance. If not for the love of his life, he'd return to Paris—a more cultured environment to his tastes—but here he sat in the shadows, watching the orchestra tune their instruments.

The sacrifice was worth it. In minutes, he'd feast on her lovely face, but that would have to be enough for the present.

Erich shifted to let a couple pass to their seats. The woman's fur wrap tickled his nose. He squeezed his eyes shut to suppress a sneeze. *Mind over matter*, the Führer's words came back as they often did. Too bad the Führer hadn't followed his own advice. Erich could have gone to South America as so many of the Reich did, but that would have distanced him continents away from Tamar Visser Feldman. Or he could have taken a pill, as many of his compatriots and the Führer had. A weak man's way out, to his way of thinking.

As many of his fellow officers from the regime had done, Erich could have gone back to Germany after the war—back to Ilse and his son, Dieter, who'd have reached manhood by now. A tinge of discomfort sought entrance. He brushed it away as he did all thoughts that kept him from his goal. His wife was too much like himself—Deep waters, deadly waters. He didn't trust her. Had their son inherited the empty space where the soul should be? There he went again waxing religious. The only object of worship he adhered to was about to enter the stage.

Although he delighted in seeing her, he was tiring of this disguise. He'd accumulated enough money through the art he'd taken to offer Tamar a life of travel, romance, and culture. Romance. How he ached for her—how he'd paid the price for her. His eyes closed, and he leaned against the velvet chairback. Yes, Jewish blood ran through her veins, a travesty in his opinion, and there'd have to be purging before there was pleasure, but he was a patient man.

Fortunately, his old wounds had healed, and as long as he took the medication, he could hold the tremors in his face and hands at bay. This time he had to do things right. Slow and steady wins the race.

A week had passed since Tamar and Daniel had traveled to Zwolle to meet with Margot. Nine days had passed since she'd last seen Karl Sneider, but he was ever present in her mind. Even tonight as she sang "My Name is Mimi," to the half-filled audience at Haarlem's opera production of *La Bohème*, she thought of him, cowering and refusing to eat or speak.

Then she forced her thoughts back to Mimi, who for the next few hours she'd become for the audience. Unlike Violetta of *La Traviata*, Mimi was a woman of simple tastes who loved the scent of roses and lilies, a well-knit tea towel, and the sliver of sunrise that peeked out over the roof next door. It was easier to become a character she liked, and she liked this genuine woman of simple tastes.

The moment arrived—Her voice melded with the woman she played, and she became one with the character. At times the melding didn't happen, but tonight, she became Mimi, and her voice took on deeper shades of meaning.

Three curtain calls and a standing ovation were the response to the troupe's performance, and Tamar was thankful. Still, it bothered her that Haarlem's opera goers hadn't embraced her as they had Margot. The theatre manager blamed poor attendance on the economy. Haarlem had been slow to revive itself after the war, but six years had passed. The producer suggested offering German and Austrian operas next season, instead of the Italian and French ones they'd been showing since the war. Maybe after five years, the Netherlands was ready to welcome back Mozart and Wagner, the countries of their enemies. Still, deep down Tamar wondered if the producers regretted giving her the lead role. Stop that—she told herself. Comparing herself to others only made things worse.

Once she'd removed her stage makeup and the black wig that weighed a kilo, she put on her street clothes and hurried home to her family. Daniel never complained about having to take care of the children two nights a week, and he was patient with them. She had married well. Yet, the time was coming when Mr. Boelen would blame the low coffers on the fact that her understudy took her place for the third performance each week. Two nights away from the twins and Daniel were all she could give, especially since he was on call most nights.

Her thoughts went back to Margot. What had made her come forward as if in a trance and sing? Huh. It was just like what happened with her son, crying out for his mother after a year of not speaking.

When she arrived home, she climbed the stairs to their third-floor bedroom. The light was on, and Daniel sat propped up against the bedstand, but a light snore emanated from him, and the book he'd been reading sat on her side of the bed.

She changed into her nightdress, then treaded across the hall to check on the twins. Although there were more than enough bedrooms on the floor above, the twins had decided to stay in the same bedroom across the hall from their parents. She lightly kissed each of them. Something sticky remained on Peri's cheek that smelled of syrup. That boy. He'd probably sneaked a taste of it when Daniel wasn't looking.

Tamar was just about to cross over into her bedroom when there was a knock on the door three floors below. Who could be calling this late at night? An older couple lived in the house on the left, but they were visiting family out of town. The house on the right belonged to her babysitter, Mrs. Libnitz, but she went to bed early.

She hurried into the bedroom to wake Daniel, but then thought against it. The knocking started again. Tamar slipped into her robe, stepped into her slippers, and headed downstairs.

Through the beveled glass, she could see a short person and another head. Tamar opened the door just as the doorbell rang.

A short woman in a habit stood there holding a child in a hooded jacket on her hip.

"Sister Adela, is that you? What are you doing here this late at night?" She stepped aside. "Please come in."

Her eyes opened wide. "Yes, I'm Sister Adela. You're the opera singer—" She covered her mouth with her free hand. "I didn't expect to see you. I'm here to see Dr. Feldman. He gave us his card a few days ago." She sniffled and brushed away tears, then entered the foyer. "I'm so sorry to bother you this late, but I didn't know what else to do."

"Who is this? Is this who I think it is?"

"Yes, ma'am. I've brought little Karl. The boys got to him tonight, sometime between supper and bedtime. When I went in to say nightly prayers with them, Karl wasn't in his bed. When I asked the boys where he was, they clammed up—they did. I finally found him out on the roof. They'd dared him to go out there, then locked him out. Imagine leaving him out in the cold in his pajamas. He was shivering like a wet kitten."

"Oh, the poor little boy. Does Mrs. Van Pelt know you brought him here?"

The diminutive woman lowered her eyes. "No, Madame. I'll lose my job over this, but I just couldn't leave the lad in that place any longer." She swiped at her eyes.

Daniel came thundering down the stairs and joined Tamar in the foyer. "What's going on?" He tied the robe's sash. "Sister, is that Karl Sneider?"

"Yes, sir. He's in a bad way."

He motioned for her to give the boy to him. "Here, let me see him." He took the boy into his arms. "He's shaking like a leaf."

Sister Adela nodded. "Don't know how long he was out on the roof. The boys left him out there. Good thing it didn't start raining."

"What happened?" he asked, carrying the boy over to the only chair in the room.

Tamar turned on the light. After Sister Adela told Daniel what she'd discovered when she entered the boys' dormitory, Tamar added, "Mrs. Van Pelt doesn't know Sister Adela brought him here."

He lifted Karl's pajama top and probed with gentle fingers around his mid-section. Then he rotated his arms and legs. "Nothing's broken." He ran his fingers over the boy's skull. "Ah, there's a goose egg. That might've been the result of when that boy ran into him on the playground." He lifted Karl's eyelids, then told him to stick out his tongue. The boy complied.

"Outside of the bruises on his legs and that bump on his head, I don't see any fractures or sprains. It looks like he has a case of conjunctivitis. I can give you some drops to put in his eyes, Sister. Having said that, I am concerned about his distended stomach. I'd be surprised if he weighs ten kilos. He's not even in the lowest five percent for weight at his age. He's malnourished. What is the orphanage doing about this?"

Sister Adela's lower lip quivered. "Nothing, sir. We have so many children to watch at meal time, I'm afraid he's been overlooked. It could be the older boys steal his food when we're not watching." She wiped her eyes with a handkerchief. "I didn't know what else to do, so I found the card you gave us at the playground. I will be fired for doing so. The director doesn't like bad publicity."

Daniel lifted the child to his chest and rubbed his back like a mother would do with a toddler. "What is the normal protocol for taking care of a sick child? Do you have a doctor onsite?"

"There's Dr. Braam, who lives a block away from the orphanage. He's retired and getting on in years, but he comes if needed."

He handed Karl back to Sister Adela, then took his hat and coat from the coatrack and put them on. "No harm's been done so far. I'll accompany you back to the orphanage and tell the director you brought the child to me because I'm a doctor, and you had my card on hand. Mrs. Van Pelt surely can't fire you based on doing what's best for the child."

Tamar grabbed his arm and pulled him away from the sister and the child. "You can't take Karl back there," she whispered. "He'll just get hurt again. The boys forced him out on the roof. He could've been killed. If Sister Adela hadn't gone in to check on the boys, he would've been out there all night."

"You're right to be worried, but this isn't the right way. Do you honestly believe Mrs. Van Pelt will acquiesce to Karl staying here? She'll charge us with kidnapping, and Sister Adela will lose her job. He's a ward of the province. We can't break the law."

She wrapped her arms across her chest. "The law won't protect him, especially when the director is so worried about the orphanage's reputation. We have to protect him, or he won't survive."

He pulled her into a hug. "Trust me. I'll meet with Mrs. Van Pelt and tell her what happened. Perhaps she'll be convinced that Karl will be safer at our house until his mother is released from prison."

She shook her head. "It won't work. How about you leave him here with me while you speak with her? Tell her we'll return him if she gives you assurance that she will deal with the boys who left him out on the roof as well as provide Karl protection and—"

Sister Adela interrupted their conversation, her voice shaky. "Doctor, even if I lose my job, it's best to leave him here. The director doesn't like to be crossed. I'm sorry. I shouldn't have involved you, but I wasn't thinking straight."

Tamar posted her hands on her hips. "Don't even think that. You did the right thing in bringing him here." She took the boy in her arms. "Daniel, go with her. Maybe the director will listen to you."

He went to the door, his jaw tight. “I still think we should take Karl back; otherwise, she can send the police to get him; then we’ll be charged with kidnapping, as will Sister Adela. We can’t let that happen.”

“But we’re trying to protect the child.”

He shook his head. “The law’s on her side. Please let me take him back.”

She stared into his eyes. Daniel was right. “As you wish.” She handed the boy to her husband. “I’ll be praying every second you’re gone.”

Chapter Ten

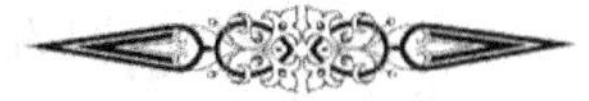

"Oh, Mrs. Lynde, please, please, forgive me. If you refuse it will be a lifelong sorrow on a poor little orphan girl. Would you, even if she had a dreadful temper?
Oh, I am sure you wouldn't. Please say you forgive me, Mrs. Lynde."

~ L.M Montgomery, *Ann of Green Gables*

Daniel and Sister Adela didn't speak the whole way to the orphanage. His thoughts filled with how he planned to approach the director. From what Tamar had told him, she was not an easy woman to deal with, and she wouldn't be receptive to a doctor acting outside his jurisdiction. He was quite sure he'd made the right decision in returning the child for legal reasons, but that didn't make it morally right.

The orphanage was dark when they arrived, the only light coming from the lantern over the entry. Sister Adela used a key to unlock the front door, which opened into a small waiting room with a receptionist desk on one side and a half a dozen wooden chairs lining the other two walls. The sister stopped, turned on the light, and pointed at the chairs. "Wait here. I'll go wake her up." Worry lines framed her face.

A sense of foreboding weighed heavy on his shoulders. He placed Karl in the seat next to him, the boy's head propped on his lap. A myriad of disturbing thoughts assailed him, but he prayed for a receptive response from the director for the welfare of this poor child, bereft of parents and friends. He thanked God for Sister Adela, who'd taken a huge risk in bringing the child to their door. Daniel prayed that she wouldn't lose her job.

A strident voice and the pounding of footsteps came from the stairs just past the reception area. "This is highly irregular, Sister Adela. How could you shirk your responsibilities like this?"

A tall, thin woman strode toward him, dressed in a long brown robe, her hair hidden under a black net. Without a greeting, she stopped by the desk, motioned with her head toward the office door behind it, and said, "Follow me, Doctor." When he picked up Karl, the director lifted a hand. "Leave him there. He'll be fine." She disappeared into the office.

Karl's eyes opened and darted around, his lip trembling. "It will be okay, Karl. You stay here, and I'll be right inside that room." He pointed at it. The boy rubbed his eyes.

With a fortifying breath, Daniel entered the office. Sister Adela sat in one of two chairs facing the director, her hands folded on her lap. Daniel took the seat next to her. The director had donned black glasses that magnified her eyes.

"Doctor…Feldman," she read from his card. "Sister Adela has informed me of what happened tonight. As I told her, she didn't follow protocol. We have our own doctor who could have examined the child. She shouldn't have brought an outsider such as yourself into this private matter. For that, I offer you my apology for interrupting your sleep."

"Thank you, but no harm has been done. Sister Adela had my business card and did what she thought was best under the circumstances—"

"Under the circumstances, she should have awakened me and followed the rules we've established. It appears that Karl is fine, so we thank you for bringing him back where he belongs." She stood indicating the meeting was over.

Daniel remained where he was sitting. "The child's lips were blue with cold, and a quick check of his body showed many contusions and a large swelling bump on the occipital part of his skull. He needs medical attention."

"Which we will provide for him in the morning when I contact our doctor. Thank you for coming."

He wasn't ready to concede defeat. What he wanted to say would certainly elicit a negative response. "I'd like to confer with the doctor about my findings. Do you have his business card?"

The director remained standing, stuffing documents into a folder. "That would be highly inappropriate. We will deal with this in-house." Steely eyes stared back at his.

Daniel could hold back no longer. "Then, I would like to keep the boy with me until such time as your doctor can examine him. Days ago, I witnessed an older boy run into him on the playground. The bruises over his body and the fact that older boys locked him out on the roof show that he's not safe in this place. You and your staff cannot watch him all the time. I'm sure his mother would want her son's safety above all things." He stood, refusing to break eye contact with this imperious woman.

Mrs. Van Pelt leaned forward over her desk. "I spoke to Mrs. Sneider, and she informed me about your wishes." She smirked. "Yes, Doctor Feldman, Margot told me you and your wife visited her in Zwolle, but I have assured her that her son is in no imminent danger. You are aware that younger children can benefit from their interactions with older ones. It's called socialization."

For the first time, Sister Adela spoke up. "That child needs more help than we can give him. Please, Madame, let the boy stay with the Feldmans, at least until we've had a chance to deal with the boys who locked him out on the roof. He could have fallen off." She stood. "You can fire me. Perhaps I deserve it, but I was only thinking of the welfare of the child. Karl Sneider needs medical help and a place where he can feel safe. He hasn't talked since he arrived a year ago until the day he heard Mrs. Feldman sing."

A shrill alarm went off. Mrs. Van Pelt ran to the door. "It's the middle of the night. What did those boys do now?" She whipped around. "Sister, come with me. Go home, Doctor Feldman." The director sped out the door.

Sister Adela started to follow then stopped. "Take him," she whispered then slipped out of the office.

The alarm continued to clang. Crying came from the reception area. Daniel hurried out to the chairs where he'd left Karl. He was sitting up, rubbing his eyes. His arms lifted when he saw Daniel. "Papa," he sobbed.

"Oh, sweet boy." Daniel hugged him to his chest. Was he so starved for adult affection that he mistook him for his father? He hadn't seen his papa in almost two years. At his age, he probably didn't remember him.

The alarm continued to clang, causing him to cover his ears. Daniel headed to the door, opened it, and stepped outside. His next decision would have huge repercussions, which was why he held the door open with his foot. Daniel thought back to what the director had said about her conversation with Karl's mother. Margot had heeded his warning and called the director. From what Mrs. Van Pelt had said, she'd assured Margot that Karl was safe at the orphanage, so Margot had relented and had not given permission for him to stay with them. That meant that the minute Daniel removed his foot and the door locked behind him, he could be charged with kidnapping. *Lord, forgive me for breaking the law.* He removed his foot.

The evening had cooled in the half-hour Daniel had been in the orphanage, and it was raining lightly. With a shiver, he wrapped his jacket around the trembling boy and stepped up his pace. His mind ran through the possible outcomes of taking Karl. If the boys were responsible for the alarm going off, maybe the director would relent at least temporarily while she dealt with them. More likely she would call the police, who would show up at his door and arrest Tamar and him. That possibility almost had him whipping around, returning to the orphanage, and pounding on the door.

No, outcomes were in God's hands. All Daniel had to do was to take the next right step. A four-year-old had been locked out on a roof in the middle of the night. He'd brought the issue to the director, and she'd refused his request. Since the staff was too small to supervise the children at all times, Karl Sneider was still in danger. *Ergo*, the next right thing to do was to bring the child home with him.

When he reached his house, he shifted Karl to his other arm, opened the door, and climbed the steps to the kitchen. The moment he entered the room, Tamar flew to his side and took the child. Daniel dropped to a chair and took a sip of Tamar's tea.

She joined him, propping Karl on her hip. "Oh, you poor boy." She sat down. "From the look on your face, I deduce things didn't go well."

He leaned back in his chair and closed his eyes. "It was the weirdest thing. Apparently, Margot had called Mrs. Van Pelt about Karl's condition, but the director had allayed her fears and assured her the orphanage was the right place to 'socialize' her son." He added bunny ears. "Just when she dismissed me, the alarm went off, and she and Sister Adela dashed out of the office. So, there I was, faced with a dilemma. Was the alarm's timing a signal from God to take Karl? Or would the police show up at our door to arrest me for kidnapping?"

Tamar ran her hand down the side of his face. "We can't worry about what might happen, or it will drive us crazy. It's no accident that Karl is back in our lives. God wants us to look after him until his parents can. Why else would all the events in the past week have taken place? Think about it. You saw a boy harm Karl with your own eyes. The warden allowed me to sing for the prisoners and you to meet with Margot. Sister Adela used your card to bring Karl here after being locked out on the roof. Then the alarm."

He nodded and winced at his pounding head. "The director is an intimidating woman. She is more worried about the orphanage's reputation than the welfare of one little boy."

"See? If she's so worried about the place's reputation, she won't tell the police. If anything, she'll come by herself or send Sister Adela to retrieve him, if she still has a job."

"From your lips to God's ears." He shuddered. "That woman scares me. I get the feeling she doesn't like to be crossed."

"Tomorrow may be a long day. Let's put this one to bed and get some sleep ourselves." She stood very slowly so as not to wake up Karl, who was fast asleep against her chest. "Will you lock up? I'll wait for you."

Once he turned off the kitchen light, he joined her at the bottom of the stairs and took the child from her. The century-old creaking stairs were steep and narrow enough without having to protect a child, although Tamar was used to climbing them.

She turned to him, sporting a jaunty smile. "Not to worry. We have one advantage—we know that a four-year-old was left on the roof at night at the orphanage. Mrs. Van Pelt wouldn't risk that information leaking out to the police or the newspaper."

"You may be right. Guess I don't have to worry about losing my medical license just yet." A sobering thought came to mind. "Do you think we should tell Margot what happened to Karl? She has a right to know, as does her husband, but I don't know where he is." Daniel reached the fourth floor and carried him into their bedroom and laid him on the settee that usually served as a place to throw their clothes for the next day. He covered him with an afghan Neelie had knitted for them for Christmas.

Tamar didn't answer until they'd both climbed into bed. She propped herself up on one elbow. "Something's different about Margot. It's like she's lost herself. At least she called the director. That shows she cares about her son's well-being."

He punched his pillow then rested his head on it to face her. "I'm not sure what we should do. Hopefully, Margot would have sufficient proof to allow us to keep Karl here. However, hearing that her son was locked out on the roof might put her over the edge. She's holding on to a bare thread as it is."

He leaned over and kissed her, then turned off the lamp. Then he stared at the ceiling, eyes wide open. The shadow of the English oak branch outside their window swayed like a metronome, but it wasn't putting him to sleep. He rolled over on his side to face his wife. "Tamar, what if the director calls Margot first?"

Tamar's eyes opened with a start. She swiped hair out of her face. "What did you say?"

"Sorry. I didn't realize you were already asleep. I said, what if the director calls Margot tomorrow morning? Wouldn't that information be better coming from us? Then we can assure her that Karl's not in any danger."

She yawned. "Wish we could call her now. If someone called me and told me my child had been kidnapped, I'd…I don't know what I'd do, but at least I'd be able to do something about it. You're right, Daniel. We need to tell her before the director can get to her."

Chapter Eleven

"Stronger than lover's love is lover's hate. Incurable, in each, the wounds they make."

~ Euripides, *Medea*

Margot jerked her arm away from the attendant who accompanied her to the warden's office. What had she done now? Maybe someone had slipped on a floor she'd mopped. The shoes Margot wore were so big the only way they stayed on her feet was if she shuffled along. She could just imagine what she looked like. Her hair, chopped off and uneven, needed a wash. Her fingers were reddened and cracked from the scrub water.

At one time she'd been pretty. Her face had adorned the marquee outside Haarlem's opera house for months. Posters of Margot's Carmen, Violetta, and Juliette hung on walls all over Haarlem and Amsterdam. Then the war ruined everything for her, but the war was over, and she was biding her time. As soon as she got out of this place, Margot van Ormer's name and face would be back on those marquees as the head soprano. She'd given them a taste of her voice the other day when she stole the show from her former understudy. Imagine that—she had single-handedly brought a roomful of inmates who'd never stepped foot in an opera to their feet with a single song!

They reached the warden's office with the attendant's fat fingers clamped around Margot's arm. How was her husband faring in prison? Were they making Klaus wash floors? She couldn't imagine how her dapper husband handled wearing prison garb. Funny how Klaus seldom came to her thoughts. Their son, the things they'd lost, yes, but not her husband. They had been drifting apart for months before their arrest. It was Klaus's fault, although he always maintained if she wasn't such a diva, they wouldn't have to live off the proceeds of stolen art.

The attendant knocked at the door. A male voice ushered them into the office. The warden remained seated behind a steel desk. Margot had never met the man, but she'd seen him from a distance in the cafeteria. He tried to convey a friendly demeanor, calling them guests and spouting his goal to help them become productive citizens. She didn't need to be rehabilitated; she just needed to get out of here.

He motioned to the single seat in front of him, then told the attendant she could wait in the hall. Opening a file, he scanned a form then smiled. "Mrs. Sneider, I'm the warden, Dr. Frank. I wasn't present when you sang, but I've heard about how favorably our guests responded to your singing, but that's not the reason for this meeting." His face sobered, as if he were searching for the words to say. "I received a phone call earlier this morning. It seems your son has experienced some trouble at the orphanage."

"What happened to Karl?" When Margot stiffened, he lifted a hand. "Not to worry. The gentleman who called me—a Doctor Feldman—wanted you to know that Karl is safe and is staying with him and his wife at their house until you advise him what you want him to do."

A wave of rage swept over her. "Who gave him the authority to take my son away from the orphanage?"

He leaned forward. "Settle down, Mrs. Sneider. The last thing I want to do is upset you, but I'll tell you what I know. It seems last night one or a few of the boys dared your son to climb out on the roof, then they locked him out there."

She gasped and covered her mouth with her hand. "So, it's true. They are bullying my son. How could the director allow that?"

The warden handed her a tissue. "He wasn't harmed. One of the employees went up to check on the boys, and she discovered what they did. In an effort to protect your son, the employee took the boy to Doctor Feldman's house. It was after midnight."

"Why him of all people?"

He shrugged. "All I know is once the doctor checked him over, he took him back to the orphanage and met with the director. She hadn't been told about the incident but said she would handle it."

Margot blew out a breath. "So, why am I here?"

"An alarm went off, and the director and the other employee dashed out of the room to handle the emergency. Doctor Feldman didn't want to leave your son in the reception room, so he took him home." He leaned forward. "Your son's fine, but the doctor wants to know if he should keep him at his house or take him back."

Competing thoughts vied for dominance. What was best for Karl? What was best for her? If it weren't for Tamar Feldman, she wouldn't be in this rat-infested hole, and Karl would be living at home with her and Klaus—safe. Tamar had ripped away her freedom, her home, her family, and her career. The answer was clear. She sat up. "I want Karl to be returned to the orphanage."

The warden's face registered surprise for just a moment, then returned to a more impassive expression. "As you wish. I'll take care of it." He nodded toward the door.

As she returned to her cell, second thoughts assailed her, but she pushed them away. The director had assured her Karl was safe. It wouldn't hurt for Karl to learn how to stick up for himself. Bullies were a part of life. When Margot was a child, hadn't she endured the taunts of the other children in her apartment building whenever she told them she had better things to do than play silly games with them?

Karl had to learn to stand up for himself like she did, or he'd never make it. Music had been her best and only friend at school. Her goal to be a famous opera singer kept her going when the kids avoided her on the playground. It didn't matter. She had reached the pinnacle of success—fame, admiration, and love from her fans. Were her fans still there? She had to get out of here—for Karl's sake and her own.

Chapter Twelve

"In the tapestry of life, an orphaned thread can create the most beautiful design
of resilience and strength."

~ Unknown

Laughter bubbled from Karl when he followed Peri's example, jumping over a crack in the sidewalk on the walk back from the park. The sound of his laughter was a melody to Tamar's ear. Her twins had eagerly welcomed Karl, and he'd smiled for the first time this morning. They'd made the right decision to rescue him from the orphanage.

Earlier that morning, when she'd made their usual Saturday breakfast of *pannenkoeken* with raisins, apples, and syrup, the twins had clapped their hands in delight. Karl had stared at his plate without picking up his fork, until Peri aimed his pancake-filled fork toward his open mouth and flew it in like an airplane into a hangar. Soon Karl followed suit, and he finished half his plate of food. He still hadn't spoken, but the twins would have him talking through games and songs in no time.

The phone was ringing when they entered the side door to the house. Tamar ran up the stairs to the kitchen to answer it before it stopped. A male voice responded to her greeting.

"May I speak to Dr. Feldman, please?"

"He's at work. I can give you his work number."

"Is this Mrs. Feldman?"

"Yes, it is." She wished Daniel was home to answer this call.

"This is Dr. Frank, the warden from Zwolle Prison. I just met with Mrs. Sneider and told her what happened at the orphanage. She prefers that you return her child to the orphanage."

"Oh," was all she could say. "Is there another place I could take Karl that would be safer than the orphanage? He's doing so well here. His color has improved, he laughed, and he ate half his breakfast."

"Mrs. Feldman, I'm simply the messenger. Mrs. Sneider is the child's mother, and it's her wish that you return the child. Good day, Madame."

Tamar stood there, phone in hand with no strength to replace the receiver. What was she to do? She'd made it a practice never to call Daniel at the hospital, but did this emergency warrant interfering with his work?" A voice broke into her thoughts.

"This is the operator. What number are you trying to call?"

She glanced at the receiver in her hand, then quickly lifted it to her ear. "Would you call St. Elizabeth Gasthuis please?"

The operator at the hospital patched her through. A female voice answered. "Burn Unit."

"Yes, this is Mrs. Feldman. May I talk to my husband please?" She winced. Daniel didn't anger easily. In fact, she'd never seen him angry after seven years of marriage, but she'd never crossed the line between work and family.

"Hello, Tamar. What's wrong?" His voice was harried.

"I'm sorry to bother you at work, but Dr. Frank called from the prison and said Margot wants us to return Karl to the orphanage. What should I do?"

A huff resounded through the receiver. "Why now? I'm just about to prep for surgery. Call Neelie. She'll tell you what to do." Click.

She stared at the phone. Luckily it was Friday, so it was Neelie's day off. Her tante would tell her what to do. She dialed zero and gave the operator Neelie's number. Laughter came from the parlor. Zari admonished the boys to stop jumping on the sofa. That's all she needed—returning Karl with extra bruises and bumps on his head.

Neelie finally answered with a breathy voice. "Hello."

"Neelie, I'm sorry to call you at the wrong time."

"It's so good to hear your voice, Tamar. I was just outside pruning the bushes when I heard the phone ring. It's a lot of steps to my apartment. How are those grandchildren of mine?"

"They're fine. In fact, they're upstairs making a ruckus with Karl."

"Karl?"

After she spilled the whole story, she said, "I need your advice because I'm at a loss as to what to do."

"Hm. That *is* a dilemma. Why would that woman demand that her son be taken back to a place where the children would hurt him? Is her rancor towards you so strong that she'd put her son in danger? That defies logic even for Margot."

"According to the warden, the director assured her Karl was safe at the orphanage, and she told her that learning to stand up for oneself was good for socialization."

"Pshaw is what I say. There's a fine line between socialization and bullying." Neelie spewed out a laugh. "He's four years old and a tiny one at that. What he needs is a safe environment. Why, he'd be safer here than at that place."

An idea erupted. "Neelie, didn't you tell me the rehab center is taking prisoners?"

Neelie's sigh came through loud and clear. "Not one of my better ideas. They've changed the whole atmosphere of the place. We brought in two inmates from Amsterdam and one from Zwolle."

"Why did they send them away from the prison?"

"Apparently, they were being targeted by other inmates…I see where you're going with this. Much as I'd like to take Karl, we aren't equipped to take children yet. We're short-staffed as it is. Now we have to keep the inmates from escaping, so each of us has to spend two nights per week at the center."

Tamar leaned against the kitchen door. "I see what you mean. Why did you start taking them if you couldn't trust them?"

Neelie breathed a sigh. "We needed the extra funding. You can't see my face through the telephone, but I have a cut on my cheek where Hendrika, one of the inmates, slashed me with a knife. How she got it, I do not know. We must have gotten careless. It hasn't been good for our old Jewish residents. They're not used to other residents taking their seats or grabbing their food. That's not the type of environment you want to bring a young boy into."

"What if Margot was able to take care of her son at your place? You wouldn't recognize her, Neelie. She's so thin—waifish even. It's as if she's a shell of her former self. Yet when Margot sang, her voice was stronger than I ever remember it. It was like she was in a trance." A lengthy quiet followed her words before Neelie spoke.

"Bringing Margot and her son here is something to consider, but the government doesn't work that fast. In the meantime, you have to make a choice—Take the boy back and hope the director will keep a closer eye on him, or keep him and be charged with kidnapping—"

"And we'd both be arrested, and our kids would end up in the same orphanage with that same director—" A shudder traveled down her spine. "Can you imagine what would happen to Peri if he was locked out on the roof?"

"He'd slide right off, laughing all the way."

"Yup, all the way to the hospital."

Neelie chuckled. "So, what are you going to do? No, let me ask that in a different way. What is the right thing to do?"

She groaned. "I always thought when there were two choices, neither of which was good, God gave us a third choice. What's my third choice, Neelie?"

"Maybe you should remain where you are for the time being. Sometimes doing nothing is the best advice. Is there any way you can stall until Daniel's home? Another thing you could do is find a way to meet with Sister Adela to see if anything has changed at the orphanage. That's my advice."

"An extra few hours will give me time to prepare Karl for going back. Thanks, Neelie."

Tamar hung up but remained in the kitchen, the sounds of laughter pealing from the parlor. She'd call Sister Adela first to see if they could meet somewhere away from the orphanage. If she could assure her that Mrs. Van Pelt was taking steps to protect Karl, Tamar would return him to the orphanage, but if not—she didn't have an answer yet.

Tamar removed Haarlem's telephone directory from the bottom shelf of the baker's rack and flipped through its pages until her finger landed on the number for the orphanage. She took a fortifying breath and dialed the number, hoping she could get through to Sister Adela.

"Haarlem Mennonite Orphanage, Hanneke speaking. May I help you?"

Not the director. Relief swept the tenseness from her shoulders. "Good afternoon, may I speak with Sister Adela please?"

"She's in class right now. May I take a message?"

"She's in class?."

"Religious classes, ma'am. She should be finished shortly."

"Yes, I need to speak with her today if possible. Here's my telephone number." She recited it then thanked her and hung up before she could ask for Tamar's name. A glance at the rooster clock above the sink showed it was four o'clock. She'd have to stay inside until Sister Adela called her. *If* she called her.

The twins and Karl had managed to fill the parlor with weaving paths of dominos. So much for vacuuming or dusting. She returned to the kitchen and removed the makings of banana bread to accompany the meatball soup for supper. Her hands were covered with dough when the phone rang. "No," she said as she ran to the sink to clean off her fingers. No time. She grabbed the receiver, feeling the sticky concoction adhering to her hair. "Hello?"

"Hello, this is Sister Adela. You called?"

"That was fast. This is Tamar Feldman. I didn't want to say my name. What I wanted to know was if it was safe to bring Karl back to the orphanage, in your opinion." She could hear her cover the receiver and say something to someone.

Her voice returned though it was muffled. "Meet me on the south side of Saint Bavo's. Can you come now?"

"Yes, we'll be there." Tamar covered the bowl of dough with a towel, then turned off the oven and the burner on which the soup simmered. She mounted the steps to the parlor and stopped at the top of the stairs so as not to knock over a path of dominos which now had taken over the whole floor. "Children, grab your jackets. We need to go to the square."

Peri, who sat in the middle of his little kingdom, dropped a domino onto the floor. "Aw, we were waiting for Papa to come home so we could show him what we built."

"We'll only be gone for a short time. Come along." She helped Karl to his feet from where he sat on the periphery of the city of dominos.

Zari put down her book and gingerly climbed off the sofa, skirting the row of dominos. Despite her efforts, the side of her foot brushed a few dominos over.

"Oh, look what you did. All that work down the drain," Peri groused.

Zari knelt down and pulled a domino out of the trail, effectively stopping the chain reaction. "You shouldn't have put them so close to the sofa."

"You should have watched where you put your big foot," he said, his stormy eyes on his sister.

"C'mon, you two. I have to meet with Sister Adela from the orphanage. If you stop arguing, maybe we can buy a box of ice cream for later on tonight." She hated rewarding bad behavior, but she didn't have time to waste.

While they hurried the five blocks to Saint Bavo's Cathedral, she fought against the need to carry Karl even though he dawdled behind the twins. It was best for the boy to strengthen his legs instead of relying on adults to carry him. She slowed her gait and called for the twins to slow down. When they reached the corner, she took Karl and Peri's hand and waited for the cars, a bus, and a gaggle of bicycles to pass, then they crossed the street that led to the south side of the large cathedral.

On the way they passed the old side of the hospital where Daniel worked. The historic picture over the door's arch which read 1728 A.D. showed two men in tights and short pants carrying a sick man on an old-fashioned stretcher. When they arrived at the cathedral, Sister Adela was standing in the shade of the majestic church, her eyes darting at the passersby.

She offered a nervous smile when she saw Tamar and the children, then peered at Karl who hung back behind Peri. "Oh, Miss, his coloring has improved indeed. He looks happier than I've ever seen him. Thank you for meeting with me here. I didn't think it wise to speak in front of curious ears."

Tamar nodded. "Karl's appetite has improved, and he's enjoyed going to the park and playing with the twins." She pulled them close. "Sister Adela, meet my children, Zari and Peri."

"Pleased to meet you, ma'am," Zari said, then elbowed her brother.

"Hello," he said, a slight frown spreading across his face. "Are you going to take Karl away from us?"

"I don't wish to," Sister Adela said, then looked at Tamar.

Not wanting to speak in front of the children, Tamar pointed at a kiosk that sold baked goods. "Why don't you three go pick out some stroopwafels for dessert." She fished some coins from her pocket and handed them to Zari.

Once they were out of earshot, she turned to Sister Adela. "I received a phone call from the warden in Zwolle where Karl's mother is being held. He said Margot wants Karl to be returned to the orphanage, but I need to make sure he'll be safe there. That's why I called you. What do you think?"

She shrugged. "I don't know what to say. Last night, one of the boys set off the alarm again. When the director and I reached their dormitory, the room was a disaster. Here it was the middle of the night, and the boys were having a pillow fight. Mattresses were turned on their sides, and feathers from the pillows were flying everywhere."

"What did Mrs. Van Pelt do?"

"The minute she entered the room, they stopped what they were doing. They're afraid of her. It didn't take them long to clean up the room and get back to bed. No one would admit to who triggered the alarm. She told them she'd handle the problem today, and then she sent me to bed."

"Did she handle the problem?"

"I don't know."

The children were returning, so Tamar had to hurry. "Did the director say anything about Karl?"

"Don't know. I didn't see her." Sister Adela turned as the twins and Karl scampered up. "He's a different boy," she whispered. "It's not a good idea to return him just yet, but I'll take him with me if you wish."

Tamar smoothed Peri's hair which stood up on end. "How about we accompany you back to the orphanage? We have to honor his mother's request, even if it is misguided."

"Orphanage!" Peri shouted, "You can show us around, Karl." He seized his hand and skipped ahead.

"Peri, stop at the corner. You're going to get run over by a bicycle." When they caught up to the two boys, Tamar took Peri's other hand. "Sweetie, we don't have time to go into the orphanage. Papa will be home soon, and we need to make dinner."

His face stormed. "Then why are we going?"

Good question. "We can at least see the orphanage from the outside. Maybe we can visit another time." Her response seemed to have mollified him for the moment. He and the other two children jumped over the cracks in the sidewalk, chanting a little ditty as they did so. It gave her time to think and pray. *Father, show me what to do. I'm at a loss.*

Fifteen minutes of idle chatter took them to the brown brick, four-story building with yellow trim. They stopped at the corner to let a car go by. Peri looked up as he balanced on the curb. "What's that place?"

"That's the *weehuis*," Sister Adela said.

Peri spewed out a laugh. "*Weehuis*—that's a funny name—like a little house, but it's not."

"No, lad, it's a house for wee ones. An orphanage." Sister Adela said, eliciting a guffaw from Peri and a "makes sense" comment from Zari.

Karl clung to Tamar's leg. With a fortifying breath, she picked him up and took Peri's hand. "Come along, Zari." They crossed the street to the door that led to the office. "Here, Sister Adela. Take him—"

Just then the door flew open, and Mrs. Van Pelt stepped out. "Sister Adela. We wondered where you went. The sandwiches need to be made for supper." Her eyes landed on Tamar, and they narrowed. "Mrs. Feldman? What is the meaning of this?" The director reached for Karl, but he tightened his hands around Tamar's neck, tangling in her hair.

"Don't make me go!"

Tamar jumped back to evade the director's hands. "I'm sorry, Madame. I cannot return the boy." She whipped around and called the twins to follow. What had she just done? How long before the police came knocking, demanding the return of the boy, and taking her into custody?

Chapter Thirteen

"Revenge is the act of passion; vengeance is an act of justice."

~ Samuel Johnson

"Look, it's the opera singer. Hey, diva, how about a song?" A tall inmate with black hair and gray roots took a drag of her cigarette, then moved to block the entrance to the showers, her arms folded tight against her chest. She gestured for another woman who was brushing her teeth to join her. Gray roots lifted her chin. "Cat got your tongue, Diva?"

Margot pushed her bucket forward. "I need to get in there and clean. Move aside, ladies."

Why was everything a battle here? She uttered a sigh. "Please, ladies, let me into the shower. You want it clean, don't you?"

"Here, let me help." The short one kicked the bucket over, dirty water spilling in all directions. Now she'd have to start over, but that was the least of her problems. The last time these two had cornered her, she'd ended up in solitary with a split lip and a black eye. Margot backed up, bumping into someone behind her. She didn't even need to look. They had her cornered. Her hands gripped the mop, her only weapon. In a single bound, she darted to the left and whipped around to face them.

Gray roots spewed out a laugh. "You think that mop's gonna keep you safe, honey?"

"What do you want from me?" Her hands shook as she aimed the mop's handle at the three of them. "I didn't do anything to you." Her voice broke into a sob. She swallowed.

The scarfed woman who'd stood behind her doubled Margot's size. "The lady asked you for a song. Give her what she wants."

Margot fought to stop her lip's tremble. "What do you want to hear?"

"Something lively. Something fun, like that other opera singer sang. The one about the general," Gray Roots said.

"I don't know that song." With a sideways glance, she estimated the distance to the bathroom's door. Could she make it before Big Girl caught up with her? She wasted no time in running out of the room.

The German lady from the cafeteria waited just outside the door. "Follow me."

Clamoring footsteps sounded from the bathroom/shower room. Margot wasted no time in following the woman, who led her to the supply closet. They slid in, turned off the light, and stood in the dark.

Once the footsteps outside the room were at a safe distance, Margot released the breath she'd been holding. "Thanks for the rescue. I'm sorry, I don't remember your name."

"You're welcome. My name's Ilse." The slight woman with a brown braid inched open the door. "I think we're safe." She opened the door further, and they slipped out.

A tear dropped down Margot's cheek. "I don't know how much more of this I can handle. Now I gotta go back and finish the job, or the guards will write me up again."

"I can stand as a lookout for a few minutes, but I'm starting a new job in the cafeteria. Dishwashing mainly, but I hope to graduate to cooking. That's what I do best."

Margot offered a weak smile. "You're a bit too small to take on the three of them."

Ilse winked. "You'd be surprised what a desperate woman can do."

They entered the bathroom, puddles of dirty water covering the floors leading to the shower. While the German woman stood guard, Margot quickly mopped up the water, hurried back to the closet to replenish the bucket with clean water, and made quick work of the showers. It wasn't the best of jobs, but it would suffice. Time was limited until Gray Roots returned with her assistants. With a quick glance around the bathroom, she hurried out into the hall to stow the mop in the closet.

"I hate this place." The voice behind her made her startle. She whipped around.

"You scared me. Guess I'm on tenterhooks. Thanks for watching guard over the bathroom." She sputtered. "Can't believe I just cleaned a bathroom. I used to hire others to clean mine." She shook her head. "How did all this happen?"

Ilse patted her shoulder. "Don't give them another thought. You're better than they are; in fact, they're not fit to clean your shoes. Remember who you are—a famous opera soprano! They're just envious. So why the doldrums?"

"My son, Karl. Remember that singer from the other day—Tamar Feldman? The warden called me in and told me she and her husband took my son from the orphanage. Can you believe that? Said the boys in his dorm locked him out on the roof. The warden wanted to know what to tell her."

Ilse's eyes flamed. "She kidnapped your son? Isn't she a Jew?" she spat out.

"Yes, to both questions. I told the warden to tell her to return my boy immediately. The director assured me he's safe at the orphanage. She said he'll never grow up if he's constantly coddled."

"I certainly wouldn't trust Feldman. You can't trust their kind. They'll take everything you got if you let them. Even husbands." She shuddered.

Her remark gave Margot pause. "Sounds like you speak from experience."

"You'd be right. That's why I'm in this backward country. To reclaim what's mine." Her lips tightened, but she offered no more information.

Margot had so many questions, but they'd reached Ilse's cell. "Thank you for your help today. I owe you one."

"Just keep your eyes peeled in all directions. Something will open up, I guarantee it." She slipped in, and the door clanged shut behind her.

Filled with more questions than answers, Margot headed to her cell. She'd left her cell door propped open. The guards allowed those who were working to do so, since they didn't have time to lock and unlock their doors. Of course, the inmates took advantage of that small freedom, which had left her vulnerable to the three who'd accosted her in the bathroom. She pulled the door shut and listened to the lock engage. Time was running out. She had to get out of here before they killed her.

Pulling the blanket around her, she curled up into a ball, so her feet didn't stick out of the short blanket. Mixed thoughts vied for predominance. If what the warden said was true about Karl being locked out on the roof, then Tamar had rescued him from a dangerous situation, but how had she known about Karl being on the roof? Too many questions didn't have answers and wouldn't unless she got out of here.

She turned over, her hip digging into the concrete bench, and she punched the pillow. Her voice had provided the door to success. It had provided a means of escape from the tenement apartment she'd grown up in. Could it be the key to open the cell door? How strong her voice had been when she sang Violetta's song, and what a great ovation she'd received. Who would have thought a group of ruffian inmates would have stood to their feet. Margot flipped over again. She wanted more. She wanted her life back. If music had rescued her before, it would rescue her again.

Perhaps she could meet with the warden, saying she'd changed her mind about Karl even if he'd already been returned. He'd most likely say it was too late, then she could offer to sing for the crowd again. Somehow singing would be her ticket out of the place—she felt sure of it.

A plunk-like sound reached her ears. Something lightweight fell to the floor just a few feet away from her bed, then muffled footsteps. What was Gray Roots doing now? Margot blew out a heavy breath and pushed to a sitting position on the concrete slab. Did she have the energy to go see what awaited her? A dead bird didn't make that kind of sound. It was more like a gentle thud.

She pushed to her feet and took measured steps, not wanting to step on anything foul. Only the ubiquitous shimmer of light from down the corridor broke the sheer darkness in the cell. In the dim light, she knelt beside a folded square of paper. Did she dare read it now? Some threat about what would happen to her if she didn't pay for their protection? She'd received a few such notes before.

Picking it up, she unfolded the paper and stuck her hands between the bars of the cell door for a glimmer of light to read it. Her shoulders lifted and fell in a huff. Why couldn't they just leave her alone? This handwritten scrawl was unlike that of the previous two notes she'd received.

Meet me by the ivy 1600.

Tamar paced the floor, waiting for the knock on the door. She could see it all now. Two policemen would be standing there. They'd demand she turn over Karl, and when she refused, they'd put her in handcuffs right in front of her children and take her away.

Daniel hadn't said much when he arrived home late while she and the children were eating supper. His eyes had landed on Karl, then he gave her a slight nod and proceeded to ask the twins about their day. After supper he'd offered to do the dishes while she put the children to bed. When she returned downstairs after reading them a story, Daniel had already gone to bed.

She hoped he wasn't clamming up, the way he had for the first three years after the war. His way of avoiding the pain of memories of the labor camps was to work harder at the hospital. Unlike Daniel, she wanted—no needed—to talk, to face the past. Now, with Karl sleeping upstairs, she longed for Daniel's touch, his words of consolation. Had she done the right thing in bringing Karl back to the safety of their house?

Grabbing a dishtowel, she mopped up the water around the sink, then headed to the parlor to pick up the toys and put them in the box that sat in the corner. With a quick glance around the room, she turned off the lamp, and trudged up the stairs to their bedroom. The room was dark, with only the steady sound of his breathing. She undressed in the dark and slid into bed. Tomorrow was Saturday, which meant dressing the children for shul. Sleep was long in coming as worries sprouted about how the director would respond to her taking the child.

"Are you still awake?"

Her eyes flitted open. "Yes, I don't know what to do." She flipped over, resting her head on her arm. In the dark, she could make out Daniel's profile—his aquiline nose, strong jawline, and eyes that stared up at the ceiling. "I met with Sister Adela, fully prepared to take Karl back. Sister Adela said things hadn't changed at the orphanage and advised me to keep him."

"What happened?"

"I didn't want to take him back, but since Margot was his mother, I knew I had to return him. The children and I accompanied Sister Adela back to the orphanage. When we reached the place, I picked up Karl to cross the street, and just as we reached the door, Mrs. Van Pelt came out, demanding to know what was going on. Karl's arms around my neck tightened so much I couldn't breathe. He begged me not to leave him. Zari started crying, and Peri clung to my leg. I couldn't do it, Daniel. So, I turned on my heel, apologized, and hurried away. Now I've made things worse. She's sure to call the police." A weighty shudder spewed out. "Could you just hold me? Tell me what to do?"

He didn't answer right away. Had he fallen back asleep? He worked so hard, but he was never too tired to play with the children. She could handle this by herself with God's help. Tamar turned over on her side, resigned to a fitful night. At least she didn't have to worry about working tomorrow, and perhaps the police would wait until Monday to arrest her.

"You know what just occurred to me?" His voice caught her by surprise.

"What?"

"This house—this very house—what did Neelie use it for during the war?"

"To shelter Jews."

"And?"

She gasped. "To hide babies…orphans."

He turned and pulled her into his arms, kissed her head, then whispered in her ear. "Exactly. God answered your prayer. Now, let's get some sleep."

Chapter Fourteen

"Beware the fury of a patient man."

~ John Dryden

Margot huddled in the shade of the stone wall that separated the yard where inmates were allowed a time of recreation from real freedom on the other side. Barbed wire and a guard's station prevented any escape attempts. Derisive laughter came from a group of women sitting on the benches in the center of the yard, smoking rolled cigarettes. Other females walked laps around the oval track, three of whom were the ones who taunted her. Some sat in the grass, lifting their faces to the hot afternoon sun that beat down. Cackles and quick glances at her came from the group who circled the track when they approached where she was standing.

She'd been waiting for the writer of the note for the better part of an hour, the ivy creeping up the wall her only clue to the place where they were supposed to meet. Soon they'd have to form lines to return inside. Something was up. Margot could feel it in their whispered conversations, too far away to hear. It would have been better for her had she accepted their offer of protection, but she didn't need any friends. They weren't her type, and she didn't plan on staying here any longer than she had to. She closed her eyes and wrapped her arms tight across her chest to ward off the sense of unease as well as the chill in the shade.

"There you are," a voice startled her, and she opened her eyes to see the small frame of the woman named Ilse. "Sorry, I had something to take care of." She scratched beneath the scarf that held back her hair.

"What did you mean by that note? Didn't know where it came from." She tilted her head to the women walking the track.

Just then, the loud order to line up came from a guard's megaphone. Margot pushed away from the wall, brushing off a spider crawling down her arm—the least of her worries. "Better be quick. What do you need to tell me?"

They headed toward the two lines forming. "Yesterday, I heard tell that they're planning to ambush you when they can get you alone. Said they intended to wipe the pretty smile off your face once and for all."

A slither of dread traveled down her. She'd proven she could defend herself against one but not three. "Why me?"

The woman next to her shrugged. "Envy? Sometimes keeping to yourself doesn't make you any friends. Just my opinion. You know the saying, 'keep your friends close; keep your enemies closer still'?"

They reached the back of the line. "I gotta get out of here," Margot said. "I was thinking of offering to sing again. Maybe the warden would let me out early if they thought I had something to offer."

The line started moving. Two guards stood on either side while the line trudged forward into the prison corridor. One of the guards pounded his stick on the floor next to Margot's foot. "Silence," he commanded.

Margot shuddered at the sound of it. Her hours were numbered. She couldn't take another beating by the women. Even worse was the quiet cold of the solitary cell that awaited her if they got to her.

Once Ilse reached her cell, she lingered by the door. "I heard of a place in Amsterdam where they take inmates who can't make it in a place like this. I'll see if I can find out more about the place. In the meantime, keep an eye out on your surroundings." Ilse trailed her fingers along the bars then entered her cell.

A tiny flicker of light filled the pit in Margot's stomach, much like the dim light that shone into her cell as the afternoon sun gave way to the early falling darkness of autumn. A song she used to sing to Karl when he whimpered issued uninvited to her lips.

"Sleep, baby, sleep,
Outside there walks a sheep,
A sheep with white feet,
Who drinks his milk so sweet."

Her life was a mess, and her child needed her. Imagine how he felt being left alone on a roof in the dark. They were both in a prison of sorts. It was Tamar's fault that Margot was in this despicable place, and it was her fault that Karl was out on that roof. How could he understand that his mother hadn't abandoned him? She had to find a way to get him back. Escaping wouldn't work. Even if she was successful, she'd never be able to return to the opera. No, she had to curry the favor of the warden—convince him to be released early, but her hearing wouldn't come up for another six months.

A plan began to take shape, although the details remained fuzzy. Perhaps she could demand to see the warden. Tell the guard it was a matter of life or death. Margot had managed to save ten guilders she'd received for selling some cigarettes she'd found in the trash. Her eyes were always alert to things that could be sold from the trash. She didn't trust the guards, but maybe they could be bribed. In the meantime, she'd keep a low profile and try not to be alone at any given time.

A guard walked past, shining a flashlight into the room as she did every few hours during the night. It usually woke her up, but tonight she hurried to the door. "Madame, I need you."

The tall stern woman focused the light in Margot's face, making her cover her eyes. Of the four or five guards, this one never smiled. "You feel sick?"

"No…yes." She coughed to give weight to her plea.

"You'll have to do better than that, diva."

Margot backed up. What did she expect to happen in the middle of the night? The warden wouldn't even be working at this hour. "I'm fine. I need to talk to the warden, but I'll wait until tomorrow morning."

"Don't get your hopes up. He's a busy man."

A week passed with no Gray Roots and her cronies. It was just as well Margot didn't get to meet with the warden. Chances were her request had never made it to him. Outside of the taunts from behind the bars when she mopped the corridor floor—"Give us a song, diva."—there hadn't been any further threats or showdowns. She stopped peering over her shoulder at every rustle or voice when she cleaned the restroom. Ilse hadn't left a note or given her an update, so Margot relaxed, working out a plan to secure an early release instead of worrying about being attacked.

She splashed cold water on her face from the sink before she used a rag to clean it. Afraid to take showers, she waited for the others to leave before she did. If she were caught cleaning herself instead of the floors, it would mean another week in solitary, so the sink was the only safe option.

After dabbing her chest and her arms with the rag, she resumed cleaning the counters and the three stalls, forcing herself to think of other things—like the libretto of her famous opera. When she'd played the lead role back in 1943 before the war began, she identified with Violetta, the courtesan—the woman who rejected societal norms and lived for frivolity. How could she not? That had been her own life. Hadn't Margot merely pointed at a pair of shoes in the show window, and whoever was on her arm at the moment bought them for her? Yes, even a Nazi officer or two. A twinge of an unfamiliar feeling assaulted her to the point that she felt compelled to wash her hands and put on fresh gloves. She suppressed whatever it was and returned to Violetta.

Now, after being forced to live in this place, she understood a part of Violetta she hadn't experienced when she'd played the role—the suffering Violetta, the sacrificial Violetta, the dying Violetta. Mere histrionics, Margot had thought back then. Now she understood what it felt like to be looked down upon, to be mocked, to be powerless.

Violetta had been forced by the father of her lover, Alberto, whom she truly loved, never to

see Alberto again, and she'd reluctantly agreed to let him go. Margot had always thought Violetta foolish. Why give up the man she loved? She should have fought for Alberto. It wasn't until Violetta was on her deathbed that Alberto came to her bedside and was with her when she took her last breath.

Separated from the man she loved. Margot hadn't felt that type of love for a man. Even her husband was a means to an end—her career with the opera—and he was a generous man. Before they were arrested for the art Erich Bergman had hidden in their house, Klaus was close to reopening Haarlem's Opera, which had been closed by the Nazis since the fall of 1943. With its opening mere months away in September 1949, Margot had been taking singing lessons to strengthen her voice, which had suffered from too many cigarettes.

Everything began to fall apart after that understudy of hers entered her life after the war. Yes, Karl had taken a liking to her and her twins, but so had her husband, Klaus. In fact, she'd caught them at the piano, practicing one of Margot's arias, instead of Tamar cleaning the kitchen after lunch. *The nerve of a Jewess—aspiring to rip the lead soprano role from me in my home!* Now that woman had her son.

A twinge of sadness filled her at the thought of Karl. He didn't deserve to be abandoned, left to fend for himself in an orphanage. Apparently, her own mother hadn't wanted to keep the child. Perhaps if Margot had brought him over for a visit a few times, her mother would have agreed to keep him. If truth be told, Margot hadn't wanted to travel to her old neighborhood—that part of her life she'd left behind when she scored her first big role at the opera.

She was cleaning behind the last toilet when a voice directly behind her made her stop and close her eyes. This was it—the end.

"Lookie what we have here." Snickers followed. She peered around for anything she could use as a weapon. Nothing. The only thing she had was the rag in her hand and the bucket at her foot with its milky water. She knew from the sound of the voice it was Gray Roots, and the snickers behind it meant there were more than one.

"Wish I had a camera. Think maybe I could sell a picture of the diva cleaning a toilet to one of them movie mags?"

Margot swiveled around and climbed to her knees so she could face her foes. She would have climbed to her feet, but for the hand on her shoulder. Three of them blocked the stall's door. There was no way to get out of here. Maybe humor would buy her some time. She posted her palms under her chin and pretended to pose. "How's this?"

Gray Roots spewed out a laugh and folded her arms across her chest. "Won't sell any copies. Think you need a hair wash. That might help sell some." In a flash, she pressed her hands against Margot's shoulders, forcing her to lean back until her head touched the water in the bowl. Despite her struggles to get loose, her nose and mouth were forced under the water by the hands that pressed down on her neck. Gray's fingers pressed down on her airways.

A thought penetrated the fury of the moment as her hands fought to release Gray Roots' hold on her. Instead of fighting it, maybe she should let the end come. Maybe there'd just be sleep on the other side. A better bed. Maybe there'd be freedom. God.

Mama, Karl's little face appeared, his blue eyes imploring her, his little hands reaching for her. No, she had to fight for Karl.

With her last bit of strength, she pulled her head out of the water, her flailing hand formed into a fist. She choked out a breath at the same time her fist walloped Gray Roots in the nose. Where had that power come from?

Blood spewed in an arc as the large woman keened backward, uttering a string of profanity as she fell onto the floor.

"What's the meaning of this?"

Gray Roots' cronies froze, their eyes on the source of the voice.

"The diva tried to kill me. I was just washing my hands when she attacked me. Could you get me a paper towel to clean up all this blood?"

A guard's voice. "Grab her a paper towel. You two, take her to the clinic. Did the toilet flood? What's with all this water?" Footsteps, then the sight of a tall female guard, head small, body large, came into Margot's oscillating view. "You're supposed to be cleaning instead of fighting. What's the meaning of this? The warden will have your head."

Margot tried to lift her head, but a spasm of coughing ensued to the point that she vomited all over the front of her already wet prison garb.

The tall woman's pin curls appeared from under her cap. She posted her fists on her hips. "So, you have the grippe. Is that your excuse for busting the gal's nose? What did you do? Pull her into the stall and beat her up? It's not going to be pretty when the warden hears. Solitary for sure."

What was the use of telling the truth? Gray Roots would exact her revenge if she did. There'd always be a next time. "I'll clean it up right away." No good would come from telling the guard what really happened. She and the other guards were probably in the pockets of Gray Roots and her friends.

"See that you do." Once her sensible shoes strode out of the bathroom, Margot pushed to her knees, fought the wave of vertigo, then used the toilet's rim to stand. The room spun, which engendered another bout of coughing and throwing up. Nobody cared. Nobody would help her to the clinic. Nobody would help her clean up the mess of water around her or help her clean off her soggy, stained prison dress.

At the sink she dabbed at her dress with a paper towel and splashed more water on her already-wet face. The red marks on each side of her neck where Gray Roots had held her under the water were starting to turn a shade of purple. She surveyed the pallid face that stared back at her. Dead eyes. Lines framing the mouth. She parted her lips and noted the chipped tooth that had occurred when she was shoved to the floor. When she pushed away from the sink, the back of her head rebelled with shocks of pain. Her fingers gingerly touched the goose egg that was forming where her head had connected with the toilet bowl's rim.

When the vertigo passed, she wheeled the mop and bucket over to the floor outside the bathroom stall and cleaned up the blood of the woman who'd tried to kill her. Where had that power come from to punch Gray Roots? She'd almost given up by that point. It must have been the thought of her son. His voice.

After she finished cleaning up the mess, she plodded to her room, locked the door behind her, and dropped onto her bed. This was without a doubt the lowest point of her life. Why hadn't God saved her? Another thought followed that one. Why should he? She'd never given him a thought in her life, or when she did, she always told herself God was for old people. When she was old, she'd think about him, but until then, there was too much fun out there to be religious.

Memories drifted in, cloudy memories from her time at the opera—from the best time in her life. That woman in the orchestra—the older one who played violin. During rehearsal, Margot had heard her talking about God as if he was real. Not some stained-window version. What was the violinist's name. Cornelia? Neelie for short, but she couldn't remember her last name. She'd told Tamar that God would give her the answers she needed to solve some problem she was having.

She'd rolled her eyes at the violinist's words. Religion was for weak people, not for sopranos who averaged five encores a show. After today, though, maybe religion was what she needed. She certainly had questions that needed answers. *God, are you out there? More likely the devil is in a place like this.*

Chapter Fifteen

"If your enemy is hungry, give him food to eat; if he is thirsty, give him water to drink.
In doing this, you will heap burning coals on his head, and the LORD will reward you."

Prov. 25:21,22

Neelie hated to admit defeat, but what choice did she have? One of the elderly Jewish residents had pulled her aside and whispered that Hendrika, one of the inmates, had knocked one of the men out of his chair, claiming it was hers. Since that time, the man had stayed in his room refusing to eat. As she waited for the warden at Zwolle to answer the phone, Neelie gingerly traced a finger over the scar on her face caused by the same woman. Even if it meant less money coming into the rehab center, Hendrika had to leave immediately.

"Good day, this is Dr. Frank speaking."

Neelie cleared her throat. "Good day, this is Mrs. Neelie Visser calling from Amsterdam. I manage the Jordaan Rehabilitation Center, and I'm calling about one of the inmates you sent."

"Ah, Mrs. Visser. I hope she is fitting in well. What is the reason for your call?"

A sigh preceded her words. "No sir, she is not doing well. Last week she grabbed a knife from the drawer and used it to cut my face. I take responsibility for that because one of our aides must have left the drawer unlocked."

He gasped. "Oh, I am sorry. She never showed any signs of aggression here. Clearly, I was wrong. I hope you haven't sustained any permanent damage."

"No, I'll have a bit of a scar but nothing more. What concerns me is the fact that she's been treating our Jewish residents with some degree of malice. Yesterday she knocked an eighty-three-year-old man off his chair in the dining room, and she's been stealing their food. Now he's refusing to eat. I can't have this, Dr. Frank. Our elderly residents have already lost their families, homes, and friends to the holocaust. They deserve respite, healing, and sanctuary. For that reason, Hendrika cannot remain here. Please understand."

"I see, but what about the contract between Zwolle and your center? It runs until the end of the year."

"Believe me, we need the money, especially since we're having to hire more aides. However, I can't put our residents' lives and security in danger—" A thought interrupted—one that brought hope and fear in the same moment. "Wait, I may have a solution. You have an inmate there, a Mrs. Margot van Ormer—that's her stage name. I'm not certain what her real name is…hello, are you still there?"

"Yes, I am. Are you referring to the singer, Margot Sneider?"

"Yes, I believe so. I used to work with her at the Haarlem Opera before the war. She was the lead soprano."

"Oh, may I assume you're suggesting a prisoner swap?"

Her lips tightened as did her chest. Was she asking for more trouble? Margot had never been friendly to her. She'd been the essence of a diva—demanding, tumultuous, and pompous. She hadn't been kind to Daniel or Tamar. Yet there was that son. "Yes, to be honest, Margot is not one of my favorite people, but I know her son, Karl, is not doing well at the orphanage. It's for his sake I'm making this suggestion. What if I brought her here and allowed her to have her son with her, as long as she took care of him?"

"Hm. Her son isn't my concern, but you should know that Margot has been in a fight or two herself. The guard said she punched another inmate in the nose, sending her to the clinic. Her file is sitting right in front of me."

Was she making a huge mistake? There was a reason inmates ended up in Zwolle instead of one of the main penitentiaries. Hendrika was much worse than the two inmates from Amsterdam's prison. From what Tamar had told her, Margot was a mere shell of what she used to be, but if she broke someone's nose, would Margot be a danger to her Jewish residents? *Lord, keep me from making the biggest mistake of my life.*

"Mrs. Visser, are you still there?"

"Sorry, yes. I was just weighing and praying, so to speak. Hopefully, Margot will fare better than Hendrika has. Perhaps the fact that we have a common interest in the opera will help her acclimate to a new level of freedom. Especially if her son is close at hand."

"As you wish. Just know that there is no changing your mind after this. Hendrika won't have an easy time back here. She was picked on by the other female guests—that is what we call them here. Our guards can't be everywhere, and a pecking order forms, despite our best efforts to teach them social skills. I'm fairly sure your Margot was 'pecked on' as well, which is why I am in favor of your proposal. We might as well do this quickly. Mrs. Sneider will be at your center at noon tomorrow. Please prepare Hendrika to be ready to leave at that time. Good day, madame."

The phone call had long ended by the time Neelie pushed to her feet. What exactly had the warden meant by 'preparing' Hendrika? If she told her now that she was going back to Zwolle, Neelie would have to post a guard at every window and door to keep her from escaping. Even if she told her tomorrow to pack up her belongings to be ready to leave at noon, Hendrika would be sure to escape. It wasn't as if the doors locked people in as they did in Zwolle. She had no choice but to lie to the woman, and Neelie didn't lie. Tomorrow would be a very messy, regrettable day for everyone, except for Margot van Ormer.

A rustle and a thud caused Margot to stir from a restless sleep. As soon as her eyes acclimated to the dim light, she slipped off her cot to retrieve what looked like a folded piece of paper lying just inside the bars. She steeled herself for a threat. It had been three days since the bathroom incident, and she still hadn't been called into the warden's office. Three days since she'd last set her eyes on Gray Roots or her friends. The calm before the storm.

Margot took small, measured steps toward the spot where the note lay. After peering out, she bent to pick up the note which had some weight to it. Her jaw tightened as she opened it, two pebbles dropping to the floor. Why? She breathed easier when she saw the scrawl wasn't Gray's. The writer of this note—Ilse, she presumed—was a fan rather than a foe. She moved to the bars to read it. Breakfast dishes clinked in the distance. Ilse must have thrown it on her way to her work detail in the kitchen.

Word has it one of the ladies is moving to that halfway house in Amsterdam. Maybe your Gray Roots. Heard you broke her nose.

The irony of it all. The bird who chirped the loudest got the worm. At least, Gray wouldn't be around to harass her anymore. She doubted Gray's minions would take her place. Mere followers—sycophants. She'd learned *sycophant* was where the word 'fan' came from, and she'd had her share of them before the war. Maybe that was it. A person got a moment of fame. She'd test that if she ever got out of this place.

"Line up," came from down the hall.

Margot didn't have much of an appetite for the same watery porridge they had every morning, but it was a chance to get out of her small space. She pocketed the note and stood at the door, waiting for its clang. Like clockwork, the door opened and she shuffled into the line, then waited with the other women for the verbal cue to move forward.

With the possibility of solitary confinement imminent, Margot took her seat, noting a few whispers and head nods aimed at her. They'd probably heard about the fight. She ignored them, focusing on the lumpy mixture on her tray instead. The dungeon—that's what she called solitary in her head—was a cold space with nothing but a thin blanket. The September nights would make it even colder—at least she assumed it was September. Meals were the only thing to break up the long hours each day, but often the guards forgot to deliver them.

She poked at the porridge. Maybe she should pocket the spoon. She forced herself to eat three bites, swallowed with a shudder, then lowered the spoon to her pocket.

Just then, someone poked her in the back. “Warden wants to see you.”

Without looking around, she covered her bowl with her napkin, then stood and picked up her tray.

“Leave it.”

All eyes were on her as she preceded a male guard through the cafeteria. A few snickers reached her ears. She refused to react. A pall fell over her, tinged with anger that Gray Roots was rewarded for bullying her while she’d be staring at the gray walls, trying to take her mind off the bitter cold.

They reached the office. She waited while the guard knocked, just like last time when the warden had told her about Karl. He seemed like a nice man, the busy type. Should she tell him what really happened? He probably wouldn’t believe her or care if she did.

The door opened, and the guard ushered her in. This time the warden didn’t look up when he pointed at the chair across from him, then fingered through a pile of manila folders. When he did meet her eyes, they held no warmth. She stared at her fingernails, uneven, cuticles growing like weeds—

“Mrs. Sneider, looks like this is your lucky day.” He huffed as if it gave him no pleasure to say so.

Her eyes met his. “I don’t understand.”

“You’re being reassigned to a halfway house in Amsterdam.”

Her jaw dropped of its own accord. “Thought I was going to solitary for—” She’d said enough. “What about Gray Roots? Thought she was going there.”

“Gray Roots? Not sure I know who that is—” He spewed out a laugh. “No wonder she attacked you.” When she started to speak, he held up his hand. “I know what they told me, but I have my own opinion of what happened. Let’s agree to leave it in the file, okay with you?”

She nodded. "What do you mean by a halfway house?" Her breaths were increasing in speed and volume. "Does this mean I'm being released?"

He raised a hand. "No, that is not what I mean. By halfway house, you will finish your sentence of—" He opened a file and ran a finger down a page. "Fifteen months. You will complete what is left of your sentence in a rehabilitation center." He leaned forward, a frown replacing an otherwise benign expression. "The manager of the facility actually requested you by name. Apparently, she worked with you at the Haarlem opera. Name's—" He picked up a slip of paper. "Mrs. Visser. Name sound familiar?"

"No, but there were a lot of people who worked there, and it's been seven years." Maybe a fan had come through, maybe a maid or the woman in charge of wardrobe. Names were not her forte.

He nodded. "You'll be replacing a previous guest from this establishment, but it didn't work out because she didn't follow the rules and caused problems. Now she'll finish her sentence here, and hopefully she'll live to walk out the door. Do you understand what I am saying?"

She met his cold eyes—cold enough to cause her to shiver. "Yes, sir."

He leaned forward on his elbows. "While you'll have a few more liberties, you are still required to follow the rules. This facility you'll be sent to has only recently been open to our 'guests'—" He paused and stared at her. "The fact that your predecessor is being returned to this establishment tells me that our relationship with the rehabilitation center is tenuous at best."

Margot frowned. "May I ask what type of rehabilitation center it is?"

He looked up from rifling through his papers. "What do you mean?"

"Is it for…convalescing patients or for recovering alcoholics?"

"Neither. It's for Jews who survived the concentration camps. You aren't Jewish, by any chance?"

Her hand went to her chest. "Me? Absolutely not." The forcefulness of her words had the warden studying her.

He frowned. "Would you rather stay here with…what did you call her—Gray Roots?"

Her lower jaw dropped. "No, sir."

"I have to be sure that you'll follow the rules. That means you treat the staff and elderly residents with respect, you don't try to escape, and you help whenever and wherever you're asked to. Do I make myself clear?"

She nodded with vigor. Anything was better than the Zwolle bathrooms.

The warden stood. "Very well. You are a test case. Our future relationship with the halfway house falls squarely on your shoulders. I will be calling Mrs. Visser on a regular basis. If I receive good reports, it may help your cause when you sit before the parole committee. *Verstehen sie*?"

"I understand." The gods must be looking down on her with favor. Or maybe it was the God her grandmother and the violinist used to talk about nonstop. The violinist…Neelie. Could she be the one who asked for her to be transferred to her rehabilitation center? How had she even known she was at Zwolle?

The warden was holding the door open waiting for her to leave. She bolted to her feet. "I'm sorry, sir. My mind is full of thoughts." She peered up at him, then met his eyes. "Thank you very much, Doctor Frank. I will do my best to make you proud."

Chapter Sixteen

"You cannot do a kindness too soon, for you never know how soon it will be too late."

~ Ralph Waldo Emerson

Tamar's heart stirred at the sharp trill of the phone. She still didn't feel comfortable answering it, as usually it meant bad news. Even more so now that Karl was napping upstairs while the children were at school. She swallowed then answered before it stopped ringing. "Yes? I mean, hello?"

"This is the operator. Are you Mrs. Tamar Feldman? I have Cornelia Visser on the line."

"Yes, I am. Please patch her through."

Neelie was giggling when it was finally just the two of them on the line. "You sounded so nervous. How are you?"

"You're right, Tante. Phones make me quake inside. I don't know why, except Karl is here with us, and I expect the police or the orphanage to be calling any moment, but they haven't. That makes me more nervous."

"It's understandable. You were a mere child when the Nazis took your house and your parents. By the time you'd moved in with me, phones were verboten in Haarlem. We had one, but we kept it hidden. Then when you moved back to Haarlem after fleeing from the camps, only the concierge of your apartment had a phone. I remember because she always seemed to be in a bad mood when I called and asked to speak to you."

Tamar untangled a strand of her hair from the telephone cord. "I wasn't exactly a mere child when the Nazis occupied the city. I was working full time at the opera, but you're right—I lived a sheltered life, so I'd never dealt with utilities or rent. In fact, this phone I'm talking on is the first I've ever owned, but I'm sure you didn't call to talk about phones."

"You're right. I have good news and a request."

Tamar leaned her head against the kitchen wall and closed her eyes. When was the last time she'd heard good news? "What is it?"

"You remember I told you the last time we talked about the inmate from Zwolle who slashed me with a knife from the kitchen?"

"Yes, but that's not good news."

"It took me a while to think it through, but I decided Hendrika could not remain in our rehabilitation center. She was bullying the aides and the residents, so I called the warden and informed him about her behavior. He agreed to come get her, but he reminded me that our contract didn't end until the end of the year. It came to me in a moment—a God moment, if you will. I suggested we swap Hendrika for Margot because I knew her and was aware of Karl's problem adjusting to the orphanage. When he didn't dismiss my idea, I told him Margot wasn't my favorite person, but we had a common love of music, and maybe that would help her regain her place in this world."

Tamar couldn't suppress her gasp. "That is good news, Neelie. Such good news. *Baruch atah Adonai*."

"Yes, praise God," Neelie said. "Before I offer to bring Karl here, I need to make sure I made the right decision. The warden said he'd allow the swap this one time, but if it doesn't work, the contract with Zwolle will come to an end." Her sigh resounded all the way from Amsterdam. "So, I'm taking a big risk in bringing Margot here. I'm hoping the chance to have her son with her will be a carrot to motivate good will and behavior on her part."

Neelie was possibly saving her and Daniel from prison. All the tension she'd been carrying the last few days erupted in a flood of tears. "Thank you. Now what is the favor you requested? Anything you ask, we will do."

"I know this is a last-minute request, but I need you and Daniel to be my reinforcements here at the rehab center. Jan's in Paris, or I'd ask him. The aides are smaller and older than I am, as are most of the residents."

"Reinforcements? I don't understand."

"Tomorrow Zwolle is going to bring Margot here and at the same time pick up Hendrika to return her to the prison."

"That's a good thing, isn't it?"

"Think about it. This rehabilitation center is not a prison. The doors and windows open and close as they do in every building. What's going to happen when I tell Hendrika that they're taking her back to Zwolle?"

"Ah, I see. She'll bolt. When are you going to tell her?"

Another sigh preceded Neelie's words. "I'm not going to tell her because there's no way I can keep her here if she decides to escape. So, here's my request. Would you consider coming to sing for the residents tomorrow around eleven in the morning? Daniel could be here to guard one of the doors. I wouldn't bring the children tomorrow, if I were you. When the guard shows up with Margot, perhaps I can convince her to sing a song or two. That will give the guard time to take Hendrika away peacefully, I hope."

Tamar blew out a forceful breath. "Sounds like a spy story. So many things could go wrong, but I'll help you any way I can. Mrs. Libnitz will watch the children tomorrow. She's a widow and works in the nursery at shul. I can't wait until all this trouble—" A loud rapping on the door sounded from the first floor, the force of which she'd last heard when the Nazis demanded entry into this very house seven years earlier.

"They're here, Neelie. The police. What should I do? They'll arrest me and take the children. Daniel's at work." Her breath came in fits and starts.

Neelie's voice was low and measured. "Grab the kids and go hide in the attic. The room's still there. Stay until the police leave, then bring the kids here. Call Daniel when you reach the train station and tell him to come here. Margot will be reunited with her son sooner than anticipated. Now you go, and I'll be praying for you."

The banging at the door continued. Tamar hurried up the stairs where the children were playing with pick-up sticks, which were strewn all over the floor. “Children, we’re going to play a new game. It’s called the quiet game. Follow me up the stairs, and I’ll show you a wonderful hiding place, but you must not make a sound. Understood?”

A gleeful expression spread across Peri’s face, but he settled at the pointer finger to Tamar’s lips. Zari’s frown showed she understood something was amiss. “Isn’t someone at the door?” she whispered.

“Yes, but we’re going to pretend to be away. Trust me.” Tamar offered her a poor excuse of a smile, then ushered the three children to the attic on the fourth floor.

“Eema, where are we going? We’ve never been in there before. You told us we couldn’t.”

“Hush, Zari. Remember we’re playing the quiet game.” Zari was right. They’d not let the children enter the attic for a variety of reasons. One was to prevent Peri from climbing out of the window onto the ledge. Maybe when he was older, he’d understand the danger, but Tamar had her doubts his temerity would give way to caution.

Rapping sounded again from the first floor, but distance made it fainter.

Peri held Karl’s hand, as if he knew he had to be the big brother. It warmed Tamar’s heart. “Eema, someone’s knocking on the door.”

Tamar reached up to release the hook from the eye at the attic door, hoping Peri wasn’t watching too closely. She lowered her head to fit through it. Memories washed over her so violently that she held onto the wall until the fugue passed.

“What’s wrong?” Zari whispered loud enough to be heard across the canal. She gripped the side of her dress. “Don’t you feel good?”

“I’m fine, *liefje*. Shh.” Her eyes took in the whole room. So many memories. Neelie’s storage boxes took up most of the attic, since she’d lived here all her married life, and her husband’s family had lived in this house for over a hundred years. Houses like this one along the canal were Haarlem’s oldest treasures. Daniel and her storage boxes took up half a corner—mainly Daniel’s medical books and her children’s outgrown clothes.

To her right on the wall hung the full-length mirror. The Mirror. Horrible memories returned, but she stuffed them away to be opened later. Instead, Tamar felt along the wall adjacent to the mirror's left side for the button. When her fingers landed on it, she pressed it, hoping it still worked after so many years.

Rapping came a third time from below. They weren't giving up. If it were the police, they would have a warrant that would allow them to search the house, just as the Nazis had done back in the day. Of course, they hadn't needed a warrant. Perhaps today would be a good time to tell the children the story about the little room behind the mirror.

The door creaked as it opened, setting Tamar's jaw on edge. Gasps flowed from the lips of the three children as the room behind the mirror came into view.

"It's like magic," Peri said, louder than he should.

"Magic," repeated Karl.

"Why is this room here?" Zari grabbed onto Tamar's belt, then inched forward. "Looks like the nursery at shul."

Tamar rested her hands on the shoulders of the boys. "Let me go in first to make sure it's…safe." She had refused to look in this room, even when she'd spent time up in the attic unpacking or looking for their passports. Sometimes she heard noises coming from above when she was on the floor below. Telling herself it was a squirrel usually calmed her beating heart.

This house…this attic held the past she'd worked so hard to sublimate. She'd lived here only three months back then—lost in a whirlwind of fear and grief. No more of that. Now it was time to face those phantoms of the past.

Three folded cribs lined the back wall. Other than that, the narrow room was empty except for a stack of law books—Jan's most likely. He'd lived here during the years his mother, Neelie, was in the camps. If he hadn't, the Nazis or their sympathizers would have taken over the house as they had so many along the canal.

When Peri and Karl started jumping up and down, she clamped a hand on their shoulders and pointed toward the wall. "Go sit over there. Remember, we're playing the quiet game. You must not speak. Do you understand?"

The boys glanced at each other and nodded, imitating her finger against their lips. Tamar took measured breaths to calm her heart, then joined them on the floor.

"Why are we here, Eema? Is it because of Karl?" Zari queried.

"Maybe." She couldn't lie to her daughter. "Would you like to hear the story of this little room?" All three children nodded with vigor. "All right." Where to begin? She couldn't tell them the whole truth. The story was hard enough for an adult to handle, much less young children. "Once upon a time, before you were born, before Papa and I were married, he and I stayed at this place."

"In this little room?" Peri asked, then pointed at the cribs against the wall.

A laugh almost burst out, but she caught herself. "No, silly. I wasn't a child then, but I was young and still lived with my eema and abba."

"Did Papa live with you and your mother and father?" Peri asked.

Leaning against the wall, Tamar pulled her son close to her side. "No, your father worked in the Dutch Resistance. He was a very brave man. Your uncle Seth also worked for the Resistance, and so did I after the opera house closed down."

"*Re-sis-tance.* Isn't that a bad word?"

Hm. She'd never thought of that before. "It could be, I guess. You'll learn about this in school someday. Back in 1943, way before you kids were born, there was a war here in Haarlem. A man named Hitler wanted to control the whole world, so he and his soldiers marched into town and took over. Your father and many others didn't want the leader and his soldiers to win, so they resisted, but they had to do so in secret."

"Wow. So, was this the secret room Papa hid in?" Peri asked, his eyes wide.

"No, son." Karl's eyes were starting to close, so she brought him onto her lap and rocked him as best she could. "No, at least not at first. Many of our people, the Jews, hid from the bad soldiers, but if they became sick, they couldn't go to the doctor, so your papa went to them to help them, and so did I."

Zari leaned her head against Tamar's arm. "How did Papa and you know where to go if they were hiding?"

"Good question. Papa would receive a secret message, then he and I would sneak away."

When Peri yawned, Tamar put her arm around his shoulders. "Have you heard enough for today?"

"No," he whispered. "Tell us more."

"Okay. Do you remember the house where I used to babysit for Karl?"

"Yeah, the tall house with all the pictures and statues. We used to take our naps under Karl's crib," said Zari. "I liked that house."

"That is where I grew up. Karl's bedroom was my bedroom when I was little. My eema and abba had a jewelry store on the first floor."

Zari sat up and shifted to look at her. "That's a co—what's that word?"

"Coincidence? It could be, but I prefer to think of it as a God moment. Think about it, Zari. Karl is with us right now because we took care of him when he was little. He needed us then, and he needs us now."

"Karl had good toys," Peri piped in.

Tamar ran her hand through Peri's curls. "That he did, Peri. Let me tell you what happened next, back when I still lived in that house with Uncle Seth and your grandparents. The Nazis—that was the name of the bad soldiers—they broke into the jewelry store and smashed it up. I wasn't home when it happened, but they took my eema and Papa, so I couldn't stay in the house anymore. I had to go hide, and Tante Neelie invited your papa and me to stay with her in this house."

"So, you stayed in these cribs?" Peri asked.

She giggled. "No, I was too big. Your papa and I worked together, but we weren't married then. Many other people were hiding in the house, including orphan babies from Amsterdam. We had to stay in the house all the time, but we sang and played games. It wasn't all bad, and sometimes we practiced hiding in case the soldiers came to the house. This secret room was built to hide the orphans."

Zari's mouth fell open. "Why did you have to hide babies? They couldn't hurt anyone."

Tamar pulled her daughter close and shifted to ease the cramp in her leg. Karl was sleeping, and she didn't want to wake him up.

Her children had been spared from the horrors she'd endured, but she'd been in her early twenties when the Occupation had started. Were they too young to handle the whole story?

For now, she'd forego telling them about the camps and Erich Bergman, the Nazi, who'd sent them there. One day, when they were a little older, she and Daniel would tell them the whole story. "Your Uncle Seth was also in the Resistance, and he rescued the babies from the orphanage in Amsterdam and brought them to this house. They'd be a few years older than you now. I hope they found happy homes."

"So why did they have to sleep up here?" Peri yawned and stretched out his arms, hitting Zari in the chin.

"Ow. Why'd you hit me?" Zari groused.

"Quiet, Zari. He didn't mean to." How much detail should she go into? Did she even want her children to know about antisemitism at six years old? She'd first felt the disdain of other children for her religion when she was about ten years old. Out on the playground, Anneke, one of her classmates had forbidden Tamar from swinging next to her. Tamar still remembered what she said. "We don't want your kind here. Go play somewhere else."

Not having a clue what Anneke meant by 'your kind,' Tamar waited until her father had finished the prayer at the dinner table to ask her mother what it meant.

Instead of a quick response, her parents had shared a knowing look at each other, the kind she never understood, then her father had said, "Let us finish dinner first, then we'll talk about it in the parlor."

By the time Tamar reached her thirties, memories from childhood grew hazy in her mind, but she remembered every little detail of the discussion that followed in the parlor. Eema had sat next to her father on the sofa, their arms linked at the elbow, as if they were one person. Seth sat next to her throwing a ball into the air and catching it until Abba made him stop. The air crackled with tension. Were they going to tell Seth and her that they weren't their parents? Was that what it meant to be "your kind"? She didn't know if she was ready to hear what grim news they were about to learn.

Surprisingly, her father asked a question. "Do you know why we celebrate Purim?"

Seth raised his hand, then quickly retracted it. "Sorry. Thought I was in school. Isn't it the story of our people during the exile from Israel?"

"Yes, son, it's the story that took place during the diaspora." Her abba must have noticed her confusion. "It's the time when our people, the Jews, were kicked out of Israel and had to live in other countries. Sometimes Jews aren't welcomed into other countries, as was the case of Megillat Esther, although her real name was Hadassah. She was a beautiful young woman whom the king of Persia wanted to marry, but she was a Jewess. Haman, the king's assistant discovered that she and her uncle, Mordecai, were Jewish, and convinced the king to kill all the Jews in the land."

"Why? What did the Jews do wrong?" Tamar had asked. "What did they ever do to anyone?"

Her father lifted his shoulders. "As you know, God played a joke on Haman. He was hanged on the same gallows he had built to hang Mordecai and Hadassah on. Irony, no? Then the king of Persia made an edict that all Jews were to live freely while in Persia. That's why we celebrate Purim."

Seth's eyebrow furrowed. "Why do they call it Purim if the holiday is to celebrate the Jews in exile?"

"Good question, son. As you know, *purim* means 'lots' in our language," her father said, a smile spreading over his face. Abba had always loved it when his children asked questions about the Torah or the other books. "It seems Haman had cast lots to determine the day for the hanging of Mordecai and his niece, so we celebrate Purim to show that Yahweh takes cares of his people and always will."

Chapter Seventeen

"The true measure of any society can be found in how it treats its most vulnerable members."

~ Mahatma Gandhi

Tamar gasped when she realized she'd almost fallen asleep. The kids' breaths were measured and even, but this wasn't a time to sleep. She pressed her ear against the wall as if that would help her hear anything three floors below. When she didn't hear anything, Tamar gently shook the three heads that leaned against her arm and chest. Time to throw a few clothes into a bag, call Daniel, and head for the train station. She hoped the house wasn't being watched.

After saying a quick prayer for safety, she whispered, "Come, children, it's time to continue the adventure. I want you to follow me down the stairs, and remember, we're not going to say a word. We're still playing the quiet game."

The kids lined up at the door, and Peri said much too loudly, "Be quiet."

Tamar felt around the doorjamb for the button to open the door from the inside. She hadn't been in this room since early 1944, and even when they did the drills, Job Hamel was usually the one to open and close the door. Finally landing on it, she pressed the button.

The door squeaked open, and she pressed a finger to her lips as they filed out of the attic. She slipped the hook into the eye, hoping Peri wasn't watching too closely. While he couldn't reach it, he'd pull a chair out of the bedroom to do so. She turned to the children. "We're going to head downstairs, but I want you to continue to play the quiet game. We're going on an adventure. How about we take a train ride to Oma's work? I'm going to fill a bag with some of your clothes, then we'll leave as soon as we can after I call your father. Does that sound like fun?"

"Are we part of the Resistance?" her daughter said.

She tousled Zari's hair. "In a way, yes." How much to tell these children? They reached the bottom of the stairs that ended at the parlor. Nothing seemed to be out of place except for the toys strewn across the floor. It didn't appear that whoever had knocked on the door had entered the house. Maybe she had overreacted. She blew out a breath and changed her mind. "Kids, please put your toys away while I call Abba. Be as quiet as mice."

A smile spread across Peri's cheeks. "I'll be the boss and make sure the toys are put away."

"Perfect." She retraced her steps to the children's bedroom and her own, stuffing two changes of clothes and their pajamas and toothbrushes into a carpetbag. Was she making accomplices out of innocent children? This was one of those sticky situations that defied the rules of legality. Karl's well-being was more important than following the letter of the law. She had to do the next good thing, and that was protecting the children.

Her life certainly had been one of breaking the law—first by sneaking out of the Nazi-occupied ghetto with Daniel to offer medical aid to those Jews who no longer fit within the law of the land. Then she, Daniel, and Neelie had paid the ultimate price by ending up in the concentration camps of Vught and Westerbork for hiding the orphans in this house.

Her past was catching up with her. Maybe protecting orphans was God's calling on her life. Karl needed her protection. She'd take the next step and hoped God would see her through it.

The children had forgotten about the quiet rule. No matter, they'd be out of here soon. She hurried down the stairs to the kitchen and asked the operator to call the hospital's burn unit.

One of the nurses answered and put her on hold. She buoyed up her strength, hoping Daniel could take off the next day or two.

"Dr. Feldman speaking." His harried voice sent her heart thumping.

"Daniel, this is Tamar. We had a visitor. The police, I think, but I didn't answer the door. We hid in the attic crib room." She paused. The absence of his response spoke volumes. "I'm taking the kids to the rehab center in Amsterdam. Neelie said Margot will be transferred from Zwolle to her center tomorrow. She asked you and me to meet her there before noon tomorrow. There's no time to find a babysitter, so I'll take the kids with me. I can't stay here any longer. We're on the way to the train station. Can you take a few days off and meet me there later tonight?" She finally took a breath.

"Why does Neelie need both of us there?"

"Sorry, in my haste, I didn't fill in the blanks. There's going to be a prisoner swap tomorrow. The inmate from Zwolle who's been staying at the center isn't working out, so when the guard brings Margot tomorrow at noon, he'll be picking up Hendrika to return her to the prison. Neelie is worried that Hendrika will try to escape when she finds out, so she's asked me to sing—more as a distraction than anything—and she'd like you there to stand guard at a door. Neelie said her two aides are no match for Hendrika."

"Ah, so she wants me for my brawn."

"Don't we all." She giggled. It felt good to laugh after the afternoon's tension. "Do you think you'll be able to help?"

An uncomfortable pause preceded his answer. "I'll see what I can do. Be safe. Tamar, you did the right thing. I'm glad you didn't let them in."

A sigh escaped. "Thank you. You don't how much that means to me."

"You're worth it. Wait, does this mean what I think it does? Is Karl going to be reunited with his mother?"

"That wasn't the original plan because Neelie's not set up for taking care of children, but since I don't have a babysitter, it might just work out that way."

"From your lips to God's ears. Love you, Tamar. Be careful. If I can find a replacement, I'll be there tomorrow morning."

Riotous children's laughter came from the parlor. As she hurried up the stairs to grab the carpetbag, she stopped at the parlor. "Each of you pick out one toy to bring with you and put the rest in the toybox." She checked her watch. "You have seven minutes." Giving the twins a time frame always brought out their competitive side.

It occurred to her that the journeys to and from the train station might be too much for Karl, so she headed up to the attic to retrieve the twins' stroller. *Wise move, Tamar. You would have had to carry Karl and the suitcase.*

She stopped before unlocking the attic door. Her breath was coming in fits, but it wasn't only because she'd just climbed four sets of stairs. Memories from two years ago came back, of the time Tamar had to go through all the storage boxes to find their passports. She'd been sitting on the floor opening one box after another when a rustling sound seemed to come from the crib room. Then something dropped. Her heart beat at a *vivace* pace. If they hadn't needed their passports the next morning, she would have hightailed it out of the attic. Instead, she calmed her heart by telling herself it was probably a squirrel. A week later she found out what…or rather, who, had made the noise.

With a shudder, she entered the attic, now a bit more sinister than it had been less than an hour ago. Her eyes scanned the room until they landed on the stroller. Good. She grabbed it and hurried out of the room, remembering to lock it. "Time to go, kids," she said when she reached the third floor. The children sat shoulder to shoulder on the sofa, Zari in the center reading them a story. If she'd had time, she would have delighted in the scene but not now.

Peri peered up. "Can I ride in the stroller?"

"Not right now. Maybe later. We're going to continue the quiet game, okay?" She brought her finger to her lips, then lowered her voice. "The next part of the game is to sneak out of the house. We'll leave by the side entrance, then scoot around back to the alley. When we're sure the coast is clear, we'll head to the train station."

Peri's eyes lit up like candles. "Oh, that will be so fun. Can we buy some candy at the station?"

"We'll see. For now, let's tiptoe downstairs, then Karl can ride in the stroller because it's a long walk to the station. Go on with you now, but wait until I come down to open the door."

The twins clamored down the two sets of stairs, whispering so loud the volume had surpassed their indoor voices. Karl lingered behind, his thumb in his mouth.

She grabbed their suitcase, then went over to Karl and bent down next to him. "Are you okay?"

He nodded, but his eyes said the opposite. Tamar pulled him in for a hug, then kissed the side of his head. "We're going to have a good time, but you let me know if you get tired or just want to slow down, okay?" He nodded. She took his hand and lifted the suitcase in her other. By the time she reached the first floor, the twins were vying for who could jump the highest.

Once she'd quieted them, she opened the door and peered both ways. Seeing no one, she put Karl in the stroller, hefted the suitcase's strap over the handles, and motioned for the twins to stay behind her. She should have stopped to pray with the children, but she didn't want to worry them, so she hummed a Psalm from shul. They headed to the small lane behind the house and kept to the shadows, the only sound the click of their footsteps and the squeaky wheels of the stroller.

Once they'd reached the bridge three blocks from the house, Tamar allowed herself to take a breath. They waited for three cyclists to whiz past, then she took Peri's hand and hurried across the street that skirted the canal. Peri skipped ahead pointing at a boat filled with bicycles that passed under the bridge. "What's that, Eema?"

"Come back, Peri. Let's stay together. Sometimes people throw their broken old bikes in the water, so the men lift them out with that pulley to keep the canal clean."

A frown covered his face. "That's weird. Can I throw my tricycle in the water? I'm too big for it now."

"We'll see." They'd crossed to the other side of the canal with only four blocks remaining until they reached Central Station. Her heart wouldn't relax until they'd boarded the train to Amsterdam. She felt like a criminal, and maybe she was. Hopefully, once Karl was reunited with his mother, the orphanage wouldn't press charges against her, but Mrs. Van Pelt didn't seem the type to show any grace.

When she felt a pull on her skirt, she glanced down to see Zari studying her, her little brows furrowed. "What is it?"

"Are we doing something wrong, like a sin?"

How to answer her daughter's perceptive question? "No, we're not committing a sin, sweetie. We're trying to keep Karl safe. I think God would want us to do that."

"If we aren't doing something wrong, then why did we have to play the quiet game and sneak out of the house? Isn't sneaking like lying?"

Out of the mouth of children. She offered her daughter a smile, which wasn't easy because smiling was the last thing she felt like doing. In a way, Zari was right. The lines between right and wrong weren't always easily discernible. "Sometimes sneaking can be lying, but remember what I told you in the room in the attic? During the war, it was against the law to hide orphans from the police, but the babies would have been in danger if we didn't hide them, so I think God would have wanted us to hide Karl."

Zari didn't answer right away, but her mouth was working as it did when she was trying to make sense of something. Six-year-olds shouldn't have to deal with issues that didn't fall easily into the right or wrong categories.

Tamar brushed stray hairs out of Zari's eyes. After assuring herself that Karl was sleeping, she whispered, "I'll tell you a secret, If everything goes well, we may have a surprise for Karl tomorrow at Oma's center."

Her eyes lit up. "Are you going to sing for the people there?"

"I'm planning to. Papa might join us as well if he can get off work." When they reached the station, she gripped Peri's hand and told Zari to hold on to the stroller. The thick crowds hurrying in all directions would provide the perfect opportunity for Peri to disappear. They took their place at the back of the shortest queue before the cashier window.

Apprehension returned full-force. The way she'd held her breath each time she'd lined up to show her papers to the Nazi guards to keep Jews in the ghetto and the others out. Her dark blond hair had been her foil as well as the disinterested expression she'd practiced in front of the mirror, and it had always worked. Now, seven years later, she adopted the same expression as she purchased four one-way tickets to Amsterdam and hurried the children to the platform.

Since the train had already arrived, she didn't have time to stop at the store to buy snacks. Peri's little lip poked out in a pout as they passed it, but she reassured him they'd stop at the herring kiosk outside the train station when they arrived. Peri always delighted in holding the herring by its tail over his head and letting it drop into his mouth.

When all the incoming passengers stepped off the train, she held back. How was she going to get the children, the suitcase, and the stroller up on the train by herself? A crowd of impatient people side-stepped her to board the train. "Zari, Peri, take each other's hand, and you go up first, but wait for Mama in the landing."

"Madame, would you like some help?" a voice said behind her.

She turned to see a man with thick glasses and a homburg. Although it was a warm day, the man wore a winter coat and a scarf. Odd. Maybe he was going north. "Please, if you could take the stroller, I can manage the suitcase." She unraveled the strap from the carriage's handle.

The man inclined his head and took the stroller, motioning for her to precede him up the train's stairs. She took the twins' hands and boarded the train. Her view from the landing showed every seat was already taken, so she turned to the man. "Would you help take the stroller up to the second level, please?"

"Yes, madame."

Tamar headed up the stairs to the second level, then wiped off the moisture that collected on her face. "I see a bank of four empty seats facing each other." When he nodded, she headed to claim it before someone else did. Good, there'd be room to stow her bag and the stroller between the seats.

Something about the man gave her pause. Had she met him before? She turned to the man to thank him, but he'd already left. Maybe she'd be able to do so when they arrived in Amsterdam.

Pulling Karl out of the stroller, she set him on the seat next to Peri, who'd already claimed one by the window, then let Zari take the other window seat while she stowed the stroller and bag on the floor between them.

Within a minute, the train's horn blew, and they were off. Tamar leaned her head against the headrest, closed her eyes, and released a sigh. She didn't want to relive this day for a long time. As a young girl in her twenties, she could have handled a day filled with intrigue and uncertainty. No, that wasn't true. During the Occupation and her time in the camps, she'd done what needed to be done to survive, but she certainly hadn't enjoyed it. The two bright stars during those years were Neelie Visser and Daniel. They'd told her about Yeshua, and He had carried her through.

She opened her eyes when Zari tugged on her arm. "What is it, darling?"

"The man who helped bring Karl onto the train—did you see him?"

"Yes, I had my hands full with the suitcase and holding onto your hands. He was wearing a wool coat and a scarf. It's not winter yet, so that seemed out of place. Why, did you recognize him?"

Zari tilted her head. "He's the man who helped Peri out of the tree. The man who knew your name."

She stared at her, trying to make sense of it all. Zari was waiting for a response. "Haarlem's a small town, so it's possible we'd see the man again. Do you remember his name?"

Zari twirled the end of her braid around her finger, then scrunched her face which brought a smile to Tamar. She could just imagine Zari's pained expression when she took her math and spelling tests at school.

"Mr. Vogt, I think. He helped you in the park when no one was there, and he helped you today when no one was there to help. That means he's an angel, doesn't it, Eema?"

She patted her daughter's knee. "Maybe so. I don't know." Haarlem was not so large that it was possible to run into the same man twice. Was Zari right? *How did he know my name*? *If he did, why didn't he mention it this time*? She shook her head. *I should be grateful instead of questioning his motives*.

Farms whizzed past for twenty kilometers. Fewer farms and more houses appeared when they approached the small towns near Amsterdam. She'd think about the man named Mr. Vogt on another day. Tamar had enough to worry about. She'd hidden herself and her children from the police who may have been at her door. She'd ferreted Karl, the child she'd kidnapped, out of Haarlem. Tomorrow she'd be part of the conspiracy to keep Hendrika, a prisoner, from escaping once she discovered she was going back to Zwolle. Then there was Margot being reunited with her son. The next twenty-four hours had their fill of problems without adding to them.

He took the only free seat six rows behind Tamar and her children. Three children this time. Her twins must be five or six years old by now. He'd seen them from his vantage point in the attic of the Sneiders' home two years before. Was the child Margot and Klaus's son—the whimpering boy who sucked his thumb? Erich had had to slip behind a tree when Tamar glanced back over her shoulder with a furtive expression on her face. He knew who she was running from. The folded document taped to the door revealed the answer—a warrant to appear at the police station and relinquish the child. Tamar Kaplan Feldman was escaping. How delicious to think she wasn't above breaking the law. Could he use that to his advantage?

She'd almost caught him in her attic when she entered with the children, but he'd hidden behind a large box in the corner. Had she noticed the cigarettes butts he'd left in the secret room? He'd have to be more careful in the future. Just being in the same house with her made him feel close—intimate even—as if she were married to him instead of that brooding doctor.

He'd followed her to the train station, keeping to the shadows behind her. She'd lined up outside the train to Amsterdam. When he noticed her struggling to carry the stroller up the train steps, he'd offered his help, savoring the scent of her hair as he pulled the child out of the stroller. How he missed her scent. Tamar hadn't even noticed him, too busy ushering her children up the train steps. The little girl's eyes had met his and remained there for too long. She recognized him and would probably tell her mother, which was why he'd disappeared as soon as the group was settled.

He pulled off his scarf and loosened his coat, resisting the urge to brush off the crumbs that had landed on his sleeve from the woman sitting next to him. His lower lip twitched and pulled down—a sure signal he was nervous.

The frailty of a driven man. Tamar was his weakness. The führer's words returned—mind over matter. Get rid of anything that interfered with the cause. Women were distractions and nothing more. Use them and lose them. Maybe the führer had been right. Erich had tried to forget Tamar, but she held a power over him—her voice, her sweetness, her innocence.

He couldn't forget their last few minutes together in Paris. She'd met his eyes as he'd slipped the pill between his lips from her place on the bed, her hands bound. *I forgive you*, she'd said. Forgiveness signified authority over him—as if a Jewess had any authority over an Aryan officer. But she did have power over him. He'd broken under her gaze.

Chapter Eighteen

"Something of vengeance I had tasted for the first time; as aromatic wine it seemed, on swallowing, warm and racy: its after-flavour, metallic and corroding,
gave me a sensation as if I had been poisoned."

~ Charlotte Brontë, *Jane Eyre*

The rattle and clang of the cell door woke her up, but Margot hadn't slept more than an hour that night. She rose to a sitting position and swiped hairs away from her eyes and mouth.

The tall guard motioned for her to stand. "Stop dawdling. You'll come with me, Sneider. Bring your things."

So, the warden hadn't lied to her. It was really happening. The tiny residue of hope she'd suppressed rose to the surface, bringing tears. Inmates didn't cry, especially in front of guards and other inmates. The guard was already stripping the cot of its pillow and sheet.

Margot peered around. Was there a souvenir she wanted to keep from hell? Two things. She picked up the pillow now sitting on the ground next to the bed. While the guard's back was to her, she used her two longest fingers to poke through the hole to the stuffing within. There she kept her only treasures: her pitch-pipe tuner and a picture of her son. She maneuvered them through the stuffing to the hole, then pulled them out and stuffed them in her pocket.

With a final glance around her home for the last year, she said under her breath, "Good riddance."

The door clanged behind her for the last time. Last time. *I vow never ever to return here. Whatever it takes. I'll be the model prisoner.* Since arriving at Zwolle, she'd tried to keep to herself, not to cause trouble. It wasn't her fault Gray Roots and her clan had ganged up on her.

What time was it? She always used the light from the corridor to distinguish night from day. When she passed the cells, the residents within didn't stir, so it must be early. All except one, that is. Ilse held onto the bars of her cell, her head peeking between them. It was almost as if she knew.

Margot slowed her pace for just a moment. Ilse had been her only friend at Zwolle. In fact, she'd been her only friend ever. Margot touched her hand. "Thank you for everything."

"Don't you forget me," Ilse whispered. "I'll find you. We'll meet again."

What did she mean by that? Margot stared at her for a long moment until the guard's voice startled her.

"Come along, Sneider. If you wanna go back to your cell, it can be arranged."

Margot nodded at Ilse, then hastened her pace to catch up to the guard, the one who was tight with Gray Roots. They passed the empty lunchroom, then headed down the hall, the warden's office door closed and dark. She wished she could thank him.

When they reached a side door, the guard stopped abruptly and placed handcuffs tight around her wrists. The metal bit into her skin, but she wouldn't complain. They reminded her she wasn't a free woman yet. The minute the door opened, she was ushered through it, the wind biting into the skin under her thin dress.

A man with a few days' growth of whiskers and a cigarette hanging out of his mouth jumped out of a van that idled at the curb. The smell of rotten food assailed her from the garbage cans. She lifted her cuffed wrists to cover her nose.

"This the transfer?"

"Yes, Good riddance is what I say. Don't forget. You'll be bringing another one back." The guard pushed her toward the side door and ushered her into the back.

Though the heater blew full-force, the wind outside kept it at bay, and Margot held her arms close to her chest to fight off the cold. Closing her eyes, she leaned her head against the seat. This was a second chance for her to make good, to stay alive until the day she was released. Anything would be better than Zwolle. She wasn't crazy like the others. Whatever it took, she'd do what she must to survive—to sing once again.

Once they were on the road, the guard turned up the radio, singing off-key with a crooner, punctuated with curses aimed at drivers who cut him off. She didn't care, as long as the curses weren't directed at her. At some point she must have fallen asleep—the first good sleep she'd had in a long while.

The blast of a horn startled her awake. Through the front window, tall buildings loomed on each side of the street. Amsterdam. Her thoughts turned to the rehabilitation center—her future home for the next year and a half. Why had Cornelia Visser—Neelie— singled her out to finish her sentence at the center? How had she even known Margot was at Zwolle? Was it common knowledge? She cringed at the thought.

Aha, her breath hitched. Tamar Feldman must have told her. Tamar Feldman—the little understudy who'd stolen her son from the orphanage. Margot had hired her to babysit Karl, and what did she do? She conned Margot's husband with those big blue eyes that belied her Jewish roots. In no time, Klaus had asked her to sing for him, convinced she'd be a wonderful addition to the opera. Then the little fiend had told the police about the art she and Klaus were holding for Erich Bergman. Since when was keeping an associate's property a crime? It wasn't as if they'd stolen it. Yet here she sat in the back of a prison van with handcuffs digging into her wrists.

If Margot remembered right from her opera days in Haarlem, the violinist and Feldman were close. Odd that a Nederlander would befriend a Jew. It was because of Tamar and her kind the Nazis had closed down the opera, which had ended Margot's career. The woman had stolen everything, and now she was trying to steal Karl.

The van screeched to a halt on a side street. The driver expressed his thoughts of Amsterdam's drivers in a diatribe as he pulled over to the curb. He jumped out and opened the side door. "Hurry up. I don't have all day. We're to enter by the back door."

Margot pushed to her feet, not having anything to hold on to and almost plummeted forward into his arms.

"Whoa, careful now. You almost knocked me over." He threw his cigarette on the ground and led her by the elbow to the alley behind a nondescript building, his other hand carrying a paperbag. Did it contain the dress she'd been wearing the day she was sent to the first prison? Anything was better than the rag she wore. Maybe the bag held her purse. Lipstick and a comb—all her earthly goods.

They reached the door, and the driver knocked. Minutes passed before a man answered. Dr. Feldman. What was he doing here? He smiled at her. Her nostrils flared in response.

"Margot Sneider, it's good to see you." It was? She nodded in response. He peered at the man behind her. "I'll need your help to make the exchange. We haven't told the other one she's leaving. When she finds out, she won't react well, so we're going to have to make the switch carefully. Come on in. We'll take off Mrs. Sneider's handcuffs and put her in Mrs. Visser's office."

Neelie Visser had an office? The driver removed her handcuffs, murmuring about this being out of his job description, and they climbed the stairs to an industrial-sized kitchen. A woman ladled steaming soup into dozens of bowls, its aroma eliciting hunger pangs from Margot's stomach. She peered up and nodded a smile at Margot and the driver, as if it were a normal activity to see a prisoner escorted through her work space.

They passed through the kitchen into a larger room with a dozen large tables skirting what looked like a dance floor with a small stage on one side. Elderly people shuffled in and took seats at the tables, some in wheelchairs pushed by aides. So, this was her new home with all these old people. It was better than fighting for her right to exist at the prison.

"You're probably wondering why I'm here," Dr. Feldman said to Margot.

"Yes. Well—" Did this have something to do with her son? The only other two times she'd seen this man was when he'd made a house call to check her raspy throat and at the prison when he informed her of Karl's condition at the orphanage. If Margot hadn't known better, she would've believed him and turned over Karl to him. Good thing the director had set her straight.

"Here we are." The doctor gestured to an office, its door slightly ajar. "I'll let Neelie inform you of what's going on." He nodded toward her and left.

Her heart beating against her chest, she opened the door to a bright office, the desk covered with piles of folders. A grayer version of the woman she hadn't seen since her opera days peered up at her, a smile lighting up her face. She stood and planted both hands on her desk.

"Please, Margot, have a seat." She picked up a pile of files and placed it to the side. "It is wonderful to see you after all these years." Her face held more wrinkles, but her eyes still held an intelligent twinkle that helped her anxiety to calm. "I don't know if you remember me. My name is Neelie Visser. I was part of the orchestra in Haarlem's opera. First-chair violin for *La Traviata.*" Her smile widened. "That was a long time ago, wasn't it?"

"I remember you." A bit. She remembered few of the staff, her role too big to give them much thought. Her eyes took in the floor-to-ceiling bookshelves on the left side of the small office. Margot lowered herself into the proffered chair. How times had changed. Now she was the needy one. She wished she'd had the opportunity to run a brush through her hair and wash her face. "I don't really know why I'm here." She had so many questions.

"I personally asked the warden to bring you here, and I hope you'll enjoy finishing your sentence in this place."

"Why me?"

"All your questions will be answered later, but for right now, we have to handle a problem, which will require you to stay in my office until we've transferred Hendrika to the van that will take her back to Zwolle. That's why I asked Dr. Feldman and his wife to come today. As this isn't a prison per se, we have to make the exchange without losing the prisoner. Hendrika hasn't been told that she's returning to Zwolle, and she won't be happy. If you don't mind waiting in here until she's on her way, we'll answer all your questions when I return." She stood, the smile vanishing. "We don't use handcuffs in here. Please respect my request to remain in here. Understood?"

"Yes, ma'am." Margot's eyes drifted to the window. Freedom was only a few feet away. Did she dare?

Chapter Nineteen

"The smallest act of kindness is worth more than the grandest intention."

~ Oscar Wilde

Tamar tapped the microphone. It responded with a loud grumble as if she'd awakened it from a long nap. She offered an apology to the dozens of residents who frowned in her direction. Tamar scurried to the soundboard to turn down the volume. After a fitful sleep on Neelie's sofa last night, she felt quite sure her voice would sound better at a lower volume.

On an ordinary day here at the center, the twins would entertain the residents with their antics, warming them up before she sang, but this was no ordinary day. The twins and Karl were sequestered with an aide. Tamar was to entertain the residents while Neelie, Daniel, and the driver ushered an unwilling inmate out of the building and into the prison van.

Their plan could go wrong in so many ways. Neelie had mentioned as she quickly passed that Margot was sitting in her office. Surely, she would hear Tamar singing. How would she react? Tamar returned to the dais and greeted the guests, some of whom were playing cards. A few others' heads nodded in slumber. "Good afternoon. Lunch is delayed today, I'm sorry to say, but I hope you'll join in and sing with me."

"Where's the kiddos?" a gruff voice bellowed from the center table. "They're the ones I paid to come see."

Guffaws erupted. "Sidney, when was the last time you paid for anything?" came from a voice in the back.

She tapped the microphone again. "They'll be out a little later."

"Good," Sidney responded. "Except that little scamp always steals my dessert."

"And mine."

At least the residents seemed to be in a good mood. Peri always brought out the best in them. She started with "*A Brivele der Mamen*," a Yiddish song the older generations were familiar with—"A Letter to Mother"—especially those who'd immigrated. Everyone in the room joined in singing and swaying. Perfect timing because their collective voices drowned out the female inmate's protests coming from the kitchen.

After a few more songs, Neelie's head peeked through the door, and she signaled it was time to wrap up. Tamar thanked the residents and told them the attendants would soon come to take them to lunch.

Neelie opened the double doors, so they could enter the dining room. From where Tamar stood, her smile looked forced. Had the woman escaped or hurt someone as they put her into the vehicle? She turned off the microphone and joined Neelie at the door to the dining room.

Up close, Tamar noticed lines creasing either side of Neelie's smile, her jawline taut. "What happened? Did Hendrika escape?"

She stopped to give the aide instructions on cleaning the room Hendrika had vacated, then she turned back to Tamar. "No, she put up some resistance, called me words I've never heard before, and slashed the driver's cheek with her handcuffs. He'll need some stitches when he returns to Zwolle. In the meantime, I gave him a few bandages and a wet cloth to stop the flow of the blood." She breathed out a slow sigh. "So, Hendrika's gone, but we have a different problem."

"What is it?"

"I left Margot in my office. Told her to stay there until I came for her. I thought I could trust her." She shook her head. "Apparently, I can't."

"She's escaped?"

"She's not in my office. I'm in big trouble. I should have insisted on special locks put on the door, and keeping a few pairs of handcuffs on the premises." She shrugged. "I didn't know what I was getting into."

Tamar linked arms with her aunt. "How could you know? If Margot had only been patient, she would have reunited with her son. Now she's a fugitive. We'll have to call the police and Doctor Frank at the prison."

Daniel sauntered in from the kitchen, swiping sweat from his brow. "Sorry, I didn't see her. Went up and down the streets around the center, but she could be hiding anywhere. Chances are she used your phone to call somebody to come and get her. She could be kilometers from here by now. Sorry, Neelie. I'll check around the outside again just to be sure."

"No, Daniel, you've done enough. You're right. I completely forgot about the phone in my office. Here I thought she could be trusted. How naïve I was."

Riotous laughter came from behind the door where Tamar had sequestered the twins and Karl. Good thing someone was happy in this center. Now that Margot was gone, what would happen to Karl? Maybe they should just take him back to the orphanage. It was just a matter of time until they'd be forced to do so. She cut a sideways glance at Neelie. "Ready for this?"

"As ready as ever."

Tamar opened the door and stepped back to let Neelie enter first.

A gasp escaped from Neelie's lips. "What are you doing here?"

What had Peri done now? Tamar steeled herself and peeked around Neelie's shoulder. What? Margot sat cross-legged on the floor of the small bedroom, Karl resting his head against her chest looking perfectly content. *Thank you, Father God.*

Peri used Zari's shoulder to stand up, who frowned at him and told him to stop. "Look, Eema, I built a house. See? I'm standing in the kitchen." He pointed to the outline of squares made with colorful wooden blocks. "Here's the door." He carefully stepped through the opening, knocking over two of the blocks. "I told Karl he and his mother can stay in it, if Oma says it's okay. Then they'll have their own house. Can they stay here?"

Margot's tired eyes looked up at Neelie, and her lips turned up slightly as if they had no energy to move more. "I'm sorry I left your office. It's just that I heard the sound of children laughing. It had been such a long time." Her lip quivered, and she kissed her son's head. "I didn't know what I had until I lost it. May I keep him?"

Neelie's lips curved. "You spoiled our surprise, Margot, but yes, for the time being, Karl can stay here. However, there are a few things you need to know. First of all, this center is not equipped to take care of children, and we don't have enough staff to do so either, so Karl will be your responsibility and yours alone."

Margot kissed the top of Karl's head. "Of course, I will take care of my son. Mrs. Visser, I am thrilled and surprised for what you have done. How did you know?"

"You have Tamar and her husband Daniel to thank for that. They were the ones who alerted me about Karl's sad situation at the orphanage. When the warden at Zwolle insisted that I take another inmate, you came to mind. The pieces fell into place, and I believe it was God's doing."

Tamar's heart went out to the slight woman sitting on the floor with Karl on her lap. Who would have ever thought Margot would deign to sit on the floor, much less choose to hold her son and not pass him off to a nanny. Had prison softened Margot—carved off those hard edges that made her look down on everyone? Then Margot's eyes landed on Tamar, who stood behind Neelie, and the smile vanished.

Margot's eyes narrowed. "You mean when the Feldmans kidnapped Karl? How could breaking the law by stealing another person's child be God's doing?"

Daniel's voice sounded from behind her. Tamar whipped around to see him standing there. She grabbed his hand. "As I told you at Zwolle, he hadn't spoken a word and was covered with bruises. Whatever the director of the orphanage told you was a lie. We felt he would be safer with us."

Neelie broke in. "You must realize this family has put their own safety in jeopardy, and now I have as well. I brought you here legally, but I don't have the government's permission for your son to reside at this center. We hope that the director will drop all charges against the Feldmans when she learns that you have been reunited with Karl, and you take responsibility for him and yourself while you're completing your sentence."

Margot didn't respond, but a furrow formed between her eyebrows. "I heard her sing at Zwolle, and I heard her sing today. Her career seems to be growing."

Tamar was suddenly lost for words at the abrupt change of subject. "My main focus is my family, but I work part-time at the opera. We're doing *La Bohème* three times a week. I play Mimi—"

Margot rolled her eyes. "I've never liked that opera. The leading role is a commoner. The costumes are plain. The setting is what—a dark and dirty attic? It must be depressing going to work."

Tamar suppressed her urge to respond. Neelie had taught her an important lesson when they were at Vught—something Tamar wished she'd remember more often. Neelie had said, "Don't listen to what people say; listen to what they mean."

What Margot said was not what she meant. While she demeaned the role Tamar played and the sets and costumes, Margot missed being the lead soprano in Haarlem's opera and wished she could regain her old life. Knowing that quelled the anger rising within her, and Tamar smiled her agreement.

"Maybe you two can sing together for the presidents, Eema," Zari peered up at her with expectant eyes.

Tamar had forgotten the children were present. She stifled a giggle. "You mean residents? Maybe so." Their time here was done. Hendrika was on her way back to the prison. Margot had reunited with her son, so perhaps she and Daniel wouldn't be taken away to prison. "C'mon, children, let's pick up Oma's blocks and put them back in the container. It's time to go home."

"All my work on Karl's house?" Peri groused.

She entered the room and knelt down next to Zari. "They can build their house later. Let's each pick up twenty, okay?" She could feel Margot's eyes burning into her back.

Neelie entered and took Karl from Margot's arms. "Let's return to my office. We need to go over the rules and expectations for your stay here."

"Before she leaves, I need to know one thing," Margot said.

Tamar swiveled on her knees to face her. “What do you want to know?”

Margot’s jawline was tight. “What made you think you could kidnap my son and get away with it?”

Daniel answered from the doorway, “We did it for you.”

Chapter Twenty

"Revenge may be wicked, but it's natural."

~William Makepeace Thackeray

Ilse fingered the knife in her pocket as she peered around the corner of the kitchen into the corridor that led to her cell. Aletta aka Gray Roots and her sidekick Flor had transferred their aggression to her the day Margot had transferred out of Zwolle. They'd been waiting for her when she returned from work in the kitchen and every day since then. Aletta had moved from taunting her that first day to shoving her to the floor on the second. The third day Gray Roots tripped her and kicked her in the thigh, her assistant howling with delight.

Unlike her predecessor, Ilse hadn't reacted with fear. Although she was centimeters shorter than Margot, she was as fast as a red fox and twice as mean. All the anger she'd stored from her husband's abandonment sat in her gut ready to spew out. Even her son, Dieter, had followed suit and abandoned her when he turned eighteen. Father and son were whittled from the same block of wood. The rejection from both her men had fueled her rage at the women, which had caused them to back off, at least temporarily.

Ilse had noted the dull knife used for cutting potatoes on the kitchen floor. She'd kicked it underneath the long metal table, wedging it with her toe behind the far leg. Hopefully, no one would notice it missing before she retrieved it.

A plan formed in her mind. If she were found with a knife, even a dull one that could hardly break through the skin, she'd be sent to solitary, and there'd be no chance of parole. Was standing up to Gray Roots worth relinquishing her future? As long as the knife lay hidden under the far corner of the table, Ilse could carry on until her sentence was completed, but not with Gray Roots harassing her. No, if she had to use the knife, she'd also have to escape.

When no one was looking, she pretended to drop the broom she'd held, grabbed the knife, and shoved it in her pocket.

The kitchen offered a way of escape. Whenever she took the garbage out to the dumpster, the only thing standing between her and freedom was the garage door. A few weeks before, the head cook had berated her for not taking the garbage out in time for the truck to pick it up. A casual question had elicited the information that the garbage was picked up on Tuesday afternoons. Now two weeks later, she'd delay taking out the trash to right before her shift ended, then she would hitch an odiferous ride with the onions and potatoes to freedom, but before that she had a score to settle.

She fingered the paper that hid the knife from view. No way would she take Margot's place. Today the victim would become the assailant. Ilse slipped around the corner and hurried to the bathroom. Voices met her ears before she reached its entrance. Unwrapping the paper, she gripped the knife and slipped her hand into her pocket. One move toward her, one mocking laugh, and all the wrath she'd suppressed over the past few years would empower each thrust into the gut of that woman.

"Don't be such a baby. Just pinch your fingers around the louse and pull it off the hair's shaft. Can't believe I got lice." Aletta leaned over the sole mirror in the restroom, a cigarette hanging out of her lips. Flor fingered through Gray roots' bangs. "Hurry up."

Flor winced and squeezed her eyes shut. "Here goes. Hope I don't get them." When her eyes opened, she glimpsed Ilse in the mirror's reflection. "Hey, look who's here. Let's get the Kraut to pick out the rest. That's probably where the lice came from."

Aletta opened one eye and peered at Ilse through the mirror. "Get over here."

Ilse shuddered despite her bravado. Lice were always present in places like this, but she'd managed to avoid them so far. Chances were they'd make their acquaintance with her scalp in the dumpster, but one place she wouldn't touch was Gray Roots' scalp. "No thanks." Ilse stood there, ready for the jerk of Gray's head, the threats, the sneering curled lip.

She didn't have to wait more than a few seconds. Aletta whipped around, fairly knocking Flor to the ground. "Who do you think you are, Hitler's mistress? Get over here."

"Don't think so. I have better things to do than be contaminated by your pets." She clenched the knife so tightly her hand was cramping. Slipping her hand out of her pocket, she kept it hidden in the fold of her garb.

With one lunge, Aletta bridged the distance between them and grabbed for her neck but ended up with a fistful of hair. In that moment, Ilse thrust the knife into her side, once, twice before it clattered to the floor. Aletta's partner screamed, then raced out of the room as Aletta fell against Ilse's chest almost taking her down with her. Ilse jumped to the side and slipped out of the room, reaching the supply room moments before footsteps clamored around the corner.

Flor's voice melded with the guard's as they passed the closet. Had she killed Gray Roots? She didn't think so. The knife was a dull one. Even so, Ilse had seconds to escape.

Once she'd reached the kitchen, she slowed her pace, grabbed the two full garbage cans that sat in the corner by the door, and tried to look as calm and ordinary as she could. No one seemed to notice her, except Beatta, the head cook. She motioned with her head toward the door since her hands were busy kneading bread then went back to chatting with the other cook.

Ilse dragged the cans out to the dumpster, which smelled of rotten meat. She slid open the side window, and threw the garbage cans' contents inside the receptacle. She peered back at the entrance hoping the guard wouldn't warn Beatta. With no time to waste, she threw a garbage can into the dumpster. It would give her something to sit on instead of today's leftovers. Then she used the other garbage can to climb onto, and dove inside.

The smell overwhelmed her, and she squeezed her watering eyes shut. Mind over matter, she repeated to herself. Think of the goal. It suddenly occurred to her that the single garbage can at the foot of the opening would lead anyone looking for her to know what she'd done. She almost fell as she leaned over to pull the garbage can through the opening, then forced the door closed, ushering in darkness.

She sat on the side of the garbage can and leaned her back against the side of the receptacle, refusing to think of what was pasted to the pocked wall. If she'd been a praying woman, now would have been the time. Her husband's abandonment had ended any religious leanings inside her, but she could hope that the truck would come on time. According to the clock in the kitchen, it was a matter of minutes.

Hope worked. The sounds of the garage door opening and the accompanying rumble of a motor were better than rousing beer songs to her ears. It sounded like it was backing up slowly. A door opened—she assumed it was the truck's door. The driver would hitch the garbage can to the truck, which he'd drive to the landfill somewhere out in the country—at least that was how it worked in Germany.

Just then the dumpster began to shake and lift. She fell off the garbage can, her hands landing in a mushy mess of something smelling of onions and rutabagas. Yesterday's dinner. The dumpster lifted further in the air, like the Ferris wheel outside of Cleebronn. What was happening? She covered her scream with a stinking hand.

A jerky movement preceded her being catapulted through the air into the back of the truck. With a whoosh, she slammed into something that jabbed into her ribs. She tumbled onto her back.

Shielding her face against a host of empty cans and whatniks that clattered on top of her, Ilse shook her head at her stupidity. Of course. Why hadn't it occurred to her that the dumpster didn't move? Only its contents did. She'd have laughed if she hadn't been afraid to open her mouth. With a screech, the empty dumpster lowered to its place in the garage.

The truck jerked forward, and soon Ilse was peering up into the afternoon light. She'd made it out of the garage, but she hadn't reached freedom yet. There were two or three more buildings at Zwolle, each having their own cafeteria and dumpster. Until she left the grounds of the prison, she'd cover her face and hold her breath, hoping nothing heavy dropped on her head.

So, this was her lot in life. A husband who'd abandoned her. A son who'd fled the minute he turned eighteen. An escaped prisoner on the lam.

Fortune had shone down on her when Margot van Ormer's haughty demeanor made her the center of gossip and derision at Zwolle. Add to that, Tamar Feldman—the object of Erich's affection—stood mere meters in front of Ilse. Imagine that—two sopranos showing up at the same prison—the two objects of her own revenge.

Time to make a plan. The truck was moving again, slowing down but not stopping. Ilse envisioned the driver waving at the entrance guards as he left the prison. She was one wall away from freedom. Fluffy clouds floated in the blue sky above. Beautiful, but she didn't have the luxury of enjoying them. Her eyes took in her surroundings. Four tall, rusted walls made it impossible to scale. She'd have to find a way over them when the truck came to a stop. Chances were she'd be injured when she jumped from the wall's height, but she'd have to take a chance. A broken rib or hip was better than a return to Zwolle.

In the meantime, she stumbled over the remaining garbage to reach the far wall—the one furthest from the cab. Just as she'd thought, a ladder was attached to the wall, most likely used by the cleaners to wash out the truck. She gripped its rungs and climbed up to the top, holding on tight when they rounded a corner. Ilse didn't have a plan—how could she? She'd have to think on her feet. Take every opportunity that presented itself. Keep her mind on the goal—to exact revenge on her husband and everyone that stood in her way.

When the truck stopped, she peeked over the top of the side. Just a glimpse in case they were in traffic. What she saw brought her a moment's relief. A country road. Green meadows on one side. A farm on the other. The perfect place to disappear.

Just then the truck started up again. Maybe she should just wait until it stopped for good at the landfill site, but who knew if they had some type of gizmo that crushed garbage, including her? Farms had barns and vehicles mere meters away. If she didn't take this chance, who knew when she'd have another? Without another thought, she slipped her leg over the top, feeling for a rung on the other side.

The truck lurched forward sending her legs flailing in the air. Her fingers detached from the rung, and she flew off, landing on her back with a thud. The breath left her in a whoosh. The truck moved forward, leaving her sprawled on the road. Her eyes refused to open. Pain spiraled down her spine. A mosquito lit on the side of her nose. Her hand lifted to brush it away. Stones dug into her back and into her legs. She opened one eye then the other. The truck rumbled down the road and disappeared from view.

Good, or was it? Which was better—dying at the hands of Gray Roots or pecked to death by scavenger birds? She wiggled her toes, then flexed her feet. They worked. She lifted her head a few centimeters off the stone-filled road. A closer glance at the farm showed no sign of life. Trees shielded the view of the house in its shadows. She needed to move, or she'd get run over, or worse, be found and taken back to the prison.

Using every bit of strength she could muster, she struggled to a sitting position. At least her body was obeying her internal commands. Every nerve cried out in pain as she used her arms to push to her knees, then to her feet. Somehow, she'd lost her shoes. She limped over the country road to the grass, which felt like kisses to the soles of her feet. Her hip raged with pain with every step, but her need to reach the nearest tree overcame her pain.

A lofty elm, its leaves just starting to fall, offered her the chance to catch her breath, which reminded her with every intake that she must have broken a rib or two in the fall. In her former life, Ilse had worked in a doctor's office, and although her responsibility centered around making appointments and fielding phone calls, she'd learned a thing or two about rib injuries. She'd have to take it easy to let them heal. Going to the hospital was out of the question.

While her body screamed for rest, Ilse couldn't risk it. That would have to wait until she found a place to hide. Thunder rumbled in the distance. The sky had darkened, and few sprinkles filtered through the leaves. Time to find a place with walls and a ceiling. She hurried as best she could from tree to tree until she'd reached the backyard of the farmhouse.

A wheelbarrow sat next to a white barn, its doors closed. A clothesline held children's clothes, a robe, and some undergarments. With the rain coming, the owner was sure to come out to retrieve the clothes. Did she dare? Ilse crept to the robe, wincing with every step, then grabbed the slip. She was just about to grab the robe when the back door opened.

A laundry basket preceded whoever was coming out the door. She dropped the slip and hastened back to the shadows beside the farmhouse. What good would a slip have done anyway? Better to cut her losses than to be caught stealing an undergarment, although the robe would have been nice.

When the coast was clear, she'd make her way to the barn. At least it would give her time to come up with a plan. She peeked around the house's edge. A tall, thin blondish woman in her forties stood there pulling children's clothes off the line, her apron blowing in the breeze. It would be easy to sneak up behind her, hit her over the head, then steal into her home. *No, I'm not a common criminal. Yes, I stabbed an inmate, but she gave me no choice.*

Once the door slammed shut, Ilse peeked around the corner seeing only an old reddish hound dog sleeping at the bottom of the steps. Sometimes it helped being a lightweight. She quickly breezed past the dog and scurried to the barn, whose double doors sat slightly ajar. Peering around, she slipped inside, stopping to let her eyes adjust to the shadowed room.

The swish of a horse's tail and the rustle of hay were the only sounds Ilse heard. She headed to the left, spying rudimentary stairs that led to an overhead loft. Her new home, at least for one night. Before she climbed to the top, she'd check her surroundings. If there were horses in this barn, there'd be water somewhere inside.

She almost ran into the trough, its liquid contents dark. No matter. After being thrown from one garbage can to another, she couldn't be picky. Ilse scooped a fistful of water into her mouth, its cold, slightly tainted taste a salve to her soul. After a few more mouthfuls, she scrubbed her face, arms, and neck, then swiped at her dress with splashes of water. How she wished she could throw away this thin, rotten-smelling dress with the word Zwolle labeled across the back.

Before she climbed the stairs to the loft, Ilse needed to take a few things with her if she could find them in this barn. If there was a horse, there'd be a blanket to warm her and a whip to protect her from curious eyes. From the amount of children's clothes on the line, it was fairly certain one of them would be coming to the barn to finish his chores. Since Ilse had grown up on a farm just outside of Hamburg, she knew the ropes.

Walking around, she eyed a lantern sitting on a bench by the horse's stall. It would be nice to have a light, but that would draw undue attention, and the family would be sure to notice it missing. A quick glance around the stall yielded a stiff horse brush, oats, a quilted stable blanket, and a pitchfork.

Her eyes traveled to the shelf above the stall. What was that? It looked like the handle of a revolver. She pulled a bucket over, balanced on top of it, and grabbed at the gun, her fingers not quite able to grasp it. Instead, she brushed the edge of the handle hard enough to cause it to drop to the ground. The gods were smiling down at her, it seemed. She picked it up then headed up the stairs, which was harder than it looked. The muscles needed to pull her weight up caused her to cry out with every step.

When she finally made it to the top, her energy had evaporated, and she fell onto the thin layer of straw that covered the floor. A few hours of sleep, and she'd be ready to start her trip to Amsterdam the next day, but first she'd need to find a change of clothes and shoes. Better yet would be finding enough guilders to pay for the train fare. She chuckled. "Erich, I'm coming."

Chapter Twenty-one

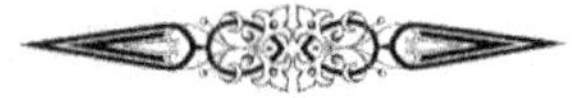

"Not everyone can be an orphan."

~ André Gide

"All right, you two, it's almost time to go to bed. You have school tomorrow."

Peri belted out a doleful moan. "Do we have to go? I'm tired, and I'll still be tired tomorrow morning."

"Ouch," Zari said, dipping her head to avoid Tamar's brush.

"Stop it. I have to get these snarls out. What were you three doing? It's like there's something sticky in your braids."

Peri spewed out a snort. "Me and Karl were gluing our hands together, but Zari stuck her big fat nose where it didn't belong—"

"I just told him to stop playing with Oma's glue. He grabbed my braids, and now they're all stuck together."

"Peri, what am I going to do with you? Go get the scissors from the kitchen drawer, and bring them up here. Walk, don't run."

After he scurried out of the room, Zari began to whimper. "Are you gonna cut it all off?"

"No, just the few strands that are glued together. You have such thick hair you won't even notice they're missing." Tamar didn't need this right now. "Peri, are you coming?" He'd probably already forgotten.

"Eema, is Karl going to go back to the orphanage?"

She regarded her daughter's reflection through the mirror. "No, he's with his mother now, so he doesn't need to. Why did you ask that?"

Zari's little eyebrows furrowed together with every pull of the brush. "I don't know. It's just that his mother doesn't act like a mother. It's like they don't even know each other."

Tamar set the brush next to the sink and swiveled her daughter to face her. "They haven't seen each other in over a year, so in a way, they have to get reacquainted. It hasn't been easy for either one of them."

Zari seemed to mull over what she'd said. "Where's his papa? Is he a Nazi like you were talking about in the attic room?"

"Why would you say that?"

"When we were in the attic, you said Nazis took away your house, and Karl and his mama and papa were living in it. So, is he a Nazi?"

Little ears. Tamar often forgot that she had to be careful what she said. Her daughter didn't need to know the whole story. "He's away, but he'll be back in a year."

"Good. Then Karl will have both of his parents, and they can move back into their big house with all the paintings."

"Not that house—" Tamar stopped when Peri ran into the bathroom, waving the scissors over his head.

She grabbed them from him. "I'll take those. Thank you, Peri. What took you so long?"

"A man was at the door, but I didn't open it. He left a letter in the mailbox."

Odd. Mail service hadn't started again in Haarlem since the war, although it had in the bigger cities. Dread filled her. The powers-that-be didn't know that Margot had been reunited with her son, so she and Daniel were still deemed kidnappers. When would this end?

Tamar made quick work of cutting away the strands of hair that were stuck together. "I'll read you a story, and then you two must go to sleep so you'll be ready for school tomorrow."

A chorus of groans followed, but they scampered into their bedroom. After reading them "The Boy Who Wanted More

Cheese," she listened to their prayers which included Zari's plea for Karl's papa to return so they could be a family, then she kissed them and closed the door halfway.

Hurrying downstairs, she peered through the window next to the door to make sure no one was there, then opening it halfway, she grabbed the envelope from the mailbox. As she suspected, the return address read *Politie Haarlem Koudenhorn.* Daniel would be home within an hour, and they could open it together.

One hour turned into three, and Tamar had almost paced a hole in the parlor's carpeting, washed the kitchen floor, and wiped the cupboards with ammonia by the time Daniel's footsteps came up the steps from the side door. The moment her eyes landed on his, she ran over and threw her arms around his neck.

"What's all this?" he said close to her ear. "Why are my eyes watering? What's that smell?"

She pointed at the envelope on the kitchen table. "That arrived today."

He sidled over to the table and glanced at it. "So, they finally caught up with us." A playful grin spread across his face.

"How can you smile at a time like this? It's not funny." She handed him the letter opener. "I waited until you came home. Why were you so late?"

"Luuk had a seizure. He's okay, but I had to wait for the tests to come back. At least he will be staying at the hospital for a while until I can find a place for him with his relatives."

"Seizures are dangerous, aren't they? What caused it?"

"We're not sure. A neurologist has taken his case and is going to do further tests. It could be epilepsy, or it could be related to a urinary infection he's had for the last few weeks."

"Poor little Luuk. My heart goes out to him."

"Mine too, but he'll be all right. Let's see what this says." He slit open the envelope and pulled an official-looking document from it.

She sat down next to him. "What does it say?"

"It's a summons for us to come to the station." He shrugged. "I expected it, didn't you? We took Karl without permission from the orphanage."

"Oh, I don't have time for this. I have rehearsal tomorrow, then the show tomorrow night." She heaved a sigh.

He pulled her onto his lap. "I'll take off tomorrow, and we'll go there in the morning. Perhaps you should take off tomorrow as well, since we don't know what's going to happen."

"Surely the police will let us go once they hear that the child is with his mother." When he didn't respond right away, she shifted to meet his eyes. "Don't you think?"

"Even so, we still took the child." He glanced at his watch. "It's not too late. Let's call the orphanage and let the director know that Karl is with his mother."

"Good idea, but you do the talking." Tamar went to the drawer by the phone where she'd put the orphanage's phone number. "They might not answer since it's after six o'clock." She handed him the slip of paper.

After he dialed the number, he put his hand over the receiver and whispered, "Pray."

Tamar stood close enough to hear a female voice answer.

"Good evening, this is Doctor Feldman. May I speak to the director please? It's important." The voice at the other end said something. "Thank you, I'll wait." He covered the receiver again. "They went to get her." His eyes closed, and his lips moved.

Ten minutes passed until Daniel's eyes opened. "Yes, this is Doctor Feldman." He winced and held the receiver away from his ear.

"No…yes…I just wanted to inform you that Margot Sneider has been released to a rehabilitation center in Amsterdam, where she'll remain for the rest of her sentence." He motioned for the address. Tamar fingered through all the scraps of paper in the drawer and handed the phone number and address to him, which he relayed to the director.

"Yes, but, Mrs. Van Pelt, the child is with his mother at the center." He held the phone away from his ear again. "I know we didn't follow protocol, but now he's out of our hands. Would you—" A pained expression spread across his face at her diatribe. "Would you call the police and tell them Karl is with Margot? Please? Then I won't have to tell them about the abuse he incurred or that a four-year-old was locked out on the roof in the middle of the night. Call. Good evening." He slammed the phone down. "Not my finest moment."

"She's not an easy woman to deal with. Do you think she'll call the police?"

He shrugged. "Who knows? We'll have to go to the station tomorrow morning while the twins are in school. I don't know what's going to happen, but maybe we should call Mrs. Libnitz next door to watch the kids if—" The rest of his words hung in the air like a dark, foreboding cloud.

"If they detain us?"

His lips tightened into a single line.

"Perhaps it's time to call Benjamin Maislin from shul. He's a lawyer and can tell us what to do."

"That's a good idea." Daniel checked his watch. "It's too late to call now. I'll give him a call in the morning before we leave."

No matter how hard she tried, Tamar couldn't turn off the jumble of thoughts springing around in her mind. From the time she was twenty-one, when the Nazis had moved in to occupy her city, she'd lived on the other side of the street from the law. At first the officers were just a quiet but constant presence on the busy streets of Haarlem—more of an intrusion than anything else. In 1943, everything had changed. When they closed down the opera, Tamar took off her rose-colored glasses. The benign officers on the corners became the enemy.

She'd joined the Resistance at her brother's bidding, still not fully understanding what was going on around her. How could anyone hate people simply because of their religion? She had to pretend when she was around them and hide things, like the yellow star she was supposed to wear to identify herself as a Jew. Her light features allowed her to bypass the guard posts in order to take messages to Jewish refugees hiding out in the country.

Even now that the war was over and the Nazis had vanished, why did she still feel the need to hide from Haarlem's police? She opened her eyes and checked the clock next to her bed. Three-forty-five. She might as well get up and make some tea. Perhaps the reason she hadn't slept was the need for time with the Lord.

She splashed water on her face, donned her dress, and ran a comb through her hair, then noting its disarray, gathered it into a proper bun. A proper hairdo for an improper meeting with the police.

Daniel's light snore came from the bed, so she grabbed her Bible and tiptoed down to the kitchen.

After steeping a quick pot of tea, she sat at the table where she and Neelie had sat seven years ago. Neelie would read a chapter from the Bible and explain it to her—how it fit with the rest of the book. At the time, they'd spoken in whispered tones, not wanting to wake up the orphan babies. They'd never been sure how much the babies' cries could be heard by the passersby on the street. For months, twelve people had hidden in Neelie's house, most of them Jews. They'd each had chores, routines, and rules to follow, but they also had fun as they sang together or played games in the quiet dark of the evening.

She opened her Bible. "I need You today, Lord. We may be arrested by the police, and Daniel may lose his job. Where would our children go if that were to happen? Please give me some words that will stay this heavy heart of mine. Lord, did I commit a crime by taking Karl and refusing to return him to the orphanage?"

Her fingers flicked through the silky pages, so thin they could disintegrate with a hard touch. She landed on Psalm 10, not knowing why, but she read through it. "Why do You stand afar off, O Lord?" Sometimes it seemed to be true, but Tamar never doubted his presence. He was there regardless if she knew it or not. Her mind caught up with her eyes as they read each verse. There it was—verse 14:

"But You have seen, for You observe trouble and grief, To repay it by Your hand.

The helpless commits himself to You; You are the helper of the fatherless." NKJV

She was helpless and fatherless. Tamar lowered her head, squeezed the book to her chest, and committed herself and Daniel to the Lord. Whatever happened that day would be in His hands. It gave her a modicum of comfort and a touch of guilt for not being at peace.

Chapter Twenty-two

"Revenge is like politics; one thing always leads to another until bad has become worse."

~ Ernest Hemingway

The stale odor, the unidentifiable green of the walls, and the scuffed floor of the police department did little to buoy up Tamar's nerves. After a lengthy wait in a queue, she and Daniel were quickly ushered into an interrogation room, as if they'd try to escape.

Officer Dekker lit a cigarette and scanned the letter they'd brought with them, then he backed up in his seat and mopped his head. "Well, if this doesn't beat all." He regarded them under bushy gray eyebrows that curled up over his glasses. "Kidnapping charge of an orphan, and you turned yourselves in. You've made our job easy." A knock on the door got his attention. "Come in."

Ben Maislin bustled in and nodded to them. He took a seat at the end of the table. "I'm the attorney for the Feldmans. When is the arraignment?"

"Right after lunch today."

He shook his head. "The charges shouldn't have even been filed. This couple didn't kidnap Karl Sneider. They rescued him from a perilous situation. When you hear the facts, you'll understand."

Officer Dekker rolled his eyes. "That's for the judge to decide. I'm sure you know that the orphanage has pressed charges, and they wouldn't have been able to do so without cause. You'll have your chance to plead your case in front of the judge."

The attorney leaned forward. "Surely you know the Feldmans came of their own volition. The child has been returned to his mother after a misunderstanding. Why don't you save the court's money by listening to what they have to say? Then I'm sure you'll release them."

The officer met his eyes. "It's out of our hands. They'll have to be there for the arraignment where bond will be set." He pushed to his feet. "One o'clock. If you want to confer with your clients, you can use this room."

"I'd rather take them to my office, which is a block away. I promise they will be present for the arraignment."

Tamar barely noticed the walk to Ben Maislin's office. She was too busy lowering her head to avoid meeting the eyes of her neighbors or members of shul. Daniel and Ben kept up a steady stream of conversation until they reached his office on the fourth floor and took seats across from Ben at his desk. Moses, the tablets in arms, seemed to be scowling directly at her from the picture on the wall. She averted her eyes. Yes, she believed in the ten commandments, but why did life always have to muddle them? When she glanced up, Daniel and Ben's eyes were on her—laughing eyes. "What?"

"Not to worry, Tamar. We'll get to the bottom of this." Ben picked up his pen. "Now, why don't you start at the beginning."

She cleared her clogged throat and told him about her singing engagement at the orphanage and her conversation with the director afterward. "Mrs. Van Pelt said she'd call Margot, but she told me not to get my hopes up. That it was unlikely that the government would allow the child to leave the orphanage. Later that week near midnight, Sister Adela showed up with the child, saying that the boys had locked Karl out on the roof."

Ben stopped writing. "You're saying an employee of the orphanage brought him to you?"

"Yes, but she didn't have permission to do so. Sister Adela was worried about the child's safety."

"Good."

"Good?" both she and Daniel said in unison.

"Since you didn't ask her to do so, you didn't kidnap the child. What did you do after that?"

Daniel squeezed her hand. "Sister Adela and I took Karl back to the orphanage, but the director didn't seem too concerned about his welfare. Mrs. Van Pelt said 'socialization' was good for Karl, and that she'd contacted his mother and assured her he was fine. As Mrs. Van Pelt stood to show me the door, an alarm went off. She huffed, 'What did the boys do now?' then she ran out." He blew out an audible breath. "This is where it becomes…complicated."

Ben removed his glasses. "It always does. Continue."

"Karl had awakened and was wailing from the alarm. I almost left, but then I thought about his crying, and the boys who had locked him out, and I couldn't leave him there, so I took him."

"Ah, the plot thickens. According to the law, you kidnapped Karl at that point, but there's a fine line between kidnapping and rescuing. What happened next?"

Tamar straightened in her seat. "I called a few days later to speak with Sister Adela, and she asked me to meet her by St. Bavo's. She urged me to keep him, since his color and his appetite had improved. We accompanied her back to the orphanage, but when the director tried to take Karl from my arms, Karl cowered in fear and begged me not to leave him there."

"What did you do?"

"I apologized to the director, moved back from her grip, and returned home. It appears both Daniel and I are kidnappers." She fought to keep her lip from trembling.

Ben set his pen down and took off his glasses. "So, Daniel, you told me earlier the parents are in prison, so the child is a ward of the province until they're released." He put on his glasses and perused his notes. "From what you said, they'll be released in a year, and his mother refused your request to bring the boy into your home."

"That's right, but Tamar and I traveled to Zwolle to meet with Margot, Karl's mother. The warden agreed to let Tamar sing for the inmates, and Margot was in the audience. As if in a trance, she started singing along with Tamar to great applause. Afterward, the warden arranged for me to meet with her, but even after I told her about Karl's condition, she was still averse to us taking the child. Believe me, she has no love for us, but that's a whole other story."

The attorney nodded slowly as if he were digesting everything they'd told him. "So, you said the mother has been released to a halfway house in Amsterdam, is that right?"

"Yes," Tamar said, "My friend Neelie manages a rehabilitation center for returning Jews from the camps, but due to lack of finances, she contracted with Zwolle to take in prisoners. Karl is now with his mother at the center." Tamar met Ben's eyes. "What's going to happen to us?"

He checked his watch. "We only have a few more minutes, so we need to prepare for the arraignment. The judge will read the charges and ask you how you plead. You will respond with, 'Not guilty.' I'm not sure whether he'll call you in separately or together. The prosecutor will summarize the province's charges, then I will speak on your behalf. At that point, the judge will determine if there's cause to go to trial, and if so, he'll set bail and a trial date. Hopefully, he'll agree with me that you are definitely not kidnappers."

Tamar's voice came out in a squeak. "So will we have to go to jail?"

Ben chuckled. "No, you'll have to post bond, which the judge will set. You'll pay a tenth of the amount to a bondsman, but as long as you show up for court, you'll be reimbursed minus court costs. It's like a guarantee that you will appear for your court date." He stood and gestured toward the door. "Don't worry. You have a strong case. In fact, you should get a medal for trying to protect the son of someone who hasn't been very nice to you."

Daniel wrapped his arm around Tamar. "See, honey, we have nothing to worry about."

Chapter Twenty-three

"Trust the past to the mercy of God, the present to his love, and the future to his providence."

~ Saint Augustine

Nothing to worry about. She clutched Daniel's hand and followed the men the few blocks to the courthouse. Dread threatened to overtake her as the worst outcomes wrestled for prominence in her mind. What if the judge put them in jail saying they were a flight risk? What if the newspapers found out that she had kidnapped the famous soprano's son? What if they both lost their jobs? How would Peri survive in an orphanage? He'd probably be first to climb out on the roof.

Her head felt heavy, and her breath quickened when she tried to keep up with the men's long strides. They arrived at a large stone building, its entrance fronted by imposing columns. Several people sat on the steps, laughing and enjoying the sunshine. She kept her eyes down as she maneuvered around them to the entrance.

The dark, foreboding hall added to her apprehension of the outcome of the next hour. People scurried here and there, seemingly comfortable in this setting, but their future wasn't on the line as hers was. Tamar whispered calming Bible verses to herself while she followed Ben and Daniel into Courtroom C. The room teemed with groups of people sitting in rows that resembled the pews of a church. Ben motioned them toward a space large enough for the three of them in the second last row. She plunked down, reaching for Daniel's hand, which she gripped like a lifeline.

Daniel turned to her and told her to relax. Easy to say; harder to do. While Daniel conferred with Ben in whispers, she tried to follow his advice, focusing her attention on the layout of the room. The front of the large room reminded her of the altar at St. Bavo's Cathedral. A wooden gate separated the spectator section from the judge's raised bench just like the altar separated parishioners from the clergy. The witness section sat empty, and a podium separated two tables where she supposed the prosecutor and defense attorney sat. At any other time, she would have enjoyed watching the proceeding, but she wasn't just a spectator.

A door adjacent to the judge's bench opened, and a man in uniform bustled into the room. "All rise. The honorable Judge Devries presiding."

The chatter stopped and everyone stood until the judge, an older gentleman with wisps of white hair combed to the side, stepped up to his chair and nodded for everyone to sit down.

He put on spectacles, leafed through a pile of folders on the desk, then looked up. "Good afternoon, ladies and gentlemen. It appears we have a full house today. Nine cases before the court. When I call your name, please don't waste the court's time by dallying. Come up to the front with your attorney if you have one. Answer each question honestly and succinctly. Perhaps we will be out of here in time for supper."

Tamar's hands fidgeted through the first few cases until Daniel stayed her hand by patting it. By the sixth case, her leg bobbed at the same rate as her heart rate. So far, every single one of the defendants had pleaded not guilty to crimes such as petty theft, intoxication, destruction of a neighbor's shed, and shooting at a neighbor's barn. The judge seemed congenial or at least benign after hearing each attorney argue for or against the arraigned, and he dismissed all six cases.

Maybe it wouldn't be so bad for her, although a kidnapping charge was more serious than shooting at a barn. A sigh escaped, loud enough for Daniel to cast her a sideways glance. The long tables of Vught played before her mind, not so different from the tables on the other side of the gate. The long line of women shivering in their slips before the Nazi guards. The gasps as each woman held out her arm to have the number burned into her skin. Some of the women had pleaded for mercy, but their pleas fell on deaf ears as the guards stamped their papers and told them to move ahead.

That was wartime, and this was six years later.

The judge called their name, and Daniel and Tamar followed their attorney to the front, through that gate, and into seats at the table on the left. The judge peered up, "Mr. and Mrs. Feldman, you have been charged with kidnapping of a child from Haarlem's orphanage. That's a serious charge. Please stand." He waited. "How do you plead?

Daniel went first. "Not guilty, Your Honor."

"Mrs. Feldman?"

"Not guilty," her voice came out in a raspy whisper. She tried again after clearing her throat. "I'm sorry. Not guilty, Your Honor."

The judge jotted something down. "Very well. Prosecutor, you may begin."

A pencil-thin man with angular features stood, reminding Tamar of the animal she'd seen in the painting, *Lady with an Ermine*, by Leonardo da Vinci.

"Your honor, according to the director of the orphanage, this couple not only forcefully abducted a four-year-old boy from the orphanage, but they did so three times, despite the establishment's pleas to return him. The motive, according to Mrs. Van Pelt, was revenge against the child's parents who are presently incarcerated."

The judge's head lifted for the first time. "Was there a request for ransom?"

"No, Your Honor. This is a case of revenge more than money. The province asks that the couple be held in custody for trial without bail, since the Feldmans may try to leave the country." The prosecutor took a seat, a bemused smile on his face.

Daniel had gripped her hand with vise-like strength. Tamar couldn't breathe. What did he mean by revenge against the parents? What lies had the director told them?

The judge didn't speak at first, but a flurry of whispers sounded behind them. "Order in the court," he finally said. "The attorney for the defense, your turn."

Ben rose to his feet and buttoned his jacket. “Your honor, this is not a case of kidnapping; this is a case of rescue. Mrs. Feldman, a member of Haarlem’s opera, was asked to sing for the children at the orphanage. During her performance, the child in question called out for her. She hadn’t been aware that he was even in the orphanage. When she’d finished singing, she went over to the boy, saw the bruises and his rheumy eyes, and recognized him as the child she had babysat for a few months two years ago. She was alarmed by his condition. According to a staff member who joined her, the child’s words when he called for her were the first he had spoken in the year he’d been in the orphanage.”

“So, she took the child?” the judge said.

“No, Your Honor. Mrs. Feldman went to the director’s office to find out about the child. As per their conversation, she asked the director if she would contact the child’s mother for permission to bring the boy into her home, at least temporarily, since according to the staff member, the child was suffering from separation from his parents and failure to thrive.”

“Then she took the child?”

“No, Your Honor. They waited to hear from the director, and when they didn’t, they visited the mother at the prison in Zwolle. I should also mention that Dr. Feldman went to the orphanage to check on the place for one of his patients at the hospital where he works, and he witnessed the child in question being harmed by one of the boys out on the playground. Dr. Feldman ran over to examine him and saw the bruises himself. Soon after that incident, the Feldmans traveled to Zwolle to meet the child’s mother.”

“What did she say?”

“She wanted the child to remain in the orphanage.”

The judge let out a whistle. “This is quite the story, but obviously there’s more or you wouldn’t be here.”

“Yes, Your Honor, a few nights later near midnight, the staff member appeared at their house with the child.”

“With the permission of the director?”

“No, the staff member asked her to keep the child since a group of boys had locked the boy out on the roof. The four-year-old would have remained on the roof had the staff member not found him later that night.”

The judge banged his gavel when a host of murmurs ascended from the spectators. "Order. So, what did the Feldmans do next?"

The attorney cleared his throat after silence was restored. "Dr. Feldman and the staff member took the boy back to the orphanage."

The judge leaned forward. "I haven't heard any evidence of kidnapping yet. Continue, Counselor."

"While the doctor met with the director, an alarm sounded, which sent the director and the employee hurrying away to find out the source of the alarm, so the doctor didn't want to leave the crying child by himself if there was a fire, so he took him home."

"Now we're getting somewhere. So did they keep the boy?"

"They kept him for a few days, then Mrs. Feldman took him back to the orphanage, but the boy shrieked when the director tried to take him, so Mrs. Feldman took him home again."

The judge wiped off his forehead with a handkerchief. "So, the child is with the Feldmans now?"

"No, Your Honor, he's with his mother in Amsterdam." Laughter filled the room until the judge rapped his gavel.

"Order in the court," the judge bellowed. "I hate to even ask. Was the mother released from prison, or did she escape?"

"She was released to a halfway house in a prisoner swap, so the Feldmans took the child to her."

The judge blew out a weary breath. "I must apologize to the remaining cases for this one taking up so much of the court's time." He put on his glasses and leafed through some papers. "Kidnapping is a serious charge, Dr. and Mrs. Feldman, and there are enough competing facts to warrant a criminal trial, so I am scheduling such a trial for a month from now. Contrary to the prosecutor, I don't believe either of you will flee, so I'll set bond at two thousand guilders each, and you may return to your home." He shook his head once more and called the next case.

Stunned, Tamar couldn't move from her seat, although Daniel had shot to his feet, as did their lawyer who was stuffing papers into a file folder. Her eyes strayed to the gate. Gates kept people in, and they kept people out. Barbed wire had done the same at Vught. Thoughts of the times she'd sat looking through its holes at the meadow on the other side. A field of green with wild flowers nodding to her in the breeze. "You can't come on this side," they taunted. Even flowers had more freedom than her future held.

"Come, Tamar. We need to leave," Daniel said.

She nodded and followed the men out, again keeping her eyes on the scuffed wooden floor. Daniel took her hand when she fell further behind. She shook her head to erase the doom-filled thoughts. Were they kidnappers? The judge must think so, or he would have dismissed the case. Was the prosecutor right? Had she taken Margot's son out of revenge?

When they reached the outside steps, Ben pulled them close when a photographer's flash momentarily blinded her. "Pesky rats," he said. "Let's return to the office and figure out our next steps."

Next step—Daniel's favorite saying. Hadn't she whispered those very words when she'd decided to meet with Margot at the prison? Look where it had landed her. Tamar didn't even remember the ensuing walk. They didn't speak until they reached his office and Ben nodded toward the seats on the other side of his desk.

Daniel plunked down. "I can't believe it." His head wagged from side to side. "The judge had dismissed every other case. I was sure after he heard our story, he'd dismiss it."

Ben took out some official-looking forms from a drawer and set his pen beside them. "Don't judge him too harshly. He's one of the good ones."

"Good ones? What does that mean?" Tamar's purse fell to the floor when she leaned forward. "We might end up in prison because of him. Then what will happen to our children? Will they end up in the same orphanage?" She clamped her lips together. None of this was Ben's fault. "I'm sorry."

Ben smiled. "Your feelings are understandable under the circumstances. Judge Devries is a fair man. A few on the bench still blame our people for the devastation that happened to our country, but Judge Devries isn't one of them. However, he won't be presiding over our case. Hopefully, we'll land one of the other judges who doesn't hate Jews." He must have noted her shudder. "Now both of you look at me."

She cut a sideways glance at Daniel, who nodded toward Ben.

"The reason Judge Devries didn't dismiss your case was because there are some questions pertaining to your intentions in taking the child. Hear me clearly—you did not kidnap little Karl. As you know, most kidnappers abduct for ransom or for other selfish reasons. Your intent was to rescue the child from danger. The judges will clearly see that when they hear your testimony—"

Tamar looked up. "There will be more than one judge?"

"Most likely, with more complex cases, there could be three judges."

Daniel interrupted. "Will Margot be subpoenaed to testify? Even though she's been reunited with her son, the prosecutor claimed we acted out of revenge. Margot is a well-loved soprano in Haarlem. The judges may be won over by her testimony—a poor mother separated by her child because of her understudy's ambition to be the lead soprano." He cut Tamar a glance. "Sorry. I know you're not like that."

The attorney held up his hand. "Let's think positive thoughts. You both did the right thing for the child under dire circumstances. The judges will see that—I'll make sure of it. Now, let's get down to business." For the next hour, he explained how the trial would proceed. "You'll need to return to the courthouse and post bond. Most of the money will be returned to you when you show up for court on the appointed date. You will also be called in for a deposition where you'll have to answer questions under oath, but it will take place in a room with both attorneys and a stenographer." He stood and motioned toward the door. "Don't worry. Live your lives, enjoy your children, but don't talk to the press. If anyone asks, just refer them to me."

The press? Tamar hadn't even thought about the press. A cement-like heaviness filled her to the point she didn't know if she could put one foot in front of the other. Why would anyone be interested in her? Yes, she sang the lead in the opera, but that was just because Margot was otherwise detained. Tamar was just a pretender, a place holder, until the real soprano was free to sing again. If it weren't for the money they'd just posted to pay the bond, she would have gathered her children and fled to a city where they could live anonymous, normal lives.

Daniel's pull on her hand got her attention. She hadn't even realized they had left Ben's office and were walking along the canal.

"You're shuffling like an old person. Let's go sit over there." He pulled her toward a bench and sat her down, kissed her forehead, then checked his watch. "We have to go meet the kids in twenty minutes. That gives us ten. Can we solve all our problems in that time?" The corners of his lips turned up.

She leaned her head against his shoulder and closed her eyes. "Why is this happening, Daniel? Didn't we pay our dues during the war? What's going to happen to us?"

He took her hands in his. "The high price of mercy—that's what this is. Our Savior gave His life—a hefty cost. We get to share a bit in that price, that's all." He pulled her close, her head resting in the nook of his neck. "We'll get through this, Tamar. Let's not worry about things we can't control. One—"

"Step at a time." She opened her eyes. "You're right. Let's go get our children. Margot has her child. Karl is safe at Neelie's, and we're not in prison…yet."

Chapter Twenty-four

"The whole idea of revenge and punishment is a childish day-dream.
Properly speaking, there is no such thing as revenge. Revenge is an act which you want to commit when you are powerless and because you are powerless: as soon as the sense of impotence is removed, the desire evaporates also."

~ George Orwell

Ilse tucked the voluminous folds of fabric into the belt of the dress, which looked more like a robe. Beggars can't be choosers. Back in Germany, she'd made enough money to purchase presentable dresses, but that was then, and this was the cost of getting her husband back. She'd found the oversized garment and a pair of boots in a trash can behind a village store. They'd have to suffice. She adopted an impassive expression, lifted her chin, and took a place behind the small line of passengers waiting for those exiting the train to leave.

She fingered the ticket in her pocket that she'd swiped from the platform. Hopefully, the conductor wouldn't look too close at it, but just in case, she'd take a seat and pretend to sleep when he came by.

As long as she looked like she knew where she was going, people didn't pay attention to a scraggly-haired, middle-aged woman. The crowd was now moving, so she followed suit, hoping her outfit wouldn't draw attention. Once inside, she climbed the steps to the top floor, finding a seat in the back corner where she could rest her head against the wall and close her eyes.

The train to Amsterdam filled up quickly, and the aisle was full of college students. The man who had dropped to the seat beside her placed his briefcase between them, taking part of her space. Just as well. She wrapped her arms across her chest and rested her eyes. The two-hour trip would give her time to plan her next move.

Her stomach rumbled. The half-eaten apple she'd found on a table at the train station was the first real food she'd eaten in two days. Tulip bulbs in a garden along the road to reach the town had made her retch, but she'd had to keep up her strength for the long walk ahead. The man next to her munched on a pastry as he read his newspaper, the crumbs falling onto his coat and into the space between them. She fought the urge to grab them.

The conductor entered the aisle, asking the people in front of her for their tickets. She squeezed her eyes shut and let her mouth hang open, breathing deeply to elicit a slight snore. She could feel his eyes on her a few moments after he asked the man next to her for his ticket. Then he moved on.

It unnerved her that she didn't know the address of the halfway house where Margot had been placed, but at least she knew of the district. She replayed the conversation she'd heard in the cafeteria.

The loud voice of the irate woman named Hendrike who'd exchanged places with Margot reached Ilse's ears from the other end of the table. Outraged that they had moved her without cause or warning, Hendrike had spouted that the center in the Jordaan district was full of elderly wartime Jews. "They didn't have to lift their fingers, while I had to work my hands to the bone."

Someone commented that she should have been happy to get out of Zwolle, like the diva had three weeks before. At least she didn't have to clean toilets and live in a barred cell with no privacy.

Hendrike stormed to her feet, her frazzled hair hanging in her face. She swiped it away with the back of her hand. "Yeah, one prison is the same as the other. Instead of hiring aides, I had to do all their work with no pay and all their leftovers."

Aletta rose from the seat across from her, planted her knuckles on the table, and leaned forward. "You blew it, woman. How stupid is that. You just didn't know a good thing when it hit you in the face."

Hendrike's face turned scarlet, and she leaned forward, their noses almost touching. "What do you know, you fat bag? The manager watched my every move. Her constant demands drove me insane."

"And they don't watch us here? Like I said, you blew it. What did you do to get sent back to Zwolle?"

She rolled her eyes and huffed. "Visser's ugly face got in mine, and I couldn't take it anymore. Grabbed a knife and slit her cheek." A triumphant smirk spread across her face.

Aletta ran a hand through her hair and spewed out a sarcastic laugh. "So now you only get to use spoons. If I'd been there, I would've counted my blessings. Anything would be better than this place."

Hendrike rolled her eyes. "Then why are you still here?"

"Cuz I can't sing opera, that's why. Heard that the diva used to work with the woman who you swiped with a knife. That's why she got the call. It's who you know."

It's who you know. Ilse didn't know anyone in this godforsaken country, but she knew how to pretend she did. A plan formulated in her mind. The rehab center was lacking workers. She knew her way around a kitchen. Once she was off the train, she'd fix herself up. Steal a proper dress, shoes, a brush, some lipstick, then make her way to the Jordaan district. She knew enough Dutch to ask for directions to the center, then she'd become the best live-in cook the manager had ever employed. Margot didn't know it, but she'd be the passport to her husband.

Chapter Twenty-five

"But mercy is above this sceptered sway;
It is enthroned in the heart of kings;
It is an attribute to God himself;
And earthly power doth then show likest God's
When mercy seasons justice."

~ William Shakespeare, *Merchant of Venice*

Neelie wiped the sleep from Karl's eyes and hefted him onto her hip. "I do believe you have gained a kilo or two since you came to stay with us." She smoothed his wispy blond hair with a spit and a polish, then kissed his cheek. "I've cut up an apple. Would you like a piece?"

"Apple," he said and grabbed for the one in her hand.

She held it just out of his grip. "Say please."

"Please give me a piece."

She handed it to him. "You're becoming quite the talker. Where's your mother? I haven't seen her since lunch." Karl was too busy with his snack to answer.

Margot was probably sleeping. It had only been weeks since she'd arrived, but she'd risen to the challenge. While she didn't talk much and smiled even less, she'd performed every task Neelie asked of her without delay or complaint, although Neelie had needed to show her how to perform the simplest of tasks. When Margot finished her chores—helping in the kitchen, sweeping the floor, setting the table, and cleaning up after, she always went to her room, closing the door behind her.

At least she hadn't displayed a sullen attitude as her predecessor had. Neelie almost wished she would show some form of life. They'd not exactly been friends before the war, but they were associates at the opera. If she could only break through the shell of impassiveness that encircled Margot—discover what was going on her head. That old American adage, "time heals all wounds," would have to suffice for now. Maybe with time, Neelie could persuade her to open up, but she had the feeling Margot was just biding her time. To escape? Time would tell the story.

A knock on the back door startled her. People didn't usually call at the back door, and Neelie had already received their grocery order for the week. She hefted Karl on her other hip and headed down the stairs to unlock the door. A woman she didn't recognize peered at her through the window—middle-aged, gaunt, wearing a coat that didn't fit the season. Maybe she just needed some food.

Neelie opened the door. "Good afternoon, may I help you?"

The side of the woman's lip curved up. "Good afternoon, Madame. I was hoping I could help you."

"I'm sorry? I don't understand." Was the woman trying to sell something? From time to time, people like her showed up at the front door, offering handmade items for sale, and Neelie always bought them, although she didn't need anything.

The woman offered her hand. "My name's…Inge...Inge Klein, and I'm a cook, a very good cook. I heard from an…associate that you might need someone to help out in the kitchen."

Was this an answer to prayer? She shook her hand, noting the calluses. This woman was used to hard work. "I'm Neelie Visser. Pleased to meet you. I am short of staff in the kitchen, but I'm afraid I don't have the budget to hire anyone at the moment. I'm sorry." She backed up to close the door.

"Wait. To be honest, I'll work for room and board. Believe me, I'm used to cooking for large crowds, and my specialties are hearty soups and stews with thick, crusty bread. My cakes and strudels are delicious."

"So, you're from Germany, Ja? I can hear your accent—high German, am I right?"

The woman's chapped lips tightened for just a minute, as if surprised by the question. "Yes, from a village near Hamburg. From the time of childhood, I've learned how to make delicious foods from scratch, and I know how to stretch a meal to save money." Inge lifted her eyes to meet Neelie's. "You can try me out if you wish. Give me a week, and you'll be satisfied, I promise you."

Something about the woman's furtive eyes niggled at her. "Mrs. Klein, do you have any references?"

"No, after I lost my husband and son, I came to this country looking for a fresh start. If you give me a chance, I'll prove my mettle. One week is all I ask."

"I'm so sorry for your loss, Inge. So many families were wiped out by the war." Neelie leaned forward to comfort her, but the woman backed up. Brittle, this one—just like many of the residents who'd come to live here after the war. Emma Bartelski, the aide who did most of the cooking, had mentioned more than twice that she wanted to go help her pregnant daughter who lived in Gouda. Neelie read between the lines that she wanted to stay for longer than a week. "All right, I'll give you a week, and we'll go from there. I must tell you that the position may only be a temporary one. Will that work for you?"

"Yes, ma'am," she said. "Would I be able to stay here during this first week? I'm new to town and don't have a place to stay." Inge's brows furrowed together, and she averted her eyes.

Oh, she'd embarrassed the woman. Neelie put Karl down and extended her hand again. "Of course you can stay here; however, we're short of rooms right now. The four aides who work here have homes of their own, except for one. You'll have to share a room with the mother of this child. They're a quiet pair, so they won't bother you."

The woman named Inge paused before nodding her assent. "Thank you for the opportunity to prove myself. May I start right now?"

Surprised, Neelie backed up a step. "Yes…Follow me. I'm sure you have a bag to deposit—" She picked up Karl again. On second thought, she should warn Margot before foisting a new roommate on her. "Wait here while I return this boy to his mother. Think he's ready for a nap." She peered behind the woman. No bag. Odd, but it wasn't her place to judge.

She headed to Margot's door and knocked, shifting Karl onto her other hip. He was gaining weight—a good thing, but not so good for carrying him up the stairs. No response came when she knocked, so she inched open the door. The room was dark, but a slight snore came from one of the beds. What to do? Karl would probably fall asleep right away since it was his nap time. She quietly laid him on the other bed and perched his stuffed bunny by his arm.

Why was Margot sleeping in the middle of the day? A lot of her elderly residents took a few naps a day. The effects of the war, she guessed. Margot might be suffering from the effects of her war in prison. She'd let her sleep a bit more, but then she needed to help in the kitchen.

Once she'd deposited Karl in Margot's room, Neelie returned to the back door where the diminutive woman waited. "Follow me, please." She led her up the stairs to the kitchen where Emma was stirring gravy for the dumplings.

The middle-aged woman, her short curls buried in a hairnet, peered up from her cooking and offered a smile and a hearty greeting. Emma's eyes landed on the stranger, then met Neelie's with an inquisitive tilt.

Neelie guided Inge forward, feeling the jerk of resistance. "Emma, this is Inge Klein. She's offered to help with the cooking for a week, and if it all works out, you may be able to spent time with your daughter and new grandchild." A tiny wisp of foreboding shivered through Neelie. Why had she agreed to hire this woman even for a week without checking her references which weren't forthcoming? Necessity bred recklessness. She'd think about it later.

Emma's eyes flashed with joy. Hopefully, Inge would be true to her words.

"Good. I'm going to show Inge to her room. She'll be staying here for the time being. After she gets settled, would you please show her what you do every day?"

"I'd be happy to. Perhaps she can help me bake bread." Emma wiped her hands on a tea towel.

Neelie led Inge into the main room. "Almost all of our residents are elderly, surviving Jews from the war. They've lost everything—their families, their homes, their purpose in life. We opened this place to help them heal, to bring them back to life." She turned to Inge who trailed behind, whose eyes traveled around the room, her face hard to read. "Will you be able to show our residents the compassion and respect they deserve?" She'd never asked such a pointed question before, but something about this woman gave her pause.

Inge offered a tight nod. "Of course. I am an efficient worker. You won't be disappointed. I see a podium by the wall. Do you do lectures here?"

"When we can get good speakers, yes. Sometimes we bring in singers, comedians—anything to lift our residents' spirits. By the way, I usually refer to our residents as guests. We've even let my niece's exuberant twins take over the stage. They've stolen the guests' hearts as well as their desserts many times." She peered at her new hire. What was her story? They'd reached her office. She unlocked the door, circled her desk, and gestured toward the seat across. "Inge, I have just a few questions before I show you to your room. What actually brought you to Amsterdam? Do you have anyone in town who can give you a reference? I can give them a quick call."

The thin woman lowered into the seat, her hands primly holding her small clutch. "I do not have any references because I don't know anyone in this country. My story is private—not one that I want to share with anyone, but I will tell you that I've come to this country to find a lost relative." Her lips clamped together in a tight line.

The woman had shut down, and no more information would be forthcoming. Neelie stared at her for a long time. There was a time when Neelie hadn't wanted anyone to know about her private life, the 'guests' she hid in her house during the war. The woman standing before her wasn't a warm person by any means, but she claimed to be efficient, a quality often hard to find.

"All right." She stood and opened her office door. "Let's go introduce you to your roommate while you're here. You've already met Karl." She led the way to the closed door at the end of the short hall and tapped on the door. "Margot was sleeping when I dropped Karl off, and he's probably sleeping now as well," she whispered, "but she needs to get up to help Emma in the kitchen."

The door inched open. Margot's face appeared between the crack, her eyes sleepy. "Do you need something?"

"Yes, I'd like to introduce you to our new cook. I'm sorry I woke you up. Could we come in, please?" The door opened a few more inches. Margot stood in her pajamas, her hair disheveled. A look inside showed Karl sitting on the floor between the two beds sucking his thumb, his stuffed bunny hanging from the same hand.

Margot's eyes widened at the sight of the woman behind Neelie, then her brows drew together. Did she know this woman, or was she bothered by being awakened?

"Do you feel sick? I'm sorry again if I woke you up."

Margot yawned on cue. "No, I was just taking a nap. That's not a problem to take a nap in my free time, is it?"

"Of course not," Neelie said. "Your time is your own, but soon you'll have to go help Emma in the kitchen, as will Inge."

Margot managed a smile and a nod in Inge's direction. "Inge? I'm Margot." The slight smile didn't reach her eyes.

"Inge hales from Germany. She'll be joining the staff for a week to start. If all works well, she'll take Emma's place in the kitchen so she can spend some time with her daughter and new grandchild." Neelie backed up to allow Inge to precede her into the room. "We're short on rooms, so she will be sharing your room for the time being. If she remains after a week, I can clean out the supply room, so she can have her own room, but for the time being, she'll be staying with you and Karl."

Inge's eyes darted around. "I won't take up much room." She nodded toward one of the two unmade beds. "Is that your son's bed?"

"He can sleep with me. You can have the bed on the left. I'll make some space for your things in the closet." Margot stepped toward the closet door in the corner and opened it.

Good. Margot didn't seem to be put out by having a roommate. Neelie backed out of the room. "I'll let you two get acquainted, but don't forget to go help Emma prepare the meal for tonight." She closed the door behind her and headed into her office. Strange. She'd expected more resistance from Margot. Maybe she was lonely for someone her own age and recognized a kindred spirit.

After the door closed, Margot's arms perched on her hips. "What are you doing here, Inge, is it?"

Ilse flounced down on the bed and peered around. "It's kind of a dump. Guess it will have to do until we get out of here."

"What do you mean by getting out of here? This is a lot better than the cells and Gray Roots knocking me around. It's not the Ritz, but the food isn't bad, I have my son, and the residents don't give me any trouble."

Ilse yawned. "So, you prefer working with a bunch of old Jews? I'd have thought you'd developed a backbone. What about your singing career? You're not getting any younger, you know."

Margot backed up and lowered onto her bed. "What are you talking about? You think I can just pick up and get my job back? I haven't had a singing lesson in years. The way I sound, they'd probably put me in the chorus. I couldn't stand that. My fans wouldn't stand for it. Not to mention the fact that I still have a year and three months of my sentence to complete."

Ilse leaned against the wall and surveyed the poor excuse of a diva across from her. The spark was gone, but the ambition was still there. She'd play that card. "Not long ago, I remember a certain soprano whose voice made everyone at Zwolle rise to their feet. You don't need any singing lessons. Even that soprano at the microphone stopped when she heard your voice. You bested her."

Margot didn't respond right away, but a glimmer appeared in her eyes that hadn't been there moments before. It was only a matter of time.

Margot bolted up, picked up the scrawny boy, and set him on the bed. Then she paced the small space in the room, her hands posted on her hips. "Even if what you say is true, the press would surely hear that I was back, and my name would be all over the papers. Fame is a treacherous thing sometimes. The police would be at my dressing room the next morning." She stopped and twisted around to face her. "I can't go back to Zwolle. What would happen to my son? I can't—" Her lower lip trembled. "How can you even suggest such a thing?"

Time to play her next card. "That woman—Tamar Feldman—" Ilse spit over her shoulder. "She's the head soprano in *La Bohème*, yes? Without competition, she'll surely get the next role. It could be Juliette or even Carmen. Think about it. She gives a reasonable rendition of the aria, 'Habanera,' and the audience rises to their feet in unison, yelling 'Brava.' After five encores and a multitude of roses thrown onto the stage at her feet, she lowers into a graceful curtsy before the stage lights dim." Ilse cut her a glance. Margot was so easy. That ambition of hers. Now for the kill.

"Tamar Feldman's a decade younger than you, is she not? She'll have the crowd eating out of her hand, as the Americans say, including all your fans." A shuddered cry spewed out of the woman pacing the small floor. Good, she'd hit her target. Go for the throat—another American adage. "Then the offers will come from Amsterdam, Paris, Milan, New York, while you'll be here cleaning rooms." Her arms pressed across her chest while she waited for Margot's reaction. It didn't take much.

The former diva's hands clenched, and she spun around to face her. A fire sparked in her eyes, and she sniffed. "The crowds are down. They won't waste money on a girl from the chorus. Loyalty counts in the opera. The house will be packed when I make my return. I was meant to play Carmen. I *am* Carmen." She raised the palm of her hand.

Ah, the histrionics. It wouldn't take long to convince her to leave this place. Ilse pushed off the bed and headed to the door. "I need to go help the cook—Emma or Esmer or something. You think about what I said. Time's wasting away, as are you. As I said, you're not getting any younger."

The diva whipped around. "Where would we go? We'd have to hide out somewhere. The minute I show my face in Haarlem, the police will be on my trail." Her eyes narrowed. "What's your interest in my singing career anyway? How did you convince the warden to let you out?"

"I took the easy way out." Enough said. She opened the door to leave, but Margot grabbed her by the elbow and whipped her around to face her.

"What do you mean by 'the easy way out'?"

She pointed at Margot's bed where her son had fallen asleep, his thumb ensconced in his half-opened mouth. "Take a seat, but this will have to be quick." After Margot lowered herself onto the corner of the bed, Ilse closed the door and leaned against it. "After you left, your favorite inmate and her minion started kicking me around. Unlike you, I refused to be a target. Got hold of a knife from the kitchen, and let's just say Gray Roots isn't such a pretty face any more."

Margot's jaw dropped. "I can't believe it. So, they didn't put you in solitary?"

"I'm no fool. Climbed in the dumpster outside the kitchen and took a ride to freedom. I jumped out when we reached a country road, even stole a gun at a farm, then headed to the nearest train station."

The diva spewed out a breath. "For a person the size of a twelve-year-old, you got some pluck. How did you convince the manager to hire you?"

Time to go or they'd fire her before she'd even started. For the time being, Ilse needed to lay low. At least there was a bed instead of a cement block or a hayloft to sleep on. "Five more minutes, or I'll get fired. I told Mrs. Visser I was a cook and needed a job. Told her she could try me out for a week—if I make it that long. Thing is—I need to find my husband, and you're going to help me. Now I have to go."

"What about my son? What am I supposed to do with him?"

"Send him back to the orphanage. He'd just slow us down, and we need to move fast." When Ilse noted her crestfallen face, she faced her. "Look, we're this close to freedom. All we have to do is walk out the back door while everyone's sleeping. Yes, we'll have to go into hiding for a while."

"Where would we go?"

"I don't know. Someplace out of the way. Maybe you can get your voice back by singing in one of those bars where the locals go. Maybe change your hair color. Singing in one of those bars will bring in a little money, and the kind of people who go to those places don't know anything about opera. Think about your career." She took her leave.

Chapter Twenty-six

"We shall show mercy, but we shall not ask for it."

~ Winston Churchill

Tamar shuddered when the phone rang yet again. After the third reporter had called asking for an interview, she'd hung up with a heavy hand. Daniel was lucky. He could go to work and put the trial out of his mind, but it was impossible for her to do with the incessant calls. In the week since the trial had begun, she'd stuck close to home with the children and only went out to go to the courthouse and to sing at Haarlem's opera. Her voice often betrayed her because she could feel the audience's curiosity, even their disdain.

The day she was called to the stand was the worst. The flash of cameras as she entered the courthouse disoriented her to the point that she stumbled over a step. Daniel tried to conceal her under his raincoat, but the press bore in like sharks after fresh meat in the ocean.

After she took the oath, the diatribe of questions began from the prosecuting attorney, pummeling her with questions laced with inuendo and sarcasm. Tamar tried to answer as Ben had instructed her—give short answers, look at the judges, maintain a positive, confident demeanor—but he hadn't taught her how to respond to the assassination of her character.

Ben had tried to undo the damage in his cross examination, painting her as a compassionate mother rather than an envious, vindictive member of the chorus. But the evasive eyes and tight lips of the judges showed he'd been unsuccessful. Poor Daniel had fared only slightly better when he was called to testify.

It would all be over tomorrow. There'd be no more questions. Both attorneys would give their final summations, and the judges would leave to decide whether Daniel and she would be able to regain their normal lives with their children or be separated for years from each other.

The night before had been the worst when she and Daniel had called Seth and his wife, Hadassah, in New York. Tamar had broken down in sobs while Daniel explained that they needed someone to take the twins if the verdict went the wrong way. How could she live without Peri and Zari? Would she ever even see them again?

At least they'd have a good life in New York. Hadassah and Seth had lived right across the hall on the fourth floor of Tamar's former apartment, so the children knew them well. It had been two years since Seth and his wife had moved to New York. Would the twins remember them after two years?

Again, she'd forgotten to pray when the thought of losing everything crashed over her to the point she'd thought she'd drowned.

A glance at the twins showed them building a wall of blocks on the parlor floor. Tamar made it to her bedroom before dropping to her knees by the bed, a torrent of tears splashing down from her cheeks. "Oh, Lord…Oh, Lord God…" When "help" was all she could muster, she quoted disjointed lines from verses she remembered from shul, then gave way to moans and groans too deep for words.

Finally, quiet descended like a heavy blanket offering no comfort. She rested her head on the bed for a moment. Time to be the mother she was and tend to her children. Her lips wobbled at the thought their days were numbered. Would her children even remember her? Kidnapping had to be one of the big three crimes along with murder and robbery, the level of crime that resulted in a life sentence. They'd probably add another ten years because she was a Jew. Ben had said the judge didn't appear to be antisemitic, but he'd said the same about the judge who had ordered the trial.

Images of an older, wizened version of herself played in her mind. Perhaps with good behavior, she'd be released in twenty-five years. She'd be in her mid-fifties then, her mother's age when she'd last seen her. Daniel would be a few years older. Would their love survive that many years apart? The twins would have families of their own by then. Although Hadassah and Seth would make sure to remind them of their parents, maybe it would be easier and less humiliating for them not to know that their real mother and papa were convicted kidnappers.

Such imaginings weren't doing any good. She struggled to her feet. The last thing the twins needed was a memory of a dour-faced mother. She shuffled to the bathroom and splashed water on her face. A look in the mirror showed swollen eyelids and splotchy cheeks. Great. She splashed some more water on her face and gently patted her eyes. Daniel would be home soon, and he had enough to worry about without adding to his burden.

She was just hanging up the hand towel when a voice, not much louder than a whisper, said her name. She couldn't tell if it was a male or female voice, but she knew that she knew. "Yes, Lord?"

"*I will never leave you or forsake you. Do you trust me*?"

Her fingers covered her lips, and tears spiraled down her cheeks. "Yes, I do."

"*That's my daughter*."

Her chest started quaking. *My daughter*. The voice of her Messiah. She blew out a breath and fell to her knees. He'd answered her prayer in person. A warm blanket of peace descended on her, wrapping her in deep comfort.

Pushing to her feet, she joined the children in the parlor in the small space that wasn't covered with wooden blocks. Instead of telling them to clean up the mess, she sat there, enjoying their childlike babbling on their project. Zari ordered Peri around, as she was wont to do, while Peri built a tower that was sure to topple any minute. Tamar savored every precious moment with them.

Footsteps sounded from the foyer below. Daniel was home. She couldn't wait to tell him about the voice. He entered the kitchen and called out, "Where is my family?"

"We're up here." Tamar stood and brushed off her dress, swiping at strands of hair that had stuck to the tears on her face. She'd forgotten about dinner. This trial had disrupted their routines, but she didn't want their last day together to be a hectic one.

Daniel's eyes landed on her, and they smiled if eyes could do so. She couldn't help herself; she touched her cheek against his, letting it remain there for more than a long time.

"What's all this?"

She sighed, kissed his nose, and backed a few centimeters away. "I'm just trying to savor every moment with…" She motioned with her head toward the twins.

He nodded his understanding. "I stopped at the store and bought some fresh bread and corned beef at the deli, so we don't have to go to too much trouble for supper." He turned to the children, who hadn't looked up from their towers. "Your papa's here. Remember me?" He knelt down and pulled Peri onto his lap.

Peri burst out laughing when Daniel tickled his stomach. "Look what I built. It's the pizza tower you told us about. See? It's leaning."

"Ah, the Tower of Pisa. Close enough. How about you two knock it down and start cleaning up. I brought home your favorite dessert."

Peri's eyes widened. "Gummy moustaches? Yay."

Daniel glanced up at Tamar and rolled his eyes. "Not exactly. Will strawberry ice cream do?"

"That's my second favorite dessert. C'mon, Zari. Let's knock them down." Peri pushed to his feet, knocking into Zari's tower over in the process.

The girl's face descended into a frown. "Papa, look what he did." She pushed him into his own tower, which sent the blocks flying.

Daniel crept over to her on his knees and picked her up in his arms. "Peri didn't mean to do that. It was an accident." He kissed her cheek. "Now, you two get to work cleaning up all the blocks. Then we'll have a nice, quiet dinner, okay, sweetie?" He offered a rueful shrug to Tamar. "If you don't mind making the sandwiches, I'll help them clean up in here. Then we can enjoy our time together."

She nodded, understanding the depth of his words.

After the kids were in bed and the dishes done, Tamar pulled Daniel into the parlor, leading him to the sofa. "I have to tell you about something that happened this afternoon." She pulled him down next to her, their knees touching.

His eyebrows furrowed. "What? Did one of those reporters harass you? You should have called me. I'll be so glad when this is all over with."

She took his hands in hers. "No, it was more like my mind was harassing me. I succumbed into tears, thinking that everything could change tomorrow, and the thought of it was too much to bear. The only words I could manage were, 'Help, Lord.'"

He folded her into a hug, running his fingers through her hair. "You've had more to handle than what's humanly possible At least, I've had my work to keep my mind off of what could happen. I'm so sorry." He kissed her head.

"Yeah, it's a lot to bear, but then God answered me in the most wonderful way. I can hardly believe it."

"What happened?" He leaned back and tucked his finger under her chin.

She told him how she'd broken down on the bed, thoughts about never seeing her children or Daniel again as she languished in a prison until she was old and gray. "Hadassah and Seth had raised our twins in New York, but by the time I finally saw them, they were adults with their own families. When I finally met them, they had no memory of me whatsoever. I was just some old woman who had brought shame to their lives." Tears rolled down her face. "You had moved on and didn't want anything to do with me."

Daniel ran the pad of his thumb under her eye to catch a tear. "You'll never lose me or the children."

"I know that, but after the third call from a reporter, I just lost my way for a while. But there's a happy ending. As I was splashing water on my face, the most unusual thing happened. I heard a voice, a whisper of sorts. The voice said, '*I will never leave you or forsake you, my daughter.*'" Tamar leaned back against Daniel's arm. "He called me His daughter." A shudder of a sob came out. "Then I knew without a doubt that everything would be fine. We're going to make it, Daniel. Somehow God will make it all work out."

"My sweet girl, thank you." He pulled her close, his own tears intermingling with hers. They remained like that for a long moment.

His lips traveled down to meet hers, and the longing she'd felt for his closeness filled her to the fullest.

Chapter Twenty-seven

"Pity would be no more, if we did not make somebody poor.
And Mercy no more could be. If all were as happy as we."

~ William Blake

Despite the reassurance Tamar had received from God's message the day before, anxiety filled her, and she held onto Daniel's hand as they bypassed the slew of reporters. She kept her head down while climbing the steps of the courthouse. Soon they were in their seats next to their attorney, whose grim face did not elicit hope. He scoured his notes since he would be giving his closing statement first.

Why did the prosecutor get the final word when it was her life at stake? Tamar's breaths came in starts and stops, and she fought to steady them. In a matter of an hour, her life would be in the hands of the judges, all of whom were men. Would they even understand the mother's heart, or would they see her as a vengeful woman as the opposing attorney described her?

She was so lost in her thoughts that she almost remained sitting when the bailiff said, "All rise." Luckily, Daniel pulled her up and continued to hold her hand. They were in this together, so she held on tight. When they were seated, Ben buttoned his jacket and approached the dais.

"Your Honors, this trial should never have happened. My clients did what any compassionate adults would do—they saw a battered child and sought to rescue him. Put yourself in that orphanage where little Karl sat in the front row. It had been two years since he'd last seen Mrs. Feldman, yet her voice broke through the hurt and abandonment he felt. Mrs. Feldman's voice sparked a familiar chord with him, and he called out, 'Mama.'"

Ben circled the podium and paced in front of the judges. "Put yourself in this couple's place. You see a little boy with bruises on his face, arms, and legs, so you visit the director's office to discover why the child has injuries and why he hasn't said a single word in the year leading up to the concert. Was it a crime to ask if they could take little Karl to their home? No crime at all."

He peered at the judges. "You have heard that Margot Sneider didn't give permission for the Feldmans to take the child, but she didn't have all the facts. The director told her that her son was fine, and living with the other boys would help make him grow stronger. Even so, the defendants traveled to Zwolle to meet with her in the prison. Does that sound like the actions of kidnappers? And yes, Mrs. Sneider refused to let them take care of the child. Ask yourself this, if you discovered that a four-year-old child was locked out on the roof in the middle of the night, what would you do?

"Now, let's look at the facts, with regard to the charge of kidnapping. When the Feldmans saw the bruises on the boy's face and heard that he hadn't spoken in his year at the prison—pardon me, orphanage, they followed standard procedure by meeting with the director. Do kidnappers follow standard procedure?

"Next, it wasn't the Feldmans who took the child after he was locked out on the roof, but a concerned employee who brought the child to them, so there was no apprehending of the child. That same night, Dr. Feldman returned the child to the orphanage, only to discover that the director and the staff had to deal with an emergency elicited by an alarm in the middle of the night. Dr. Feldman couldn't leave the child, shaken by the alarm, so he took him. What was his intent? To demand a ransom? To seek revenge? No, you'll agree that his intent was to rescue the child, not to kidnap him.

"Again, Mrs. Feldman took the child back to the orphanage, but the boy was so upset at seeing the director, he whimpered and clung to her neck. Ask yourself this: Was Mrs. Feldman's intent to kidnap Karl Sneider when she made the quick decision to take him back to her home, or was it out of concern for the child's welfare?

"Now that the child is back with his mother, this whole case is moot, so why did the province waste the taxpayers' money? The prosecution will spin a tale about revenge, long-held grudges, and envy that Mrs. Feldman held against Karl Sneider's mother. Consider the facts. The Feldmans' intent was to protect Margot Sneider's child—a four-year-old who refused to eat, a little boy who refused to talk, a child covered with bruises. I submit to you that the Feldmans did not kidnap the child. They rescued him. By God, make your decision to free the defendants by rendering a 'Not Guilty' decision. Their future is in your hands. Thank you." Ben looked long and hard at the judges, then returned to his seat.

Quiet reigned in the courtroom until the judge called for the prosecutor's closing remarks. Tamar studied the faces of the judges, but she couldn't decipher what their expressions reflected. One judge rifled through papers; the other two shifted in their seats. How could they not be moved by Ben's closing statement? Maybe they were inured to his impactful words. Maybe their minds were on other things—like future cases or getting back to their families. How she wished women could sit on the bench. They'd understand how a mother felt.

The prosecutor stood and buttoned his jacket. With a shake of his head, he began. "Such histrionics." He rolled his eyes for effect. "As learned men of the bar, I'm certain you can see past the play for your emotions, but the facts of the case speak for themselves. A four-year-old child was abducted from an orphanage, against his mother and the director's will. In other words, the two people who were legally responsible for Karl Sneider's life had not given their approval. The abduction without consent satisfies two elements of the crime of kidnapping. Add to that the fact that the child was not returned to the orphanage when the defendants had opportunity makes this a heinous crime. The defense argued that, as a physician, Dr. Feldman's intent was based on his assessment that the child was suffering in some way. However, the orphanage's own doctor did not have the opportunity to examine the child."

The prosecutor spun toward the bench. “Most of you have children.” A few of the younger men nodded. “If you do, you’ll agree that boys often have bruises on their legs from playing soccer or stick ball—you name it. It’s in the school of outdoor play that boys become men. They learn in the school of ‘hard knocks,’ to coin an American metaphor. Who among you has suffered a kick to the shin or a shove of the arm while playing with your friends? Even if the Feldmans’ motivation in abducting the boy was borne out of altruism, I submit to you that they overreacted, did not go through the proper channels, and tore the boy away from his home for the last year. Any psychological damage Karl Sneider has suffered as a result of the abduction will manifest itself later in his life.”

He paced back in forth, his hands clasped behind his back. “Our country’s justice system is based on following certain rules concerning our personal rights and freedoms. As long as the courts maintain those rights and freedoms, order overcomes chaos. What we cannot allow are emotions to overcome our good sense. Emotions are all the defense can offer. Dr. and Mrs. Feldman abducted Karl Sneider not once but twice. They kept him in their house and refused to open their door to the summons officer. Then they secretly took Karl to the train station and dropped him off at a friend’s place of work in Amsterdam.

“You’ll remember the testimony of Karl’s mother, Margot Sneider. When asked about her relationship with the defendant, she said, ‘strained.’ When I asked her to explain what she meant, she said, ‘envy and resentment.’ Mrs. Sneider went on to elaborate—” He took a small piece of paper from his jacket pocket. “‘‘Tamar has always been envious of my success in the opera. I brought in the crowds each night. I suppose it was natural to feel that way as she was just a chorus girl, and the crowds have not been good since she’s been the head soprano. She also envied my home and even tried to steal my husband away from me.’”

Gasps and murmurs erupted after his last statement. Tamar kept her head down; it was too heavy to lift. So, this was how it was going to end—her reputation ruined, her family destroyed—all based on innuendo and lies. The prosecutor’s last words would remain in the minds of the people in the courtroom. She’d always be remembered as a bitter woman, motivated by envy and resentment.

The prosecutor stopped in front of the bench and posted his arms on the railing, eying each one of the men. "You know the law as well as the facts. Do not let emotions cloud your judgment. You need to decide three issues regarding the facts of the case: Did Dr. Feldman and his wife take Karl Sneider from the orphanage? Two, did they take him without the permission of those responsible for the child? Lastly, did they move the child to another location to evade the police? If the answer to these questions is yes, then you must render a guilty verdict. Do your civil duty, Gentlemen." He returned to his desk. "The province rests, Your Honor."

After the prosecutor's final words, the judges left to render their decision. Her whole future lay in the decision they made. If she were one of them, she would have voted guilty. Margot had won.

Ben leaned forward after seeing her crestfallen face. "Not to worry. The judges won't be fazed by his remarks when they go over the facts of the case." He reached over and patted her hand. "Let's go back to my office. I asked my secretary to bring us sandwiches and coffee." He stood, closed his briefcase, and led them out of the courthouse.

Daniel huddled her close as they made a pathway through the reporters who crowded on every step and clamored for her attention.

"What do you have to say to Margot Sneider's accusation?"

"Any truth to the prosecutor's words?"

"Is it true you stole the child simply to get back at her?"

When they rounded the corner, Tamar finally lifted her eyes. She felt as if there was a large A tattooed on her forehead like the one in *The Scarlet Letter*. How would she ever live with the shame of it all?

Daniel must have read her thoughts because he told Ben to go on ahead. Then he pulled her toward him. "Tamar, it's going to be okay. Ben said that's the way prosecutors operate, but the judges will know that his words were pure lies. The truth is what we need to hang onto. I need you to be strong. This will all be over soon." He kissed her forehead. "I love you more than anything. Don't let them get to you."

She leaned into his chest, the lapel of his jacket rough against her cheek. For once his words didn't console her. Their future lay in the hands of three men who might be won over by the words of the prosecutor. Even if they came back with a not guilty verdict, her reputation was sullied forever.

"C'mon, we need to catch up." Daniel took her hand and picked up his pace, dragging her behind.

She hurried to catch up with him. "How long do you think it will be until they make a decision?"

He glanced at her and shrugged. "Ben will have a good idea. I hope it's not too soon."

"Why do you say that?"

"The more they talk about it, the more time they have to analyze our case. We don't want them making a quick decision."

They caught up to Ben and followed him into the elevator and up to his office. As Ben had mentioned, the credenza was filled with sandwiches, small cakes, and coffee and water. He pointed toward the table and told them to get some lunch. Tamar poured herself a cup of water. Her appetite had vanished, and she was quite certain she wouldn't be able to keep any food down. She took her seat across from Ben.

Once Ben had returned to his seat and placed a napkin over his sandwich, he leaned forward. "I can tell by the crestfallen looks on your faces you're worried about the outcome. Don't be. Yes, the prosecutor gave a powerful speech. What else could he do? Since the facts of the case are weak for his side, he had to impugn your reputation, Tamar. Don't worry. The judges can see through the veil of inuendo the prosecutor cast. We have a very strong case, and the judges will see that."

Daniel lifted his head, his eyebrows forming a V. "What if they decide for the prosecution? Will we have to go to prison?"

Ben took a bite of his sandwich and chewed before answering. "Immediately, I'd file an appeal, for which I have ten days to do so. You'd have to sit through another trial, but there'd be three new judges, and as I said before, we have an air-tight case."

His words did little to mollify her. Daniel's tight jaw indicated he felt the same. The two men started talking about matters unrelated to the case, which gave Tamar time to ponder. What had she heard in the bathroom at home? In the midst of all that was happening, she'd almost forgotten. The mere whisper of a voice had said, "*That's my daughter*." She repeated the words to herself. She'd cling to them when the judges returned with their verdict.

"What did you say?"

She glanced up to see Ben looking at her. "Oh, nothing. It's just a memory from yesterday. I was—" The phone rang.

Ben grabbed it and put the receiver to his ear. "Right." He hung up. "That was fast. The judges have returned with their verdict."

Chapter Twenty-eight

"Now is the winter of our discontent made glorious summer by this sun of York;
And all the clouds that lour'd upon our house in the deep bosom of the ocean buried.
Now are our brows bound with victorious wreaths, our bruised arms hung up for monuments; Our stern alarums changed to merry meetings; our dreadful marches to delightful measures."

~ William Shakespeare, *Richard III*

Daniel's eyes brimmed at the slump of Tamar's shoulders as they took their seats, waiting for the judges to file out. He wanted to comfort her—tell her that everything would return to normal in just a few hours, but that would be cruel to give her false hope, when he couldn't be sure of their fate.

He moved his chair closer to hers, so they could lock arms—lock their very souls as they awaited the verdict. If anything, he was numb—his normal way of handling unpleasant news. He'd learned to wrap himself in a cocoon-like blanket. How wrong he'd been to close himself off to Tamar, when she'd needed him the most. Yes, he'd asked her to forgive him, and she'd been generous with her response, but old habits were hard to break, and he felt himself descending into that cocoon again.

Enough about himself and more about her—the bride he loved, the mother of his children. She deserved better. He looped his arm around her shoulders, not caring how it looked to the court.

Tamar cut him a sideways glance, her eyes filled with a mixture of apprehension and gratitude. She rested her head against his shoulder, the shudder in her breath traveling down to a slight tremor in her hand. "The despair I felt at Vught doesn't match what I feel now. Maybe because other people didn't depend on me during the war. I try to remember the words I heard yesterday— 'Trust me. I will never forsake you, my daughter,' but I keep forgetting."

He kissed her temple. "It's understandable. Whatever happens, know that I love you, and I'll do whatever it takes to protect you and the children."

She managed a weak smile that vanished in an instant. "I know you will, but what can you do from a prison cell?" Her brow furrowed. "It never occurred to me that we might receive different sentences. Is it possible that one of us will be exonerated and the other convicted?"

He patted her leg. "Let's not think the worst. We have to hold on to hope."

The steady chatter behind them quieted when the three robed judges filed in.

"All rise," the bailiff said. The rustle of the spectators standing reached Daniel's ears, and he pulled Tamar to her feet. The moment the judges took their seats, Daniel started to sit, but Ben motioned for them to remain standing.

The shuffling of the judges' papers seemed inordinately strident to Daniel's ear. *Let's just get this over with.* Somehow standing when the spectators behind them sat made him feel more like a criminal. Simply the fact that their future was out of his hands brought a vulnerability he'd rarely felt since their year in the labor camps. The yellow stars they wore on their arms and the tattooed numbers on the inside of their forearms gave testament to the hatred people had for them.

The judge on the left interrupted Daniel's musings. He swallowed past the heavy ball in his throat. Steadying his breath,

Daniel lifted his eyes to the men who would decide their fate. He had to be strong for his wife and twins, but he felt anything but.

The robed man offered no smile, not even a little help to allay Daniel's fears. "Ladies and Gentlemen, members of the court, Dr. and Mrs. Feldman, we have come to a decision. May I say that this case should never have come to the court based on the facts as they apply to the law of the province. Having said that, there are three issues evoked from different interests of the parties involved based on who has legal responsibility for a child. Issue one: Does an incarcerated mother or father forfeit their parental rights when custody has been removed from them? Issue two: Does an institution forfeit their *in loco parentis* rights when the child's life is endangered? Issue three: How far does the province's 'duty to rescue' law reach in light of the present case?

The bench will answer each question one by one. With regard to the parents' rights, the law states—" The judge put on his glasses. "'If the victim is a minor, consent must come from a parent or guardian."

A gasp escaped Daniel's lips. The judge must have heard because he met Daniel's eyes. "'However, if the legal parent or guardian is absent, unconscious, delusional, or intoxicated, consent is implied." He took off his glasses. "In the present case, since Mrs. Sneider was absent, so to speak, her consent is implied."

One down. Daniel could feel tears brim in his eyes. He cut a glance at Tamar and squeezed her hand. Her tightened jaw moved slightly, and she squeezed back.

"As per the second question, concerning the legal rights of the Haarlem Mennonite Orphanage, the institution operates as legal guardians *in loco parentis*. The prosecution has submitted, quite correctly in two incidents, that the Feldmans indeed abducted the child according to the definition. In other words, they transported the child away from the orphanage without the director's permission."

Murmurs rose from the spectators to the point that the judge pounded his gavel and called for attention in the court.

Tamar swayed and dropped to her seat, her eyes closed. The bailiff rushed over as Daniel knelt to take her into his arms. Daniel glanced up. "Could you bring me a glass of water?"

After the bailiff nodded and left, Daniel set her back in the chair.

"Shall we take a recess, Dr. Feldman?" came from one of the judges.

Tamar's eyes fluttered open, darted around her, then met Daniel's eyes. "What happened?"

Daniel glanced up at the judge. "Give me a minute, Your Honor." He ran his fingers down her cold, taut cheek. "You fainted, darling. Do you want to take a break? The judge wants to know." The bailiff hurried over with a pitcher of water and a glass. "Thank you." He poured a bit into the glass and lifted it to her lips.

She took a sip, then shook her head. "I'm fine. Don't stop on my account." She grabbed the armrests and nodded toward the judges. "I'm okay. Please continue."

"Very well. Let's come to order." The judge on the left flipped through the file in front of him. "Oh yes. As I said before, the defendants abducted the boy in question twice, but the law also requires an intent at the time of abduction. The requisite intent comes in four forms: One, to hold for ransom or reward, or as a shield or hostage; two, to facilitate the commission of a felony or flight thereafter; three, to inflict bodily injury or terrorize the victim or another; or four, to interfere with the performance of any governmental or political function.

"As per the case before the court, the defendants did not have the requisite intent of the first three, although it can be argued that the Feldmans interfered with the performance of a governmental function. However, since the Haarlem Mennonite Orphanage is run by the Mennonite Church, it does not fall under the auspices of the government."

He held up his hand when voices rose from the courtroom. "The prosecution has argued that Mrs. Feldman circumvented the police officer's warrant when she took the child to Amsterdam; however, she did so to reunite the child with his mother. Therefore, in terms of intent, the defendants did not abduct the child with the requisite intent.

"The last issue to be determined is issue three: How far does the province's duty to rescue reach in light of the present case? Although the province doesn't have a Good Samaritan's law as many other countries do, Section 323c of the Criminal Code states that 'any person is obligated to provide assistance in case of an accident or general danger if necessary, and is normally immune from prosecution if assistance is given in good faith and follows the reasonable person standard.'" The judge took off his glasses and leaned forward. "The court has decided that Dr. Feldman and his wife acted in good faith and passed the reasonable person standard when they took the boy from the orphanage." A small smile spread across his face. "As a result, we find the defendants not guilty of kidnapping. You may go home to your family, Dr. and Mrs. Feldman. Court dismissed."

This was it? They were free to leave? Daniel stood there, unable to move. His lower lip wobbled as the realization overtook him.

Ben clapped him on the back. "See, didn't I tell you? We did it. Yes!" He pumped his fist in the air then grabbed Daniel's hand, shaking it. "I'd say we should go out and celebrate, but—" Ben nodded toward Tamar.

Tamar. He whipped around to see tears rolling down her cheeks, her fists covering her lips. "Oh, my sweet girl." He wrapped her in his arms and dissolved into his own tears at the shudder of her shoulders. "It's over. We can go home to our twins and forget this ever happened." He kissed her head. "I love you so much. Let's go home, darling." Swiping at his eyes, he helped her to her feet. "Justice was served today."

She peered up at him. "Can we pray?"

Ah, he'd forgotten to pray. "Of course." Holding her tight against his chest, he prayed verses from Psalm 30—one he'd learned as a boy in shul:

> "I will extol You, O Lord, for You have lifted us up,
> And have not let my foes rejoice over us.
> O Lord my God, weeping may endure for a night,
> but joy comes in the morning."

"Sorry," he said. "My own prayers always fall short of King David's."

"Mine as well." she breathed out a shuddery breath, but a slight smile curved up her lips. "It's all over, isn't it? I've forgotten what normal feels like." She wrapped her arms around his waist.

Ben leaned toward them. "There will be some documents to sign at the clerk's office. I'll take you there. Sometime this week, could you come to the office to fill out paperwork? Then you can put all this behind you."

"So, it's really over?" A shadow of doubt still lingered inside him. "Is it possible the prosecution will appeal the decision?"

Ben shrugged. "They have ten days to file an appeal, but it would be a waste of the taxpayers' money. Trust me, it's over."

She grabbed her purse, linked arms with Daniel's, and leaned against his arm as they slowly followed Ben out of the courtroom. Luckily the room had emptied except for a few stragglers whose eyes seemed to follow them. Security officers in the hall shooed onlookers out the door before they reached it. One guard signaled for them to wait. For what? She felt like a celebrity—a notorious one at that.

The security guard gestured for Ben to approach. Daniel took her hand to follow him. At least she and Daniel were not leaving in handcuffs never to see their children again. The thought of the twins not having to deal with reporters outside her door gave her a modicum of comfort. Since she and Daniel had been exonerated, they'd be able to return to their old life. Picking up the twins at school, reading them bedtime stories, shopping at the market without eyes following her every move. How she longed for simple things that she'd taken for granted before. Freedom was now a valuable commodity that she'd cherish from now on.

Camera lights flashed in her eyes, causing her to blink again and again as reporters surrounded her. Voices rivaled with each other to catch Daniel and her attention.

"Are you happy with the verdict, Doctor?"

"Mrs. Feldman, are you going to return to the opera?"

"Don't answer, you two," Ben yelled over his shoulder. "I'll handle this." He raised his hand to quiet the crowd. There had to be a hundred people pushing toward them. The flashes caused her to sway against Daniel's side. He shielded her with his arm.

The crowd quieted somewhat. "Gentlemen, if you'll be patient, we'll answer your questions, but you must understand that this couple has been through a lot. Please, give them a chance to breathe." They remained on the top step while a court employee set up a microphone. Ben took his place behind it, pulling the two of them beside him.

"Today, justice has been served. This case should never have come to trial. Dr. and Mrs. Feldman's rescue of an injured child was intentionally recast as a kidnapping by the prosecution, but the court proved rightly that each one of us has a duty to protect those people who cannot protect themselves. Now I'll open it up to your questions."

A voice rang out from the middle of the crowd on the stairs. "Are you saying the orphanage abuses the children. Is that what you're saying?" A flurry of questions drowned out Ben's words.

Ben covered the microphone with his hand until the crowd quieted. "I'm not saying that. The Mennonite Orphanage of Haarlem has an excellent record for providing a safe environment for the children in their care, but sometimes kids fall between the cracks. This holds true of any institution. At those times, each one of us has a duty to keep the child safe, whether by informing the authorities, or in certain situations, as was the case with my clients—one has a duty to protect the child. Are there any more questions?"

A voice came from the bottom of the stairs behind a crowd of photographers. "Mrs. Feldman, would you please expand on what the prosecutor said in the court—that you harbored envy for Margot Sneider as the lead soprano of the opera?"

Daniel instinctively tightened his grip of her arm. When Ben cut a sideways glance at Tamar, Daniel gave him a quick shake of his head. Ben turned back to the crowd and waited for the noise to die down.

"Gentlemen, because the prosecutor had nothing to go on in terms of motive, all he could do was grab at straws—anything to impugn my client's character and good name. Any connotation he invented to ruin her reputation was quickly dismissed by the judges. The facts speak for themselves. Mrs. Feldman had babysat the child years before, and it was only after she saw the bruises on his legs and arms and discovered that he hadn't spoken in a year that she went straight to the director's office to find out why. You'll remember that a staff member of the orphanage brought the child to her house after the four-year-old was locked out on the roof. You have to ask yourself—if he were a child you knew, wouldn't you have done the same?"

When the crowd of reporters settled down, he tapped on the microphone. "If there are no more questions, I'd like my clients to be able to go home. Give them space."

With Tamar sequestered between Daniel and the counselor, they made their way down the steps. Ben's words must have mollified the crowd. They moved back to allow them room to exit the premises.

Once they were a few blocks from the courthouse, Ben stopped them at the corner by his office. "Remember to stop by in the next week so we can put this case to rest." He smiled. "We couldn't have asked for a better outcome. God was definitely protecting you."

Chapter Twenty-nine

"Before you embark on a journey of revenge, dig two graves."

~ Confucius

Margot swiped at the tendrils of hair that fell in her eyes, then wrung out the mop. This was not part of the plan she'd made for her life at the age of forty-two. She supposed she should be grateful to Neelie Visser. Certainly, her responsibilities at the center were a big improvement on her daily chores at Zwolle, although it didn't escape her thoughts that she could and should be singing *Carmen* instead of mopping floors. Yes, Neelie had arranged for her to be reunited with Karl, and he was putting on weight and speaking in complete sentences instead of just grunting and pointing.

"Look at those hands." Ilse stopped next to her and hoisted a sack of flour over her shoulder. Her face scrunched as if she'd smelled rotten meat. "They're more painful-looking than they did in Zwolle."

By instinct, Margot slid her chafed hands into her pockets. "Aren't you supposed to be preparing lunch in the kitchen?"

Ilse dropped the sack to the floor with a thud. "Anything to get away from Emma's curious eyes. One day I corrected her when she called me Inge. Why did I have to pick a name so close to my own?

Ever since, Emma keeps on asking me questions about my past. I'll be glad when her daughter goes into labor. Maybe then I'll get some peace." She yawned aloud. "You know, that would be the perfect time to bolt out of here."

Margot blew out a huff. "That again? Can't you just let it drop? Yeah, these hands have seen better days, but I refuse to go back to Zwolle. Look what happened to the last girl who was here. Now I have Karl. My sentence will be over in a year, two months, and three days. I don't like it, but I can last that long."

Ilse's face contorted. "You've become soft. Think of it. That Jewish gal is stealing your fans from right under you." She reached over and grabbed Margot by the chin. "Your face appears as bad as your hands. Look at those lines around your lips. You're aging, girl. If you stay in here too much longer, no amount of makeup will help you win the lead soprano roles. You'll be relegated to the chorus." Ilse's shove caused her to fall next to the mop pail.

Dark water splashed onto Margot's hair. "Stop it. Why did you even come here? You could have gone anywhere—taken on a new identity instead of ruining my life. Why don't you just leave!"

"Because I need you to help me find my husband."

"Why would I know anything about your husband?" Margot pushed to her feet and moved the wheeled mop bucket away from her.

"Does stolen art ring a bell?" Ilse wrapped her arms across her chest. "Erich's always had a thing for opera singers—especially lead sopranos. Are you getting the picture?"

Hm. What in the world did Ilse…oh— "Are you talking about Erich Bergman? The guy whose art we stored for him? I'm not going to find him. Look what he did to us." She posted her hands on her hips. "That weasel of a man is your husband? If it weren't for him, Klaus and I wouldn't be in prison." She spit over her shoulder.

"You're right. He's a weasel." She chuckled. "Sounds like you don't harbor kind thoughts of him."

"Of course I don't." Margot examined her fingernails. "I thought he was dead. Didn't he die in Paris? That's what our attorney said." She shook her head. "I can't believe Erich Bergman is your husband!"

Ilse nodded. "He can't be dead. He's too mean to die. I have to find him and make him pay for what he did to me and my son."

Margot stood, her eyes widening. “So, all this was a setup? Is that why you pretended to be a friend? You thought I could lead you to Erich? The last time I saw him, he looked like he was about to die. He showed up at my door dressed in a doctor’s coat, but he was in bad shape. His face was swollen. He could hardly make it up the stairs, and he demanded I give him medicine. Is he a drug addict?”

Ilse shrugged. “Like I said, I haven’t seen him in nine years. Last time Erich called was in 1944. Our son was only twelve at the time; now he’s nineteen, but he left home at eighteen. Why was he in such bad shape?”

“Not sure. He was ready to throw a big rock through the window of my house. Because he was wearing a lab coat, I mistook him for Tamar’s husband and let him enter. I’d been expecting Feldman to make a house call to treat my throat. I should have recognized your husband. He didn’t exactly look like a Jew.” She spewed out a breath.

“Erich’s about as far from a Jew as can be. You know he worked for the Third Reich in Haarlem. He called me from there. That’s when he told me about you. Said you were a Nazi sympathizer.”

Margot waved a dismissive hand. “I was just looking out for myself. It was so dreary during the war. The opera had closed, and the only nightclubs open were in Amsterdam. Klaus introduced me to your husband at the Spiegel bar. Said he could open doors for me to perform for the members of the Reich at some of the clubs they’d taken over.”

“You didn’t answer my question. What was wrong with him when he came to your house?”

She posted her hands on her hips. “Apparently, a fire had broken out in the warehouse in Amsterdam where he had been storing the art, and he got caught in the fire. His skin was yellow and his eyes desperate. In fact, he looked years older than he had during the war. I hadn’t seen him in years. He always dealt with my husband, Klaus, to store the art he’d bought at auctions. In return he’d give us a few pieces to sell.

“When he showed up at my door, he was in great pain. His hands were shaking, and he looked like he was going to pass out. I gave him a drink and some aspirin.” She shook her head. “I thought it strange that he didn’t carry a medical bag, but I was so frazzled at the time. He pretended to look at my throat, then said it was red and irritated. Told me to stop singing and give my throat a rest. How naïve I was."

Ilse shrugged. "Now you know the truth. Erich always was obsessed with opera singers. He'd mentioned you and Tamar Visser. That was what Erich called her. Visser was her name before she married that Jew, wasn't it?

"You kidding? It was Kaplan. Tamar Kaplan—she was my understudy in *La Traviata*. She ruined the opera. They closed it down because of her kind. So why would you even bother trying to find your husband? What's the point? It won't end well even if he's still alive."

She studied her nails. "I just need one shot. After years of not hearing from him, I figured you or that woman could lead me to him."

Margot rolled her eyes. "What a fool I was, thinking you were a friend, but you're just using me." Could anyone be trusted anymore? She'd never been good at choosing friends; in fact, she'd had few female friends, even when she was in school. Margot preferred men, especially the ones with power and influence. Yes, powerful, rich men drew her like a magnet. They were the ones who opened doors for her. The talent agent who'd promised to make her a star back when she was a teen. The singing coach who gave her free lessons. The opera manager who arranged for her to have a private audition with the producer. Of course, there was always a price to pay.

"Margot, we're both stuck here. You're not getting any younger, but if we work together, we can help each other out of this rathole."

Ilse's voice brought her back from her thoughts. Margot stood and stretched her aching back from bending over the mop bucket. "Even if I could leave this place, I couldn't help you. I don't know where your husband is. Klaus told me he died in Paris. The police killed him for some reason. Figured he got what he deserved after making us take the fall for his crimes." She peered at the slight woman with wrinkles framing her lips. "Why would you even want him back after he abandoned you?"

She spewed out a stream of profanity, then lowered her voice when Margot motioned to her to stop. "I don't want him. I want him to pay for forsaking me and his son." Angry tears cascaded down her cheeks, as if they'd burst through a dike in the canal. "We had a good life. Erich had a job as an accountant before he was drafted into the army. We went to the ballet and the opera. Erich and Dieter shared a love for the violin. He was teaching him how to play, and they'd put on concerts for me and the neighbors."

She swiped the tears away with the back of her hand. "Dieter was only twelve years old when his father left. He worshipped Erich and would do anything to please him. Dieter joined the Hitler Youth Organization to please his father. When the war ended and no calls came, Dieter thought he had died, but I knew better. It would have been better if he had," she spat out the last few words and covered her forehead with her hand. "Now my son is like his father."

"What do you mean? He can't be that old yet."

"He's almost nineteen. Eight years without his father. He's angry, full of rage. Dieter left home one night after we had an argument. I haven't seen him since." Her lips tightened. "When I arrived in Amsterdam from Germany, a police officer followed me from the train station. I knew I was in trouble, so I led him into an alley and killed him with the gun I'd brought from home—one of my husband's old ones. That's how I ended up in prison, then in Zwolle."

This was a side Margot hadn't seen in the woman before her. The vulnerable side. Ilse was fighting for her family, even if it was to get her revenge against Bergman. She'd never trusted the man. The way his lip pulled down. The coldness in his face. The way his eyes followed Tamar around the nightclub in Amsterdam. The only time she'd ever seen an ounce of compassion in the man was when he talked about his son back in Germany.

Compassion. When had that ever been important to her? From the time Margot was a wee one, nobody had shown her a millimeter of compassion, including her mother, sister, and grandmother. She'd learned early on to harden her edges. Fame would take her where she wanted to go, and later the men. Margot shoved away such wanton thoughts and stuffed compassion deep inside. If this was a game Ilse was playing, Margot had to have the upper hand. "Ilse, I still don't get it. Why would you risk your life for Erich Bergman? He abandoned you and your son."

"I want him and that little minx to die."

Margot blew out a breath. This wasn't going to end well, and she'd be the one to pay the price. The very idea of returning to Zwolle and Gray Roots filled her with instant disgust coupled with anxiety. Yes, the walls around this place pressed in like vises. Ilse was right. She was aging, and no longer could she hit the notes. What would happen to Karl? Even though she harbored no good will toward Neelie Visser, deep down Margot knew she had a good heart. Neelie would make sure her son received good care.

Just then Ilse removed a cigarette from her pocket, shoved the window open a few millimeters, then lit it with a match by swiping it over the brick outside the window.

"You know you're not allowed to smoke in here." Margot wrapped her arms across her chest.

Ilse rolled her eyes. "One of the old men traded a few cigarettes for a little extra brown sugar for his porridge. The boss won't make an appearance until later in the afternoon. Do you want one or not?" She took a rolled cigarette from her pocket and held it toward her.

How long had it been? Back when she and Klaus lived in the big house on the corner, back when money came easily. She took the proffered cigarette, lit it, and took a deep exhale, which led to a bout of coughs.

"You're out of practice, woman." Ilse slapped her on the back a few times.

After Margot took a few drags, she felt herself relax. She viewed the woman before her. "So, what's your plan?"

She studied her for an uncomfortable few moments. "If I tell you, I'll have to kill you if you tell anyone else." She leaned against the wall, her eyes in slits, reminding Margot of a Gila monster she'd seen at the zoo before the war.

"Why would you say that? Who would I tell?" Something deep inside advised her to stop this conversation. It wouldn't end well.

Ilse took another puff then tapped the ashes against the outer edge of the window. "If you chicken out, Neelie will grill you about my absence, then the police will come and interrogate you for hours until you'll tell them anything just to make them stop. That's why I don't think I'll tell you anything until I know I can trust you." She leaned against the wall and folded her arms across her chest.

"Look, I'm no snitch. You can trust me. So, what's your plan?"

She exhaled a plume of smoke. "Where do you think my husband is?"

Margot thought about it for a moment. An art auction. The hospital if he looked as bad as he did the last time she'd seen him. "The opera?"

"Haarlem's best. I listened to the radio the other night. Found out they're doing *La Bohème* for the next month or so, and you know who plays Mimi, Mondays, Thursdays, and Saturday nights?"

"Tamar Feldman singing Mimi? That should be me singing that role. No one does a death scene like me. Remember Violetta in *La Traviata*? I packed the house every night before the war started."

"The only way you'll ever play Mimi is to get rid of her. *Verstehen sie*?"

Chapter Thirty

"What armies and how much of war I have seen, what thousands of marching troops, what fields of slain, what prisons, what hospitals, what ruins, what cities in ashes, what hunger and nakedness, what orphanages, what widowhood, what wrongs and what vengeance."

~ Clara Barton

Daniel stifled a yawn as he leafed through his messages. How would he get through the day with only two hours of sleep? Tamar had tossed and turned all night as she often did before her performances. The hecklers in the audience had upset her, but she tried to put on a good face for the twins and him. She couldn't hide her anxiety when she slept.

One message from the administration office gave him pause. Oh no. They wanted a firm date when Luuk would be released. Granted they'd been able to keep him under the radar for years with each ensuing skin graft, but the time had come to set a release date. Because of all the drama he and Tamar had endured in the past few months, he'd put off finding a placement for the ten-year-old.

He knew what the ultimatum meant. Either find a place for Luuk, or he'd be sent to an orphanage. What would happen to a scarred Jewish boy who'd not seen the light of day outside of the hospital for years? There was no point seeking an extension from administration. Funds were tight for the hospital, and the powers-that-be had little compassion for patients who'd outstayed their welcome.

Daniel glanced at his watch and checked his schedule. If he could finish his rounds this afternoon, he could visit Luuk's grandmother in the hofje this morning. He asked the attending nurse for the file on Luuk Gochman. After jotting down the grandmother's address, he told the nurse he'd be back after lunch.

The cool wind of the morning made him button up his jacket and step up his pace. Fortunately, the retirement center she lived in was only two kilometers from the hospital. He headed across the bridge over the canal and passed the train station, arriving twenty minutes later at the address.

He remembered the last time he'd been to the hofje eight years ago when he was still in medical school. A shudder escaped at the chance he'd taken as a member of the Resistance. He'd stood outside the door, waiting for the Nazi soldier to pass before he'd entered to offer medical assistance to a Jewish man who was suffering through the last few days of his life. Daniel had ferreted some morphine from the hospital to help the man with pain. The man probably hadn't lasted more than a day or so, but at least the medicine had made his time on earth more bearable.

How long had this retirement center been able to shield its Jewish residents from the German officers? He shook his head to sweep away such maudlin thoughts, then opened the door to a long, dark tunnel that opened up into a light courtyard. The place hadn't changed in eight years—attached cabins facing the center courtyard, all alike except for different colored doors. An older couple sat on a bench holding hands facing a small fountain, the woman leaning her head against the man's arm. Someday that would be Tamar and him, side by side, enjoying each other in the winter of their lives.

Daniel approached the couple, noting the woman's eyes were closed. The man whose corduroy cap partially hid bushy white eyebrows smiled up at him. "Good afternoon," he whispered cutting a sideways glance at his wife.

"Hello, would you be able to direct me to Mrs. Gochman's home?"

"Why yes, she lives in the corner hofje, the one with the red door." He nodded toward the corner on the left. "Lenore doesn't get out much anymore."

"Thank you." Daniel headed toward the hofje tucked in the corner. The rosebush next to the porch was overgrown with weeds, the single chair on the porch covered with rust. Why hadn't he thought to bring Luuk to visit his grandmother? It would certainly do them both good, especially if that was all that remained of their family in town.

"I'm coming." A withered voice responded to his knock. A minute passed before the door inched open to reveal a shriveled woman with a rounded back who barely reached his waist.

"Mrs. Gochman. I'm Doctor Feldman from St. Elizabeth Gasthuis."

Her bespeckled eyes lifted to meet his. "I didn't call for a doctor. You must have the wrong address."

"Do you have a grandson named Luuk? I'm here to ask you some questions about him."

Her eyebrows furrowed as if she was having trouble remembering, then she nodded. "Ah, little Luuk. How is he doing? It's been so long since I last saw him. Please come in, Doctor." She stepped aside and used her free hand to usher him through the door.

He stood in the small space by the door and let her pass. "Luuk is doing very well; in fact, he's ready to be released from the hospital. That's why I am here. He needs a place to go, and we aren't aware of any other relatives except you."

The old woman moved to a chair and gestured to the only other one in the room. She took a handkerchief from her apron and dabbed at her eyes. "I've wanted to visit him so often, but I don't walk so good, and well, this is no place for a child. I wish—" She covered her trembling lips with her knuckles.

He leaned forward. "If you'd like, I could bring him for a visit. It would mean a lot to Luuk." When she nodded, he continued. "Could you tell me if there are any other relatives of Luuk's that I could contact about his care?"

She shook her head slowly. "The camps took all my children. My youngest son, Abel, and his wife, Rachel, were the only ones who left Dachau. Then the fire took them." Fresh tears fell down her cheeks.

He leaned forward to cover her hand with his. "I know." Words failed him. Sometimes words weren't necessary. They'd all lost family, but telling her wouldn't make her feel better. They sat there, not moving, the only sounds her sniffles and the ticking of the cuckoo clock above the kitchen entry.

After long moments she straightened in her seat. "You must be parched. Would you care for some tea? I was just making a pot."

"That would be nice."

Mrs. Gochman used her cane to push to her feet. "I'll be right back." She hobbled to the kitchen, leaving him the opportunity to look around the living room. A spinet piano stood in the corner upon which sat framed family photos. He ambled over to take a closer look. The picture in the middle showed a large family seated around a Passover table. Another framed picture showed a fortyish couple exchanging rings. Were these Luuk's parents? He picked up a picture of a middle-aged version of Lenore Gochman holding a baby of about six months. Luuk's eyes smiled back at him.

"Ah, you've found my only picture of my grandson. That was taken in happier days."

His hostess was having a hard time setting down the tray of tea cups. "Here, allow me." He hurried over to retrieve the tray before it fell to the ground. Noting her shaky hands, he poured her a cup then his own.

"Thank you." She dropped to the chair as if her energy had expended. "These days the slightest activity takes my breath away. My curse for still being alive."

He took a sip of the lukewarm tea. "It's not easy, is it? Your husband. I didn't notice him in the picture of your seder meal at Passover."

She closed her eyes and nodded. "He was taken in the Great War."

It was time to ask her again before she fell asleep. "Mrs. Gochman, are there any members of your family still alive that I could contact about Luuk?"

"Sadly, no." She opened her eyes. "What's to become of him?" She leaned forward. "An orphanage is no place for my grandson. Why don't you take him."

Why indeed? His family was finally getting over the turmoil of the trial, and to take another child into his home after such upheaval left him gutless. Before he made that decision, he and Tamar would have to include the twins in that talk. However, he was sure they'd be excited to have Luuk join their family. At the present, though, he didn't have an immediate answer for that question.

"All I can tell you is I'll do my best to find him a good family to live with, and I'll bring him for a visit with you. He'll like that." Daniel gulped down his tea, stood, and took the untouched teacup sitting in front of her. "I need to get going." He held up a hand when she grabbed her cane. "Don't get up. I'll take this tray to the kitchen and be on my way." He reached down and took her hand in his. "Thank you for the impromptu visit."

He headed to the door after setting the tray on the kitchen counter. A glance back showed her eyes already closed and soft measured breaths coming from her open lips. Would he be able to keep his promise?

After grabbing a sandwich at a local restaurant, he headed back to the hospital to complete rounds and procedures assigned for that afternoon. As he picked up Mr. Feinstein's file, someone tapped on his shoulder. Turning around, he peered into the face that he'd wanted to avoid—Mr. Cas Anholts, the hospital head administrator, who'd cut funds from his mother if he could. "Hello, Cas, I'm just on my way to do rounds. Do you need something?"

As Daniel turned to head to Mr. Feinstein's room, it became clear that Anholts hadn't taken the hint.

"You're not fooling me, Daniel. I know Luuk is the little pet of the burn unit, but he's costing the hospital every day."

Daniel suppressed the urge to roll his eyes. "I hardly think a ten-year-old boy is breaking the bank. I know you have to cut expenses, but at the moment, he has no relatives alive to take him, and a boy with as many scars as he has would be abused by other kids at an orphanage."

They reached Mr. Feinstein's door, and he started to enter when Cas's arm stopped him. "I want him out of here by the end of the week. That leaves you three days. Do you understand?" He handed him a sheet of paper containing a handwritten list. "Here's a list of families in Haarlem that have signed up to adopt children. I'm sure one of them would be a suitable fit for our boy."

"Thank you." He peered down at the list. Three potential families who might give Luuk safety, love, and the future he deserved. It was an option he hadn't anticipated. A pang of sadness filled him. He'd grown attached to Luuk over the years and couldn't imagine not joining him for a chat or the reading of a book. Three days didn't give him much time to interview the families, but he'd make it a top priority.

Friday arrived and Daniel had whittled the families down to one. He'd rejected an older couple who appeared only to want a boy to work the farm for them. Luuk was regaining his strength, but he wasn't ready for plowing yet. Daniel excused himself and told them he'd be in touch. In touch to inform them they'd not be getting the boy.

The second house Daniel visited was a mess. The porch swayed as he entered the house. The glass from the front window had shattered and lay in a pile on the ground outside. Who knew how long it had sat there. He turned and walked away without knocking on the door.

The third family lived in a prim and proper house, pretty flower boxes adorning the windows. He counted five children's bicycles leaning against the fence. How would Luuk fare in a house full of children? For the last three years, he'd become an old soul with only adults to socialize with. Still, it might be therapeutic for him to live with a large family.

The door flew open when he knocked. A red-haired boy about eight and a girl with blonde braids stood there.

"Who are you, Mister?" the girl said.

"I'm Dr. Feldman. Are your parents at home?"

The freckled girl scrubbed a hand over her nose. "Nope. Only Elke is here. Why do you want to talk to her? Is she sick?"

Daniel chuckled. The inquisitiveness of children. Why had she called her mother by her first name? "No, that's not why I am here. Would you go get your mother?"

"She ain't my mother. She ain't Cuno's mother either." She dug her elbow into the boy's side.

"Ow. Stop it."

"Children, enough of that. I'll take over." A woman with a scarf over her hair bustled the children away, brushed off her apron, and stood to her full short height. "Sorry about the kids. I'm Elke Bakker. May I help you?"

He held out a hand which she took and gave it a vigorous shake. "My name is Dr. Daniel Feldman from Saint Elizabeth Gasthuis. The business administrator at the hospital gave me your name. He said you'd signed up to take an orphan into your family. Is that right?"

"That depends," she said, fingering a jewel-studded heart hanging from a necklace.

"Depends on what, may I ask?"

She backed up. "We can talk over a cup of tea. Shall we?" She beckoned Daniel inside.

The interior of the house was as clean as the outside. Mrs. Bakker motioned to a chair in the kitchen. Sunflowers adorned the space above the refrigerator and the center of the table. "Would you like some tea? Won't take but a minute to steep."

He'd had enough tea for a month. "No, thank you. Is it true you applied to take in a child with the province?"

She poured herself a cup then took a seat across from him. "I did, but that was a few years ago. My husband and I now have four children that we've taken in, and we have one of our own. Still, I'd like to hear what you have to offer."

Offer? Something didn't seem right in this perfect little home. "It's clear that you have your hands full. I understand." He pushed against the table to stand. "I won't take any more of your time."

"No, wait," she said, staying his arm until he sat down again. "As you can imagine, raising four children is expensive. Taking on a fifth would add more to our monthly budget. We'd need more money for food, clothes, bedding—" She counted on her fingers. "Not to mention, school supplies, vitamins, and wear and tear of the furniture. Since you mentioned you were a doctor, I can only assume your orphan requires medical care." She met his eyes. "How much money are you offering us to take the boy off your hands?"

He hadn't anticipated a mercenary motive. "I'm sorry to have wasted your time, Mrs. Bakker. It didn't occur to me to consider finances, and you're right—taking a child into a home carries expense with it. I should have checked that out before visiting. Tell me, what would be an approximate amount of money you'd be seeking for taking Luuk?" He rose to his feet.

She stood, folded her arms across her waist, and leaned against the kitchen entry. "I'll need to know about the boy's illness."

"A year after Luuk and his parents returned from the camps, his parents were killed in an apartment fire. Luuk survived, but he suffered extensive burns to his arms, legs, and the right side of his face." Daniel couldn't help but smile. "That ten-year-old is a fighter. He's survived a half a dozen skin grafts. Luuk is smart, inquisitive, and a joy to be around, but I fear that the scars will leave him vulnerable to the taunts of children. He's gone through enough. I have to make sure he will be in a safe environment."

A frown furrowed her brows. "So, you say the boy was in the camps. Does that mean the boy is a Jew?"

"Yes, Luuk is Jewish. Will that be a problem?" The ensuing pause spoke volumes. "Thank you for your time, Mrs. Bakker. I'll see my way out."

As he passed her, she grasped his arm. "Not so fast. Since Luuk will incur some medical expenses, the amount of money I'll need is 100 guilders. As for the boy's religion, he'll have to adapt to Christianity. You must understand that I can't run a household with a multitude of religions. It would confuse my children." She walked him to the door. "Also, I can assure you that my children will be forewarned about Luuk's scars. They're good kids, so I don't think they'll give your orphan any trouble, but as you know, kids will be kids."

Kids will be kids didn't bode well for Luuk, but Daniel kept his thoughts to himself. A family, even with questionable motives, was better than the orphanage for the boy. He took out his business card and handed it to her. "If you have any questions or problems that arise, please call me." Daniel bade her goodbye and left. He hadn't thought about the fact that Luuk would not be able to keep his faith. Although he and Tamar were Messianic Jews, they still kept kosher, celebrated Passover and the other festivals, and worshipped God in Hebrew at shul. How could he honor the promise he'd made to Luuk's grandmother to put him in the best home? Still, out of the three families, Mrs. Baaker's home was the safest, and it was better than the orphanage.

He returned to work with one main misgiving—Luuk's religion. Deep down Daniel knew the best environment for Luuk was with him, Tamar, and the twins, but the timing was all wrong. Although the trial was over, his family was still reeling from its effect. Reporters still showed up at the worst times—the hospital, the opera, outside their house. Out of nowhere, a journalist with a microphone often appeared, hitting them with a barrage of questions.

If he was the only one who'd been disadvantaged by the trial, Daniel could live with it, but all he'd had to suffer was having to leave the house for work hours earlier than need be, in order to evade the reporters. However, if wasn't just him.

Both Peri and Zari had suffered the taunts of the kids on the playground. Peri was able to discount what they said, but Zari had come home with tearstains streaked across her cheeks. She refused to talk about what happened on the playground, but the joyful smiles that had lit up her face had tamped down.

Of the four of them, Tamar had suffered the most. She hadn't had the luxury of sneaking out of the house in the dark. She'd had to face the reporters on the sidewalk on her way out. Even worse were the audience members who heckled her during curtain calls.

All these thoughts played in his mind as he knocked on the door of the administrator.

"Come in," said the harried voice from within.

When Daniel inched the door open, Cas Anholts waved him in with his free hand, the phone's receiver in his other. "I'll be right with you." He nodded toward the chair across from him. "Yeah, we'll have to grab a round of golf.... Sure, invite him, and that will give me a chance to make a plea for the new wing...That's the plan. I'll name it after his grandmother if need be, so long as the funds come from his deep pockets...Keep in touch. Bye."

Daniel took a surreptitious glance at his watch. He didn't have all day with rounds awaiting him, but Luuk's future took precedence.

Cas took a sip of his coffee. "What can I do for you, Doctor?"

"I just returned from checking out the three families on the list, and I narrowed it down to one family in particular." He handed him the information. "The woman seemed interested even after hearing about Luuk's disabilities. Do the families get paid for adopting the children? The mother mentioned needing payment for the costs for taking him."

He shrugged. "I'm sure they're remunerated for taking in a child, but that's between them and the provincial government." Cas peered at the document over his glasses. "Good. That will make the board happy. I have to give an account for every patient that stays more than ten days. Thank you for taking care of this." He stood, indicating the meeting was over.

Throughout rounds, he thought about what he had just done. Had he settled too quickly on a potential family for Luuk? When he reached the boy's room, Luuk was at the window staring out at the grounds below. Daniel joined him, noting the wistful look on his face. "How are you doing, Luuk? Would you like to take a walk with me outside? It's a beautiful day."

His face broke out in a gleeful smile, although the corner of it pulled down a bit. Was it worth another round of plastic surgery? The boy had been through enough. "Do you want me to push you in the wheelchair, or do you want to try walking?"

His nose wrinkled into a frown. "I can walk myself." Luuk took his hand and pulled him to the door.

"Slow down, buddy. We have to stop at the desk and tell them where we're going, and I only have fifteen minutes, okay?"

"Okay," he sighed and opened the door, which took a while since he had trouble cupping his fingers around the knob.

The misgivings Daniel had felt before deepened. While here at the hospital, the staff celebrated each improvement Luuk made, but it would be different in a household of children. Once they'd alerted the nurses station they'd be outside on the grounds for a short time, Daniel let Luuk run ahead, his gait ungainly, to reach the elevator first. Any burst of movement was good for the boy.

When they stepped outside, Luuk gripped the railing and struggled down the stairs to the lawn. Daniel resisted the urge to help him. He'd have to learn the hard way, it seemed. Luuk headed to one of the nearby lofty linden trees that lined the sidewalk. He wrapped thin arms around the trunk of the tree. "This feels so good." He touched the trunk with his nose. "It smells so good too."

Daniel chuckled at his antics. "The tree's a bit too big to hug."

The boy peered over his shoulder, a smile embracing his lips. "I know, but it reminds me of my papa. He was tall and strong like this tree, and I used to stand on his feet and put my arms around his legs, and Papa would walk me around in a circle." His lips tightened. "I don't want to forget him, but sometimes I can't even remember what he looked like, but I remember how strong his legs were when he walked me around."

"I get it. My dad died in the war, and I think about him every day. I'm glad you remember him."

Luuk backed away from the tree trunk then wiped his hands on his pants. "This is my favorite place because the tree is always here when I look out the window." He smiled up at Daniel and took his hand.

Chapter Thirty-one

"Folly is often more cruel in the consequences than malice can be in the intent."

~ Aldous Huxley

Tamar hadn't left the house in three weeks, except to buy food at the market on Saturday or to go to work at night. The press had not taken the judge's warning to heart. Right after the trial ended, reporters had camped out in front of her house, making it impossible to take the children to school or for Daniel to leave for work without microphones being shoved in his face.

If they'd lived in a big city like Amsterdam, news of their trial would have made the back page of the newspaper, but Haarlem was small enough that their story made the headlines day after day. Fortunately, after three weeks only a reporter or two remained outside, so it was easier to sneak out to the back alley and avoid them. In just a few hours, she'd slip out the back to head to the opera house for tonight's performance.

Attendance at the opera had skyrocketed since the trial. She didn't fool herself into thinking spectators filled the seats because of her performance. The audience was more like the crowds that stuffed the courtroom to see a would-be kidnapper. In fact, she'd received a few heckles along with the roses at the end of each performance. She longed for the days when she'd become less of a curiosity.

At any rate, the stage managers and producer, Mr. Boelen, were thrilled with the profits they'd made over the last few weeks at her expense. Tonight, she'd have to buoy up her reserve to face the public once again. How she wished Tante Neelie lived closer. She always allayed her fears and helped Tamar see God's purpose in the trials she endured.

She glanced at the clock. Why not call her? She hated to bother Neelie at work, but by the time Tamar returned from the opera, it was always too late to call. Perhaps Neelie could carve out a few minutes to chat. Tamar called the operator who patched her through to the rehab center.

"Hope Community Center. May I help you?" An unfamiliar voice with a slight accent said.

"Good afternoon. May I speak with Mrs. Visser, please?"

"May I ask who's calling?"

"Is she busy? I don't want to bother her."

"Please hold, and I'll transfer you through to her office."

Tamar glanced at the clock. Soon she'd have to leave for the opera. Mrs. Libnitz from shul would meet the twins at school and keep them at her house until Daniel could pick them up after work.

"Neelie Visser. May I help you?"

"Tante, this is Tamar. I'm sorry I called during your work day. Are you free to talk for a few minutes?"

Neelie chuckled. "I always have time for you. We haven't talked much since the trial. How are you and Daniel doing? Are you still surrounded by reporters?"

How she loved her adopted aunt. "It's so good to hear your voice. We're becoming old news now, which is a relief. There've been a few hecklers at the opera, but it's to be expected, I suppose."

Neelie tsked. "That makes me so mad. Haven't you two suffered enough?"

"It's okay. How are Margot and Karl doing? Is she following orders better than the last girl from Zwolle did?"

"Yes, Margot definitely is more trustworthy than her predecessor. I don't know if I told you, but I hired a German woman named Inge to help in the kitchen while Emma Bartelski is out of town taking care of her new grandson. She took a two-month leave of absence to help her daughter."

"German? How did you find the woman?"

"Inge showed up at my back door dressed in rags. If I hadn't needed an immediate replacement for Emma, I might have been more circumspect. Belying her appearance, she confidently expounded on her cooking and baking skills, so I hired her on the spot against my better judgment." She blew out a breath. "Fortunately, she's turned out to be a proficient cook, although there's something about her—"

"What is it, Tante? Did she give you references? Has she done something to make you regret your decision?"

"Nothing in particular, and no, she didn't have any references, but since the war ended and so few people returned, it's hard to find willing workers. It's just a feeling I have about her."

Hm. It wasn't like Neelie to rush to decisions, especially when it came to the rehab center. "What is it that makes you uneasy?"

"I'm just not sure if I can trust her. Inge and Margot share a room, and whenever I approach them, they grow silent as if they share some big secret. Maybe I'm just imagining things."

"I doubt you're imagining anything. Your hunches have always been on target. What are you going to do about it?"

Neelie sighed. "They've both fulfilled their responsibilities, so I thought about letting them accompany me to the market—supervised, of course. I'm sure they're growing stir crazy being cooped up in here all the time."

"Isn't that against the rules? What would Warden Frank say about you taking Margot out of the place?"

Neelie's voice softened to a whisper. "I'd get his approval before I did anything. Margot has sung several times for the residents here, and Inge has accompanied her on the piano."

Tamar laughed. "Aren't you a bit concerned that Margot might try to escape?"

"As you know, this place isn't a fortress. The doors can easily be unlocked from the inside, and she could escape any time." Neelie heaved another sigh. "It's just that I can sense Margot's malaise. She dotes on her son, but she seems so lost, so sad all the time. Guess

I'm getting soft. On a happier note, how are my grandchildren doing? When are you going to bring them for a visit?"

"They enjoy school, but they become restless having to stay in the house all the time. Now that the press is no longer hovering outside our door, I'll be able to take them to the park. Much as I'd like to bring them to Amsterdam for a visit, I'm not eager to run into Margot, and I'm sure she's not eager to see me. You know how she testified against me at the trial, saying I was having an affair with her husband, and that I 'kidnapped' her son purely out of envy."

Neelie spewed out a chortle. "Those were pure lies. When I see her with Karl, it warms my heart, and I forget what a diva she was back before the war. Guess I hoped her time in prison had chiseled off her rough edges, but she's turned out to be a pretty good worker. She never complains. It's just that—"

"Just what, Tante? Your intuition is usually correct."

"It's just I have this feeling that something bad is going to happen. Silly but true."

"Maybe we shouldn't invite trouble." Tamar glanced at the clock. "Oh, I have to get ready to go to work. I'm going to practice with my singing coach at five. He's helping me move from spinto to dramatic, so I won't be so raspy at high D."

"What in the world does that mean?"

She giggled. "Sorry. Opera lingo. It means he's helping me stretch my diaphragm so I can be heard over the orchestra. I'd better go. Love you, Tante."

"Wait." What is it, Anna?" Neelie must have covered the phone with her hand. "I can't believe it."

"What is it, Tante?"

"They're gone. My worst fears are realized."

"What do you mean by 'they're gone'?"

"Anna, one of the new assistants, just told me the women's room is empty. Margot and Inge have escaped. What should I do?"

Despair laced her aunt's voice. "Are you sure? What about Karl? Did they take Karl?"

"They're all gone. I'll need to call the police and the warden at Zwolle. Sorry, I'd better go. I'll let you know what's going on as soon as I find out."

Margot cursed when her foot lodged in a crack in the sidewalk. “Slow down, Ilse. Karl’s not light. What are we going to do with him? Where are we going?”

Ilse glanced back. “Why don’t we drop him off at the orphanage. I’m sure they’ll be happy to have him back.”

She gripped her son closer. “No, I gave him up once. I won’t do that again. Tell me where we’re going.”

A man on a bicycle teetered past them, obviously inebriated. The two women and child plastered themselves against a wall, Ilse spitting expletives at the man. She pushed away from the wall and brushed herself off.

“Tell me again why we are doing this?”

She blew out a scoff. “I have one goal—locate my husband and make him pay.”

Margot shifted Karl from one arm to the other. “How do you know where he is?”

“Where do you think?” Ilse glanced around then gripped the handle of a wagon that rested next to someone’s house. She pulled it behind her as if it belonged to her.

“What are you doing? Put that back.”

Ilse spewed out a laugh. “Save your arms and put the kid in the wagon. We’ll return it tomorrow. Maybe.”

Margot complied. “He’ll be more comfortable in the wagon, but we gotta be careful. We’re fugitives from the law.”

Ilse tsked. “Nobody’s going to call the police about a missing wagon. C’mon, let’s step up our pace. We’ll stop in a few minutes at a park, and I’ll fill you in on the plan. Then you can let the kid use up some of his energy.”

Four blocks took them to a small green space next to a Catholic church. Margot dropped onto a park bench and slipped Karl out of the wagon. “Now don’t go too far, and be careful not to stumble over the uneven cobblestones.” She turned to Ilse. “I know I’m not going to like it, but tell me the plan.”

Ilse opened her satchel and removed two teacakes. "You can share yours with your kid. This should tide us over for a while." She took a bite. "Made these this morning, and they're already as hard as rocks."

Margot took a cake and bit off a small bite.

"As I told you, Erich's been obsessed with the opera ever since he heard that woman Tamar sing, and of course, you."

Margot wiped the crumbs off her dress and called Karl over to her. She broke off a piece of the cake, gave it to him, then lifted her hand. "Know this. Never once did I have designs on Erich Bergman. There was always something sinister about him. The guy didn't have a soul."

"He did at one time, but that's a moot point now. Apparently, Erich's had some plastic surgery done on his face, so it will be hard to find him. The only place where we'll likely find him is at the opera. I got my hands on a program for *La Bohème*, and guess what? Peter Winter is listed in the list of board members."

"The name sounds familiar. Wasn't he an opera singer a long time ago?"

Ilse shook her head. "He was a German composer—one of my husband's favorites. From the time Dieter started taking violin lessons, Erich talked about Peter Winter to the boy. Told him that nothing would make him happier than to have him emulate Winter's life and become a famous composer."

"Sounds like good advice to me. Wish my husband was here to impart some wisdom to Karl." Margot knelt to wipe Karl's nose with her handkerchief.

Ilse waved a dismissive hand. "Talk is cheap. Do you think that Erich's advice mattered when he failed to return after the war and abandoned his wife and his son? Dieter didn't pick up his violin once after 1945, but what he did pick up were a love of beer and bad company. It probably didn't help that for years I'd look out the window and burst into tears. Dieter grew to hate his father, as did I. Then Dieter disappeared, and I haven't seen him in over a year."

Margot peered over her shoulder. "So, is that when you developed your plan to find him?"

"More or less. At first, I figured if he were to see me and his son again, he'd come back to us. Then reality hit like a ton of bricks. Erich Bergman had moved on. So here I am. My motive is to confront Erich and make him pay up for the years he took away from me and my son. I'm sure he's hidden money somewhere."

Margot sat on the bench, removed her shoes, then rubbed her feet. "Ouch, these shoes aren't helping much. I've gone soft." She looked at Ilse. "You haven't told me the plan yet."

"Simply put, we're going to go to the opera tonight. See if we can find Erich. I stole some money from Neelie's office. Enough to buy two tickets. The seats won't be good, but we're not there for the show." She raised her brows. "We could have some fun at Tamar Feldman's expense, if you know what I mean."

Margot stared at her for a long moment. "No, I don't know what you mean."

She chuckled. "Follow my lead."

Margot shook her head with vehemence. "We can't go to the opera in these rags! What would we wear? Has your bitterness made you crazy?"

Ilse didn't answer right away, then shrugged. "Simple. We steal a few dresses and shoes. Some makeup."

Margot lifted a hand. "No way. I'm not going back to Zwolle. I can't."

"Didn't you used to live near the opera somewhere? The house where Erich visited you that time when he was sick?"

She pulled Karl onto her lap. "I haven't been back there in years. I'm sure it's been sold, or the bank has it locked up."

"Great. Lead on. Maybe we can find some of your old clothes there." Ilse wipe one hand against the other as if it was an easy solution.

Margot looked at her friend. Had she lost her mind? "What if someone's living there? I'm sure all of our belongings have become the property of the province."

"Maybe not. Let's check it out. Here, I'll pull the wagon." Ilse took Karl and hefted him into the wagon.

A half-an-hour walk took them to the four-story house on the corner of the Barteljorisstraat.

Ilse pointed at the for-sale sign on the front door. "Good news, but it doesn't mean someone's not living there."

Margot peeked in the front window. "Huh, they haven't moved the dry-cleaning business out of here. This was just a front for me and Klaus. Strange that it's still here. The 'Be back shortly' sign's still up."

Ilse picked up Karl who was rubbing his eyes and bounced him on her hip. "Where's the key?

"What? I don't have a key. Are you loopy?"

"Everyone has a key. You know that. Hiding on the lintel or under the mat." She put down the boy and tried to feel along the top of the door but couldn't reach it. "Let's go around to the back. See if anyone's living here."

Margot put Karl in the wagon. "Stop whining, Karl. Remember this house? Maybe later we can go to the park we used to go to." She followed Ilse who had already disappeared around the corner of the house. "Wait. What are you going to do?"

When she caught up with Ilse, she was at the back of the house, feeling above the lintel of the back door. "Where does this door go?"

"It leads up to the kitchen and living room, then up to the bedrooms and the attic. I'm sure there's no key there," Margot said.

"Aha!" Ilse dropped to her knees beside the door, and with her finger traced the outline of a brick. "Watch and learn. Everyone has one of these. Don't you know nothing?" She jiggled the brick from its place in the wall, then peered in the hole created. She pulled out a key and waved it in Margot's face.

Margot batted her hand away. "We can't break in there. What if someone's home?"

"Like I said—watch and learn." Ilse wiped the key against her dress, inserted it in the lock, and motioned for Margot to be quiet. A quick turn of Ilse's wrist opened the door. Margot entered, Karl on her hip, memories accosting her. She nodded to the stairs. "Careful," she whispered. "They're squeaky." As she started up, Ilse grabbed her arm.

"Let me go first. We need to move quietly in case someone lives here."

When they reached the kitchen level, Margot stopped at the door, listening for any signs of life, then tiptoed to the refrigerator and opened it. "It's been cleaned out," she whispered. "That might mean my closets have been cleaned out as well."

"Let's go upstairs. We don't want to press our luck," said Ilse.

Margot shifted Karl to her other hip. Fortunately, he was ready for a nap. She followed Ilse to the next level then pointed at the credenza. "The art's all gone. Doesn't surprise me. Either the police or your husband took it all." She pointed to the short staircase straight ahead. "That leads to the attic." She eyed the bedroom at the top of the stairs. "This was Karl's bedroom. I might just put Karl in the crib if it's still there. Our bedroom was at the end on the right."

She opened Karl's door. "Look, Karl, your bed. Everything else is gone, but the bed and the chair are here." She placed him on the bare mattress. "Get some sleep, but don't make any noise."

Ilse was going through the medicine chest in the bathroom. "Nothing's left, but I did find this is in the bottom drawer." She held up a floral shower kit.

"My makeup. There should be a brush in there. What I wouldn't do for a long shower, but they probably turned off the water."

Ilse turned on the faucet. The water spit out at first then came out in a normal stream. She turned on the hot spigot, and after a long minute, the water heated up. "I don't think anyone lives here. We'll know for sure when we go through the bedrooms. Let's go. If no one lives here, we can stay here for the next few days."

"Let's hope so." Margot led her to the master bedroom and opened the door. The bed had been stripped, and the massive piles of art were gone. She hurried to the closet and opened it. Most everything was gone, but in the corner enveloped in plastic were some of her cocktail dresses. She ran over to the dresser and opened the drawers. "Everything's gone except some formal dresses…and some of my lingerie." She picked up a pair of hose and rubbed it against her cheek. "Oh, this feels so good. Never again will I take silk and satin for granted."

Ilse opened the armoire. "It seems no one is living here. We'll stay here, but we'll have to be careful. We wouldn't want a curious neighbor calling the cops, would we?" She headed to the door. "Let's check out the attic." Margot took one last glance at the dresses in the closet, then followed her up the few stairs that led to the attic.

Ilse yanked at the door without success. "It probably hasn't been opened for years. Help me." Together they pulled on the knob, and finally the door creaked open to reveal a room full of boxes. "What is all this stuff?"

Margot shrieked and swiped at a cobweb. "I've never been up here. What a mess. Attics have always scared me. So dark and dirty, and you don't know what's hiding in them—rats, spiders—"

"Maybe you should have spent a little time up here. This is a treasure trove. We could probably pawn some of this stuff and make a small fortune." She held up an old shawl that lay on the floor. "With a little cleaning, this might work as a wrap for the opera." She started digging through the boxes. "You start at the other end. Open that window to let some fresh air in."

Margot swiped at her eyes and sneezed on cue. "I can't stand all this dust." She maneuvered around stacks of books and torn-open boxes to reach the window and open it. "I hate attics. When I was a kid, my mother used to make me stay in the attic as a form of punishment. I always imagined ghosts and dead bodies lingering in the dark corners."

"Silly girl," Ilse said. "Get to work, and we'll be out of here. Make a pile of things we can pawn. Jewelry, candlesticks—that kind of thing. The more we find, the better our escape will be."

For the next hour, they worked their way through dozens of boxes. Most contained children's clothes, old books, broken furniture, and the like.

"Look at this," Ilse said. "A box of Judaica. Your husband wasn't Jewish, was he?"

"Of course not—" Margot stood and stretched her back. "We bought this house at an auction right after the war. It came real cheap. The downstairs had a jewelry store that had been vandalized—glass everywhere. By the time we bought it, all the good stuff had been stolen."

"Look what I found!" Ilse held up a pistol. "I'd recognize this gun anywhere. Erich had a Luger just like it. Could this one be his?"

After an hour of scales, Tamar's voice warmed up, and she was able to reach the top of her range. Tamar put everything Neelie had told her out of her mind except her performance a mere two hours away. Thoughts of Margot and the mysterious German woman finally gave way to the character she'd play tonight in Puccini's *La Bohème.*

Mimi, the simple embroiderer, who lived in a garret of an old house on Paris's left bank.

Tamar summoned memories of her trip to Paris with Daniel and her aunt. Closing her eyes, she remembered the rounded roof lines of the apartments across the street from their hotel and the young tenants who sat out on the roof, trying to catch a hint of the summer breeze. In the winter, there'd be no sitting outside. Tamar could almost feel the dark and dank rooms behind their windows that her character, Mimi, had to endure.

The opera started with Mimi running out of matches to light the candle that provided the only light for the cold attic room. She'd summoned the courage to ask the stranger named Rodolfo who lived next door for a light for her candle. For "Mi chiamano Mimi,"—my name is Mimi—Tamar's first song, she needed to show Mimi's vulnerability and awkwardness at meeting her handsome neighbor.

Mimi had grown to adore the poet—the man, Rodolfo, although she'd had to hide when his girlfriend, the beautiful Musetta, came to visit. Each time, after Musetta left, Mimi waited for Rodolfo to come find her, his proclamations of love for Mimi calming her fears. Then the coughing started. She'd blamed it on the cold room that no candle could warm, but Rodolfo wasn't fooled. His worried eyes informed her that her incessant coughing foreshadowed the fateful end of her life.

Tamar bathed herself in the character of Mimi as she waited in the wings. Breathing deeply, she summoned a shiver, remembering the cold she'd experienced in the labor camp with only a thin blanket to cover her body.

The stage manager nodded for her to make her entry. Tamar shuffled onto the stage, rubbing her arms. Applause broke out as she made her way to the table in front of the faux window that looked down on the Paris street. She picked up the candlestick and sang her first lines, by this time totally immersed in Mimi. When she'd used her last match, she hastened downstage to Rodolfo's room, where she stared into the eyes of the man who would become her first and last love.

The man's kind eyes gave her the strength to tell him the truth. Tamar sang Mimi's one and only aria. In the song, she said that Mimi wasn't her real name but Lucia, although she knew not why.

Yes, honesty was the foundation of an abiding relationship, but honesty also engendered vulnerability.

The story progressed igniting Mimi's insecurities whenever she felt she could never live up to Rodolfo's urbane lifestyle. She was a simple seamstress, who could only afford a ragged dress she'd found in the trash. To evoke Mimi's insecurities, Tamar remembered how she'd felt when, as a twenty-one-year-old, she'd watched from her window whenever Daniel came to collect her brother, Seth, for one of their secret meetings. Later her brother had told her about his and Daniel's work for the Resistance.

During the intermission, she ran her lines while the makeup artist added a yellow tone to her skin, then applied deep furrows to her brows and lines around her lips. A glance in the mirror showed a woman who'd aged twenty years, ravaged with tuberculosis.

She summoned the only memory she'd had of being deathly ill at Neelie's house during the war, when the cold intruded her bones through her thin dress. She'd fainted on the steps leading to her bedroom, and Daniel had carried her up and covered her with many quilts. Daniel had always been there for her, just as Rodolfo had stayed with Mimi until she breathed her last breath.

Fully prepared for the last scene, Tamar became Mimi, her voice strained but strong enough to reach the back of the auditorium.

The crowd responded with three curtain calls, where she curtsied on the arm of Rodolfo and accepted the bouquet of roses from the director. It was then that the heckles started, but she pretended she didn't hear them.

The curtain started to close when a female voice resounded above the applause.

"Tamar Feldman stole my husband. The woman should be in prison instead of on that stage." A wave of murmurs sounded from the audience. The voice spoke again. "Tamar Feldman is a kidnapper and an adulterous woman."

Was that Margot? How had she?— Tamar shielded her eyes and glanced into the silhouetted heads of the audience, but the lights blinded her.

"Get rid of the kidnapper," the woman screamed again and again. Another voice joined the woman's, an angry female voice. Others joined in. Then the chants of 'kidnapper' turned into a loud chorus of boos.

How naïve she'd been. Her children's faces floated before her eyes, then Daniel's face. Fleeting images that disappeared as if they'd been taken from her. Her life was ruined. The heat of the room overtook her. Black spots appeared before Tamar's eyes, and like the character she portrayed, she slid to the floor.

Before he could stop himself, Erich scrambled down the stairs and raced up the side steps to the stage. The chants of the crowd continued and strengthened. Who had started the protest? No, it couldn't be. What was Ilse doing in Haarlem? He scanned the shadowed forms of the audience, most of whom stood to their feet. Up in the balcony, a short woman stood next to a taller woman in the aisle, their fists raised, their voices louder than the others. Could the shorter one be Ilse? No, his imagination was running away from him.

When he reached the center of the stage, cast members and stagehands milled around Tamar, her eyes closed, her pallid skin the color of death. He shoved aside the wretched people gawking at the love of his life.

"Hey, old man," a stagehand groused and pushed him back.

Erich teetered to the side, then righted himself. He'd forgotten his disguise in his quest to rescue Tamar—too late now. His main focus was the woman lying on the stage floor before him. He dropped to his knees much too nimbly for the man he portrayed. Tears brimmed then streamed down his cheeks. Where was the doctor?

He ripped off the glove that belied his age and gently brushed strands of hair that swept across her forehead. A woman from the chorus held Tamar's hand. He fought the strong urge to knock her back and grab the hand that belonged to him alone.

"What happened?" a man's voice behind him said.

An older woman dressed in costume rolled her eyes. "Obviously she fainted. Do you think she's pregnant? Maybe the heat of the bright lights caused her to lose consciousness."

Stupid woman. Hadn't she heard the taunts from the rabble during curtain call? The very idea that his Tamar would kidnap a child. Although Erich didn't believe in saints, Tamar was the closest to one he'd ever encountered. That innate goodness, those wide eyes that showed her deepest thoughts, that voice that could melt butter.

Two men dressed in costumes approached, carrying a stretcher. "Move aside, old man," one of them said. They lowered the stretcher and carefully placed her on it.

No one pushed him around and got away with it. He clenched his fists but caught himself before he blew his cover.

"Who are you?" the woman wearing a scarf glared at him. "What are you doing up here on the stage?"

"I'm her father," slipped out before he could squelch it.

One of the men carrying the stretcher stared at him for a long moment. "Well then, follow us."

Erich shoved up his glasses that had fallen to the bridge of his nose and followed Tamar backstage. Conversations buzzed about what had happened to her. As he passed a bulky woman, he caught her words.

"Yeah, anyone that would kidnap a child wouldn't have a problem stealing someone's husband."

The stagehands who circled her guffawed at her remark, while one said, "Tamar Feldman is no kidnapper. Leave her be."

Erich stepped up his pace to catch up with the men who carried the stretcher. They stopped at a door at the end of a hall, which sported a large golden star and the name Tamar Feldman written under it. So, this led to the inner sanctum of the woman he'd loved for almost a decade.

"Get the door, old man," a porter told him.

"Of course." He pulled the door open and stepped back so they could enter first. His eyes took in the whole room upon entry. Somehow its simplicity surprised him, but upon further thought, it didn't. His Tamar was no diva. The simple costumes hanging on the rack spoke of a woman of simple tastes, and like Mimi, Tamar was not one to put on airs. A dressing table sat in the middle of the room, the mirror above it illuminated by a dozen lightbulbs.

"She's waking up," one of the men who had lowered the stretcher to the floor, said.

Erich hadn't given thought to how he'd explain his lie. Maybe he should bow out before someone discovered his deception. But he couldn't. Something drew him like a magnet. Her head turned slowly side to side, and her fingers rubbed at her eyes. Even though stage makeup covered her face, the pallor was obvious in her neck and hands.

How he wanted to take her into his arms and comfort her, and that's what he'd surely do if there weren't the stretcher bearers and two stage assistants in the room. Of course, due to corrective plastic surgery he'd undergone, she wouldn't be able to recognize him.

The last time he'd seen her was in his room in Paris where he'd bound her. No amount of assuring her of his love erased her fears. Her last words to him had daily echoed in his mind though he tried to suppress the memory. She'd watched him swallow the pill he'd hidden in his pocket. "I forgive you," she'd said, her eyes filled with what he interpreted as pity. He didn't need her pity; he needed her adoration.

A middle-aged woman bustled through the drawers of Tamar's dressing table. "Ah, I found the smelling salts. Hope they're still good. They've been there since before the war. Margot's cache, I believe." She hurried over to Tamar and swished them under her nose.

Pushing aside the woman's hand, Tamar blinked then opened her eyes. "Where am I?"

"Ah, Miss, you're back. Thank the Good Lord. You fainted during curtain call." She kneeled down next to her. "You're in your dressing room now."

Tamar tried to prop up on her elbows, but she fell back. "What happened, Elsbeth?" She shook her head from side to side as if to dispel a fugue. "Oh, I have such a headache."

The woman named Elsbeth removed the wig Tamar wore. "What did I tell you last week? You need to eat a good meal before you perform. You probably fainted from hunger."

For the first time, Tamar's eyes locked on Erich's. "Who are you? You look familiar."

Elsbeth's eyes darted from Tamar to him. "Surely, you recognize your father, don't you?"

"Father? I don't have—"

"Lie down, Miss Feldman. You're not thinking straight. Why don't you rest until your strength returns."

Erich took the opportunity to slip out of the room before the others called his bluff. At least he'd seen her up close for the first time in months. She had grown more beautiful with time, if it were even possible.

From his place on the stage, Erich noted that the crowds had dissipated except for a few curious onlookers. His eyes rose to the balcony where he'd spied the two women who appeared to have started the chant, but the balcony was empty. Somehow, he knew the heckler was his wife. She'd come back to exact revenge on him for abandoning her after the war. Ilse wasn't a stupid woman. She'd known about his obsession for sopranos.

The stage hand appeared from behind the curtain, not ten meters from him. "What are you doing up here, sir? You need to leave, or I'll call the security guard to remove you."

"I'm leaving." Erich almost let him have it. Did the stage hand not know that as the opera's silent board member, Erich signed his paychecks? He hurried down the stairs and up the side aisle to the lobby, keeping his eyes peeled for his wife and the other woman. If Ilse had come to town to find him, she'd be out for his blood. He'd need to keep a low profile until the hubbub passed over, then he'd step up his plan to seize the woman who should have been his wife all along.

Chapter Thirty-two

"Teach me to feel another's woe, to hide the fault I see, that mercy I to others show, that mercy show to me."

~ Alexander Pope

When Daniel finally trudged into the house, he stifled a yawn and plodded up the stairs. A stab of guilt assailed him. The three-hour emergency surgery followed by the night resident calling out sick meant that he hadn't been there to pick up the twins at the scheduled time. He'd tried calling Tamar, but she'd already left for the opera. Mrs. Libnitz had said they could stay at her house until tomorrow morning. Bless Mrs. Libnitz.

Rubbing his eyes, he tiptoed through the kitchen to the parlor, not wanting to wake up Tamar, who was a light sleeper. He stopped at a movement on the sofa. Tamar sat there, still dressed in her street clothes. He steeled himself for her reprimand, which he deserved. "What are you still doing up?"

Her face held little color. Something was off. He took a seat beside her and pulled her into a hug.

She rested her head in the niche of his neck. "I was surprised to see the twins weren't in their beds. What happened?"

"I had an emergency surgery and had to fill in for Dr. Gruber, who called out. Mrs. Libnitz said the twins could stay with her tonight. I'll pick them up tomorrow morning. Sorry."

She blinked. "What? Oh, no need to say sorry. We both know emergencies can happen." She peered up with a weak smile.

"How was work tonight?" he said.

She shrugged. "Let's talk about your day first. Sounds like you had a busy one."

"I spent most the afternoon interviewing three families that would be open to taking Luuk. Narrowed it down to one family, though I wasn't overly confident in my choice. The woman seemed to be more interested in what money she'd receive than in the child, and she also mentioned that he would have to assimilate into their family's religion. No more Passover meals for little Luuk."

She squeezed his hand. "Doesn't sound so good, but it's better than the orphanage for a boy with scars."

"That's what I thought. What about you, darling? How did the performance go?"

When she didn't answer right away, he pulled away so he could face her. Tears brimmed in her blue eyes. Her face was devoid of color.

"What is it, honey? You must have been fraught with worry when the kids weren't in their beds. I'm so sorry I put you through that."

"It's not that." Her lips trembled. "I can never sing in the opera again."

"What are you talking about?"

She closed her eyes as if to summon her composure.

"What happened, darling? You can tell me."

She stood and began to pace. "I was taking my final encore when a woman in the balcony accused me of not only being a kidnapper, but also of stealing her husband. Said I should be in jail. The whole audience joined her in chanting 'Kidnapper.' I fainted right there on the stage." She stopped and whipped around to face him. "I can never sing again; in fact, I can't stay here in this house any more. It's only going to get worse. I've had enough."

Daniel bolted to his feet and folded her into his arms, feeling her shudders against his chest. "Oh, honey. Surely, it's not that bad. You've had hecklers before. Remember what Ben said? He told us not to let the press or the public get to us, or they will have won. We're innocent." He pressed his forehead against hers. "You're not a kidnapper, and you're not an adulterous woman. The truth is all that matters."

She shook her head. "It was different this time. Before there'd be a heckler or two, but they were drowned out by the rest of the audience. Tonight, it was as if everyone in the seats joined in the chant." She released a dolorous sigh. "The producers want to meet with me tomorrow. I think they're going to fire me." She pressed her head against his shoulder.

He kissed the top of her head. "Let's go get some sleep. Tomorrow in the light of day, everything will look better." Empty words.

The comfortless gray sky did little to instill any confidence in her. Tamar kept her eyes on the sidewalk in case one of last night's rabble-rousers passed her. She'd walked this path so many times to work, euphoric at times at the prospect of being able to play Mimi, a character she'd fallen in love with. Now she felt like Marie Antoinette on her way to the guillotine.

Isaiah 26:3, the verse she'd read earlier in the morning, had given her a bit of comfort. "Thou wilt keep in perfect peace whose mind is stayed on Thee." But its promise ebbed as she approached the opera house. Would she be dismissed, even blackballed forever from singing in the opera? She'd be happy to return to the chorus if the producers saw fit to demote her. That tremble returned to her lower lip. How could she face Mr. Boelen with a tear-streaked face? No, she'd hold her head high and look him straight in the eye. She'd done nothing wrong, but public opinion was making her question her moral character.

As she always did, Tamar headed to the side door, but it was locked, and no amount of knocking yielded a response from Han Baas, who guarded the door like a bulldog. Of course, he wouldn't be working since this wasn't a rehearsal or performance day. She smoothed the stray hairs that had escaped her scarf and returned to the lobby door and entered, surprised that it was open.

The dark lobby was devoid of the crowds whose loud din usually spurred her excitement as she waited in the wings during intermission. She'd become adept at interpreting the warmth of the audience's chatter. Lighthearted meant they were enjoying the performance. Murmurs meant she hadn't connected with them during the first two acts.

Now the only sound was the echo of her footsteps against the floor, as grim as the wooden floors of the courthouse three weeks ago. Tamar tried to assuage her heartbeat as she had during the court case. Then she'd been fighting for her very life—for the future of her husband and twins. Now she was simply fighting for her job. If truth be known, she'd miss singing, but it was a small thing compared to her life with Daniel and the children.

The din of male voices became louder as she approached the producers' office. From the sound of it, there were at least three people awaiting her presence. The door was only open a few centimeters. Before opening it, she took a few measured breaths to calm her erratic breathing.

Conversation evaporated as the eyes of three men turned to face her when she pushed the door open, its screech announcing her presence.

"Good day, Mrs. Feldman." Not Tamar as he usually called her after a performance. Mr. Boelen, his severe eyes negating any signs of favor, motioned with his head toward the middle seat of a long table. The two other producers' expressions were unreadable as they took their seats across from her.

Without responding, she sat in the proffered chair, folded her hands on her lap, and gulped past the lump in her throat.

Unsmiling, Mr. Boelen remained standing, his head cocked to one side. He studied her as if she were a specimen in a petri dish. "I am sure you know why we've called this meeting." He waited for her response.

She merely nodded, her eyes on the document in front of her.

The producer began to pace the length of the table as he was wont to do when he was the bearer of bad news. "As you know, attendance had been low since the start of *La Bohème*, but attendance took an upward rise after your trial. One can only surmise that our patrons were eager to see you perform after all the publicity you received." His pacing stopped, and his eyes bore into hers. "However, after last night's performance, we cannot continue to have the reputation of our opera sullied by the outcries of certain members of the audience. We've worked hard to build our clientele, but several of our most prestigious patrons have already threatened to cancel their financial support unless you are removed as the lead soprano—" He leaned his arms on the table.

Tamar swallowed past the lump that ached in her throat. "I am so sorry."

"We are sorry, but we're going to have to terminate your contract. I am sure you understand that we cannot maintain our reputation for excellence when the audience explodes into a circus."

"I understand." She pushed to her feet. "Do you need me to sign anything?"

He nodded toward the file in front of her. "Please sit." His eyes showed a spark of compassion. "We realize this isn't your fault. Be that as it may, we have to look at our financial line. Yes, attendance is up, but you'll agree it's not for the right reasons. One of our new investors has suggested you take a leave of absence. When the theatrics settle down, we want you back, but in the meantime, we'd like to suggest a temporary solution." He gestured for her to sit back down.

She lowered to the seat, her eyes on his. What possibly could he suggest? Mr. Boelen began to pace again.

"There's an ocean liner, the *Queen Mary*, out of Liverpool that would like to present two shows of *La Bohème* on its trip from England to New York. Would you be willing to play Mimi for the passengers? The ship doesn't offer a venue as large as this one, so it would be in a more intimate setting, but the new investor is willing to cover the cost of the production. He assures us that it will be a boon for the ship in the long run as more people will be exposed to the opera."

Mr. Boelen returned to his seat, but he didn't sit down. "The contract states that you would agree to do three trips to New York and three back. That would last six weeks. You'd be required to do two performances per week for a total of twelve performances. Each crossing is five days long with two days at the port to restock and refurbish. I was told you have a brother who lives in New York City.

Perhaps you can stay with him in the intervening days. What do you think?

All eyes were on her. How could she answer so quickly? She cleared her throat, which didn't help. "What about my children? My husband? Are you suggesting I leave them for a whole month? I don't think I could do that."

He leaned forward, leaning on his knuckles. "We realize you'll need to confer with your husband. The investor didn't mention your husband coming, but perhaps we can negotiate for him to accompany you. However, I don't believe the *Queen Mary* is a suitable place for your children. Remember, we're only talking about six weeks. By that time, your detractors will have moved on to other scandals. Go home. Talk to your husband. The trip begins on Sunday, ten days from now. We'll need an answer in three days at the most."

"Very well," was all she could muster. The producers stood signaling the meeting was over. They smiled for the first time, most likely relieved that she'd be gone.

If he wasn't playing the role of an aged man, he'd have kicked up his heels. His cards were falling into place. The owner of a bar on the seamy side of town had believed his tale that the Gauguin painting of a Tahitian girl was an original and had paid him the price he asked without any bartering. Said it would bring the locals in, so he'd recoup his losses in no time.

Two things he'd learned since the war ended. Money spoke louder than appearance, it seemed. Even though he was the newest member of the opera board of directors, the producers had accepted his suggestion to send Tamar packing without discussion, especially since he'd arranged for her to take the *Queen Mary* gig.

When he'd been part of the Third Reich, loud threats and force put everyone in their place. Those tactics had stopped working when Hitler and his cronies were killed or disappeared. Yes, money talked more than threats, and the Botany 500 suit he'd bought didn't hurt.

He'd learned the second lesson after the war ended. Wrap what he wanted in the package of what the other person wanted. What the producers wanted was to sell more tickets and reduce any vestige of scandal. Of course, he only wanted one thing.

Chapter Thirty-three

"A dark cloud is no sign that the sun has lost his light; and dark black convictions are no arguments that God has laid aside His mercy."

~ Charles Spurgeon

As he was hurrying down the hospital stairs to head home after a long day, a door opened above, and a voice sounded. "Doctor Feldman, there's a phone call for you. It's Dr. Anholts, and he says it's urgent."

"Very well." Daniel turned and trudged up the stairs. Why now? He hadn't been off in ten days. The flu had hit the burn ward with a vengeance, and the other attendings had called out sick. His throat felt raw, and all he needed was sleep. The last thing he wanted to do was bring home germs to Tamar and the twins.

Once he reached the third floor, he blew out a breath and opened the door. The administrator dare not ask him to work another shift. He'd fall over. Tamar needed him home.

Sister Griet was holding the phone out to him. "Glad I caught you in time."

He took it. "Dr. Feldman here."

"Sorry to bother you, but I thought you'd want to know. The little boy you found a family for a few weeks ago has apparently run away from his new home. The mother's as angry as a peahen and said he wasn't fitting in. Said he had trouble doing his chores. Do you have any idea where he'd have gone? I don't have time for this."

Daniel heaved a sigh. "I'll take care of it." He called Mrs. Libnitz to inform her of his delay, then handed the receiver back to the nurse. "Thanks, Sister."

"Is it little Luuk? Is he sick? How I miss that boy."

"Yes, apparently, he's run away from his new home. It's been what—three weeks? He could be anywhere. Where do I begin to find him?"

The old woman shook her head. "He can't have gone far on those spindly legs. Isn't he living out on a farm?"

He nodded. "A few kilometers outside of Haarlem on the way to Amsterdam. I need to call Tamar. It could be a long night."

She sent him a weak smile. "If anyone can find him, it's you, Doctor. I'll send a prayer upward for the two of you."

It was times like this he wished he'd bought a car or at least had his bicycle at work. Daniel started off toward the edge of town then spun around. His bike would allow him to cover more territory. He covered the blocks between the hospital and home quickly.

When he arrived, he retrieved the bicycle from the alley behind the house and pedaled toward the outskirts of Haarlem. His breath came in spurts due to his speed and the fact that he hadn't exercised his limbs in a long time.

Darkness had descended hours ago, and except for the din coming from some local restaurants and bars, the town was fast asleep. Most of the houses he passed had nary a light inside.

His thoughts returned to Luuk. What would happen to the boy now? Only one answer echoed back to him, but what would Tamar and the twins say? Weren't their lives complicated enough without adding another child to the fold? *Lord, help me find Luuk. Then tell me what to do with him.*

Daniel veered onto the country road he'd taken to reach the farm. Why hadn't he thought to ask when he ran away? That would have at least given him an inkling as to how far he could have traveled.

Where does he like to go?

Whoa, where did that come from? His head whipped around to see who had spoken, but the only sounds were country ones—a babbling brook, the swish of tall weeds that lined the country road, the moan of a turtledove.

Where does he like to go?

Ah. He shook his head at the smallness of his faith. He'd asked but hadn't expected an answer. Good question—one he should have thought of immediately.

He turned the bike around and returned to the hospital. In spite of the distance and the sweat that was dripping from his brows, the road back to town was easier, most likely because he knew the answer.

Twenty minutes took him to the edge of Haarlem and another fifteen took him to St. Elizabeth's Gasthuis. Instead of dismounting his bicycle, he pedaled straight for the lofty linden tree that sat in the courtyard behind the hospital. The cloudy night offered little light, but he made it to the tree.

"Luuk, you here, boy?"

He waited for a response but heard none. What was that? A whimper from the other side of the linden had Daniel jumping off his bike and circling the tree. There, huddled against the trunk was the little boy. Daniel approached him slowly, not wanting to scare him away.

He rose to his feet. "Leave me alone."

"Luuk, it's me, Dr. Feldman. Don't be afraid. I won't let anything happen to you."

A brief appearance of the moon shed light on the quivering small form in front of him. "Don't be afraid, Luuk. Trust me. I won't hurt you." He stepped toward the boy who retreated and stumbled over a root. Three steps took him to the boy. Daniel gently lifted him into his arms. He'd lost at least five kilograms. Had the family starved him? He rested his head against his shoulder. "I'm so sorry, Luuk. Why did you run away?"

"I couldn't do the work fast, so they sent me to bed without dinner." Tears splashed onto Daniel's neck. "I wasn't good enough."

Daniel patted his neck. "Oh, Luuk, you are so good. You'll come home and live with us. The twins will love you." He hadn't had a chance to talk to Tamar or the twins about this. How he wished they'd understand. "Let's go home," he whispered, then headed to his bicycle. When he reached it, he placed him on the bar and pedaled to the street.

Luuk clung to his neck making it difficult to steer. This may have been the first bicycle ride he had ever had. "It's okay, son. We'll be home in no time."

When he arrived at the house, lights came from the dining room. Tamar must be home. He hoped she'd understand why the twins were still with the neighbor. Luuk had fallen asleep against his chest, so he lifted him onto his shoulder and carried him up the stairs to the parlor.

Tamar sat on the sofa, her arms tight across her chest.

"What is it, honey? What happened?"

Her eyes drifted from Luuk's sleeping form to Daniel's face. "I'll tell you later."

"What happened, Tamar? Was it your meeting with the producers today?"

Her lips trembled, but she didn't answer. Daniel rested Luuk on the other end of the sofa and covered him with a blanket, then he sat and gathered Tamar onto his lap. "Tell me, darling. No matter what happened, we'll make it through."

She shook her head. "They basically fired me. Said they couldn't afford to let a scandal, even if it was based on a lie, ruin their bottom line."

He pulled her head close to his chest. "I'm so sorry, honey. It's not fair. You did nothing to deserve this."

Her voice was muffled. "They offered me a job on *the Queen Mary* for six weeks. *La Bohème.* I'd play Mimi—two shows one way; two shows back. I'd have to stay with Seth between trips. The producers need an answer within three days."

"You mean you'd be going by yourself?"

She sat up to meet his eyes. "They said it could be written into the contract for you to go, but not the children." Her eyes traveled to the sleeping boy on the table. "Now it's your turn."

He took her hand and stroked her knuckles. "Luuk ran away from the family he'd been placed with. The administrator asked me to find him. After coming home to get my bicycle and pedaling halfway out into the country, I came to my senses and found him in his favorite place."

"Where was that?"

"By the tree behind the hospital." His eyes traveled from the sleeping boy to his wife.

She folded her arms across her chest. “You want him to stay with us. Am I right?”

He shrugged, then took her hand. “Luuk’s been hurt so much—” Daniel lowered his voice. “There are no other options for him. With his burn injuries, it will be a while before he’ll regain his strength.” He pulled her toward him. “I know this is a terrible time to take on another child. It couldn’t be worse. What do you think?”

She didn’t speak right away. Every second of silence made him falter. “If it’s God’s timing, we’ll make it work, but what about the contract to work on the ocean liner? We couldn’t possibly ask Mrs. Libnitz to watch three children for six weeks, but who else could we ask?” Her head shook quickly. “I couldn’t stand being separated from them for six whole weeks.”

He tipped her chin up. “If this is God’s doing, He’ll find a way to make this work. What if you told the producers that you’d only take the job if you could also take the three children? We could make it part of the contract.”

“I’m not sure if I have any bargaining power, but you’re right. If it’s God’s will, He’ll make sure everything works out. If not, I won’t take the job, and I’ll become a full-time mother.” She smiled for the first time. “Could you take a leave of absence? Maybe you could be the medical person onboard.”

“Why not? I can deal with vomit from seasick passengers as well as the next guy.”

She burst out laughing. “The very thought. Never would I have believed when I left the meeting today that I’d ever laugh again, much less be the mother of three. Life with you has never been boring.” She wrapped her arms around his waist.

Chapter Thirty-Four

"Vengeance and retribution require a long time; it is the rule."

~ Charles Dickens, *A Tale of Two Cities*

The Queen Mary was more of a city than a ship. She and Daniel needed more than four hands to keep their three young ones from getting lost—or worse. The children wanted to explore every nook of the ship, so Tamar had been thrilled that Tante Neelie had offered to take a leave of absence to watch the children.

Neelie's offer had surprised her. Tamar hadn't even thought to invite her when she'd called her to seek her advice about whether to take the job or not.

"Who's going to watch the twins?" Neelie had asked.

"I don't know. Mrs. Libnitz is always available to babysit when I have a performance, but for six weeks? I couldn't bear to be away from my children for that long."

"Why don't you make bringing the children and Daniel a condition of accepting their offer? In fact, make me part of the offer. I'll watch the kids while you perform. It will be fun. I don't get to see them enough as it is. What do you think?"

Words escaped her. Was this the Lord's working? Was He taking a bad situation and turning it into a gift? "I don't know what to say. What about the rehab center? Who will take over for you for six weeks?"

Tante Neelie didn't answer right away.

"Hello. Are you still there?" Tamar said. Perhaps they'd gotten disconnected.

"I'm here," she said. "With all that's happened to you two lately, I didn't want to add to your burden, but remember when I told you Margot and Inge had escaped?"

"Of course."

"They took Karl and cleaned out the whole room, so I know it was planned. I had to call the warden in Zwolle. He wasn't happy to learn I'd lost Margot. There won't be any replacements coming from that prison. Margot will land on her feet, but I worry about little Karl. He's so vulnerable."

"Did you call the police?"

"Of course. They said there was nothing they could do, but they'd keep me posted. I'm just hoping Margot has someplace safe to take Karl. If she doesn't, it's possible she'll take him back to the orphanage in Haarlem. Who knows?"

A dark cloud of guilt landed on her. "This is all my fault. If I hadn't gone to the director to take Karl out of the orphanage, he wouldn't be in danger right now."

"Now, sweetie, you can't take on guilt that doesn't belong to you. You did what God called you to do with Karl, but this time it's his mother's doing. I didn't tell you this, but when I called the warden and mentioned Inge's name, he said something surprising."

"Don't keep me in suspense, Tante."

"He said that another prisoner—a woman from Germany named Ilse—had escaped from Zwolle mere weeks after Margot had left Zwolle. It's possible the woman who showed up at my door, begging me to hire her to be the cook, was in reality Margot's friend from prison."

"Ah, 'now the plot thickens very much upon us,' as the saying goes. You're right. Well, I'm just relieved you're able to come with us. But since you lost your cook, how can you possibly take a leave of absence, and who will replace you for six weeks?"

Her aunt chuckled. "I've been doing this job for a long time, and I don't mind saying that I could use a change of scenery. He'll work out the details. You just wait and see."

Daniel and Neelie were right. The producers readily accepted her request to bring her family and Neelie on the ocean liner for six weeks, provided she and Daniel took full responsibility for the children. When Daniel had been granted a six-week leave of absence from the hospital, he'd offered to work in the ship's infirmary, as long as his pay would include a daily tutor/nanny for the twins.

The ship was so big Tamar and the family had gotten lost every time they left the confines of the two staterooms assigned to them. Tamar and Daniel's room contained two single beds which they pushed together; however, the beds were so short Daniel's long legs hung over the end by a half a meter. A desk and a chair were the only other furniture, which sat under the porthole that overlooked the ocean below.

A small bathroom containing a shower connected Neelie and the children's room to theirs. God bless Neelie whose voice reached through the door. "Peri, no jumping on the bed." And "Luuk, you know better. Zari, why don't you read the boys one of your books."

On their first night on the open sea after leaving from Liverpool, they encountered rough water, and the odor of vomit permeated the air. Neelie had knocked on the connecting bathroom door at two in the morning, her face ashen.

Tamar took one look at her aunt then called Daniel, who had just fallen asleep after being called out to deal with a sick passenger. "I'll be right back." She lightly shook his arm. "Sweetheart, wake up. Neelie's seasick."

"Wha' is it?" he said through closed eyes.

"Neelie needs you." He sat up, shook his head, then climbed to his feet until the boat's sway sent them both onto the bed. When the shaking stopped, they headed to the door.

"The boys and I should have listened to you, Daniel," Neelie said through fingers that covered her mouth. "We should have chosen thin soup and water instead of the rich dinner and chocolate cake offered by the waiter. The boys have green faces that look like mine. Zari seems to have weathered the storm and is still sleeping."

He chuckled. "You aren't alone. I've been called to the infirmary a half a dozen times to treat seasickness." He reached into his pocket and pulled out a bottle. "Here are some tablets that will help your stomach. You take our room, and we'll stay with the kids."

Two moaning boys lay atop their bed covering their eyes. Zari had awakened and sat on the edge of her bed. "What's that smell?"

"Your brothers and aunt are sick," said Tamar from her place on the boys' bed. She lightly brushed the hair from Luuk's wet forehead.

"Is this the way it's gonna be every night? Cuz if it is, I wanna go home," Peri groused.

Daniel approached with a glass of water and a wet washcloth. "You boys are seasick. A half a pill each will suffice." He gave Luuk the medicine then did the same for Peri.

"The pill burns my throat," said Luuk. "My tummy doesn't feel good."

Daniel wiped his brow. "You'll feel better soon. From now on, if the captain says there's going to be bad weather, we need to avoid eating a lot, then you two won't be sick, okay?" Just then the bell rang from their stateroom. "Duty calls. You two get some sleep." He kissed their heads, then grabbed his medical bag and left.

Early the next morning, Tamar woke up to the sun shining through the porthole. She wasn't ready to go to rehearsal with two sick children and a sick nanny, but her first performance was a day away.

The slop bucket wasn't helping assuage Margot's seasickness. Ilse didn't seem to notice the way the ship swayed from one side to the other but slept through the storm in the upper bunk bed. Karl was asleep as well, thank goodness.

Margot wiped her forehead with a handkerchief she'd found in the attic. She'd always wanted to take a trip on an ocean liner, dress in fancy gowns, and dance the night away. This voyage wasn't anything like that. The best they could afford from pawning things from the attic were third class tickets in the bow of the ship near the propellors.

Despite Margot's reluctance to leave the country, Ilse had convinced her the timing was perfect. She'd come in the back door waving a newspaper. "Guess what?" she said. "Tamar Feldman has been fired from the Haarlem Opera, and she's going to be performing *La Bohème* on the *Queen Mary*. No doubt Erich will be aboard that ship, so you know what we have to do."

Margot had rejected the idea, even using her husband, Klaus as a reason to stay in the country. "He'll be out in a year, and he'll be looking for me and Karl."

Ilse had rolled her eyes. "I haven't heard you talk about your husband since I met you. He's moved on, sweetie. Look, we can make a fresh start in America. I already bought us some false IDs with some of the money we made—even one for the kid. From now on, my name is Anika Jaager, which means 'hunter'—appropriate, don't you think? And your name is Lotte Bakker. It's best to keep Karl's name the same, so he won't spill the beans, as they say in America. Lotte Bakker will become a famous opera diva in New York. It's the American way."

Lotte Bakker, hmm. Ilse had a point. What Margot wanted more than anything was to reestablish her career. "What do *you* want to do once you get to New York?"

"Haven't thought that far ahead. I have a more pressing issue." Her eyes brightened. "Imagine Erich's reaction when I use his own Luger on him."

The plan was coming together like well-fitted gloves. Erich couldn't believe his luck. Luck? No, a well-thought-out and executed plan brought results more than luck or Tamar's God did. He stared at the roiling waves six floors below. No one was out on deck now. The passengers were too busy losing their dinners, which afforded him the opportunity to leave his room and get more fresh air than the porthole offered. He chuckled when a man pushed through the door and vomited over the railing.

Yes, he was days away from reclaiming what was his. Once the Queen reached New York, he and Tamar would disappear and begin a new life together without the encumbrances of children and religion and former spouses. Until then he'd play the role of a doddering old man. He'd wait until all the players were in the ship's banquet hall, where Tamar would be performing.

Who would have thought his wife would make the trip from Germany and show up at Haarlem's opera? He'd hoped she would have moved on, but she'd always had that jealous streak. When he'd heard Ilse's voice from the balcony bellow to the whole house about Tamar's character, it had surprised him at first, then it didn't. He could almost feel his wife's vindictive eyes—and something else, a coldness borne of festering bitterness. His wife had probably filled Dieter's mind with vitriol about him. She'd come to exact revenge for abandoning her and the boy, but didn't she understand? The war had resulted in many living casualties. Families were torn apart, not just from death but also from absence. Tamar was his family now, but he had to get rid of her family first.

Chapter Thirty-five

"Vengeance is in my heart, death in my hand, Blood and revenge are hammering in my head."

~ William Shakespeare, *Titus Andronicus*

The banquet hall wasn't what Tamar had expected. She'd hoped for an auditorium-like venue, similar to the opera house she was used to. Instead, she counted fifteen rows of folding chairs with an aisle down the middle. No orchestra pit preceded the stage which was one step above the floor level. The primary school she'd attended had more steps up to the stage than this one did. She peered around. The walls and the dance floor were made of beautiful polished brown wood. Torch-like lamps and sconces provided an ambiance of light. A gold frieze hung on the wall above the stage. Yes, it was a beautiful room—just not for an opera.

Her chin had wobbled when the cruise director, Mr. Perry, had shown her the room, but she'd managed to suppress her disappointment. The officer dressed in a white suit with striped epaulets told her there'd be a pianist that would be available for two rehearsals before the performance. No, she would not be playing Mimi in *La Bohème* with a supporting cast. No, there would be no costume fittings or directors or set designs. Instead, she'd be singing for an hour twice a night—songs of her choice, and if she wanted to add a song or two from the opera, she could. However, for the second show, the chairs would be removed so the passengers could dance. She'd simply be a nightclub performer providing background music.

According to Mr. Perry, there were other performers in various bars and pianists in the lobby and dining halls, all vying for the passengers' attendance. "An ocean liner is like a smorgasbord of entertainment. Expect passengers to come and go throughout your performance. Choose the right songs, and they'll stay for a while." He must have noticed her tight jaw line. "This isn't what you expected, is it? It never is."

She'd offered a weak smile and decided to be honest. "I'd been told I would be performing the lead in *La Bohème*, but I'll do my best to pick songs that will reach a wider audience."

He patted her hand. "A miscommunication, obviously. We were told you were the lead soprano at a Dutch opera, but we aren't set up to offer a big show like that, and frankly, our passengers aren't the kind to sit and watch anything for very long. Do you think you'll be able to fulfill your contract?"

Could she? Tamar met his eyes. "I've sung in a prisons, hospitals, and even in a Nazi bar. I can sing for your passengers."

He heaved a sigh. "I'm relieved. At this point, I don't know who I'd find to replace you. Your pianist, Faith Weesner, has crossed the sea with us many times. She'll be able to offer suggestions for suitable songs. You two will get along famously—I can already tell."

The cruise director had been right. Faith, who hailed from London, was a godsend helping her prepare for the two performances. It hadn't occurred to Tamar that most of the passengers would speak English, which meant choosing ten new songs that would appeal not only to a non-opera crowd, but also to an English one. Fortunately, Tamar was familiar with the torch songs of Lena Horne, Ella Fitzgerald, Doris Day, and Etta James.

They'd practiced for hours the day before their first performance until her voice grew hoarse—songs like "At Last," "My Funny Valentine," and "Dream a Little Dream."

Faith had allowed her to add a song from *La Bohème* and one Dutch song, but she had balked at a hymn from Shul. "I'm sorry, but the passengers aren't the religious type." When she'd noted Tamar's disappointment, she rolled her eyes. "Okay, we'll try it out, but the idea is to keep the crowd from leaving. Now I advise you to baby your voice tomorrow. Drink plenty of warm water with lemon and honey, and you'll be fine for tomorrow night. No rehearsal."

The next day Faith had looked over the dresses Tamar had brought and shook her head. "You need something a bit more 'professional.' I have some dresses that might fit you since we're about the same size." They'd settled on a beaded white gown and matching mesh cape, accented with dazzling gold beads, and short white gloves. Faith adjusted the neck line. "This will be perfect for tonight's shows, but we'll have to raid my closet for future ones. When you get to New York, you'll need to do some shopping."

Tamar regarded herself in Faith's full-length mirror and turned side to side. "This is so elegant, and it's a far cry from the rags I wore in *La Bohème*." Tamar turned to her accompanist and took her hands. "I'm so grateful, Faith. God sent you at the right time."

Faith rested a hand against Tamar's cheek. "You'll be fine. The audience will love you. You have an innocence and an honesty that will draw them to you. Don't worry." She checked her watch. "Practice how you're going to introduce the songs. I sense you've been through a lot in your life, but don't tell them things that will make them feel bad. I know that sounds horrible, but it is what it is. Again, you'll have the audience coming back for more."

Chapter Thirty-six

"If you prick us, do we not bleed? if you tickle us, do we not laugh?
If you poison us, do we not die? And if you wrong us, shall we not revenge?"

~ William Shakespeare, *Merchant of Venice*

Only half the chairs were filled when Tamar tapped the microphone to make sure it worked. Faith had said people often came late because there were so many other things to do on the ship. Tamar's voice cracked when she introduced herself, sounding like an insecure teenager. What had she been thinking, taking on this job with songs she didn't know and with so little time for rehearsal? Two couples hurried in as she announced the first song—"Dream a Little Dream."

Her voice sounded stilted, unsure even, which was exactly the way she felt, yet she carried on. Sometimes it took a while to find her voice, and although Faith was an excellent pianist, some of the songs they'd chosen needed a full orchestra behind them. A couple slid from their seats and slipped out the side aisle. This did not bode well. She glanced at Faith who gave her an encouraging smile.

Tamar didn't have to be Ella or Doris or Etta. All she had to do was be Tamar Feldman.

The song ended to a tittering of applause and another couple hurrying out, replaced by four people who sat in the back row. Before introducing the next song, she told them a bit about the twins, just as she'd rehearsed. It was then she noticed Daniel leaning against the back wall. When their eyes met, he nodded and touched his lips then pointed up. Buoyed by the strength of his presence, she began her version of "At Last," that would have made Etta James proud.

When she finished her last song, a smattering of applause replaced the roses of the opera, but this was a different kind of audience who scrambled to be the first out the door. Okay, this was her new job. With no dressing room to change into her street clothes, she stepped off the stage to return to their state room when Daniel strolled toward her.

Words didn't come. Tears were close to the surface. Daniel folded her into his arms and kissed her forehead. "You did great, honey."

"I don't know what I expected. I feel like a performer in one of those carnival side shows."

"I know. You looked so sultry up there, like Marilyn Monroe." He straightened his arms to look at her dress. "Here's one member of the audience that wants an encore. Let's go back to the room."

"You're funny. I have to change into another one of Faith's dresses for tonight's show, and I want to spend some time with the twins and Luuk before they go to bed."

He pulled her close and kissed her temple. "You sang wonderfully. This is just a different kind of audience. They're like Peri and Zari in the candy store."

They walked hand in hand back to the lift that would take them to their floor. The operator nodded at them as they entered, his eyes lingering on Tamar's dress. She cringed and averted her eyes. Daniel squeezed her hand and pulled her close to his side.

"Let's take the stairs from now on," she whispered as they exited the lift and slipped her arm inside his elbow. "So, tell me about your day."

"Not much to tell. A child cut his foot on a piece of glass. A few upset stomachs, and a hangover or five. I have to say this has been a nice change for me—almost like a vacation of sorts. It's so rewarding to see Luuk playing with Peri. He's adapted well. I get to spend more time with them and you, which I love. Neelie said she needed a change as well and is enjoying spending time with her grandchildren. How about you?"

"I don't know. It could be stage jitters, but I just have this feeling something bad is going to happen."

"What do you mean?"

Tamar shrugged. "Wish I knew. It's like there's a darkness over everything. A prickly feeling like when you walk down a dark alley at night, and you hear footsteps behind you." She gripped his arm. "We have to keep a close eye on the kids, okay? Never let them out of our sight."

He wrapped his arm around her shoulder. "You're shivering. Don't worry."

She blew out a breath. "Sorry I sound so maudlin. It's probably just jitters. I'll feel better after tonight's performance is finished. Once I get into a routine and know what to expect, it will be all right. It's probably nothing."

The late show went flawlessly. Once Tamar got used to the chatter, the scraping of chairs, and dancers not paying a bit of attention to her singing, she relaxed. The audience wasn't coming to see her perform; they came for the dancing. It was liberating in a way. She and Faith were there merely to create an ambiance for the crowd, which ebbed and flowed throughout the evening.

After a few days, Tamar had to admit that taking this job was a godsend. On her two days off, Tamar spent time with the children, reading to them, taking them for walks around the ship, and spending time in the playroom and library. Daniel and Neelie would join them for meals, sitting out on the deck chairs, and enjoying some of the events the ocean liner offered. Tamar's favorite thing was watching the stars with Daniel's arm around her. The stars were so vivid against the backdrop of the dark sky and black sea that she could trace the constellations with her finger.

Neelie had gained a few pounds from the rich food—at least that's what she said. The color had returned to her cheeks, and the worry wrinkles had smoothed out. She refused to take time off during Tamar's free time, so the two of them would find adjacent deckchairs out of the wind, cover themselves with the blue blankets, and chat or fall asleep.

During one of those times, Tamar mentioned the foreboding feelings she'd experienced. "I know it's silly, but I just have this feeling that something's afoot."

Neelie removed the cucumber patches from her eyes she'd nabbed from their salads at lunch. "What do you mean by that?"

"I don't know why, but there's this gray pallor that hangs over everything on this ship. It's just my imagination, but something bad is going to happen. I tell myself I'm being paranoid or a killjoy because what could be greater than this trip with you, Daniel, and the children?" She reached for Neelie's hand.

Neelie sat up. "Why would you think such a thing? Your shows went well, and you sang your heart out. The audience was like putty in your hands, except for the inebriated patrons. I'm quite sure your last two shows tomorrow will be just as good because you'll know what to expect. The children have behaved and they're happy. Luuk has adjusted, and the color has come back to his cheeks. Daniel is a lot more rested. What could possibly go wrong?"

"Guess I'm inviting trouble. Maybe it's the fear of the unknown or the guilt that I lost my job and made you and Daniel leave yours."

She raised a dismissive hand. "Pshaw. I needed a break, and I have so enjoyed this ocean liner. It's like a city, and for a few days, we're its citizens. I'm looking forward to visiting New York for the first time, aren't you? You'll spend time with your brother and Hadassah."

Tamar offered a smile. "Yes, I'm looking forward to seeing Seth and Hadassah and meeting my nephew, Yair, but—"

Neelie studied her face. "Something's really bothering you. Have you prayed about it?"

"No." She sat back and closed her eyes. "Ever since I started singing at the opera back in 1943, there's been trouble. First my parents were killed and we had to go into hiding, then the camps. It just seems we Jews weren't meant to be happy—" Tamar opened her eyes and gripped Neelie's hand. "I am so sorry. After all you did for me and Daniel—hiding us in your home, going to the camps because of me. You didn't deserve that."

Neelie patted her hand. "You have always been like a daughter to me, and I love you and your family. The reason I ended up at

Vught was because of an obsessed Nazi." She spit over her shoulder. "But Officer Bergman is dead. He can't hurt you or me anymore."

"What if he isn't? I saw him swallow that pill in that Paris hotel room before the police could wrestle it away from him, and there was that look in his eyes—as if he had won. Do you think he could have faked his own death?"

Neelie shook her head. "You're inviting trouble again. I understand. You've been through a lot this year with the case and the trouble at the opera house." She touched the lingering scar on her cheek. "I've had my own problems with the staff. Hendrika stabbed me with a knife. Then Margot and Inge escaped, and I lost the contract with Zwolle." She pushed to a sitting position. "God never said life on this side of heaven would be easy."

"I know." Tamar heaved an audible sigh. She took Neelie's hand. "I caused a lot of my own problems. Took risks like meeting up with the orphanage's director. What did I think she was going to do—release a child to a stranger? Then singing in a prison in order to meet with Margot?"

"Well, here we are. You and I staring at the roiling waves without a trace of land in sight. We'll be in New York the day after tomorrow. Let's not give our troubles a single thought. We can't worry about what's going to happen tomorrow. Jesus said, 'Each day has enough trouble of its own.'"

Chapter Thirty-seven

"When we, by the working of mercy and grace, be made meek and mild, we are full safe; suddenly is the soul oned to God when it is truly peaced in itself: for in Him is found no wrath."

~ Julian of Norwich

Tamar stood behind the curtain and watched the seats fill up. This was the last night before they arrived in New York, and Daniel and Neelie were bringing the children to hear her sing professionally for the first time in their lives. She hoped Peri would behave.

Tamar ran her hand against the beaded white gown Faith had lent her. This was undoubtedly the most exquisite dress Tamar had ever worn. She felt the edges of the matching mesh cape, then adjusted the dazzling gold and diamond necklace around her neck. With her hair styled in a French twist, she looked like Doris Day, and would add "All through the Day" to tonight's lineup of songs.

A glance at the twins brought a chuckle. They were already squirming, and the show hadn't even begun. Neelie patted Peri's legs and bent over to say something to him. His protruding lower lip showed he wouldn't last long, even if it was his mother singing.

At least she only had to do one show tonight. The director had asked her to autograph glossy pictures of herself after the last show, as was the normal practice for entertainers on ships. It seemed like a waste of paper, but she'd agreed to pose for the photographer earlier in the week. She was quite sure few patrons would linger in the room afterwards, and she'd be able to spend the last night with her family.

The lights lowered and Faith took her seat at the piano. Showtime. She walked out to a smattering of applause, Peri and Luuk's squeals dominating. Suddenly a heavy foreboding weighed down her shoulders. Not now. Not when the five people she loved more than life were in the room. This was nothing more than stage fright. She swallowed hard and took hold of the microphone.

If there had been a more beautiful angel, Erich had never seen her. Tonight, he'd have his angel. He'd wait until everyone left the room, and if his words couldn't persuade her, his fist could. Until then he'd bask in the sultry voice that belied the white dress she wore and the cape that almost looked like wings. He would have preferred that she sing an aria or two instead of the simple tunes of the times, but the subtle curves of the gown with its décolleté bodice brought a resurgence of emotion that simmered below the surface.

He'd hoped the fickle crowd would quickly depart to other entertainment spots on the boat, but then the emcee had mentioned an autograph session after the show. His plan to take her was further delayed by the presence of the doctor, the violinist whom she called Tante Neelie, and the twins. Where the third child had come from, he had no idea, but there were three sets of squirming legs between the violinist's seat and Dr. Feldman's. Perhaps it was Margot Sneider's offspring.

Erich had kept close tabs on Tamar during and after the kidnapping trial. He'd read every newspaper article, sat in the back row of the courthouse, and even stood outside her house. The house. How well he knew it. The first time he'd heard the voice of the angel was from the first-floor lobby when he'd come to pick up his repaired violin back in 1944. From that moment on, he had to have Tamar Visser. She'd been his obsession, but the one and only love of his life had let others persuade her away from him. The aunt, the husband, even the children—they were all expendable.

Hadn't he given up his life for her—his face in the fire, his family back in Germany? She'd been his one weakness, and Erich did not tolerate weakness in himself. Tonight was the night. As the Americans would say, let the chips fall as they may.

Chapter Thirty-eight

"Malice is of the boomerang character, and is apt to turn upon the projector."

~ William Makepeace Thackeray

The line of people that formed in front of the table spanned the length of the room, almost back to the stage where she'd performed an hour ago. She'd already gone through two cartridge pens by signing a message on each of the glossies. However, the cruise director had gestured with his hand to speed it up, so she merely signed her name on each.

Tamar didn't fool herself into thinking the long line had anything to do with her singing. People liked mementos of the various activities of the cruise, and an autographed black and white of her face would add to the pile of decks of cards, banners, and cocktail napkins.

The twins and Luuk had hung around for a while until Peri had zigzagged around the adults too many times in his effort to hide from the other two children. Daniel had motioned that he was taking the children back to the cabin but would leave Neelie with her.

A tall bespectacled man with a British accent asked her to sign the picture with the words, 'To Byron, all my love, Tamar.' She stifled a grin and scribbled the words down. Why not? She and Neelie would have a good laugh afterwards. Finally, the line dwindled to a dozen people. She covered a yawn, the warm room making her yearn for a good night's sleep. How the woman in front of her could wear a mink stole, she had no idea.

"Sweetie, you sing really good." Long red nails shoved the glossy toward Tamar. "Make it out to Trixie. Maybe someday you'll be so famous I can get a good price for this."

Tamar's jaw was beginning to ache from smiling so much. She finished signing the picture and slid it back to her. "Thank you, ma'am, for coming."

"Call me Trixie. Ma'am was my ma. See you, doll." She strutted away, the last person in the line.

Tamar leaned back and closed her eyes for a few seconds. Such a relief not to have to sing for another week. When an opera closed, the last performance was always a sad affair, but she felt no sadness. She couldn't wait to see her brother Seth, Hadassah, and Yair who'd be a year old. Her first nephew.

Her eyes flew open at a shriek from somewhere in the room. The lights had been dimmed, and it was difficult to see. A barrage of Dutch words sounded. Was that Neelie's voice? "Let me go. Tamar, run!"

Tamar bolted to her feet. "Neelie? Where are you?" She tripped against the leg of the table as she rounded it. All she could see was the shadowy image of the last row of chairs. The doors were closed, and the only light came from a sconce by the stage. Where were the attendants? "Neelie, speak to me."

The shadow of someone came up the center aisle—a man, and he was carrying someone who was flailing and fighting.

"Let her go." She looked around for a light switch. Anything to take away the advantage the darkness had over her. She rushed to the door and tried to open it, but something blocked it on the other side. "Help! If anyone can hear, help!" She tugged on the door, letting in a centimeter of light.

The man had slowed and was standing mere meters from her, his hand over Neelie's mouth. Her feet kicked at his shin, and he swore. Something about him was familiar—a middle-aged man. At least that's what she could deduce from his demeanor.

"Why are you doing this? Let her go." What she needed was a weapon—something to stop him. She felt in the pocket of her dress. A cartridge pen and a key would have to do. She gripped the pen tight in her fist. "Put her down this instant. Let her go!" Her voice, already weak from singing sounded shaky at best. Had the table not been close enough to lean on, her legs would have given way.

"Tamar, I don't want to hurt her, but I will. You take her place, and I'll let her go." The voice was gravelly, and there was a tint of an accent—German. Could it be Erich Bergman? No, she'd seen him die in that hotel room in Paris. His face was in the shadows, but the way he stood, the gruffness of his voice—there was no doubt it was he.

For the first time, the glint of a knife flashed from the man's hand held next to Neelie's throat. If she agreed to take her place, could Neelie escape and get help? She had to take a chance. *Lord, save her. Save me.*

"I'll come. Just don't hurt her." If it was Erich Bergman, could she convince him to believe her? She took a step in his direction, then another. "Let her go." What could he do to her on a ship this size? The answer was obvious. The sea would mean certain death. Hadn't he said all those years ago he'd rather die with her than let her live?

"Move, or she dies." The knife dug into Neelie's throat, making her gasp.

"Don't. I'll come." She stepped closer, now seeing his face for the first time. Erich Bergman—thinner, the perpetual scowl still turning down one corner of his mouth. Her voice came out in a whisper. "Let her go."

He thrust Neelie forward, grabbed Tamar's hand, and jerked her to his side. The edge of the steel-cold knife dug into her neck. Neelie bent over a chair in a paroxysm of coughing.

"Run," she managed despite the knife touching her skin. Thoughts of Daniel and the twins played like a movie in her head. The dimple on Daniel's right cheek when he smiled. Peri's fat little legs in perpetual movement. Zari's wide eyes when she discovered a new word in a book. Tamar closed her eyes. This was how it was going to end. No. She jerked against his hold.

His arm tightened around her neck, the smell of tobacco and garlic accosting her nose. "I don't want to hurt you, Angel. We're going to walk out of here without any fuss. I've got it all figured out. We'll start a new life in America. In time you'll…love me." He pushed her toward the far door.

"Don't trust him, honey. He's deranged." The voice came from the stage area, a female voice, but not Neelie's.

Erich whipped around to face the owner of the voice, his knife piercing her skin.

Tamar's breath hitched when a trail of warm liquid trickled down from her neck. Footsteps approached from the other side of the room, not frenzied steps but deliberate ones. A woman came into view, the darkness covering her face, but Tamar could tell she was short.

"*Guten abend*, Erich. What has it been—eight years?"

Tamar's eyes were riveted on the diminutive woman as she slowly walked toward them, a gun pointed at Erich's heart.

"Hello, Ilse. It has been a long time." His head tipped toward her. "The years haven't been kind, have they?" He chuckled.

Tamar took advantage of the distraction to pull away, but his hold tightened. Had Neelie left? She couldn't tell in the dark.

"Always the sweet talker." The woman moved a step closer. "You always liked the pretty ones, didn't you?"

The door at the far end of the room creaked. Neelie must be trying to leave. The woman glanced over her shoulder. "The door's blocked. Come over here where I can see you."

Although Tamar's hands had stopped shaking, the drama unfolding had taken her attention away from her dire position. The woman's rancor left no room for negotiation. Someone wouldn't be walking out of this room tonight.

"I'm a good shot, and I won't hesitate to shoot you. Now come closer so I can see you." The gun in her hand darted between Tamar's captor and Neelie. "Recognize this luger, sweetheart. You won't believe where I found it. In the attic of a house in Haarlem. Margot Sneider's house. By the way, Neelie, Margot's here with her boy in steerage."

Footsteps sounded before Neelie came into view. Her eyes widened at the sight of the woman, but her steps didn't falter. "Inge. Why?"

"Ilse's the name. Nothing personal. Simply a means to an end." Ilse motioned toward Bergman. "I had a score to settle with this one. Join your friend."

Neelie shuffled to Tamar's side, their hands touching. Just the touch of her aunt's hand brought a modicum of comfort to her.

"There, isn't that a pretty picture? My husband falling for a Jew. Never in a million years would the thought have entered my mind. It had to be the face and the voice." Inge's lips curled into a sneer. "So, you abandoned your wife and your son who adored you for a pretty Jew." She sniffed and swept a hand over her eyes. "I should kill all three of you right now. I'm already an escaped criminal. What difference would it make?"

Someone banged on the door. Voices sounded from behind it. When Ilse cast a quick glance in that direction, Bergman whipped around and bolted away. Ilse shot at her husband's retreating form but missed. Neelie fell to the ground.

"No!" Tamar screamed. She dropped to the floor next to Neelie and wrapped her arms around her. "Don't leave me, Tante. Please, God, bring her back." When Neelie didn't answer, she rocked her back and forth. "Please, God."

The lights went on, and two men in ship uniforms swarmed in. One of the officers grabbed the gun from his holster and trained it on Bergman's wife. "Drop the gun, ma'am. Hands up."

Tamar glanced down at her aunt, whose eyes were closed. "Tante? Can you hear me?" She released her hand and felt around for blood, finding nothing until her hand landed on Neelie's upper arm. Out of the corner of her eye, she saw Bergman hiding behind some chairs. "He's getting away."

"Who's getting away?" one of the officers said.

"Bergman. He's the woman's husband. He held a knife to my throat." Tamar motioned with her head to the last row. One of the officers hurried in that direction.

Neelie stirred, blinked, and lifted her arm to shield her eyes from the light. She winced.

"Don't move. Ilse shot you in the arm." Voices sounded from the hallway. Three more officers streamed in the closest door. Tamar called out. "Over here. My aunt's been shot."

One of the officers came over and bent down beside her. "I'll call the medic."

Just then Daniel bolted into the room, his eyes darting in all directions. Tamar lifted her arm. "Over here, Daniel."

He dropped down beside her. "Are you okay? When the alarm sounded, I heard—"

"I'm okay, but Neelie's been shot in her arm."

"Oh, Neelie—" He gently tore her sleeve. "Tamar, get me a towel from my bag to staunch the blood. Neelie, lie back and relax. We'll have this out in no time."

She rifled through the medical bag, pulled out the towel, and handed it to him, but he put up his hand. "You press that against the wound while I get something to clean it up. From what I can see, though, it looks like it just grazed her skin." Tamar applied pressure to the wound. Neelie's eyes were now squeezed shut, her breath emitting in short spurts.

Daniel's voice steadied. "Good job, honey. Now take the towel away and I'll have a look." He used a large pair of tweezers to open the wound. "No bullet. Good. I'll just clean this up and dress the wound. It'll sting, Neelie, but that will forestall any infection. You'll need to rest." He called a staff member over and requested a wheelchair to take her back to their stateroom. "Tamar, you go with Neelie. One of the crew is staying with the kids—"

"Not so fast, Doctor." The captain of the ship approached. "We'll need to take both ladies' statements before they can leave."

Daniel stood to his full height. "Can't this wait until tomorrow? The woman's suffered a gunshot wound."

"No, it can't." He beckoned to an officer to join him. "Get their statements, but be quick about it."

After she and Neelie gave an account of what happened, the officer released them to return to their rooms. Tamar bent down and kissed her aunt's forehead, then turned at the scuff of footsteps. "Looks like they're taking Erich and his wife out of here in handcuffs. Wonder if they have a jail here."

Neelie chuckled. "Hope there's only one jail cell on this boat. That would be the best punishment for them both."

Chapter Thirty-nine

"After life's fitful fever he sleeps well. Treason has done his worst. Nor steel nor poison, malice domestic, foreign levy, nothing can touch him further."

~ William Shakespeare

Margot stirred from her sleep at the pounding on the door. Ilse's bed was empty. Had she forgotten her key? She almost said, "I'm coming," when a man's voice on the other side of the door bellowed, "Open up."

Nothing good could come from opening that door.

The pounding continued. More voices sounded from the corridor. Karl was stirring. She pulled him close to her side. "Shh. Go back to sleep, sweetie." She lightly brushed damp hair away from his face. The room was so hot it was a wonder he wasn't screaming. She debated covering his mouth with her hand. No, that would just make him cry. Her time was up. She kissed her son's temple. "I love you, baby." And she did. What would happen to her son if she opened that door? For the first time she was more concerned about Karl than herself.

More knocking. “Lotte Bakker, open this door. We have your roommate in custody. We need to come in.”

So, this was it. Tears splashed onto Karl’s head. Why did it take this long to realize how much she loved him? She kissed him then closed her eyes tight and leaned against the wall. For the first time in forever, she prayed.

Sleep evaded Tamar. She stared at the fan hanging on the wall, its whir adding little movement to the stale air in the room. Her mind replayed all that had happened. Seeing Bergman and his wife being led away in handcuffs had eased her mind for a moment, but the man was invincible—a wily fox whose obsession had defied death and the police more than once.

Something Ilse had said floated back—something about Margot. Hadn’t she said Margot was on the ship? That could mean only one thing. Tamar’s life was still in peril. If Ilse had trained a gun on her, surely Margot was in on it. According to Neelie, they’d escaped together. Something else Ilse had said came to mind. She’d said Margot’s son was also in steerage. Karl was on this ship.

Daniel’s measured breathing meant she shouldn’t wake him. The children were sleeping on the pullout sofa, so Neelie could get a good night’s sleep. Tamar would have to figure this out by herself. It stood to reason if Ilse was arrested for attempted murder, the ship’s security officers would search her room and find Margot and Karl. What would happen to the boy if she were arrested?

This is all my fault. A slideshow of memories played in Tamar’s mind. If she hadn’t made such a big deal out of saving Karl from the orphanage, he wouldn’t be in as much danger as he was now. If Margot was on this ship, it meant she’d be arrested again for escaping Neelie’s custody, which would leave Karl more vulnerable than he was at the orphanage. What right did she have to interfere with anyone else’s child when she couldn’t be the mother she should to her own children?

Her head swayed back and forth on the pillow. Look at all the trouble she’d caused—even to the point of leaving her twins without either parent, had both she and Daniel been convicted of kidnapping Karl. *Lord, what a mess I've made of things. Margot would have been out of prison in a year or so, had I not told her about Karl's condition. Forgive me for making things worse for him.* Tears erupted and rolled down into her hair then onto the pillow.

"What's wrong, honey?" Daniel's arm went around her shoulders and pulled her close. "Did you have a bad dream?"

She motioned for him to whisper since the kids were sleeping only meters away. "Sorry I woke you up. You go back to sleep."

"You've been through a very traumatic event. Of course, you'd have trouble sleeping." He pulled the blanket up to her neck. "Do you want me to give you something to help you sleep? We have a big day tomorrow."

"No, it's too late now. I just feel like such a failure. Everything that happened tonight started with me. If I hadn't insisted that Margot know about Karl, he would at least be safer in the orphanage than he is on this boat once she's arrested. Our kids wouldn't be on this boat if I hadn't meddled in Margot's affairs. I'm such a bad excuse of a mother."

"Look me in the eye." Daniel framed her face with his hands. "Stop it. You are a wonderful mother, a wonderful wife, and a wonderful friend to a woman who doesn't deserve your friendship. You did the right thing."

When she lowered her eyes, he shook his head. "Nothing I say seems to make a difference with you. You're a great mother. Sure, nobody's perfect on this earth, but you do your best. So, you're late once in a while. So, the soup had too much salt in it."

She smiled. "That was Peri's doing. He loosened the top of the shaker."

He winked. "There's a smile. I certainly haven't been the perfect father, working all the time. You saw a problem with Karl and addressed it the best way you could. I still think God put you in that orphanage at that time to help that boy." He took her hands. "Since I can't convince you that you're a good parent, I'm going to pray that God gives you a sign of some kind, okay?" He whispered a prayer in her ear. "Amen. Now try to get some sleep." He nestled her head in the crook of his arm.

Tamar had just fallen asleep when a soft knock on the door woke her. She looked around the dark room and heard the measured breaths of Daniel sleeping beside her. One of the children coughed and stirred. Why would someone be knocking on her door at this time of night? Maybe she'd just dreamed she heard it. Then there was another soft knock. Tamar gently shook Daniel's shoulder.

He bolted up almost hitting her chin. "What is it?"

"Darling, shh. There's somebody at the door." She donned her robe and tied the sash then followed Daniel to the door, stopping to turn on the light in the bathroom, so as not to wake up the children.

He opened the door slightly. "I don't believe it."

Tamar peeked around from behind his shoulder. She gasped. There stood Margot with Karl propped on one hip. Her eyes radiated fear against her thin, wan face. The woman who had always appeared so tall and sure now looked so thin an ocean breeze could knock her over. She visibly swallowed.

"I'm sorry to interrupt your sleep, but I need your help." When Karl stirred, she switched him to her other hip as if his weight was too much to bear.

"Come in." Daniel moved sideways to allow her entrance.

"Is Neelie here?" she whispered.

"She's next door. Do you want me to get her?" said Tamar.

She peered into the hall behind her. "I don't have much time, but I need to…make things right, if that's even possible." Her eyes filled with tears.

"Here, let me take Karl. It would be best if we talked in Neelie's room. It's just next door." Tamar nodded at the sleeping children on the sofa.

"Follow me." Daniel entered the bathroom they shared with Neelie and gently tapped on her door.

Within a minute, Neelie opened it, her arm in a sling. Her eyes widened at the sight of Margot and the child. "Come in." She offered the desk chair to Margot, but she declined. "What's this all about?" Neelie asked, slowly lowering to the chair while Tamar placed the sleeping child on the bed and sat down next to him.

Margot began to pace. "I don't have much time, so I'll be quick about what I have to say." Her hands formed fists then released. She turned to face them. "I have made a supreme mess of everything, and I'm sorry. An officer demanded to come in my room. He called me by name and said Ilse had been arrested. I didn't answer the door, and he finally went away. I don't know what she did that got her arrested, but it had something to do with her husband—making him pay for abandoning her and her son." Margot stopped in front of Neelie and nodded toward the sling on her arm. "Did she do that?"

Neelie nodded. "How did you get involved with her?"

"I didn't until she helped me out of a scrape at the prison. She's small but mighty when she's mad. Then when she showed up at your place, she convinced me to escape with her by dangling the carrot of an opera career in front of me. Against my better judgment, I listened. Another bad decision."

She turned toward Tamar. "You know what? Tonight, after the officer left, for the first time in my life, I prayed. Told God I was so sorry for the mess I made of my life and all the people I've hurt, including little Karl and the three of you. That's when I got this impression—not a voice really, but a strong sensation that I was to find you three—that you would tell me what to do. I know you will never be able to forgive me, but I still have to ask." Her head lowered.

Tamar bolted from the bed and wrapped her arms around her. "Of course, I forgive you." Daniel and Neelie joined her, each echoing her words. They remained in a huddle until Margot's tears were spent.

"This has been quite the night," Neelie said retaking her seat. "Never in a million years would I have thought any good could have come out of it." She chuckled. "Margot, you never do anything small."

Daniel leaned against the desk. "So, what are your plans now, Margot?"

She lowered herself onto the bed and smoothed Karl's hair. "I'm going to turn myself in. Since I escaped from your place, Neelie, I'll have at least five to ten years added to my sentence. I'm okay with that as long as I know Karl will be safe and sound." She peered at Tamar. "I know it's a lot to ask after all the trouble I've caused you and Daniel, but would you consider raising my son while I'm away? I never appreciated how good you were to Karl, but I couldn't see beyond my own nose. You're a wonderful mother—much better than I could ever hope to be."

"Whoa." Tamar covered her mouth. "Are you kidding me? You hate me."

"I hated you; more likely, I envied you." She shook her head. "I don't have that luxury now. Fact is, I need you."

Tamar stared at her for a long time. Could she trust this woman? She turned to Daniel.

He lifted a shoulder. "What's one more child?"

Tamar wrapped her arm around Daniel's waist. "We would be happy to take care of Karl, and we'll make sure he knows what a great mother he has."

"Thank you," Margot whispered. She kissed her son's head, tears falling in rivulets down her cheeks.

"Would you like me to go with you?" Daniel said.

"No, this is one walk I need to do by myself." She trailed her fingers down Karl's cheek, handed them a rucksack, then turned and left.

After they closed the door, Tamar leaned against it. "I can't believe what just happened. Margot entrusted her son to me?"

Daniel pulled her into a hug. "Honey, this is the sign."

"What do you mean?"

"Who would have thought God would use Margot to tell you you're a great mother?"

The End

Did you miss the other books of the series?

A Song for Her Enemies
What Hides Behind the Walls

www.ingramcontent.com/pod-product-compliance
Lightning Source LLC
Chambersburg PA
CBHW051940220626
47052CB00004B/726

* 9 7 8 1 9 6 8 7 9 2 3 1 2 *